REFUGE

AUTUMN 1108 SR* (*SAINTS RECKONING)

Waves washed over Natalia as she struggled to breathe, and all seemed lost until a firm shake broke the icy grip of the haunting nightmare. Athgar stared down at her, his grey eyes filled with worry.

"Where am I?" she asked.

"Aboard the *Golden Chalice*." He smiled. "You had us all worried. You've been out for days."

"And the ship?"

"Damaged. The hull took a beating from that spell of yours, but the captain reckons we'll make port."

"And what port will that be?"

"Korvoran," said Athgar. "In the Duchy of Reinwick."

"Yes. I remember now." She tried to sit up, but her spinning head forced her to close her eyes.

"Try not to move. You've been through a lot."

"What did I do?"

"You conjured a maelstrom that sent our pursuers to the bottom of the sea. My sister won't trouble us again."

"I remember the sea trying to swallow us."

"Yes, we almost sank, too, but when you collapsed, the maelstrom ceased. You've been down here ever since. Galina said you were bleeding quite profusely; that spell was nearly the end of you."

She reached out to take his hand. "I'll be fine," she soothed. "Though my head feels like someone kicked it. What of the others?"

"All up on deck, safe and sound. Now, lie down and rest. You must conserve your strength."

"Why? What's happened?"

"Nothing yet, but we should be in Korvoran by late afternoon. That's when the real work begins."

"Get the others down here," she said. "We need to discuss how to proceed."

"There'll be plenty of time for that once we're ashore. Now get some sleep."

He turned, but she called out to him, "Athgar, please don't leave. Stay with me. I'd feel the better for it."

He smiled. "For you, anything."

Stanislav leaned against the railing.

"Quite a sight, isn't it?" A voice interrupted his thoughts.

He turned to see Belgast walking across the deck. "I never would have taken you for someone who liked the sea."

"Because I'm a Dwarf?"

"Well, you must admit, there's little in the way of standing water up in the mountains."

"That's because up there, it's all snow." Belgast also leaned on the railing. "You know, it's quite peaceful."

"Peaceful? The deck rolls beneath our very feet. I'd hardly call that reassuring."

"Really? I would have said it's relaxing. It almost lulls you to sleep."

"Well, don't get used to it. Unless I'm mistaken, that's the coast of Reinwick."

Belgast squinted. "So it is. Tell me again why we chose to go there?"

"Because it's rumoured the family no longer has any influence there."

"That still doesn't get us back to Therengia."

"True, but at least it'll give us a slight reprieve from the Stormwinds."

"Have you ever been to Reinwick?"

"Yes, but not for some years."

"And?"

The mage hunter shrugged. "There's not much to tell. The last I heard, the duke was a man named Wilfhelm Brondecker, though, in truth, I doubt he would remember me."

"Why's that?"

"I only met him the once, and was one of dozens introduced to him— not exactly the type of thing that endears you to someone."

"And what was your opinion of him?"

"I didn't see him enough to form an opinion. As I said, I only met him once."

"Yes," said Belgast, "but surely you know his reputation?"

"And how would I know that? I was in the business of finding potential mages, not socializing with the nobility."

"But you met him; you said so yourself. If you weren't socializing, then why were you there?"

"I was there to pay my respects to Larissa Stormwind."

"I thought they banned the family from Reinwick?"

"They did, but that came later."

"Just how long ago were you there?"

"Let me think, now. I believe it was in ninety-five."

"So you haven't been back for over a decade?"

"No. Look, it's not as if I had much choice where I travelled in those days. The family employed me, and my job was to go where the rumours took me."

"So, what's that got to do with Larissa Stormwind?"

"It was common practice to check in with the local family members when visiting such places, though only as a courtesy, you understand."

"And were the people there accepting of outsiders?"

"For the most part, but I suspect Athgar's eyes might draw some unwanted attention."

"Ah, yes," said Belgast. "The grey eyes of a Therengian. They don't like them much in these parts, do they?"

"No, but you must remember the Old Kingdom's borders once stretched to the Great Northern Sea. Therengians were seen as conquerors. Even today, most Petty Kingdoms fear them rising again."

"Then we'd best not mention the events in the east. I can't imagine what they might do if they found out Athgar is the High Thane."

"They won't learn it from me."

"Nor me," said the Dwarf, "but we best keep a close eye on him. I'd hate to see him get into trouble."

"A good idea. We should also avoid revealing our connections to the Stormwinds until we've got a better idea of what's been going on here."

"Did I hear you mention the family?" called out Galina. She moved closer, with Katrin by her side.

"Yes," said Belgast. "We were suggesting we keep your family name a secret for the time being."

"An excellent idea." Galina stared out at the distant shore. "I assume that's Reinwick. Does this mean we're close to the port of Korvoran?"

"I would assume so, but that would be the captain's area of expertise." Belgast looked along the deck. "Have you seen Athgar?"

"He went below to see how Natalia's doing."

"And?"

"I'm afraid there's no news on that account. She used a lot of her strength to cast the maelstrom spell. It's a miracle she didn't kill herself."

"But she's the most powerful mage on the Continent," added Katrin. "She's always been that way, even back at the Volstrum."

"Yes," agreed Galina, "and she's honed her skill even more in the intervening years. I'm sure she'll recover, but it will take some time, providing we have it."

"Why?" said Stanislav. "What are you suggesting?"

"We heard rumours that Reinwick banished the family, but they wouldn't take that as a reason to stop trying. By now, they might've found their way back into the duke's favour."

"In that case," said the Dwarf, "we must be careful who we interact with.

"The *Golden Chalice* limped into Korvoran's harbour, drawing attention from those working the docks. It wasn't that the arrival of a ship was unusual, for similar vessels crowded the place, but the *Chalice's* condition suggested it had undergone a terrible ordeal.

An odd assortment of tradesmen met them on the dock, each eager to offer their services to aid in the ship's repairs.

Athgar led Natalia across the boarding ramp, holding on to her arm to keep her steady. Katrin and Galina came next, followed by Stanislav and Belgast, who kept a sharp lookout for trouble.

"We need to find a place to stay," said Galina. "I have some funds, but they won't last forever, so I suggest we be thrifty."

"I have an idea," said Athgar. "Come. Take Natalia's arm and steady her, will you?"

Galina moved up, taking his place. The Therengian pushed his way down the jetty, trying to catch up to a trio of scarlet-clad knights.

"Excuse me, Sisters," he called out. "I wonder if you might be able to help?"

They turned, with one asking, "How can we be of assistance?"

"My companions and I just arrived, and we require lodgings. I wondered if you might be able to recommend somewhere."

She stared back a moment, noting the colour of his eyes. "I'm afraid there are not too many places willing to take in one of your... persuasion."

"Perhaps the Lydia?" offered another knight.

"That's a tavern, not an inn."

"True, but old Handley knows the area well. He might be able to suggest something."

"My fellow sister makes a good point." She pointed inland. "You see that tall building over there, the one with the red walls?"

"Yes," replied Athgar. "What of it?"

"Just north of it, you'll find the Lydia. You'll recognize it by its sign."

"A woman?"

"No, a ship. In any event, old Handley doesn't care where you're from, providing you can afford it. You do have coins, don't you?"

"A few."

"Then I suggest you spend them wisely. In any event, someone there will be better able to suggest an inn for you."

"Thank you. Your help is much appreciated."

The Lydia was smaller than Athgar expected, yet there was no denying it had its charms. The group squeezed themselves around a table, then ordered some ale, which proved surprisingly cheap.

Athgar took a sip from his tankard while watching his companions. Natalia sat beside him, paler than usual, her head resting on his shoulder. They made for a villainous-looking bunch, unkempt and dirty, a result of their rushed departure from Ruzhina.

"Well?" said Stanislav. "How do you want to proceed?"

"I suggest we take what we know to the duke," said Athgar. "But before we do anything, we need to learn more about our surroundings."

"Such as?"

"Is the family still banned from court? What is Korvoran's opinion concerning the Stormwinds, or Sartellians, for that matter? Not everyone knows they're both a part of the same family. I'd also like to know if there are any Orcs in the area, so we can get word back to Shaluhk. Lastly, and most importantly, we need to get Natalia some help."

"The Mathewites must have a mission here," said Belgast. "I'm sure they could do something."

Galina set down her tankard. "I suggest Athgar and Natalia head to the mission. I'll take Katrin and search for any sign of Stormwinds while Stanislav and Belgast try to learn more about the current duke."

"Good idea," said the Dwarf. "We can meet back here this evening."

"We still need a place to stay," added Katrin. "Or did you forget that minor detail?"

"Not at all," replied Galina, "but until Natalia's been to the mission, we don't know how much we'll have left to work with. I don't suppose anyone has any relatives here?" She looked at Belgast, but he shook his head.

"I have a lot of cousins," said the Dwarf, "but none this far west."

"Then I suggest we get to work. Are you able to make it to the mission, Natalia?"

"I'm tired, not dead."

"Still, we don't know how far away it is. Perhaps we should hire you a carriage?"

"With what?" said Natalia. "We can't afford an expense like that."

"That brings up an important point," offered Katrin. "Sooner or later, we'll need more coins."

"What are you suggesting?" asked Athgar.

"Galina and I could hire on as Water Mages. Ships are always looking for ways to reduce their travel time."

"And split us up? I don't think that's wise. By staying together, we stand a better chance of defending ourselves against the family."

"He's right," said Natalia. "Our ultimate goal should be to return to Runewald, but first, we must spread the word on the dangers of inviting Stormwinds into the courts of the Petty Kingdoms."

"Or Sartellians," added Galina.

"All well and good," said Belgast, "but we can't just stroll up to the duke and say, 'Excuse me, Your Grace, but can you kick these people out of your court? They're bad folk.'"

"We came here because he's already done that, or at least that's the rumour."

"Yes," said Natalia, "but we need to confirm that's still true before we request an audience."

"And if we do," said Athgar, "why would he even agree to see us? It's not as if we can reveal our true identities."

"Why not?" asked Katrin.

"For one thing, you, Galina, and Natalia are all Stormwinds, and if he's banned the family, he'll want no part of you. For another, if I reveal I'm the High Thane of Therengia, they'll likely lock me up, or even worse, execute me. Judging from that Temple Knight's reaction, I doubt the locals much like the thought of the Old Kingdom reborn."

"So what you're saying," said Stanislav, "is that Belgast and I have the best chance of arranging an audience."

"I suppose so."

"You know," said Natalia, "the Temple Knights of Saint Agnes will likely have a good idea of what's going on at court."

"What makes you say that?"

"It's common practice for a garrison commander to present themselves at court from time to time. It's how the Church keeps their influence amongst the Continent's rulers."

"By threats?"

"I suppose that's one way of looking at it. Having a Temple Knight around reminds them there's a professional army out there to help ensure the peace."

Stanislav snorted. "Well, if that's their objective, they're doing a poor job of it. There's always conflict somewhere in the Petty Kingdoms. Clearly, the presence of Temple Knights has had little effect."

"Aye," said Belgast. "It's true. And made all the worse by the Church's insistence on remaining neutral in all conflicts. What's the point in having knights if they're never to be used?"

"You need to understand Church doctrine," explained Natalia.

"They originally formed the Temple Knights to guard their temples. However, in recent years, they've become more of a political force, rivalling the power of Halvaria itself, were they ever able to mass in one place. My understanding is they're now scattered throughout the Continent, held in reserve until their services are needed."

"Yes," said Athgar, "and thank the Gods for that. We've already fought them twice. I shouldn't like to try a third."

"Those were the Cunars; we know the family infiltrated them."

Galina gasped. "Are you sure?"

"Positive. We discovered this in Ebenstadt right before the Holy Army marched on Runewald."

"You say you beat them twice?"

"Yes," said Natalia. "Once at Ord-Kurgad, though there were fewer to fight there. The Battle of the Standing Stones was a different matter entirely."

"Why have I heard none of this?"

"I imagine they weren't eager to share news of their defeat. When we crushed their crusade, they abandoned Ebenstadt and likely a good part of the surrounding kingdoms as well."

"What makes you say that?"

"The Temple Knights of Saint Cunar stripped the immediate area to form the Holy Army in the first place. I imagine there were a lot of empty commanderies after we slaughtered them."

"Slaughtered?" said Katrin.

"Yes. They refused to surrender."

"And they haven't tried to recapture the city?"

"Not so far."

"Novarsk did," added Athgar, "but we beat them as well. I wonder how things are going back there since we left?"

"I imagine Kargen has everything under control," mused Natalia.

"And by Kargen, you mean Shaluhk."

"I mean the both of them. They're a team, much like we are. Each has their strengths, but together, they're more potent than they are individually."

"I agree," said Athgar, "but we're getting off topic."

"You're the one who asked about Novarsk."

He chuckled. "So I was, and for that, I apologize. Now, let's get out there, and do what's needed, shall we? Does everyone remember their tasks?"

"Yes," said Stanislav. "Belgast and I will find out what we can about the duke."

"And Katrin and I," said Galina, "will look into attitudes regarding the Stormwinds."

"Or Sartellians," added Katrin. "We mustn't overlook them."

"A good point," said Athgar. "Natalia and I will locate the local Mathewite mission and see if they can help her. We'll meet back here at dusk."

"What about rooms?" asked the Dwarf.

"Everyone keep an ear out. Perhaps we'll hear of suitable lodgings while we're out and about."

"And if we don't?"

"Then we will need to rely on the generosity of the Lydia's proprietor."

The Dwarf snorted. "I don't much fancy the idea of sleeping here, do you?"

"I've seen worse," replied Stanislav. "I remember one time, many years ago, when I found myself in Torburg."

"Torburg? Where's that?"

"In Erlingen, south of here. I happened to arrive just as the army was massing, and as a result, there wasn't a room to spare."

"Where did you end up staying?" Belgast asked.

"I was forced to while away the night in a tavern. I shouldn't need to tell you, but you don't get much sleep sitting at a table."

"I can well imagine."

"What of you, my friend? Have any horror stories you'd care to share?"

"As a matter of fact," said Belgast, "I do. I once found myself in the middle of nowhere with nothing."

"Oh? And where was this?"

"A little out-of-the-way place called Ostermund."

"What did you do?"

"He found us," said Athgar, "and we lent him enough to get by."

"Yes," agreed the Dwarf. "And thus, a great friendship was born."

"That hardly counts as a suitable tale," said Stanislav. "Where's the suffering in that?"

"Ah, well. The place I ended up staying only had weak ale."

"Now that," said the mage hunter, "is truly tragic."

ASSISTANCE

AUTUMN 1108 SR

The mission of Saint Mathew consisted of a single-floor building, its wooden walls laid out in a long, rectangular shape. Athgar and Natalia presented themselves at the door, where a single Temple Knight stood guard. He, in turn, beckoned to those inside, and moments later, a knight of Saint Agnes appeared.

"Is there a problem?" asked Athgar.

"Not at all," the sister knight replied. "My name is Sister Felicity. When admitting women to the mission, it's common for one of our order to be present." She was about to say more when her eyes beheld Athgar's. "You're a Therengian."

"I am. Why? Is that a problem?"

"No. A few of your people have sought treatment here, but I would've expected there to be more, all things considered."

"I don't understand."

"Well, those descended from the Old Kingdom have few options for healing."

"Meaning?"

"The physicians of Korvoran refuse to treat them."

"And the Life Mages?"

"As far as I know, there are none in all of Reinwick," said Sister Felicity. "They are known to be very rare amongst the Petty Kingdoms, their services only available to the wealthiest of nobles, but let us not delay further. You plainly came here seeking aid. Might I enquire as to the nature of your injury?"

"I'm not the one who requires help," said Athgar. "It's my wife, Natalia."

"And her symptoms?"

"Isn't that for the lay brother to deal with?"

"There are several skilled brethren here," said Sister Felicity. "Your wife's symptoms will help me decide who is best served to aid you."

"I'm weak," said Natalia, "and lack the strength to do much. Even walking is a chore at present."

"Then follow me, and I will take you to see Brother Aleksy."

She led them through the mission to a room on one side of a large eating area.

"Brother Aleksy," said Sister Felicity. "There's a patient here for you."

The lay brother of Saint Mathew looked up from where he was writing. "How interesting," he mused. "It's rare that we see grey-eyes seeking our assistance." He held up his hand to forestall any arguments. "Not that I object to treating such a patient."

"It is his wife who needs your help."

"Oh? What seems to be the problem?" He swivelled his gaze to Natalia.

"I lack strength," she replied, "and tire easily."

"Could you possibly be with child?"

"Doubtful. Besides, I already have a daughter and suffered no such symptoms."

"Come. Take a seat, and I'll look at you."

She sat, and the lay brother moved closer, first peering into her eyes, then feeling her forehead.

"There is no sign of fever. Have you any dizziness?"

"A little."

He felt her wrist. "Your pulse is strong, and you look well-fed. Has something happened recently that might account for this weakness? An illness, perhaps?"

"No," said Natalia, eager to hide her magical abilities.

He pinched the skin on her arm and watched it closely, nodding his head. "You're a little pale. Might I ask from whence you hail?"

"Ruzhina."

"Ah. That likely accounts for the hue of your skin. Have you recently been at sea?"

"Indeed."

"Aha. Then that accounts for it."

"So, what is it?" asked Athgar.

The lay brother moved back to his desk. "All evidence seems to point to simple exhaustion. A few days' rest should set things right. I might also suggest a sleeping draught?"

"Which is?"

"A powder, which, when added to a drink, produces a soporific effect. If you are willing to wait, I can go and fetch you some?"

"Yes. Thank you," said Natalia.

Brother Aleksy left the room, leaving the pair in the Temple Knight's company.

"Say," said Athgar. "You wouldn't happen to know Sister Cordelia, would you?"

"Can't say I do. Why? Where does she serve?"

"In Krieghoff."

The Temple Knight chuckled. "I have no idea where that is."

"It lies far to the east; though, in truth, I suspect it's more southeast of here. She was an equerry. Have you one of those here?"

"No. Our horses are all acquired through the regional headquarters in Eidolon. I could make enquiries about Sister Cordelia if you're interested."

"I was merely curious," said Athgar.

"It sounds like you've travelled quite a lot. Might I ask how you came to be here in Korvoran?"

"We fled Ruzhina," said Natalia.

The knight eyed them suspiciously. "Does that make you criminals?"

"No, although the term 'fugitives' might not be far from the truth. My name is Natalia Stormwind." The knight's eyes widened.

"Members of that family are not welcome in Reinwick, under penalty of death."

"I can assure you we are not supporters of them. Rather, we are fleeing them."

"Might I ask why?"

"Let's just say we take objection to their influence in the courts of the Petty Kingdoms."

Sister Felicity remained quiet for a moment, mulling things over.

"Will you report us to the authorities?" asked Athgar.

"No. I'll not condemn a person based solely on their name. However, I suggest you keep your family affiliations to yourself, at least for the present. If word got out about your true identity, it might spur action against you."

"And by action, you mean?"

"If not arrested by the duke, then possibly a lynching at the hands of the populace. There's a lot of hard feelings these days when it comes to the Stormwinds."

"Why?"

"I'm not the person to answer that."

"Then, if I might ask," said Natalia, "to whom should we direct such questions?"

"Temple Captain Leona. She commands the order here in Korvoran. You can find her at the commandery should you seek an audience."

"Thank you. We shall definitely consider it."

Brother Aleksy reappeared, bearing a small clay pot that fit easily in his hand. "Here it is." He held it up before carefully removing the top. Inside lay a pale green powder.

"What is it?" asked Natalia.

"Ground seaflower, common enough in these parts. Mix a pinch of this into some water, and you'll find it induces sleep. Be careful, though. Too much, and you might find yourself unable to wake. I would also only use it as required."

"Why is that?" asked Athgar.

"It's a potent mixture, and a person can become dependent on it."

"Who in the Continent would want to sleep all the time?"

Brother Aleksy laughed. "It's not just the sleep, but the dreams that often accompany its administration. They say it opens the mind."

"You may rest assured I shall use it sparingly," said Natalia. "I'm quite happy with experiencing my life while awake."

The lay brother handed over the pot. "There's enough to last you a week, at least. If you need more, you know where to find me."

"Thank you."

"Now, is there anything else I can help you with?"

"Actually, yes, there is," said Natalia. "You wouldn't, perchance, know of an inn in these parts that you could recommend?"

Brother Aleksy's gaze swivelled to Athgar. "I'm afraid there's no place in all of Korvoran that will shelter the cursed descendants of the Old Kingdom."

"I beg your pardon?"

The lay brother blushed. "Sorry. I meant no offence, but you must understand how the people of Reinwick see folk like your companion here, especially with the news from out east."

"What news is that?" she asked.

"They say the Old Kingdom has been reborn, which has made people nervous. They fear it will spread and absorb all the Petty Kingdoms."

"And what do you believe?"

"I don't generally put much faith in the concept of an empire reborn, but then again, you can't deny the recent news is disturbing. Now there's even more unrest in the Petty Kingdoms as kings and dukes rush to isolate the threat."

"I'm curious," said Athgar. "What do you mean when you say 'isolate'?"

"Many have taken it upon themselves to gather up anyone with grey eyes."

"For what purpose?"

"To keep them away from the general population, of course. They're afraid they could try to rise up."

"So you're suggesting they make them slaves?"

"Not slaves so much as prisoners," said Brother Aleksy, "and I might point out the Church opposes such a move. Personally, I find it abhorrent."

"Has the Duke of Reinwick made such a move?"

"No, but our neighbour to the south, Andover, certainly has, assuming our information is accurate." He paused for a moment, then blushed. "Look at me, repeating gossip like it was something of import. Please, pay no attention to my ramblings; I beg of you."

"We should leave anyway," said Natalia. "It's getting late, and we still need to find lodgings. Thank you, Brother Aleksy, for your aid."

"You are quite welcome," replied the lay brother.

Natalia stood, taking Athgar's hand to steady herself. They left the room, making their way back to the entrance and out to the street. They had only just taken their bearings when Sister Felicity called out.

"You must pardon Brother Aleksy," she said. "He means well but tends to prattle on incessantly. I think at heart he's just lonely, but it tends to put people off."

"Not at all," said Natalia, turning to face the knight. "Was there something you wanted?"

"Yes. If you're looking for lodging, you might try a place called the Anchor. They'll take anyone provided they can pay."

"Thank you. We'll keep that in mind."

They were well out of sight of the mission when Natalia finally broke the silence. "What did you make of all that?"

"You mean the diagnosis?" said Athgar. "I believe it's accurate. A pity you couldn't tell him about your magic though."

"No. I mean all this news about the people of the Old Kingdom."

"It's alarming, to be sure, but what can we do about it? We have no power here."

"Not yet," she corrected, "but things change over time."

"What is it you're thinking?"

"A lot of land lies between here and home. It would be far easier to travel in numbers."

Athgar grinned. "You're suggesting we take Therengians with us?"

"Naturally. The Gods know we can use everyone we can get our hands on."

"We have plenty of land, that's true, but that's a lot of miles to travel, and a large group might be seen as trouble. Not to mention we'd need to find some way of feeding them all."

"Still, it's something to consider."

"And I will, in time, but right now, there are more important matters to deal with, like how to pay for our next meal."

"Yes," said Natalia. "I've given that some thought too."

"And?"

"Perhaps we could take service with His Grace, the duke?"

"And why would he consent to that?"

"There are no Stormwinds here, remember? That might indicate he requires mages at his court."

"And what makes you believe he'd be willing to hire you?"

She smiled. "Between Katrin, Galina, and myself, we can offer him three Water Mages at one price."

"And what price would that be?"

"Enough to keep us all housed and fed."

"It's worth a try," said Athgar, "but ultimately, we still must find a way home—after we expose the family's plotting, of course."

Natalia chuckled. "Our list keeps getting longer."

"What list?"

"The list of what we need to do. Now, we just added liberating the Therengians to the pile."

He smiled. "Well, we can't make things too easy. That wouldn't be our way."

"And what is our way?"

He took her hand. "I'm not sure, but whatever it is, we do it together, agreed?"

"Agreed!"

"Do you believe we'll ever learn the true reason they expelled the Stormwinds from Reinwick?"

"We might," replied Natalia, "but I suspect there are very few who know the full story. The family would do all in its power to suppress such information."

"And yet the family is no longer here."

"Not at court, but I'm certain their agents are still here, if only to keep an eye on things."

"Surely the presence of a mage would be noted?"

"They won't be mages. You remember when we met back in

Draybourne?"

"Of course," said Athgar. "I rescued you from those thugs."

She laughed. "I seem to remember it was the other way around. In any event, those 'thugs' were working for the family. Think of them as bounty hunters."

"Like that fellow Nikolai whom we ran into in Caerhaven?"

"Precisely."

"Why do they work for the family?"

"Because the Stormwinds have coins, something most of those rogues are perpetually short of."

He looked around the area, suddenly suspicious. "You don't think we're being followed, do you?"

"I doubt it. They'd have to know we were coming, and bounty hunters have no magic to receive news of our flight. Still, we should exercise caution when it comes to trusting people."

"A good point. I shall follow the advice of my ancestors."

"Which is?"

"Trust is earned at the head of an axe."

"Hardly the type of thing to endear us to the locals."

"And that surprises you? I used to think my people had it tough in Draybourne, but this place makes that city look positively inviting."

"I might remind you we met in Draybourne, so it wasn't all bad."

"True," said Athgar, "and I wouldn't trade that for anything, but things are much tougher here for Therengians than they are out east."

"It's strange to think people are treated differently simply because of the colour of their eyes."

"Many fear anything they're not used to; the Orcs are a prime example of that. Most of the Petty Kingdoms view them as no more than savage brutes, yet we both know they're more advanced than us Humans in many ways."

"True, yet Dwarves and Elves live in cities amongst men and women."

"Ah," said Athgar, "but they're much more like us. Yes, there are physical differences, but most of those are superficial. On the other hand, Orc blood is black, which makes them foreign."

"But why be accepting of Dwarves and not Therengians?"

He shrugged. "Another mystery we may never be able to solve." He halted, his gaze wandering to a nearby stall.

"Something wrong?"

He smiled. "It just occurred to me that we might have a source of income after all."

Her gaze followed his to see meat hanging out in the open. "You mean hunting?"

"I do."

"Be warned: in many places, you need the ruler's permission to hunt close to a city."

"Why is that?"

"All the land not otherwise disbursed is typically the king's property, or in this case, the duke. I doubt His Grace would take kindly to you taking his deer—that would be considered poaching."

"What a ridiculous concept. Deer are free creatures roaming the Continent's forests; it's not as if they pledge loyalty to a lord."

"All true, yet it doesn't stop them from claiming the creatures as their own. I know it's frustrating, but this is the way of things here, and we must abide by their laws."

"Even when they don't make sense?"

"Especially when they don't make sense. It will also serve you well to learn as much about these people as possible."

"To what end?"

She lowered her voice. "You're the High Thane. Eventually, you must deal with these people, which will be easier if you understand them."

"And to understand them, I must learn as much about their customs and behaviours as I can. That makes perfect sense, of course. It's just not something I'd thought about."

"That's why you have me."

He looked into her eyes before he leaned in, kissing her tenderly.

"What was that for?" she asked, smiling.

"For being you." He was about to say more, but at that precise moment, someone grabbed his arm, yanking him around violently.

"What do you think you're doing?" the stranger snarled.

"I beg your pardon?"

"Keep your filthy lips to yourself, Grey-eyes."

"I'll have you know that's my wife," said Athgar.

Without another word, the fellow struck out, punching him in the gut, knocking the wind from him. Athgar crumpled to the ground, and the fellow moved in for a kick.

Natalia raised her hands, with words of power tumbling from her lips. Frost formed on her fingertips as she reached out, touching the malcontent. He screamed in pain when ice climbed up his arm, his eyes widening in fear. Natalia kept the contact until the man fell to his knees, releasing him from the torment.

"I suggest you learn some manners," she said. "In the meantime, you should make yourself scarce."

He got to his feet, avoiding her direct gaze. Then, cradling his afflicted arm, he ran down a side street.

"Are you all right?" she asked.

Athgar stood, his breath still laboured. "He caught me by surprise. I won't let that happen again." He took in the bystanders, all looking at them in shock. "I believe we might have overstayed our welcome here. Perhaps it's time to return to the Lydia?"

"I think that an excellent idea."

"Wait a moment; you used your magic."

"What of it?"

"I thought you were exhausted?"

"I am, and if truth be told, my power has yet to return to full strength, but it was more than enough to deal with the likes of that fellow."

She took his arm, and they resumed their walk. After several steps, she giggled.

"Anything you'd care to share?"

"I was thinking how lucky that fellow was."

"Lucky? Why would you ever say he was lucky?"

"If the roles were reversed, you might have set fire to him, which would leave him… smouldering."

"You've been hanging around me for too long."

"Never," she replied.

RUNEWALD

AUTUMN 1108 SR

Graxion Stormwind straightened his back. The ride from Ebenstadt was far longer than he'd anticipated, but finally, before them lay Runewald, the capital of Therengia. "Are you sure this isn't a mistake?"

"Quite sure," replied his sergeant. "A Temple Knight of Saint Mathew gave us directions, a fellow by the name of Captain Yaromir."

"And he swears this… village is truly where their king resides?"

"Indeed, my lord."

Graxion stared at it a little longer as if his mind might will a larger settlement into existence. "Very well. It appears we must make do with what lies yonder." He urged his horse forward.

The sergeant dutifully fell in beside him while the rest of the entourage, half a dozen men-at-arms, trailed along in their wake. As they drew closer, Graxion noticed Runewald's walls were made of stone yet bore no sign of bricks.

"Earth Mages," muttered Graxion.

"Pardon me, my lord?"

"You were undoubtedly wondering how such a wall was constructed."

The sergeant shook his head, but before he could respond, he noticed someone on the wall and moved to clutch the hilt of his sword. "They've seen us, Lord."

"Hold, Sergeant. We are on a diplomatic mission, here to extend the family's hand of friendship."

"We are to stay here? In this primitive place?"

"If this is the home of their king, then yes. We must, on occasion, make sacrifices for the greater good of all."

As they approached, a voice called out from atop the gate.

"What did he say?" asked the sergeant.

"I couldn't tell. We'll get a little closer and then halt. That should avoid antagonizing them."

A door opened, and half a dozen men came out armed with spears and shields, but there was no sign of armour.

"What's this, now?" said Graxion, under his breath. "Have they no trained warriors?"

"Halt!" came a voice. "Identify yourself."

The visitors stopped. "I am Graxion Stormwind," called out the mage. "I am here to offer my services to your king."

"We have no king."

"Then I request an audience with whomever is in charge."

A lone figure moved closer. "I am Captain Raleth, leader of the Thane Guard. If you'll follow me, I'll show you where he can be found."

"Very well, Captain. Lead on."

Their host led them through the gate, revealing an odd collection of goat pens and small gardens. Beyond this relatively open area were the villagers' homes, where thick thatched roofs sat atop wattle-and-daub walls supported by wide beams.

They passed several homes, their arrival of great interest to the inhabitants. Finally, they came across another open area roughly circular, with a huge firepit at its centre, though at present, it was unlit. The largest building in all of Runewald stood to the east, a long structure with a high roof.

"Sir?" The panic in the sergeant's voice caused Graxion to swivel his gaze to where a small group of Orcs walked towards them, their eyes locked on his guards.

"Do not panic," whispered the mage. "We received reports that the Therengians employ Orc mercenaries. Try to ignore them."

"But they are savages, my lord. How can we trust them not to attack?"

"That would cause a diplomatic incident. I doubt even the ruler of this place would dare risk offending the Stormwinds."

Their host halted. "Give us your horses, Lord, then I shall escort you inside."

Graxion climbed down from the saddle, waiting as they all handed over their reins.

"Your men must wait here," said the captain.

"You heard him, Sergeant. Fear not. I shall call out if I need you."

Captain Raleth opened the door, and the mage stepped into a long room with a firepit running the length of it from left to right. Doors stood at either end, although there was no clue what lay beyond. The large Orc waiting there for them, however, was the most striking feature of all.

"I am here to see your master," said Graxion.

"I was led to believe you came to see our ruler," said the greenskin.

"I did. Is he not your master?"

"Our leaders are not our masters; they act on our behalf. In any case, he is not available. In his stead, you may deal with me."

The mage wanted to laugh but controlled his amusement. Was this savage serious, or was this all part of an elaborate prank designed to test him? "And you are?" he finally asked.

"Kargen, Chieftain of the Red Hand, and acting High Thane."

"Are you suggesting these people allow an Orc to rule over them?"

"As I said, our leaders do not rule. The people of each village elect their thanes, then they choose one from amongst their number to act as leader."

"And is Runewald your village?"

"It is the home of my people. The Orcs of Runewald are my responsibility, but we stand shoulder to shoulder with the Humans here. In essence, we are all Therengians. Now tell me, what is the reason for this visit?"

"I am here to offer you my services."

"And you are?"

"Graxion Stormwind, Master Water Mage. I come from Karslev."

"Ah, yes," said Kargen. "The capital of Ruzhina. Tell me, is the Volstrum still controlling your king?"

Graxion found himself at a loss for words for the first time in his life.

"We know all about you," continued the Orc. "Your family has selectively bred Water Mages for generations. Is that not correct?"

"I… suppose that's one way of putting it. I was not aware anyone outside of our family knew of this."

Kargen grinned. "We Orcs are often dismissed as savage brutes, yet I assure you, our scholars are amongst the brightest in all the Continent."

"Scholars? I was unaware Orcs had such things?"

"It appears you are full of misconception where we are concerned. Tell me, why did you come to Runewald?"

"As I said, I am here to offer my services."

"And what does that mean, precisely?"

"I am a powerful mage," said Graxion. "Rulers often seek us for guidance or counsel."

"How does the knowledge of magic help you guide others? One would think a scholar better suited to such a role."

"Any court in the Petty Kingdoms would be thrilled to have someone like me."

"Then I suggest you seek a position there, for we have no space for you here."

Graxion reddened. "You dare to insult me to my face?"

"I do not intend to insult, merely educate."

"But I am an accomplished mage, one of the most powerful in all the Continent!"

"Mages we have in plenty," said Kargen. "And of what use would a Water Mage be to us? We do not live by the sea."

"But I am a battle mage."

"We are not at war."

"Not at present, but that can change quickly in the Petty Kingdoms. Why, it wasn't so long ago you were fighting Novarsk."

Kargen smiled again. "I can see you have kept abreast of recent events. Doubtless, then, you will recall we defeated Queen Rada without any help from you or your so-called family."

"But mages are an important part of any army."

"As I said, we have enough already."

"Nonsense. No one can claim this."

"Shaluhk!"

A door opened, admitting a female Orc. "Yes, my bondmate?"

"This is Lord Graxion Stormwind. He claims we need to hire him to supplement our army, but I told him we have sufficient for our needs. Remind me, if you would, how many purveyors of magic there are amongst our people?"

"Twelve, at last count, although there are a number in training I do not include."

"There, you see?" said Kargen. "We do not need the help of you or your family."

"Ah," said Graxion, "but there is more to consider than simply magic."

"Go on. I'm listening."

"The Stormwinds are wealthy. Perhaps a gift might be more of an inducement to allow us into your court?"

"Why do you place such importance on being part of our court?"

"It is the way of things. The Stormwinds advise the most powerful rulers in all the Continent. We lend our expertise on many topics, not just warfare."

"Let him continue," said Shaluhk. "I would hear what he offers in terms of a gift."

Graxion smiled, for gold was always the swayer of opinions. "We can supply you with coins, enough to fill a large chest."

"Impressive," said Kargen. "Just how many coins are we talking about?"

"Thousands."

"Would that not depend upon the size of the chest?"

"I beg your pardon?"

"You claim to be able to fill a large chest, but ask half a dozen people, and all will have a different opinion about what constitutes large."

"Surely you jest," said the mage. "I'm offering you coins, enough for you to live a life of luxury."

Kargen held out his hand, and the female Orc, Shaluhk, moved closer to take it. "I already possess what riches I need. Your gold will win no favours here." He waited a moment as the visitor glanced at Raleth. "And if you believe your coins will buy the allegiance of the good captain here, you are sorely mistaken."

"You're making a big mistake," said Graxion. "It is not wise to refuse my offer."

"And yet I did just that."

"Then I shall seek out this High Thane of yours. I'm sure he will see reason."

"I know him well, and I can assure you his opinion of the matter is no different from mine. Now begone, before I take offence and order you arrested."

"You wouldn't dare!"

"Laruhk?" called out the Orc chieftain.

Moments later, a large Orc entered, spear in hand. "Yes, my chieftain?"

"See Lord Graxion Stormwind and his companions escorted from our borders."

The mage reddened. "And if I refuse the escort?"

"Then I shall let the tuskers feed off your bones. The choice is yours as to whether that is the fate you desire."

Graxion stormed from the hut. His sergeant straightened, his hand gripping the pommel of his sword. "Problem, my lord?"

"We have been insulted," replied his master. "Come. We will leave this wretched place with all haste."

They climbed into the saddle, heading back towards the gate. Halfway there, they saw huge creatures easily twice the size of their horses. Their massive heads, long and tapered, sported sharp, pointed teeth capable of tearing flesh from bone. Upon their backs sat more of the green folk.

Graxion paled. He'd faced his share of danger over the years, but never in his wildest dreams had he ever imagined such a monstrosity.

"What are those things?" said his sergeant.

"I believe they call them tuskers. Not something I'd care to pit my strength against presently."

"Agreed, Lord. Where to now?"

"We will return home by way of Ebenstadt, then north, through Novarsk. I'm sure there, we'll find those willing to entertain our presence."

"You will not," came the voice of Laruhk.

They both looked at the Orc staring down at them from the saddle. "The Kingdom of Novarsk is no longer a sovereign country, for it is a conquered land. Surely you learned this on your initial trip through there?"

Graxion glared back. He knew Novarsk had lost the recent war with Therengia. However, agents of the family assured him the nobles there were still in control. He harboured no doubts that they would welcome his coins, yet it was best not to mention his plans to this Orc.

Laruhk shrugged in a very Human-like manner. "It matters little, but I am tasked with escorting you from our lands."

"Then we shall be rid of you when we reach the border of Novarsk."

"No, they are our lands now. We will not leave you until you pass through that kingdom and out the other side. Until then, I recommend you get used to us."

Shaluhk sat by the fire, pulling Kargen down with her. "*That man is dangerous,*" she said in the tongue of her people. "*I doubt that is the last we shall hear of him.*"

"*Nor I,*" replied her bondmate, "*but it is no surprise that he came. The family was bound to visit, eventually. At least it gave us a chance to see them in person.*"

"*And they gave no indication they are aware of Athgar and Nat-Alia's journey to Karslev. Hopefully, that means they are safe, though I would be happier for some news of them.*"

"*Agreed,*" said Kargen. "*Yet, in the meantime, we must look after things in their absence.*"

"*And how fares the army?*"

"*The reforms Nat-Alia suggested are well underway, while Belgast's cousins work night and day to provide armour and weapons. They have already made enough mail to equip the Thane Guard, and there are spears enough for all. How are things in Ebenstadt?*"

"*The reports are encouraging,*" said Shaluhk. "*More Therengians join us from the west. We shall soon need to choose more sites for villages.*"

One of the doors crashed open, with Agar running into the room, Oswyn riding his shoulders and shrieking, her voice echoing off the walls.

"Hold!" called out Kargen in the Human tongue. "I would talk with you."

Agar slowed, his youthful energy held at bay. Oswyn, as if reading his mood, quieted. "Yes, Father?" said the Orc youngling.

"Tell me, what is the mood of Runewald? Are people happy?"

"They are, Father, but you knew that already."

"I did, but I wanted to see if you were aware of what goes on around you."

"You are talking of our visitors?"

"I am. What do you know about them?"

"The Stormwinds sent them."

"And do you understand the importance of that name?"

"Yes. They bear the same name as Nat-Alia but are our enemy."

"Good. Remember this lesson well in future. One day, your life may depend on it."

"I will, Father. I promise."

"Now, go fetch Tonfer Garul, will you? And keep an eye on Oswyn."

"Agar, good," said the little girl.

The pair ran off, the shrieks returning.

"They are devoted to one another," said Shaluhk.

"Yes. A symbol of the trust shared between our two peoples."

They sat silently, staring at the flames, basking in their shared presence.

It didn't take long for Tonfer Garul to find them. "I hope I am not interrupting anything?"

"*Not at all,*" said Kargen, lapsing into his native tongue. "*Come and join us. We wish to discuss something.*"

"*By all means.*" Tonfer sat opposite them. "*What is it you would like to know?*"

"*You have been working with the bard, Dunstan. Is that not correct?*"

"*It is.*"

"*What have you learned concerning the customs of Athgar's ancestors?*"

"*Much, but it might help if you could be more specific about what you want to know.*"

"*The Therengia of old stretched across an extensive region of the Continent,*" said Kargen. "*How did they rule such an expanse?*"

"*The Old Kingdom, as Humans like to call it, was broken down into provinces, each run by a governor appointed by their king. Beneath each, were other individuals, though they possessed their own title, and were collectively known as administrators.*"

"*And these were also appointed?*"

"*Yes,*" said Tonfer, "*but there was a requirement that they be able to read and write, a necessary precaution to ensure they could follow the king's missives. To that end, one of their rulers, Byrnwold the Brave, created a place of learning to teach those necessary skills. It was called the Golarus—the place of learning.*"

"*And for how long did this place exist?*"

"*That is difficult to say. They built the first one in the capital of Therengia, but that city's name is lost to us. Eventually, they built others throughout the kingdom; some reports say as many as two dozen at their height. Most of these tales only survive in oral form, so we have no actual confirmation that the numbers are correct.*"

"*Thank you. That is most informative.*"

"*Might I ask the relevance of this line of questioning?*"

"*I must consider what to do with Novarsk,*" replied Kargen.

"*Are they not an independent kingdom?*"

"*They were before invading us, but we can not leave them to their own devices, else they will simply repeat the sins of their past and war with us once more.*"

"*And so you mean to make them a province?*"

"*It is but one of many possibilities. Another would be to install a ruler friendly to our cause, but then we would have to worry about later successions to the Throne.*"

"*It is a difficult decision,*" said Tonfer. "*How will you choose?*"

"*That is a question I have long been asking myself.*"

"*We must go to Novarsk,*" said Shaluhk. "*Only by seeing the place for yourself will you be able to make your decision.*"

"*I was hoping Athgar would be home by now.*"

"*As was I, but the decision has been left to us.*"

"*Then I shall leave by week's end.*"

"*No, WE shall leave. My place is by your side, especially when this burden sits heavy upon your shoulders.*"

"*And what of Agar?*"

"*He and Oswyn will accompany us. I am certain Skora would be willing to help look after them.*"

"*Then it is settled,*" said Kargen. "*We shall go to their capital, Halmund, and see the state of things for ourselves.*"

THE ANCHOR

AUTUMN 1108 SR

"Well?" said Athgar. "Did anyone learn anything interesting?"

"Believe it or not," said Galina, "this very place figures prominently in the tale."

"What tale is that?" asked Belgast. "And am I going to need another ale to listen to it?"

"I refer to the reason for the Stormwinds' banishment from Reinwick. It all starts with the owner of this place. He used to own a ship called the *Lydia*, which still sails to this day, though admittedly under a different name —the *Valiant*."

"Wait a moment," said Stanislav. "I know that name. That's a part of the Holy Fleet, isn't it?"

"It is; their flagship, in fact. Master Handley over there sold it to the Temple Knights of Saint Agnes. That very ship uncovered a Halvarian plot to foment unrest in the region. A plot, by the way, that was abetted by a certain mage by the name of Larissa Stormwind."

"Other than Stanislav, has anyone else here ever met this person?"

"No," said Galina. "Though the name is not unfamiliar to me. I believe she was considered a powerful mage."

"And how would you know that?"

"I worked at the Volstrum, remember? I had access to all kinds of records, and I have an excellent memory."

"What else can you tell us about her?" asked Natalia.

"She was an excellent student, one of the Volstrum's best, if her marks are any indication, although nowhere near as powerful as yourself. In every respect, she was exactly what the family was looking for. Mind you, this was years ago."

"How long ago did these events occur?"

"The duke banished the Stormwinds late in ninety-eight."

"Ten years," said Stanislav. "That's a long time for the family to be on the outs. I doubt they took it well."

"I have no information on that score," said Galina. "However, I found out Larissa ingratiated herself with the duchess. There are rumours she was very angry about her husband's decision and for a while, their relationship cooled."

"Cooled?" said Athgar. "Are you suggesting they no longer get along?"

"That would be my guess, but once again, we're only getting this information second-hand. We need to get ourselves to court to find out more."

Athgar turned his attention to the males at the table. "How about you two? Learn anything of value?"

"That depends on your definition of valuable," said Belgast. "We learned more about the Holy Fleet, but I'm not sure that's of any use to us."

"Tell us anyway," said Natalia. "You never know what might work to our advantage."

"Very well. The *Valiant* was the first ship to join the northern fleet, but it wasn't the last. Another similar craft, the *Vigilant*, soon followed, and then they assembled an expedition to destroy the Halvarian presence at some place called the Five Sisters."

"What's that?" asked Katrin.

"A group of islands to the northeast of Reinwick. Apparently, they destroyed the fleet, though some accounts claim they captured quite a few ships of Halvarian design."

"That's not the best part," said Stanislav. "There are rumours the Temple Knights created a secret base in the Five Sisters, and that's where they're hiding the bulk of their fleet."

"Once again," said Athgar, "I don't see how that works to our advantage. It's not as if the Church is willing to get involved with our family problem."

"Ah," said Natalia, "but it's not a Church Fleet; those ships belong to the Temple Knights of Saint Agnes. They helped us at Ord-Kurgad. Maybe they'd be willing to help us here?"

"Help, how? There's nothing for which we need ships, at least not at present."

"Still, it might be good to cultivate some friends amongst the Temple Knights. Sister Felicity suggested we visit her captain."

"That's an excellent idea," noted Athgar.

"How about an inn?" said Stanislav. "Any luck with that?"

"As a matter of fact, yes," replied Athgar. "Someone suggested we might be able to find lodgings at a place called the Anchor. We made some enquiries on our way back here, and it's only a few blocks away."

"Then I suggest we get going. The sooner we get away from the stench of the sea, the better."

"Ah, yes. About that," said Athgar. "Don't get your hopes up. The Anchor is close by the bay."

"How close?"

"Close enough for the seagulls to be a constant nuisance, if I'm not mistaken."

"Do they serve ale there?" asked Belgast.

"I imagine so."

"Good. Then let's get going, shall we?"

The Anchor was not the most pleasant of places, with a filthy floor and an odour to match. However, it was relatively quiet this time of the evening, its dozen tables mostly empty.

They took a seat, then Galina waved over a server.

"What can I get you?" the woman asked.

"Do you rent rooms?"

"We do, providing you can pay."

"That's not a problem."

The woman took in the group. "The rooms hold two apiece. I'll let you decide how best to split up your friends."

"Then let's say three rooms, shall we?" Galina placed three gold coins on the table. "Will this suffice?"

"Most definitely," the server replied. "I'll even fetch your dinner, if you like. Breakfast is served at first light, providing you don't mind porridge."

"I love porridge," said Natalia. "You couldn't give it a hint of maple, could you?"

The look she received indicated that such frivolities were not available here.

"Never mind," said Natalia. "I do miss Shaluhk's porridge," she added as the woman left the room, presumably to see to the food.

"Well," said Galina, "at least we have rooms for the night."

"We need to look at getting more coins," suggested Katrin. "What about you, Belgast? Couldn't you take up smithing or something?"

The Dwarf's eyes bulged. "Take up smithing? Do you believe that's something you can just whip up out of nothing? It takes a fortune to set up a forge, assuming you possess the requisite skills, and I most definitely do not!"

"But I thought you were a smith in Runewald?"

"No, I run the business side of the smithy. It's my cousins who do all the work. Do you believe all Dwarves are smiths?"

Katrin fell silent.

"How much do have we left?" asked Natalia.

"Enough to pay for our room and board till the end of the week."

"Then I suggest we concentrate on the more important things for now."

"Which are?"

"Making contact with the duke."

"Are you sure that's still necessary?" asked Athgar. "We know he ejected Larissa Stormwind. Isn't that enough?"

"Not if we want to break the family's grip over the Continent."

"And how does that work?" asked Stanislav. "One duke can't kick them out of all those courts."

"True, but he has influence and allies, and the more we spread the word, the better."

"Are there any other kingdoms who've turned against the family?" asked Katrin.

"You're asking the wrong person," replied Natalia. "Galina would likely know more than I."

"There were rumours back in the Volstrum," replied Galina. "But I hesitate to lend them credence."

"What types of rumours?"

"There's a kingdom called Hadenfeld. The family's been trying to gain influence there for years. There's even a rumour they backed a rival faction during a rebellion."

"Hardly surprising, considering what we now know about them. Was the rebellion successful?"

"For several years, yes," said Galina. "They even broke away and formed their own kingdom, but it didn't last."

"Why? What happened?"

"Their king died, and then his son tried to take the Throne of Hadenfeld. It didn't end well."

"Meaning?" asked Natalia.

"They lost the war, the king his life, and as a consequence, Hadenfeld and Neuhafen were reunited."

"And the family didn't ingratiate themselves into their court?"

"No. For some reason, their offers were refused."

"How long ago was this?"

"Some years now," said Galina. "Though, come to think of it, it would've been right after they uncovered the plot here, in Reinwick. Do you think there might be a connection?"

"It could be just a coincidence," said Natalia, "but hopefully, a visit to court might provide more information."

"What is it you're thinking?" asked Athgar.

"There are several occurrences over a relatively short period. A Halvarian plot, the rise of this Temple Navy, and another kingdom refusing the family's offer of mages."

"There's something else," offered Stanislav. "Remember, that navy you're talking about is owned by Temple Knights, not the Church."

"Why is that significant?" asked Katrin.

"I'm reminded of something Brother Yaromir mentioned back in Ebenstadt. We were having a drink one night, and he let slip the Cunars were pushing their weight around."

"Meaning?"

"He wasn't exactly full of details, but it appears the majority of funds the Church collects go straight into the Cunar's coffers."

"To what end?"

"I can answer that," said Natalia. "Back in Ebenstadt, we discovered the family had infiltrated the Cunar Order."

"But you ruined the fellow, surely? After all, you destroyed the army."

"We did, but what if that one individual was only the tip of the spear?"

"Are you suggesting the family has taken over all the Temple Knights?" asked Stanislav.

"Not all of them, but they've most assuredly placed people in influential places."

"That makes no sense," said Belgast. "We know they control the empire. Why would they wish to strengthen the Cunars?"

"It's not only the Cunars," said Athgar. "It all makes perfect sense now."

"Care to share your thoughts?"

"What's the one thing stopping Halvaria from invading the rest of the Continent?"

"The Temple Knights," said Galina. "They're the biggest threat."

"Now, what if that very same Church was destroyed?"

"Don't be ridiculous," said Katrin. "You can't destroy an organization that large."

"Sorry," said Athgar. "Let me clarify. I'm not talking about the entire Church. I doubt the empire cares about that one way or the other. I'm talking about the fighting orders."

"But," said Katrin, "Stanislav said the Cunars are taking all the funds. How does that weaken them?"

"You forget—there's more to the fighting orders than just the Cunars."

"That's right," said Natalia, warming to the idea. "But the only other orders with a battlefield presence would be the Agnesites and the Mathewites."

"Agnesites?" said Athgar. "Is that what we're calling them now?"

"Hold on a moment," said Galina. "I see a flaw in your theory."

"Which is?" replied Athgar.

"If the Cunars took all the coins, who paid for this new fleet?"

"That's something I can't answer, at least not yet. We need more information."

"We need to talk to the sisters," said Natalia. "It's their fleet. They must have an idea who's funding it."

Belgast grunted. "For all we know, the family's behind that too."

"No," said Athgar. "I have a hard time believing that. Their ships conduct patrols to cut down on piracy, and they defeated a Halvarian Fleet some years ago. Hardly the type of thing they'd do to an ally."

"Yes, but there's still the matter of a secret base that's out there somewhere." The Dwarf paused a moment. "By the Gods, I should've seen it sooner."

"Seen what?"

"Why would an order of Temple Knights build a secret base? I can think of only one reason."

"Which is?" asked Athgar.

"They don't trust the rest of the Church."

"If that's true," said Galina, "then the entire organization is in peril. You were right, Athgar. Something is tearing them apart."

"That might be to our advantage," said Stanislav. "You know the old saying, 'Those who oppose the same enemies must be friends'. You've worked with the sisters before, haven't you?"

"Yes," said Natalia. "Back in Krieghoff. They helped us at the Battle of Ord-Kurgad."

"And," added Belgast, "in that battle, they faced down the Temple Knights of Saint Cunar. What was that woman's name again?"

"Sister Cordelia."

"That's right. She was the equerry or something."

"So she wasn't in charge?" said Galina. "That's a little unusual, isn't it? Leading a group of knights against a brother order without a captain?"

"She mentioned something about her previous assignment being troubled. Could that be related to all of this?"

"That would depend on where it was."

"Ilea," said Athgar. "A country on the southern coast, if I remember correctly."

"Illiana certainly never mentioned the place," said Galina. "So I doubt it's related."

"We're missing something. It always feels like someone is two steps ahead of us."

"That's because they are," said Natalia. "The family's had years to set these plans in motion, and we only just started untangling the threads."

"All well and good," said Stanislav, "but we need to make some decisions on how to proceed."

"I'll go to the Agnes commandery tomorrow," said Natalia.

"Are you sure you're up to it?"

"I'll take Katrin with me. We're more likely to get answers if we send women. No offence to you three."

"None taken," said Athgar. "We still need to locate those Orcs if we want to contact home, so Belgast and I will visit some taverns and see what we can discover."

"What about us?" asked Galina.

"I've an idea on that," said Stanislav. "I was thinking we could make some discreet enquiries about that fleet we keep tiptoeing around."

"For what purpose?"

"If they are indeed on the same side as us, we might be able to use them to spread the word concerning the family's motives."

"You believe that will work?"

"I do," said the mage hunter. "I spent years travelling the Continent, and I've yet to see a Temple Captain who didn't maintain a presence at court. Most people discount them as mere decoration, but they see and hear everything. They also wield tremendous influence, although they seldom use it."

"But you're speaking about Cunars, aren't you?"

"Not at all. The Mathewites, in particular, are highly sought after as advisors, although never in an official capacity, as that would violate their oath of neutrality. Instead, they are often consulted as a 'courtesy', which has the advantage of being deniable if things go bad."

"That raises an interesting question," said Galina.

"Which is?" replied Stanislav.

"If we assume the Cunars are in league with the family, and the Agnesites are on our side, then where do the Temple Knights of Saint Mathew stand?"

"They often work with the sisters," said Natalia. "Though that, by itself, is no guarantee where their loyalties lie. It means we must be extra careful as we go about our business, for all three orders patrol the streets of Korvoran."

"When do we approach the duke?" asked Katrin.

"That will largely depend on how we fare with the Temple Captain of Saint Agnes. I'm hoping she might be the instrument to get us there."

"Well, it's late," said Stanislav, "and we can't do any of this in the dark. I suggest we all get a good night's sleep."

The group rose, all except for Athgar and Belgast.

"Coming?" asked Natalia.

"I'll be up in a moment," said Athgar. "I still have some ale left."

Belgast waited until the others left to eye his companion. "Well? What is it?"

"Do you get the feeling we're being watched?"

"I get that all the time. It's only natural for Humans to be wary of us mountain folk."

"No, it's more than that. I just have this feeling there's more at play here. Something big that we can't quite grasp."

"Have you any proof?"

"No. Nothing more than a hunch."

"Don't ignore it," said Belgast. "That feeling may well save your life one day. Have you told the others?"

"No, not even Natalia. She'd tell me I'm imagining things."

"I doubt that. She believes in you, my friend; never doubt that."

"She has enough to worry about without my wild conjectures."

"You spent a long time as a prisoner," said the Dwarf. "I know how wearing that can be, but you have friends here that you can count on to watch your back. We'll stick together, you and I, and if we find anything to support your theory, we'll bring it to the others, agreed?"

"Agreed."

"Good. Now finish that ale, and go get up to that room of yours. Natalia's waiting for you."

"I shall." Athgar downed his ale in one gulp, then wiped his mouth with his forearm. "Good talking to you, Belgast. I'll see you in the morning." He headed upstairs.

The night wore on, but the Dwarf remained, absently sipping his ale. He was at a crossroads, his loyalties strained. On the one hand, he badly wanted to help his friends, but he'd taken an oath many years ago, an oath he'd sworn never to break. How was he to reconcile the two?

The more he thought, the more troubled he became. Until recently, there'd been no conflict, for they were two worlds, separated by time and distance. Now, however, they were getting closer, and he feared they would soon collide, with him in the middle of it. The question was where his brethren stood. Would they support his friends, or would they insist on maintaining the neutrality they'd cultivated for so long?

It was a troublesome question that occupied his mind until the wee hours of the morning. He needed to make enquiries, but to do that, he must slip away from the others. To do otherwise was to risk discovery. Guilt nagged at him, for he was playing a game of deceit that might jeopardize the very friendships he sought to protect.

He finally downed the rest of his drink and stood, feeling every bit his age. Dawn would herald a new day and perhaps, with it, a way out of this mess he'd gotten himself into.

THE COMMANDERY

AUTUMN 1108 SR

The Temple Knights of Saint Agnes' commandery was laid out in a hollow rectangle, with the lower level housing the sister knights. Natalia and Katrin were escorted to the second floor, where the company commander's office was located.

"These two are here to speak to the captain," announced their escort. They halted before a door where a sentry stood.

The guard entered the room for a moment, then reappeared, holding the door open. "The captain will see you now."

They stepped into a sparsely furnished room, where a wide window, framed by some curtains, dominated the western wall. The captain sat with her back to it, sifting through notes littering the large desk.

"Greetings, Captain. I'm Natalia, and this is Katrin."

"Good day to you both. My name is Temple Captain Leona. Please, sit." She waited as they each took a chair. "I gather you're not from these parts?"

"What makes you say that?"

The captain smiled. "My Temple Knights are very good at reporting any unusual events."

"You're referring to Sister Felicity meeting us at the mission."

"I am. It's not very often someone with your particular family connections visits Korvoran, which makes me all the more curious as to why you're here."

"We came to see you on a matter of some import, but I've yet to determine if you're the right person to speak with."

"Whatever do you mean?"

"Let's just say we have, in our possession, what some might refer to as delicate information."

"When you say delicate, you mean something you don't want getting out into the open?"

"Precisely."

"Then why come here at all?"

"In the past," said Natalia, "we worked with sisters of your order. In particular, one named Sister Cordelia."

A look of recognition crossed the captain's face.

"Do you know her?" asked Natalia.

"Not personally, but she is known to me. Might I ask the nature of your working relationship with the good sister?"

"There was an altercation—a member of another order overstepped his authority and engaged in a disreputable manner."

"And this was in Krieghoff?"

"Yes," said Natalia. "How did you know?"

"As I said, she is known to me, as are the circumstances of this… entanglement. Are you the mage she wrote of?"

"I am, though I'm curious as to why she would write to you when you clearly don't know her personally."

"She wrote the letter to my predecessor. They served together in Ilea."

"Ilea? I remember her mentioning that. It's on the southern coast, isn't it?"

"It is, though I fail to see what that has to do with your presence here today. Sister Felicity mentioned you might be fugitives. Would you care to elaborate?"

"It's a long story," said Natalia.

"There's plenty of time," replied the captain. "I have no other pressing issues this morning."

"Very well. I exhibited the potential for magic at a very young age, so much so that they took me from my mother and enrolled me in a magical academy called the Volstrum, in Karslev."

"The capital of Ruzhina?"

"Yes, that's right. There, they taught me all the skills required of a battle mage, including not only magic but politics as well. Upon graduation, however, they informed me they would breed me with a man of their choosing."

"Breed? Are you suggesting they were forcing you into a marriage?"

"No, only childbearing. They had no thoughts of an actual wedding. In any event, I refused and, with help, fled the country."

"And they've been looking for you ever since?"

"Yes, though I fear it's a bit more complicated than that. In my travels, I happened upon a man named Athgar of Athelwald."

"Strange name, that. Is he a Therengian by chance?"

"He is, and he's here in Korvoran."

Captain Leona nodded. "That would be the man who accompanied you to the mission. Have you any children?"

"A daughter, but the family tried to kidnap her. In retaliation, Athgar and I travelled to Karslev, our intent being to stop them. Needless to say, it didn't go according to plan, and so we now find ourselves on the run from a powerful family."

"And your daughter?"

"Safe at home in the care of trusted friends and family."

"An interesting account, yet I can't see how we can be of assistance. If you're looking for sanctuary, it's the temple itself you should be visiting."

"It's not sanctuary we want, but an introduction to the duke."

"The duke? Why would you want that?"

"When we were in Karslev, we stumbled upon some damaging information that might prove to be the family's undoing."

The captain shifted forward, leaning on her desk. "You have my full attention."

"Our understanding is that your order had some kind of run-in with the Stormwinds a few years ago."

"We did. I was here when it happened."

"Might I ask what transpired? Rumours are floating around, but I'd prefer to hear the truth directly from you."

"The previous captain, Charlaine deShandria, uncovered a Halvarian plot to foment rebellion in the hopes of starting a war."

"Is that why you formed a Holy Fleet?"

"No. That was in the works long before all that was uncovered. Is that important?"

"Perhaps. We suspect the Temple Knights of Saint Cunar were... infiltrated."

The captain didn't even blink.

"That doesn't surprise you?" asked Natalia.

"I've heard others speculate as you do now, but I can neither confirm nor deny it."

"Can they be trusted here in Korvoran?"

"As much as any of us can. It's been our experience that this influence comes from the senior ranks of the order."

"Our experience? You mean there are others who feel as you do?"

"I am not at liberty to divulge any information on this. Suffice it to say your story is most intriguing and definitely something that would be of interest to us."

"There's more."

"Go on."

"We uncovered evidence that the Stormwinds are the power behind the Halvarian Empire."

The captain sat back, obviously surprised. "Are you certain?"

"As sure as I can be. We found a letter my grandmother wrote. She used to be a senior member of the family."

"This is most distressing. We knew there was a connection between the Stormwinds and Halvaria but never dreamed they were the ones in charge. Have you this letter?"

"We do," said Natalia, "but there's no way to prove its authenticity."

"What you told me helps explain a lot. I shall send word to my colleagues and let them know of this discovery, but I fear there is little we can do about it at present. Why did you want to see the duke?"

"It's our understanding he banned the Stormwinds from his court. We hoped to convince him to spread the word to the rest of the Petty Kingdoms."

"That's no small order."

"Agreed, yet it's still worth pursuing. I've heard it's common for Temple Captains to spend time at court. Would you consider introducing us to His Grace?"

"You two?"

"No," said Katrin. "I'm only here for moral support. It's Athgar and Natalia who need to talk to His Grace."

"I can't promise anything," the captain replied, "but I can make some enquiries. If I'm being honest, your husband complicates matters. Descendants of the Old Kingdom are looked down on. I very much doubt he would be well-received at court."

"He's an important man," said Katrin.

"Important, how?"

"He's influential," interrupted Natalia. "He's also an accomplished Fire Mage."

"A Fire Mage and a Therengian. Anything else I should know? He's not a pirate as well, is he? Because that's about the only thing I can think of that would make matters even more difficult."

"No. We've worked with the Church before, if that's any help?"

"You speak of Krieghoff?"

"No. In Corassus, with a man called Brother Cyric."

"Cyric? How small the Continent seems."

"You've met him?"

"No, but his name keeps cropping up in all sorts of places. If you worked with Cyric, you must be trustworthy. I shall do what I can to arrange a meeting with His Grace, the duke. Is there somewhere I should send word?"

"We're staying at the Anchor."

The captain grimaced. "Not the nicest of places."

"We had little choice. We are low on funds."

"I shall make alternate arrangements for you."

"Are you sure? We don't want to be an inconvenience."

"Nonsense. You've helped us unwind a few more threads in this mystery. It's the least we can do."

"There are six of us."

The captain laughed.

"You find something amusing?" asked Natalia.

"Only in your number. Clearly, this is a sign."

"I'm not sure I understand."

"There were only six Saints," said Captain Leona, "and they changed the entire Continent."

Natalia stood, indicating that Katrin should do likewise. "Thank you," she said. "I know we're asking a lot."

The captain rose, then hobbled around the desk, revealing a leg missing from the knee down. Natalia, trained in the way of courtly manners, ignored the injury, but Katrin couldn't help but stare.

"Lost in battle," explained the Temple Captain, "but I'm still able to ride a horse."

"My apologies," said Katrin. "I don't mean to be rude, but did you consider using a Life Mage?"

"I can see you're new to these parts. You won't find a Life Mage within a thousand miles of here, at least not one willing to heal an old warrior like me."

"Old?" said Natalia. "I wouldn't have said you're much older than me."

The captain smiled. "Now you're just being polite. I'm easily ten years your senior, likely more, but such matters are of little consequence in the grand scheme of things. I thank you all the same, however. You are quite accomplished with the niceties of court."

"It was part of my training. They teach all Stormwinds how to behave in social gatherings."

Leona sat on the edge of her desk. "What else did they teach you back in Karslev?"

"Other than magic? Reading and writing, as well as the histories of all the major ruling families of the Continent. I was also a battle mage, so I received instruction on strategy, tactics, plus weapons and armour employed by the armies of the Petty Kingdoms, and so much more that I'm afraid it would bore you to tears."

"All of that, yet you're still relatively young."

"The Volstrum commences training at a young age, and I was younger than most."

"You are a credit to your academy… or perhaps not considering your circumstances, but that's a good thing. I shall send a letter to His Grace this afternoon. In the meantime, my adjutant will make arrangements for more suitable lodgings. I expect you'll hear from me late this afternoon. Will that suffice?"

"It will," said Natalia. "And once again, thank you."

They finally left, leaving the captain alone with her thoughts. As their footsteps receded, Leona called out for her guard.

"Yes, Captain?"

"Set a detail to keep an eye on them."

"You suspect a trap, Captain?"

"From them? No. But I imagine it won't take long for others to take an interest in their affairs."

"So we're to guard them?"

"Only observe, for now. Of more interest will be who goes out of their way to meet them."

"Just the two of them?"

"No, there's six, so we'll need to ensure we keep an eye on them if they split up. You can find them at the Anchor."

"Very well, Captain. I shall see to it at once."

"Well," said Natalia, stepping out onto the street. "That went better than expected."

"Do you think they believed us?" asked Katrin.

"I certainly hope so, or we may have inadvertently put ourselves at risk."

"You don't trust them?"

"It's not a matter of trust. The simple fact is the more people learn our real identities, the greater the likelihood the family will find us."

"But the family was exiled from Reinwick."

"True, but there are others who serve without taking the Stormwind name."

Katrin shook her head. "And here I thought learning magic was hard enough. I'm glad I didn't have to sit through all those other lessons. I don't understand how you know all this?"

"Did you not pay attention in class?"

"You know I didn't. I was too busy panicking over not mastering the spells."

"And now you've mastered over half a dozen. See? All you needed was a patient tutor and time to absorb theory."

"Yes, though I had to be enslaved in a mine for years on end first. That, I could have done without."

"On that, we are in complete agreement."

They wandered down the street, in no rush to return to their lodgings. The air reverberated with the shouts of merchants hawking their wares, accompanied by the endless squawking of seagulls. This all mixed in with the smell of the sea, creating a unique experience for those who'd spent their lives inland.

"I don't know if I'll ever get used to this," said Katrin. "The Volstrum was so quiet."

"It was, except for Mistress Nina. She could prattle on all day. I wonder whatever happened to her?"

"Galina would have a better idea. In any case, she was a Stormwind through and through. She'd be more likely to oppose us than help."

"I don't know if that's necessarily true. I always found her to be fair."

"Fair, yes. Forgiving? That's an entirely different matter. She was the one who ordered me to be escorted from the Volstrum. It was her fault they sent me to that mine."

"She might've given the order," said Natalia, "but I doubt she had much choice. Those in charge have strict policies regarding progress. Keep in mind I'm not defending them, only explaining their actions. I think the whole Stormwind brood needs to learn a few things about what it means to be a family."

"Don't forget the Sartellians; they're just as bad."

"Agreed. Say, do you think the duke knows they're one and the same?"

"You mean the Stormwinds and the Sartellians? I doubt it. The good captain mentioned Larissa Stormwind, but there was no talk of any Fire Mages other than Athgar."

"Yet one more thing we must speak to the duke about."

Natalia slowed, then crossed the street to a stall selling a variety of cheeses. She selected a block, holding it to her nose. "Don't look now," she whispered, "but we're being followed."

"By whom?"

"That's a good question." Natalia raised her voice, holding the food up for inspection. "What do you think of this?"

Katrin wrinkled her nose. "Not something I could see myself eating." She lowered her voice. "What do we do?"

"Follow my lead." Natalia replaced the cheese, then continued down the street, taking her time, letting her gaze drift over the various goods on display. She paused by an apple cart. "There are three of them, but they appear content to simply keep us in sight."

"To what end? Do you believe they mean to waylay us?"

"If they do, they're in for a rude awakening."

Katrin paled. "You can't take them on, Natalia, not in your current condition."

"I was more than capable of talking to the Temple Knights, and I helped when Athgar was assaulted."

"Yes, but there's a big difference between a single target and three. We both know how draining that would be."

"Well, we can't lead them back to the others."

"What else can we do?"

Natalia took her companion's hand. "Come with me. I have an idea." She sped up, pulling Katrin down a side street.

"Where are we going?"

"Towards the sea."

"To what end?"

"The docks were busy when we arrived. I'm thinking they're always so. What better way to hide than amongst a crowd?"

"You don't think those are sister knights following us, do you?"

"No," said Natalia. "They're men. Last time I looked, only women served the Temple Knights of Saint Agnes."

"Then who are they?"

"I have no idea, nor am I eager to find out." They turned a corner, revealing the harbour in all its glory. A casual glance revealed their pursuers still following in their wake.

Natalia spotted a nearby boat where someone was in the middle of unloading barrels, with a bunch already standing upright by the water. She climbed up on a barrel to better view the area.

"Any luck?" asked Katrin.

She jumped down, a smile creasing her lips. "I think I have the perfect solution, one that won't end up with us having to fight."

"Care to share what that might entail?"

"We're going to visit a ship."

"And if they follow us aboard?"

"Oh, they won't."

"How can you be so sure?"

"Because this particular ship belongs to the Temple of Saint Agnes."

"And how do you know that?"

"By its flag. Now, come. We must find our way to its mooring before our pursuers close in on us."

"I thought they were only following us?"

"They were," said Natalia, "but they sped up once we got on the docks. I suspect they might have allies down here somewhere."

"Oh, great! Just what we need, another enemy to deal with."

They pushed through a line of men hauling sacks of grain up the causeway. Finally, the scarlet tabard of a Temple Knight came into view.

"Excuse me, Sister," called out Natalia.

"Is there something I can help you with?"

"Yes," she replied. "There are three men following us. I fear for our safety."

"Then step aboard the *Vigilant*, and I shall have a word with them."

The two mages crossed the boarding plank, then watched as a pair of Temple Knights moved forward to accost the individuals, but the strangers turned and fled at the first sign of trouble.

"Who do you think they are?" asked Katrin.

"I have no idea, yet clearly, whoever it is doesn't want to talk to our saviours."

EBENSTADT

AUTUMN 1108 SR

The walls of Ebenstadt grew more distinct as the delegation approached. Laruhk and his tuskers led the way, the massive animals towering over mere horses. Following them came one hundred hunters, their Orc bows unstrung, for they were in friendly territory, not the land of their enemies.

Kargen and Shaluhk walked behind this vanguard, as did the rest of the entourage. At the tail end was Kragor, with another hundred hand-picked archers, both Orc and Human.

It was an odd sight, leading to dozens of Humans watching their approach from the city walls. Not since the siege, some three years ago, had so many Orcs gathered in one place. It was not something to be missed.

The great city doors opened as they approached, but the tuskers turned aside, content for the beasts to roam the open countryside. The rest of the column, over two hundred strong, entered Ebenstadt, maintaining their relative positions as they marched through the city. The entire procession finally halted before the Thane's Estate, the name given to the building now housing the offices of those responsible for running the city.

Kargen ordered the Orcs to disband, and the hunters quickly dispersed into the streets, eager to visit the largest city in all of Therengia. Kragor's archers formed an escort as Kargen and Shaluhk entered the building, then took up guard positions at the door.

The building's interior was opulently appointed, for it used to be a noble's estate. However, all that changed when the Temple Knights of Saint Cunar abandoned the city, leaving the wealthy and powerful to flee for their lives. It was a bitter blow to the economy, yet the people of Ebenstadt survived, even prospered, under Therengian rule.

Temple Captain Yaromir waited inside. "Good to see you two. I received word yesterday that you'd be arriving. I trust all is well?"

"As well as it can be," replied Kargen, "but decisions must be made. In the absence of Athgar and Natalia, we seek your counsel."

"I am but a humble Temple Knight and, as you know, am forbidden to interfere in local matters."

"Yet you sit in judgement over this very city. Come, Captain, you must acknowledge your order is not truly neutral, else you wouldn't have agreed to take on that responsibility."

"You make a most compelling argument. Shall we sit and partake of a meal while we talk?"

"That would be most suitable."

"Where is your son?"

"Outside," said Shaluhk. "With Skora, and Oswyn, of course. The two are inseparable."

"In that case, follow me." Yaromir led them to a side room warmed by a roaring fire. "You must excuse the coldness," he said. "The floors here are made of marble, a beautiful stone but very chilly on the feet."

As they sat, a couple of Temple Knights carried in trays of food and drink. Yaromir waited until they left before continuing.

"You indicated you came to seek my counsel. Might I enquire on what subject?"

"Novarsk," said Kargen. "But before we talk of that, let me ask you about Rada."

"What, in particular, would you like to know about her?"

"Has she shown any sign of accepting her confinement?"

"Unfortunately not," said the Temple Captain. "She is as obstinate as always. We tried to convince her of the error of her ways, but she maintains she rules by divine right. Not that she follows the ways of the Old Gods, of course. She insists the Saints themselves chose her ancestors."

"And did they?" asked Shaluhk. "We know the Saints were mortal. Could they have chosen who rules the land?"

"That would contradict what we know about them," said Yaromir. "So I must assume they did not."

"Could they have done it without the Church's knowledge?"

"Anything is possible, but the Saints preached that divinity exists only in the heart of an individual. The very idea someone rules by divine right directly contradicts that. Of course, many Petty Kingdoms maintain a similar claim to kingship, so she's not the only one who states such."

"This I understand," said Kargen. "Does Rada accept that she lost the war?"

"Only in the sense she understands she is imprisoned. She still maintains her fellow countrymen betrayed her."

"Why is that?"

"In her mind, a group of wildlings and Orcs could never defeat the power of Novarsk—her words, not mine. No, I'm afraid we will never see her admit defeat. We did, however, learn a bit more about her."

"Which is?"

"She conspired to kill her own father while he assaulted the walls of this very city. Successfully, I might add. That served us well in the short term, for it enabled us to get Ebenstadt under control. On the other hand, who can truly trust someone who kills their own father? Why, the very notion is uncivilized. And to think they call you Therengians barbarians!"

"I hoped," said Shaluhk, "that Rada might come to her senses, but it appears putting her back on the Throne would only lead to further conflict."

"I would agree," said Kargen. "We need another option."

"There was a cousin who could lay claim to the Throne," said Brother Yaromir. "Although, if I recall correctly, he was fairly young."

"Yes, a mere youngling who would be about fifteen by now. Do you know anything about him?"

"I'm afraid not," said Yaromir. "The last I heard, he was living at the Palace in Halmund under house arrest."

"Would Rada abdicate in favour of her cousin?"

"I don't believe so. She's the type who's only concerned for her own well-being."

"Yes," said Shaluhk, "and a person willing to kill her own kin will not surrender easily, as we have seen. I fear she shall spend the rest of her days locked in a cell."

Kargen was undeterred. "Then we must meet this cousin ourselves and decide if he is worthy of our trust."

"And if he is not?"

"Then we shall consider one of the alternatives."

"Which are?" asked an intrigued Brother Yaromir.

"I am of several minds. One possibility is that we appoint a person of Novarsk descent to manage the kingdom on our behalf. That would do much to mitigate the threat their realm poses to us, but we would still be subject to the whims of an individual. Another option would be to appoint a governor as the Therengians did in olden times, but I am hesitant to suggest it."

"Why is that?"

"Simple," said Shaluhk. "They had a hard enough time dealing with their own queen. Imagine what they would do when confronted by a foreigner with that claim?" She took a sip of wine. "We could promote one of their own barons to the Throne."

"We could," said Kargen, "but then we would be putting our faith in someone we have little knowledge of. They could end up being worse than Rada."

"Then what do you suggest we do?"

"For now? We follow up on our original intentions and visit Halmund. Only from there can we see what the people truly need."

"You mean want?" said Yaromir.

"No. From what Nat-Alia has told us, many Humans are only interested in one of two things: wealth or power, and the most dangerous of them all, possess both. Were we to make a new king of Novarsk, we would merely be trading one for another. Better to give them what they need, a leader dedicated to improving their lives."

"And how do you do that?"

"We appoint the most able individual we can find. Beneath them will sit others chosen for their ability to rule."

"But they have that now, surely? What you've described is how the nobility rules."

"No," said Shaluhk. "Nobles are not trained to be administrators, nor is there any guarantee those serving beneath them are competent at their assigned tasks."

"Some might argue that point," said Yaromir, "but the truth of the matter is nobles are much more likely to possess such skills due to their privileged upbringing."

"Yet it is in their best interest to ensure they chose only other nobles to rule. In no way can that guarantee fair and just treatment for the common folk."

"I cannot argue with you there, but where else would one find educated candidates?"

"Are not members of the Church well-educated?"

"They are," agreed Yaromir, "but they are sworn to a strict neutrality."

"Then we must train our own," said Shaluhk. "Tonfer Garul assures us this was how the Old Kingdom chose its governors. Can we do any worse?"

"Likely not, but remember, the Old Kingdom was torn down by the very same people who formed the Petty Kingdoms, which includes Novarsk. I doubt they'd be eager for you to rule over them."

"You make a valid point," said Kargen, "but we still require a solution to our problem. Little did we realize that when we conquered Novarsk, we would put ourselves in such a difficult situation. It now makes us responsible for these people."

"You surprise me," said Yaromir. "Although I suppose I should know better."

"Whatever do you mean?" asked Shaluhk.

"History shows us conquerors seldom care what becomes of their enemies. It's why many of the Petty Kingdoms still refuse to treat Therengians with any kind of respect."

"We are not the Petty Kingdoms," said Kargen. "Nor are Therengians like other men and women of the Continent. We believe all of us are equal in stature."

"Yet you are a chieftain."

"The tribe chooses their Orc chieftains," explained Shaluhk, "and the same for thanes."

"But isn't the title of High Thane hereditary?"

"Not at all. What would be the point of that? We want the best leaders, not someone whose only claim to the position is being the offspring of a ruler."

"But wouldn't you want Agar to become chieftain one day?"

"Only if he is the best choice," said Kargen. "What matters to us is the continuity of our way of life, and even that changes as generations pass. Is this not so in Human lands?"

"No," said Yaromir. "Though I suspect things would be better were it true. Most Human rulers covet wealth and power, and not necessarily in that order. There are exceptions, but those are rare." He took a sip of his wine. "Your people's approach to ruling is to be commended. I only wish more thought as you do."

"Perhaps they would if only given a chance. Tell me, what do you know about the nobles of Novarsk?"

"From what Rada has told me, there appears to be only one rank of nobility: that of baron."

"Is that common amongst the Petty Kingdoms?" asked Shaluhk.

"It is. There are larger realms, which may include other ranks, but barons are the most common. Of course, sometimes the ruler is a duke rather than a king or might style themselves as a prince, but it amounts to the same in the end."

"Do you have any idea how many barons are in Novarsk?"

"Twenty-two," said the Temple Captain. "Assuming none died since Rada's imprisonment. Then again, I suppose their heirs would replace them, so the number should still stand."

"And do you believe these barons would accept a foreign ruler?"

"I think they'll accept much to guarantee their treasuries. I suspect most of them expect to be executed or at least stripped of their titles."

"So how do we win them over?"

"You should start by granting a general amnesty. Let them return to running their lands and filling their purses."

"And will they share this wealth?"

"I doubt it, but at least they'll be happy, and happy barons make for a peaceful kingdom."

"It is not right," said Shaluhk. "It should not be the wealthy who dictates peace or war. It should be those most affected by battle—the commoners."

"I admire your passion," said Yaromir, "but the Continent doesn't work that way. There are always wealthy, powerful individuals who dictate how the rest of us live."

"That is your history," said Kargen, "but it is not that of the Orcs or the Therengians."

"Clearly, we must find a solution that works best for all," said Yaromir, "but I would caution you. Change is hard, especially when it requires sacrifice. The wealthy won't easily part with their coins, nor the influential, their power. I wish you well, but your decision, whatever it is, will not be an easy one."

"On that, we are in agreement."

"Tell me," said Shaluhk, "are there any members of your order in Halmund?"

"Yes," replied Yaromir. "A dozen, to be exact. A senior Temple Knight would command them, though I suppose I would be their superior in regional matters. Perhaps I should send one of my men to accompany you? At the very least, I could pass on my standing orders concerning the current occupation."

"I would happily accept such a travelling companion," said Kargen. "Might I ask who you would send?"

"Brother Maurice would be my best choice. He's an experienced warrior as well as an efficient administrator. When do you intend to leave?"

"In a day or two. First, I would like to take some time to look over things here in Ebenstadt."

"Worried we might be failing you?"

"Not at all, but if I know Athgar, he will return and wish to hear how we all fared. Better to be prepared ahead of time than to be caught unawares."

"Novarsk has other cities," said Shaluhk. "Do they all maintain garrisons of Temple Knights?"

"Finburg does, but the other towns are considered too small to warrant a garrison. After all, the Temple Knights of Saint Mathew can't be everywhere."

"Thank you, Captain Yaromir. Your insights were most valuable. You gave us much to think on."

"Indeed," said Kargen. "Now, if you will excuse us, we should find out what Agar and Oswyn have been up to."

"Yes," said Shaluhk. "Knowing those two, they will have climbed to the top of the building by now."

Oswyn brought the axe down, hitting the twig. The wooden weapon did no damage but delighted her nonetheless, resulting in a fit of giggles that echoed down the street.

"She is clever," said Agar. "She has already discovered that an axe cuts. I have yet to see another Human of her age who has realized such."

Shaluhk smiled, choosing to respond in the Orcish tongue. "*That is because she has you as a teacher. Soon, however, you will outgrow her, for their race remains in an infantile state for many years.*"

"*It will be interesting to observe her development, but I will never outgrow her, for she is like a sister to me.*"

"*Did you hear that, Kargen?*"

"*I did,*" replied the chieftain. "*I only wish Humans felt the same way.*"

"*Some do,*" said Agar.

"*Yes, my son, some do, but there are far more who see us only as savages.*"

"*Then we must teach them otherwise, Father.*"

"*You show great wisdom for your age. No doubt it is your mother's influence.*"

Oswyn leaped to her feet and ran down the road, her wooden axe held high as she did her best imitation of a war cry. Agar, ever the dutiful minder, chased after her.

"*I see much of him in her,*" mused Shaluhk.

"*As do I. I only hope their friendship continues as they age.*"

"*Why would you think otherwise? Are not Athgar and Nat-Alia still our friends?*"

"*They are,*" said Kargen. "*But we did not meet as children.*"

"*Yes, you did, or did you forget you first befriended his father, Rothgar, when Athgar was still a youngling?*"

"*I forgot that, though now I look back on it, it seems like ages since we met.*"

"*Your face betrays you,*" said Shaluhk. "*You are worried for him.*"

"*I am. They went into the land of our enemy, and we have heard nothing since. For all we know, they have been killed.*"

"*No. I would have learned about it from their spirits. They are alive. I can feel it.*"

"*Is that your magic speaking or merely wishful thinking?*"

"*Perhaps a little of both.*"

"*I wish they were back. I would be happy to hand over responsibility for Novarsk.*"

"*Have you made a decision yet?*"

"*No,*" said Kargen, "*but I would value your true opinion on the matter now that we are alone. Do you believe the Humans of that kingdom would consent to be ruled by Athgar?*"

"*We must think not only of Athgar but of those who follow.*"

"*Still, the question remains. Will they accept a ruler who is from outside their realm?*"

"*The situation is more complicated than that.*"

"*In what way?*" asked Kargen.

"*Novarsk may be ruled by a member of their own elite or by an outsider, yes?*"

"*Those would appear to be our only options.*"

"*That means you must consider who we can trust more: one of them or one of us.*"

"*When you put it that way, it seems like a straightforward choice. One of our own would be better suited from our point of view, yet this path could lead to unrest.*"

"*More so than occupying their country with our warriors?*"

"*That is the question which haunts me and one I can not answer in Ebenstadt. Only a visit to Halmund itself will provide the answers we need.*"

ASSISTANCE

AUTUMN 1108 SR

B elgast swallowed a mouthful of ale, then set down the empty tankard. "And you're sure we can trust them?"

"If you can't trust a sister of Saint Agnes, who can you?" said Katrin.

"Easy for you to say. You didn't fight off a Holy Army."

"We worked with the sisters before," said Natalia. "You of all people should remember that."

"Of course I remember that," spat out the Dwarf, "but one good knight doesn't make the entire order trustworthy. How do we know they haven't been corrupted like those Saints' forsaken Cunars?"

"He raises an interesting point," noted Stanislav. "And you must admit, up until a few years ago, every one of us would have thought them all trustworthy."

"Speak for yourself," said Athgar. "There's something wrong with an order dedicating itself to fighting."

"Isn't that what the Thane Guard does?"

"All right, I concede they're not all bad, but we know the family infiltrated the Temple Knights of Saint Cunar. Who's to say they haven't done the same to the good sisters?"

"You make a valid argument," said Natalia, "but I detected no sign of deceit from their captain. She also knew of Brother Cyric, and we know him to be trustworthy."

"There's a big difference between knowing someone and knowing OF them."

"Still, we have to trust somebody, eventually. In any case, all we're asking for is an introduction to the duke. What's the worst that can happen?"

"They could arrest us?" said Galina. "Did you tell them you were a Stormwind?"

"At first, I wasn't going to, but then Captain Leona mentioned she'd spoken to Sister Felicity. I also told her my grandmother was a person of influence."

"Anything else we should know about?"

"Yes," added Katrin. "We were followed."

"By who?" asked Athgar, his frustration suddenly forgotten.

"Three men," replied Natalia. "We led them to the docks and then informed some Temple Knights."

"And?"

"They tried talking with our pursuers, but the men ran off at the sight of trouble."

"Any idea of who they were?"

"None whatsoever," said Natalia. "They wore no armour we could see or any clothing that might make them stand out in a crowd."

"Perhaps they were thieves," suggested Galina, "looking for an easy mark."

"I don't believe so. They seemed more interested in following us than any actual confrontation."

"Still," said Athgar, "you captured the attention of someone, and we can't rule out the possibility they work for the family. I suggest we all be more vigilant in future."

Katrin laughed.

"What's so funny?"

"That was the Temple Ship's name."

"What Temple Ship?"

"The one whose crew helped us," said Katrin, "and a good thing too. Those men looked to be getting ready to take more direct action."

"Meaning?"

"I think they meant us harm."

Natalia shook her head. "No, that makes no sense. The docks were busy. Why wait until we were surrounded by others? There would be too many witnesses."

"Perhaps they don't care," said Belgast. "Gangs often work by instilling a sense of fear in the general populous. A public death would keep people on their toes."

"Yes, but something like that would surely attract the attention of the duke's men, wouldn't it?"

"I suppose you're right. Do you think they might have just wanted to scare you?"

"If that's what they wanted," said Katrin, "then they succeeded. Again, though, the question would be, why?"

"To keep you silent," suggested Stanislav. "I may be pulling this out of thin air, but consider this: they banned the family from operating in Reinwick, yet agents under its employ discover a group of malcontents—that's us—arriving at the docks. They can't act overtly for fear of being discovered, but at the same time, they have to make sure we don't reveal their secrets."

"An interesting idea," said Natalia, "but it leaves out one crucial detail."

"Which is?" asked the mage hunter.

"Nobody except us knows we recovered anything from Stormwind Manor."

"But they do know we're fugitives."

"He makes a compelling case," said Athgar. "We've all seen the family up close, and I'm sure they've worked out by now that we mean them harm. In their minds, we represent the enemy, and the Gods know they've tried several times to put an end to us in the past. Is it so difficult to imagine they'll continue to do so?"

"Then why didn't they attack us?" asked Natalia.

"My guess would be they wanted to find all of us. They likely thought you'd lead them back to the rest of our party. After that, we'd probably receive visitors bearing knives in the middle of the night."

"What we need," said Belgast, "is a safer place to stay. I wouldn't want my worst enemy to spend a night here, let alone my friends. Surely there's somewhere better we can go?"

"I'm afraid not," said Athgar. "Not if we want to stick together. It's all my fault. We could stay anywhere if it weren't for my grey eyes."

"Don't be so hard on yourself," said Galina. "We also have to consider our funds or lack thereof. That, alone, places a great restriction on where we can afford lodgings. If that means we stay in flea-ridden places like this, then so be it. At least we're still alive."

A server placed a bowl of stew before Belgast. He sniffed it, his nose wrinkling in disgust, but then a stranger entered the inn, distracting him. "Looks like we have company."

Natalia, spotting the new arrival, stood. "Sister Felicity, so good of you to join us. Have you news?"

"I do indeed," replied the knight. She crossed the remaining distance to stand before the group. "Would you care to make the introductions?"

"Certainly. Katrin, you already know, and this is Galina, Stanislav, and Belgast. Last, but definitely not least, is my husband, Athgar."

"How do you do? My name is Sister Felicity, but Natalia has already told you that. May I sit?"

"Of course. Can I get you something to drink?"

"No, I'm fine, thank you." The knight looked around the group, meeting each one's gaze in turn. "Temple Captain Leona sent me. We've made alternate arrangements for your lodging, providing that's still something that interests you?"

"Can you read minds?" said Belgast. "Because we were just discussing that very concept. What have you got in mind?"

"Here in Korvoran, the order is blessed by some wealthy benefactors, amongst them a woman by the name of Yelena Dreyer."

"Never heard of her."

"Nor would I expect you to. She owns many trading ships that ply the Great Northern Sea. Ships, I might add, which benefited immensely from our efforts to reduce piracy in the area. She has agreed to take you all in."

"For how long?" asked Galina.

"A few weeks, at least, or until you find your feet. I told her nothing of your background save that you fled your homeland and are thus short of funds."

"And she believes us to be worshippers of the Saints?" asked Athgar.

"I did not bring the matter up, but I believe she would be inclined to make that assumption."

"So we're to lie to her?"

Sister Felicity smiled. "I only ask you to take a pragmatic approach. I doubt she would openly enquire about your beliefs. In any case, our order preaches acceptance of all manners of worship, even those purporting to believe in the existence of the Gods." She raised her hand to forestall any argument. "I am not here to argue faith, merely to present you with an opportunity to improve your circumstances. Are you still interested?"

The group all looked at each other, eventually nodding.

"Yes," said Natalia. "I believe we are."

"Good. Then I'll let you finish your meal before we head over there."

"If it's all right with you," said Belgast, "I'd rather skip the food. I don't think I can stomach it."

"In that case, we can leave at once."

"Not quite," said Katrin. "We need to retrieve our things from our rooms." She disappeared upstairs, along with Galina.

"Things?" said the Temple Knight.

"A few meagre belongings," said Natalia, "nothing more. Did you bring your horse, by chance?"

"No. The house of our benefactor is only a short walk."

"That surprises me," said Stanislav. "This looks to be a less savoury part of the city."

"And you would be correct," said the knight, "but go five blocks north of here, and the change is rather dramatic. There you'll find lush gardens and plenty of wide-open spaces, just the sort of thing the wealthy pride themselves on."

The two women reappeared, Katrin carrying a large bag.

"A little heavy for clothing," noted Sister Felicity.

"Who said it was clothes?" said Natalia. "Now, shall we be on our way?"

"By all means, follow me." She led them outside, then down a block before turning north. True to her word, the street opened up, and trees became more common. Within three blocks, it felt as though they'd passed into a different world, one full of plant life. Athgar found the entire scene rather strange, for the large number of trees were all arranged in precise rows, a most disturbing sight for someone used to the wilderness' natural chaos.

"Here we are," said Felicity, halting at last. "The house of Yelena Dreyer."

They stood before an open iron gate that invited them to walk down a long pathway, leading to a large manor house made of dark grey stone. In form, it was not unlike Stormwind Manor, a two-storey rectangle building, surrounded by gardens, but the differences in details were startling. Here, colourful curtains decorated each window, while a blue-painted door with lanterns on either side welcomed them. Their new host was expecting them, for as they strolled down the pathway, the front door opened, revealing half a dozen servants and a woman, obviously someone of influence.

"Greetings," she called out. "I am Yelena Dreyer. Welcome to my home."

Sister Felicity nodded her head in recognition. "Good day, my lady. May I introduce the group?"

"By all means."

"This is Natalia," the knight began. "It was she who first contacted the order. Also present are Katrin, Galina, Stanislav, Belgast, and Athgar."

The woman's gaze wandered over the group, lingering on Athgar. She appeared taken aback at the sight of his grey eyes but managed a quick recovery.

"Come. Let us go inside where we may sit comfortably. Have you eaten yet?"

"No," answered Belgast, a little too hurriedly.

In answer, the woman turned to one of her servants but spoke no words. He obviously knew what was intended, for he hurried inside along with two others.

The new arrivals followed Lady Yelena into the house, where a riot of colours met them in the entrance hall. This woman had spared no expense decorating the place, with silver candle holders hanging on the walls and a multi-coloured tile floor so clean it reflected the light.

Eventually, they reached their destination, a sitting room with woven rugs and plump, cushioned chairs. As they sat, the servants entered, bearing drinks.

"I understand you are exiles," said Yelena.

"That's true," said Natalia. "I myself was trained as a Water Mage in the great academy at Karslev."

"Do you, perchance, have a price on your heads? I only ask out of idle curiosity."

"Not as far as we know, but there was some animosity between our former employers and us. I don't wish to speak ill of them, but it came to our attention they were engaged in illegal activities. Needless to say, they refused to change their ways, leading to our departure."

"A fascinating tale. Might I ask how you came to Reinwick?"

"By ship," said Natalia. "A merchant vessel known as the *Golden Chalice*."

"I know that name. It belongs to a competitor of mine. How was the voyage?"

"Dangerous," said Athgar. "We came across a violent storm on our crossing, which resulted in some damage to the *Chalice*."

Their host smiled. "That's the first good news I've heard today. Shipping cargo is a cutthroat business these days, so any damage to a competitor affords me a chance at an advantage."

"Might I ask how you got into the business?"

"I was born in Ruzhina: Porovka, to be exact. My late husband was master of a ship that docked there, seeking new opportunities—that's how we met. Eventually, we married and settled in Korvoran, but not before he'd grown his business to more than a dozen ships. When he died, some three years ago, I took over, enlarging the fleet to its current strength of twenty-two vessels."

Athgar looked around the room. "You've done well for yourself."

"I have, yet there is work yet to do. Things became even more profitable once the Temple Knights started their efforts to reduce piracy. As a result, I've become an ardent supporter of their cause, even going so far as to help finance the Agnesite Fleet."

"The Agnesite Fleet?"

"Yes. You must pardon the expression, but it can't be called a Holy Fleet when it's run by a single order."

"But the fleet in Corassus is controlled solely by the Cunars," said Natalia.

"True, but in that case, they take orders from the Antonine. This fleet has much more leeway in carrying out its duties. Since their efforts began, piracy has shrunk to the point where it's almost been eradicated. We can still lose ships at sea, for it can be unpredictable sometimes, but at least raiders are no longer feared."

"I only saw one Temple Ship at the harbour, a vessel called the *Vigilant*."

"Yes. It used to be a raider before the Temple Knights captured it. That's what started everything."

"I'm not sure I follow," said Athgar. "What do you mean by 'everything'?"

"Sister Felicity would probably know more about this than I, but my understanding is the *Sea Wolf's* raid spurred on the efforts to fight piracy."

"That was the *Vigilant's* original name," added the knight.

"Yes," continued Yelena, "and that hunt for pirates eventually unmasked the Halvarian threat. Without the efforts of the Holy Orders, the entire region would have fallen into war. So you see, many are thankful for their presence here."

"I'm curious," said Athgar. "Were the other orders present for any of this?"

"Oh, yes. The Cunars and Mathewites both contributed warriors to the cause. Still, it was the good sisters like Felicity here who manned the ships, or should I say womaned?" She chuckled. "In any event, if it hadn't been for their captain insisting on looking into things, we would've been doomed."

"You mean Captain Leona?" asked Natalia.

"Saints, no. I mean Captain Charlaine. She's moved on now, likely to a more prestigious assignment. After all, you can't let people like that go to waste. But enough of me. Tell me more about yourselves?"

"What do you want to know?"

"What are your intentions here in Korvoran? You mentioned you're a Water Mage. Are you seeking employment on a ship? Or perhaps a position at court? I hear the duke is lacking when it comes to mages these days."

"That's certainly an option," said Natalia, "but at this time, we're merely seeking an audience."

"An audience? How intriguing. To what end, if I might ask?"

"We received some information I think he would consider valuable."

"Have you, now? Fascinating. I'd offer to help you in this regard, but I'm afraid I possess no contacts as far as the duke's court is concerned. I tend to favour a social life built around more mercantile folk. Now, if you're looking for shipboard employment, I can most assuredly be of assistance."

"We will keep that in mind," offered Galina, "but we've yet to decide how long we shall remain in Reinwick."

"I understand completely." Yelena looked at Sister Felicity. "Has your captain made enquiries?"

"She is in the process," replied the knight, "but these things take time."

"Now, on that, we can agree. As I said earlier, I have no real connections to His Grace, the duke, but I know from my colleagues that he can often be difficult to reach. He was a bit more mellow years ago, but since the duchess's death, he's become much more solitary in nature."

"The duchess is dead?" asked Galina.

"Oh yes," replied Yelena. "She passed away about ten months ago."

"If you don't mind me asking," said Athgar, "have you any suggestions about how we might best handle an audience?"

"Do you mean in terms of behaviour?"

"Yes."

"He is, I'm told, a stickler for etiquette, so make sure you mind your manners. Are you familiar with the ways of court?"

"I am," said Natalia. "It was part of my training."

"Then you should be well-prepared. Letting him steer the conversation is the best way to raise an issue with His Grace."

"But if we do that," asked Athgar, "how do we bring anything up? It's not as if he can read our minds?"

Yelena laughed. "Why, you must lead him, of course. Talk around the subject, and try to get him to ask for more information. In that way, you'll pique his curiosity, but at the same time, he'll feel like he's controlling the conversation."

"This is getting more and more complicated."

"Naturally," said Yelena. "How else does the nobility project its air of mystique?"

RUMOURS

AUTUMN 1108 SR

"It's a simple enough question," said Belgast. "Have you seen any Orcs or not?"

"No," replied the barkeep. "And even if we had, we don't welcome their kind in civilized lands like Reinwick."

"Yet you're familiar with them."

"Only insomuch as people talk about them."

"So you have heard talk of Orcs?"

The fellow shrugged. "I hear people tell of sea monsters, but that doesn't mean they exist."

"I know they exist, you fool. I've seen them myself. All I want to know is where they can be found?"

His outburst quieted the room. The barkeep, sensing trouble, vanished into the back. A trio of men who'd been minding their own business in the corner appeared to take offence. Rising as one, they made their way to the table where Athgar and Belgast sat.

"You're being too loud," accused the largest of them.

"I'm a Dwarf," said Belgast. "This is my normal volume for talking."

"Still, you've insulted our host. I suggest you apologize."

Belgast looked around the room. "I'd love to, but it appears the fellow has vanished. You're a tall man. Perhaps you have a better idea where he went, or is the air too thin for you at that lofty height?"

The ruffian clenched his fists.

"Come now," soothed Athgar. "We meant no offence. We are here for conversation, not to fight."

"Your friend should've given that more thought before he started badmouthing the barkeep."

"I was only asking a simple question," said the Dwarf.

"You're not helping," said Athgar.

"Listen to the grey-eye," the man continued. "At least he knows his place."

Athgar reddened. "My place? And what, exactly, is my place?"

"You're a nobody, a man of no significance, fit only for cleaning the boots of others." His two companions loomed large behind him.

"Come now," continued Athgar. "Can we not come to some sort of agreement? Let us put aside our differences and part as friends, shall we?"

"In a pig's eye!" A fist flew out, but the Therengian expected it and easily dodged the blow, then raised his hands to ready a spell.

"No!" cried Belgast. "You'll burn the place down."

The warning came just in time. Athgar halted his litany mid-incantation but, in doing so, failed to see the cup tossed through the air. It struck him in the face, cutting his cheek, its contents splashing to the floor.

"That's not fair," he called out. "I dare you to try that again." As soon as the words fled his mouth, he realized his mistake. Two more tankards sailed his way, both metal. The first struck the wall beyond the bar, smashing open a container and sending scraps of clay flying in all directions, while the other broke against the wall.

Athgar jumped out of his chair, his axe in hand. Belgast stood, kicking his chair out for dramatic effect. He was easily the shortest person in the room, yet when his fist caught the huge Human beneath the chin, the fellow went limp, collapsing to the floor.

Incensed by the Dwarf's attack on their friend, his companions surged forward with fists flying. Athgar instinctively blocked a punch, his foe's knuckles scraping across the back of the axe, leaving a bloody smear. The Therengian quickly kicked out, taking his opponent in the groin. That one also collapsed, sucking in great gasps of air.

The remaining man backed up, appearing to have no wish to continue. Athgar looked at the Dwarf triumphantly, but at that precise moment, their last opponent yelled out to the other patrons. "Don't just stand there. Get 'em!"

Belgast acted quickly, throwing a chair, not to hit anyone in particular but as a temporary barrier. He then turned around and plunged through the window, breaking glass as he went.

Athgar, astute enough to recognize the danger, soon followed suit, tumbling into the street, then quickly getting to his feet, his sturdy axe still in hand. His companion craned his neck this way and that, desperately searching for an avenue of escape.

"This way," he finally screamed, then took off down the street. Dwarves are not known for being fleet of foot, so it was no surprise when Athgar overtook his comrade, but he soon slowed, allowing his friend to keep pace.

"Well, that didn't exactly go as expected," said Belgast. He quickly glanced over his shoulder, then slowed. "It appears we outran them."

"I suppose that's what comes from asking about Orcs. They don't like them around here."

"No, or your people, it would seem."

"Perhaps we hit a sore spot?"

"Or we were simply in the wrong part of the city," said the Dwarf. "It wouldn't be the first time I made such a mistake, nor, I wager, will it be the last." He halted to stretch his back before glancing towards his companion. "I'd put that axe away if I were you. It's garnering attention."

Athgar tucked it into his belt, letting his gaze drift down the road. "Looks like we're in the Artisan District. Do you think anyone here has any news of Orcs?"

"I'm beginning to think this is a fool's errand. Korvoran is a seaport and a busy one at that."

"Yes, exactly, which is precisely why they may have heard something."

"Did you hit your head on a rock? Since when do Orcs ply the seas of Eiddenwerthe?"

Athgar's face fell. "I suppose you have a good point. Still, these ships travel all across the north. Wouldn't they hear things?"

"Aye, they probably would, but they're all sailors. Of what interest to them are tales of Orcs? You might as well be asking them about giants."

"So, where does that leave us?"

"Wandering the streets of Korvoran, where we started. Do you think Natalia had any better luck getting in touch with the duke?"

"It's been several days now and still no word."

"Yes," said Belgast, "but at least the Temple Knights found us a better place to stay."

"You're only saying that because of the free food."

"It's not just the free food." A stone skidded past them, causing the Dwarf to turn around. "Oh, for Gundar's sake, they decided to pursue. No doubt they'll soon be upon us and introducing us to the cobblestones."

"I could use my magic."

"No. Do that, and you'll lose any chance of meeting His Grace. We need to stay out of trouble, not cause it."

"I'm open to suggestions." Athgar took a few steps, then halted.

"Whatever's the matter?" asked Belgast.

"They sent people to cut us off. There's nowhere to go."

Four men approached from the front, each clutching a severe-looking club, a few of which appeared stained with blood. A quick glance behind spotted six more, many carrying knives.

"I don't think they're going to listen to reason," said Athgar. "Any suggestions on an alternate plan?"

Belgast dropped his head with resignation. "I'm getting awfully tired of all this. Very well. Ready your magic. It appears we have little choice."

"Who do we attack first?"

"Those ahead. At least there's less of them."

Athgar threw up his arms, summoning his inner spark. Flames jumped about on the backs of his hands, but before he could release it, someone rushed out from a nearby store, weapon in hand, ploughing into the club-wielding villains, knocking one to the ground, and then lashing out with a hammer, striking a shin and sending another to the road.

"By Gundar," the fellow raged. "I've had enough of you street thugs. Now get out of here before I smash your skulls in!"

They quickly scattered, the injured man half carried by his comrades. Their saviour turned towards Athgar and Belgast, revealing himself to be a Dwarf.

"Sorry you had to witness that. People like that should be chased out of the city. Come, we'll go inside my shop. You can wait there until those other brutes lose interest."

"What is it you do?" asked Athgar.

"Me? I'm a smith. Didn't you see the sign?" He pointed upward.

They stepped inside, their new host turning to introduce himself. "I'm Barbek Stoutarm, and you are?"

"Athgar of Athelwald, and this is Belgast Ridgehand. We must thank you for your assistance. Without your timely intervention, we would surely have perished. I hope we haven't put you in any danger?"

"Me? Danger? Why would you think that?"

"You saved us from those thugs. Won't they want revenge?"

"Even they're not that stupid."

"Am I missing something?" asked Belgast.

"I supply weapons and armour to the Temple Knights of Saint Agnes. The last thing those thugs want is the interest of a holy fighting order. Now, sit and rest. You look exhausted." He reached under a workbench and retrieved a clay jug. "Fancy some mead? It's not as good as the stuff back home, but it's not bad."

"Most assuredly," said Belgast.

Barbek nodded towards Athgar. "And yourself?"

"No, thank you all the same. I'll stick with a clear head for now."

"Suit yourself." The smith busied himself with fetching a pair of tin cups. "So, what brings you to Korvoran?"

"We're looking for information," said Belgast.

"Oh? What type of information?"

"We're interested in finding Orcs," said Athgar. "Have you heard of any in the area?"

"That's a strange thing to ask after," noted Barbek. "Why in the name of the Saints would you be interested in them?"

"Just a moment ago, you cursed in the name of Gundar. Do you worship the Old Gods or the Saints?"

"Does it matter?"

"You did claim to work for the Temple Knights."

Barbek laughed. "Aye, and I do, but they don't care who I worship, so long as I do justice to my craft." He passed Belgast a cup before pouring himself some of the sweet nectar. "I couldn't help but notice you avoided answering the question. Are you looking for some kind of bounty?"

"Bounty?" said Athgar. "No. Why? Is there such a thing?"

"Not in Reinwick, but I understand not all the Petty Kingdoms are such understanding folk."

"Does that mean there are Orcs nearby?"

"Not in Korvoran, or anywhere else in the duchy, for that matter."

Belgast set down his cup as if something had just occurred to him. "I'm sorry, Master Barbek. I've been so self-absorbed after all our troubles that I seem to have lost my manners." He held out his hand.

The smith clasped it in his own, holding it for a moment. Something evidently passed between the Dwarves, but Athgar had no idea what it was. Had they met before?

"It's good to see a friendly face," said Belgast at last, returning to his mead.

"Aye, though I must admit to some surprise. Another member of the guild hasn't visited me in years. I received no notice that you'd be coming."

"Guild?" said Athgar. "What guild?"

"The Dwarven Smiths Guild," said Belgast.

"But you're not a smith?"

"No, but I oversee my cousins in a supervisory capacity, so I could hardly run such a place without their blessing."

"I had no idea you were so well-connected. Assuming that counts as well-connected?"

"It does, but we don't like to advertise the fact."

"Yes," agreed Barbek. "The truth is we run most of the Human smiths guilds throughout the Petty Kingdoms, but not too many people know that, so I'll ask you to keep that to yourself."

"I'll tell no one," said Athgar.

"Good. Now, let's circle back to those Orcs, shall we? Why are you searching for them?"

"I am an Orc friend," said Athgar. "And I've been an Orc of the Red Hand for years. Well, obviously, I'm not an Orc but a member of the tribe."

"Can't say that I know of them."

"Nor would I expect you to. Their home lies far to the east."

"The east? You mean in Therengia?"

"So you've heard the news?"

"Who hasn't? It's the talk of the Continent." Barbek leaned in closer, finally noticing Athgar's eyes. "Ah, I should've realized. You're from there yourself, aren't you?"

"I am, though it's not something I'd like to be spread around just at the moment."

"You can trust him," said Belgast. "We share an oath."

"Trust me about what?" said Barbek.

"This is Athgar, master of flame and High Thane of Therengia."

Barbek laughed, a deep-throated chuckle that echoed off the walls. His mirth abruptly ended when he noted his new visitors did not join in on the fun. "Oh? You're serious?"

"Absolutely," said Athgar.

"My apologies, Your Lordship. Or would that be Your Majesty?"

"Lord would suffice in normal circumstances, but I would prefer you call me Athgar. It's a little difficult to keep one's identity a secret when using titles."

"Understood. Does anyone else know of your true identity?"

"Only my travelling companions."

"Say, you're not hoping to raise the Orcs against the Petty Kingdoms, are you?"

"No, of course not. Why would you even think that?"

"Well, you are the King of Therengia asking after Orcs."

"High Thane," corrected Athgar, "not king."

"What's the difference?"

"Kings are hereditary. High Thanes, on the other hand, are selected by the will of the people."

Barbek looked at his fellow Dwarf, who nodded.

"It's true," said Belgast. "The Orcs similarly choose their chieftains."

"Am I to understand," said the smith, "that you've lived amongst them for some time?"

"I have, and I find them to be most civilized."

"Who? The Orcs or the Therengians?"

"Both."

"The truth is," said Athgar, "we want to contact our brethren back home. The Orc's magic will allow us to do that."

"I see," said the smith. "So you need to locate some Orcs here, so one of their shamans can use a spell?"

"Precisely. Do you know of any in the area?"

"It depends on how you define 'area'. I met some down in the kingdom south of here, but that was years ago. At that time, they called themselves the Ashwalkers. They lived in the western forests of Andover, though I don't know how many of them there were."

"Did they live in a village?"

"No," said Barbek. "They were a wandering folk. I came across them while on the road."

"What happened?" asked Belgast.

"Not much, if I'm being honest. I traded some of my goods with them, then went on my way."

"Goods?" said Athgar.

"Yes, knives mostly, but several fancied some axes I'd made. I remember getting a very nice pair of boots out of the exchange. They were quite possibly the most comfortable footwear I've ever had the pleasure to wear."

"Interesting," said Athgar. "I never considered they might be a clan. That will make them much harder to find."

"Clan?" said Barbek. "What's the difference?"

"Clans are a wandering people, travelling where the game is. Tribes, on the other hand, settle down into a specific area. Some even plant crops, though not to the extent we Humans do. How far away is Andover?"

"Not far at all, but I'm afraid relations between Reinwick and Andover are extremely strained at the moment. I would advise against travelling there."

"Is it a large kingdom?"

"That depends on what you consider large. It occupies more land than Reinwick, but I met them more than twenty years ago. If what you say about them is true, they could be anywhere by now."

"Orcs go where the game is plentiful. I'm sure it wouldn't be too hard for me to locate them."

"Your appearance isn't going to help you. You may think the treatment of your people is bad here, but it pales in comparison to what Andover does."

"Meaning?" replied Athgar.

"The King of Andover has ordered the execution of anyone of Therengian descent."

"Surely you jest? He kills people just because of the colour of their eyes?"

"I wish I was joking, but I'm afraid his fear of the Old Kingdom reborn is deep-rooted. It has been so ever since he took the Throne. I imagine the news about this new Therengia to the east hasn't helped any."

"That makes things very difficult," said Athgar.

"Difficult?" said Belgast. "You mean impossible, surely? You can't possibly consider going to Andover."

"What choice do I have? I must get word back to Runewald!"

"I don't envy you your task," said Barbek, "but there's a fine line between bravery and stupidity. If I were you, I'd try to devise another way of contacting the Orcs. Either that or give up the notion entirely."

"How does the court of Andover view the Orcs?" asked Athgar.

"I have no idea," replied the smith. "It's been a few years since I've been to that fabled land, and my work here has kept me quite busy. Far too busy, if the truth be told, but I can't complain. I'm finally making a decent living."

"Fabled land?"

Barbek chuckled. "Yes. Andover is often the setting for fairy tales. I think the king there must encourage it."

"What sorts of fairy tales?"

"Oh, you know, the usual—mythical beasts and noble quests. They even claim the great woods house creatures of antiquity, whatever that means. I wouldn't put much faith in the stories if I were you. They're likely just meant to scare people off."

"Why would they want that?"

"A great woods lies on their border with Burgemont and Langwal. I suspect these stories are meant to dissuade any thoughts of invasion on their part."

"Thank you," said Athgar. "You've been most helpful. And please know that if you ever find yourself in Therengia, you would be welcome."

"I thank you for the offer," said Barbek, "but I doubt I'd travel that far east."

"You never know," said Belgast. "I never thought I'd find myself this far west, but here I am."

HALMUND

AUTUMN 1108 SR

L ying astride the great Redrock River, the sprawling city of Halmund
had long ago overgrown its walls, which, as a result, had fallen into
disrepair.

To Kargen's eyes, the homes they encountered looked ill-kept and badly
needed repairs, but Agar was the first to comment on them.

"*Father?*" he said in his native tongue. "*Why do the people of Novarsk live
like this? Do their chieftains not look after them?*"

"*It would appear not, though I am surprised by how many live in such a state.
All places have their share of the less fortunate, but in our lands, the community
takes care of them. It would appear the wealthy of this kingdom have no such
thoughts for the well-being of their people.*"

Their entourage passed by a cluster of women openly begging. At first,
these individuals raised their voices, calling out for help, but at the sight of
the Orcs, they shrank back, suspicion in their eyes.

"*Why do they fear us?*" pressed Agar.

"*They are alarmed by that which they do not understand. Our ways are foreign
to them, and likely their leaders have spread stories about the barbarity of us Orcs.*"

"*But we are not barbaric, are we?*"

"*No, my son, we are not, but ignorance leads to suspicion, which opens the door
to fear.*"

"*Then we shall teach them our ways.*"

Kargen smiled. To a youngling like Agar, life was easily explained away.
However, the chieftain knew Humans could be a fickle folk, who often
spoke of one thing while practicing another. This was not true of most

Therengians, but some questioned their traditional values, even in their new homeland.

"*You are brooding,*" said Shaluhk, interrupting his thoughts. "*Tell me what ails you.*"

"*The people of Novarsk suffer,*" he replied, "*while I suspect those in charge live a lavish lifestyle.*"

"*Lavish? You are becoming quite eloquent. Is that the influence of our scholars?*"

"*I must admit I spend more time in their company of late. The more I discover about the Old Kingdom, the more I am intrigued.*"

"*You should take care, bondmate mine. Remember, the Old Kingdom of Therengia was powerful, but it still fell into ruin. We, in contrast, must build a land that stands the test of time, else our descendants will once more be scattered to the four winds.*"

"*I am aware of the danger, but I now must make decisions in Athgar's name. That, I fear, is a heavy burden.*"

"*You can trust your instincts. He left you in charge because he trusts your judgement. Do not decide based on what you believe he would do; make decisions based on what your heart tells you.*"

"*It is good you are here,*" said Kargen. "*You help me see things as they truly are.*"

"*Shadook,*" called out Oswyn.

The shaman smiled as the tiny child ran up to her.

"*Well, what do we have here?*" she said, lifting up the youngling and holding her close. "*That is the first time you used my name.*"

"*Not quite,*" said Agar. "*She has a hard time with some of her Orcish words.*" He turned his attention to Oswyn, poking her affectionately. "*Shaluhk,*" he corrected.

"*Shadook!*"

Kargen laughed. "*It appears she has made up her mind.*"

"*Then Shadook I shall be,*" replied his bondmate.

Skora's voice drifted towards them. "I'm sorry," the old woman said in the Human tongue. "She got away from me. I'm afraid I'm not as fleet of foot as I used to be."

"None of us are," replied Shaluhk in the same language. Her gaze drifted once more to the decrepit buildings. "These people are suffering. Many look like they have not eaten a decent meal in weeks."

"Yes," agreed Kargen. "I will see what we can do for them."

"I have an idea," said Skora. "Take food away from all the wealthy folk hereabouts. I'm sure they have plenty to spare."

"Are you now an expert in the wealthier members of society?"

"I have met none myself, but our newer countrymen come from all over the Continent, and they tell the same tales."

"Which are?"

"The wealthy live a life of excess, while their subjects suffer."

"Not everywhere, surely?"

"There are exceptions," the woman continued, "but by and large, the poor are mistreated, particularly those descended from the Therengia of old."

Shaluhk nodded. "I have heard those stories as well. It is astounding that such people could be made to suffer so. We Orcs have had our fair share of poor leaders, but none that would let their own starve like this."

"Theirs is a different way of life," said Kargen. "One that stresses the importance of self over service. It is precisely that belief which eventually drove us from Ord-Kurgad."

Agar perked up. "Why did we have to leave, Father?"

"Humans came seeking to destroy us."

"Yes, I know that, but why?"

"They wanted sky metal, the rarest of all minerals. Initially, we defeated them, but the Duke of Krieghoff returned with a much larger army, for he could not allow a threat to remain on his border."

"But we were defending our home?"

"He did not see it that way. From his point of view, we defeated his warriors. Even if he ignored that, his neighbours would not, seeing it as a weakness and attacking, seeking to take his land."

"So we were caught in the middle?"

"I see you grasp the full significance of it all. Yes, we were, as you say, caught in the middle."

"I will never again allow Humans to take our land," announced Agar.

"That is why our home, Therengia, must be acknowledged by its neighbours."

"Yes," agreed Shaluhk, "and to gain that, we must show strength."

"Orcs are strong!" said the youngling.

"Indeed, but we must also show the strength of our resolve. We are not alone anymore, as you well know."

"Is it true Uncle Athgar changed our lives forever?"

Kargen chuckled. "Clearly, Tonfer Garul has heavily influenced him."

Shaluhk ignored him. "Athgar and Nat-Alia were not the cause of change, merely the spark that led to the solution."

"Just as you and Father were," said Agar. "Everyone says the Red Hand would never have found our new home without you."

"He's a bright lad," said Skora, "and he remembers everything."

"Yes," said Kargen. "Though I have not yet decided if that is a blessing or a curse."

Oswyn pointed in front of them. "Winfith!"

"It appears there is a delegation to welcome us to Halmund," said Shaluhk.

A dozen Therengian warriors stood waiting, with Wynfrith, the Thane of Bradon, at their head. Kargen's escort moved to either side of the road, allowing their chieftain to receive them.

Wynfrith bowed respectfully. "Kargen, Shaluhk. Good to see you both. I received word you were coming and arranged for the barons of Novarsk to meet us at the Palace."

"They are there now?"

"No. I thought you'd like a chance to catch up on things upon your arrival. They shall gather first thing tomorrow morning."

Oswyn reached out her hands. "Winfith!"

The elder thane smiled. "May I take her?"

"Of course," said Shaluhk, handing over the child.

"My, how you've grown," continued the thane. "Why, you must be twice the size of when I last saw you."

Oswyn giggled.

"Actually," said Agar, ever the stickler for details. "She has only grown a hand's width." He turned to his mother. "How long until she reaches her full size?"

"Likely not until she is fifteen or sixteen years of age."

"Then I have a lot of work ahead of me."

"So it would seem."

"Come," said Wynfrith. "Let us continue to the Palace, and I'll fill you in on recent events." She gave the order, and the Therengian warriors began marching farther into the city, guiding the way for them. "What do you know about Novarsk?"

"Not as much as I'd like," said Kargen. "It is, or rather was, ruled by a queen and broken into regions, each run by a baron."

"Have you any idea how many barons there are?"

"Temple Captain Yaromir seemed to think there were twenty-two."

"And so there were before Rada's defeat. Now, however, the actual count is seventeen."

"Why the discrepancy?" asked Shaluhk.

"Since the war ended, several deaths and marriages occurred, which served to merge some of the baronies. Their lands vary greatly but are measured by how many knights they're expected to field."

"I am not sure I understand," said Kargen. "Are you suggesting they are granted land based on the number of warriors they can provide?"

"It is a strange custom, I'll grant you, but I'm told it's common amongst the Petty Kingdoms. The idea is that the Crown grants land in exchange for service. In this case, the service consists of a specific number of warriors, including knights."

"And how many warriors or knights is a baron expected to support?"

"Some are as low as ten men and only one knight, while others are responsible for several hundred and at least a dozen knights. The most powerful of all is Lord Valentyn. His estates are scattered over the countryside, but he maintains his home keep in the northern part of the realm. At last count, he supplied twenty-five knights and four hundred warriors to the Royal Army, by far the largest. That was before the war, of course. The numbers will probably be much smaller after the thrashing we gave them."

"That is more than we brought with us," said Kargen. "I hope he will not cause us any trouble?"

"It's impossible to say at this point. All the barons remain tight-lipped about their wishes regarding the Throne. I suspect some of them want to be made the new king themselves, or at least the prince's regents until he comes of age." She paused a moment. "What are your intentions regarding these people?"

"I am not sure. I need to speak to all the barons before making a decision. I am somewhat hampered at present by not knowing any of them, which makes it hard to assess where their loyalties lie. I look forward to getting to know them better."

"You'll find them a mixed bunch. Some seem decent in their own way, but I wouldn't trust any while out of sight."

"I shall take heed of your warning."

They continued past the old wall that had fallen into disrepair. Beyond lay the inner city, a place of commerce and wealth. The buildings here were much better kept than anything they'd seen on their way in, a testament to the riches of Novarsk.

Eventually, the Palace came into view, an enormous structure built of white stone, boasting four corner towers, although only ornamental. Extravagant gardens with colourful flowers arranged in perfect symmetry surrounded the grounds.

"This place is immense," said Kargen. "You could likely fit the entire population of Runewald within its walls and be left with room to spare."

"They are a wasteful people," said Wynfrith. "The cost to build this must have been staggering, yet I'm told this is only one of three such places."

"Three? Why would a queen need three palaces?"

"I have no idea, nor do I care to know more. I am content to command our fyrd. I shall leave the governing to you."

"She is clever," said Shaluhk. "She knows whoever rules here will be under constant scrutiny."

"From whom?" asked Kargen.

"Them." She pointed at a distant gathering of people near the Palace gates, eager to witness what was happening inside. Dressed in decent clothing, these Humans were unlike their poorer brethren. He guessed them more likely to be merchants than farmers.

"Who are they?" asked Kargen.

"The wealthy of Halmund," replied Wynfrith.

"The barons?"

"No. Natalia would call them commoners, yet amongst that group, those people would seem to hold most of the wealth."

"More than the barons?"

"Possibly, although I cannot say with any certainty."

"How do you know all this?"

She smiled. "Let's just say I've spent my time here wisely."

Next morning found Kargen ready to meet the nobles of Novarsk. He sat on the floor instead of the throne, his idea to show his guests that Therengia harboured no desire to usurp their Crown. As the barons entered, however, it quickly became apparent his attempt had not impressed them. They nervously gathered around, their eyes scanning the room, unsure what was about to unfold. Kargen stood, his sizeable green frame commanding attention.

"What is this?" snarled one of the barons. "Are we to be sacrificed to some ancient god?"

"My name is Kargen, Chieftain of the Red Hand. I come here this day on behalf of Athgar of Athelwald, High Thane of Therengia."

The angry baron stepped forward. "You are naught but a filthy greenskin. If the High Thane is to give us an ultimatum, then let him come here and do it in person."

Wynfrith stepped out from the sidelines. "And who do you think you are to make such a demand?"

"I am Lord Valentyn Sayenko, Baron of Krasnov."

"The High Thane's presence is required elsewhere at this time," she replied. "In his place, he has named Chieftain Kargen as his representative. You will deal with him, or you will deal with no one."

Lord Valentyn reddened but said no more.

"I am here," continued Kargen, "to inform you that Queen Rada no longer sits upon the Throne of Novarsk. What will replace her has yet to be determined."

"You mean who, surely?" said Lord Valentyn.

"We have not yet decided whether we shall permit you to retain a monarch."

Another baron spoke out, "Surely you jest?"

"What is your name?" demanded Kargen.

"Pavel Kolkov, Baron of Nayalov."

"Nayalov. That is one of the larger baronies, I assume?"

"It is," replied the lord. "I will not sit back and meekly accept this insult to the people of Novarsk!"

"I might remind you, Lord Pavel, we are the victors here. Your army lies in ruins, its warriors dispersed or dead, and you have only been allowed here by my invitation. I suggest if you want to keep your lands, you show a greater sense of decorum and stop making demands." Kargen let his gaze wander over the other barons. Most stared at the floor, a sure sign they'd resigned themselves to their fates, but these two, Valentyn and Pavel, still had fire in their eyes.

"There is much to consider in the coming days," continued Kargen. "During my visit here, I shall meet with each and every one of you individually. To that end, you will remain in Halmund and make yourselves available as needed."

Lord Valentyn was defiant. "And if we don't?"

"Then your title will be stripped, and your lands seized."

"You have no right."

"You brought this on yourselves. We Therengians are a peaceful people, but we will not sit by and allow our neighbours to raise arms against us."

"You are no Therengian," spat out Lord Pavel. "You're not even Human—you're an Orc."

"Yes, I am," replied Kargen, "but under the law of our land, there is no distinction between Human and Orc. You should all take that to heart over the next few days, particularly when I call upon you to discuss your kingdom's future. The fate of Novarsk is in your hands."

He nodded to Wynfrith, and then the Therengian warriors moved in, escorting the barons from the room. Lord Pavel, the last to leave, kept his eyes glued on Kargen until the end.

"*That one will be trouble,*" said Shaluhk, speaking in the Orcish tongue to ensure none but her bondmate would understand her words.

"*Yes. He and Valentyn both. We must keep a close eye on them, lest they attempt to sway the rest to their cause.*"

"Their cause? Do you fear they will raise arms against us?"

"It is a distinct possibility. Both are powerful men, and though neither could challenge us on their own, if more joined them, we would be hard-pressed to stop them."

"Then we must take measures to prevent it."

"What would you suggest?"

"I recommend we send for the Thane Guard. Their presence here in Halmund might help dissuade the barons from considering more direct action. If I used my magic to get word to Laghul, they could be on the road before morning."

Kargen nodded. *"Do so, and have them pick up Laruhk and his tuskers when they pass through Ebenstadt."*

"What of Temple Captain Yaromir?" asked Shaluhk. *"He and his men could be useful in helping the poor."*

"Ultimately, they serve the Church. I would not force him to make a decision that might put him in direct opposition to us. I will send word to him by messenger to inform him of our progress, but for now, the Temple Knights of Saint Mathew are best left in Ebenstadt. In the meantime, we shall see if Brother Maurice would be willing to learn more about the Church's attitude towards our presence here in Novarsk."

"A good idea," said Shaluhk. *"We know nothing of the Church's opinion on the matter other than they maintain a presence in two cities. We also do not know what other orders might be present. Rada may not have been the most devout of worshippers, but I suspect the Church has a strong presence here, as it does throughout the Petty Kingdoms."*

"Yes. We must be careful. Our defeat of the Cunars likely still stings. I imagine they would welcome the chance to wipe away the disgrace with another so-called Holy War."

"I agree, but I doubt they will make the same mistake twice. If they come for us again, it will be at the head of a very large army. Thus, it is imperative we solidify our hold on Novarsk as soon as possible."

THE AUDIENCE

AUTUMN 1108 SR

After more than two weeks of waiting for word from the duke, a visitor arrived at the house of Yelena Dryer. The well-dressed fellow sported a closely trimmed beard, but the lines on his face told of someone unhappy with his lot in life. Upon entering, he bowed slightly to Natalia but stiffened as his gaze turned to Athgar.

"Is something wrong?" asked Natalia.

"I seem to have come here in error," the visitor said. "My pardon."

"Are you here, perchance, to tell us the duke will grant us an audience?"

"I was… that is… I am. Yes." He stared at Athgar throughout his rambling answer, finally directing all his attention to Natalia. "My pardon, madam. I wasn't aware servants would be present."

"This is no servant; he is my husband, Athgar of Athelwald. And you are?"

"Captain Marwen, my lady. I have the honour of serving His Grace as a leader of some of his footmen."

"And the message?" said Athgar.

"He has deigned to grant you an audience today at noon… sir. Do I call you sir?"

"He is a man of some importance," said Natalia. "'My lord' would be more appropriate."

"My lord," the man corrected, although he looked extremely uncomfortable doing so.

"Will you be taking us there?"

"I have that honour, yes."

"Then tell us a little about yourself," replied Natalia.

"I beg your pardon?"

"Tell us something about your past. How long have you served His Grace, the duke?"

"Fifteen years, my lady, give or take a few months."

"And have you any experience?"

"Doing what?"

"Fighting, of course. You did say you commanded some of his footmen."

"Alas, no. I am ever ready to serve, but the kingdom has been relatively peaceful for many years."

"Yet the Church fought off the Halvarians, didn't they?"

"That was not a land battle, my lady. The enterprise was fought entirely at sea."

"Without the duke's aid, it would seem."

"I don't know who you got your information from, but several Reinwick ships accompanied the fleet."

"I didn't know His Grace controlled warships?"

"He doesn't," said Captain Marwen, "but they used merchant ships to carry Temple Knights and supplies."

"And those were the duke's?" asked Athgar.

"No, but of Reinwick. It amounts to the same thing."

"Does it, now?" said Athgar. "How very interesting."

"Do not look down on me!" said the captain. "You haven't earned that right."

"I meant no disrespect," said Athgar. "I'm merely trying to ascertain where you stand on matters. I see you bear no love for my people; how do I know I can trust you to take us to His Grace and not to some alleyway, where we'll both be murdered?"

The fellow's face turned positively crimson as his mouth flapped open, entirely at a loss of how to respond.

"He teases you," soothed Natalia. "Although, if you intended to kill us, you'd have a hard time of it."

"Why is that?"

"We've both been in battle, Captain. Athgar, even more so than me. I wouldn't like to consider your fate should you take up arms against us."

"I can assure you that is the furthest thing from my mind. In fact, quite the reverse. I'm here to ensure your safe arrival."

"What is the duke like?" pressed Athgar. "And be honest now. I assure you; no word of your opinion will leave this room."

"He is a solitary man," replied Marwen, "who rarely grants private audiences. You should consider yourselves lucky."

"And the reason for his solitude?" asked Natalia.

"He never got over the death of his late wife. His son, Fernando, now sees to many of the day-to-day details of running the duchy."

"Might I enquire how Her Grace died?"

"After a brief illness brought on by rotten food. Some speculated she was poisoned, but it was never proven. Even today, some still believe the Halvarians were responsible in retaliation for their spoiled plans."

"But that would assume the duke was responsible for their defeat, wouldn't it? I was under the impression the Temple Knights took things in hand."

"And so they did, but they would never have built a Holy Fleet were it not for Her Grace's generosity. You see, she was an avid supporter of the sisters' endeavours."

"Did the duke take any action against Halvaria?" asked Athgar.

"He banned the Halvarian Ambassador right after the plot was uncovered, but even he's not foolish enough to take on the empire directly."

"Not foolish enough?" said Natalia. "Your words betray you, Captain."

"I'll not deny the duke is sometimes lacking in reason these days. He is, as they say, decidedly old, though at times he can be rather energetic."

"Fernando is the designated heir?"

"He is, my lady."

"And is he married?"

"Not at present."

"Might I ask why?"

"I beg your pardon?"

"I'm only curious," said Natalia. "He's a grown man, is he not?"

"He is, and for some time now, but all such attempts at arrangements of that sort have fallen through."

"Why is that?"

"It is, I fear, due to the constantly shifting threats and alliances that plague the Petty Kingdoms. On one such occasion, the bride's offer was cancelled when they sided with our traditional enemy in a trade dispute. Another was lost when the young lady in question ran off with someone else."

"Aside from his marital woes, what is he like?"

"Most competent, my lady. He'll make a fine duke one day."

"Tell me," said Athgar, "are we to meet with the duke or his son?"

"The duke himself," said Captain Marwen. "Though I suspect the meeting will be short. Most are, these days."

"You mentioned his son, Fernando, looks after many of the responsibilities of running the duchy. Are we to infer he would need to approve our plans?"

"I cannot say, for I've heard little regarding the reason for this audience."

"What do you know?" asked Natalia.

"I understand that it's the direct result of Temple Captain Leona interceding on your behalf. You have a powerful ally pressing your case."

"Yet it took over two weeks to arrange an audience."

The captain shrugged. "His Grace is a busy man. I'm afraid today was the first opportunity available. I might go so far as to suggest you should consider yourself lucky. There are a great many who seek the duke's attention these days."

"And we are grateful for the opportunity to meet with him."

"Yes," added Athgar, "but if we're to see him at noon, shouldn't we be on our way?"

"Of course," said Captain Marwen. "If you'd like to get changed, then I can lead you there."

"Changed?"

"Yes. I assume you wish to wear your finest attire. You are meeting with the duke after all."

"These are the only clothes we have," said Natalia. "I'm afraid His Grace must put up with us as we are."

The disparaging look the captain bestowed upon them left no doubt about his feelings on the matter, but then he remembered himself. "Yes, of course. In that case, perhaps we'd best leave now. Our destination lies some blocks away. Have you a carriage?"

"No, we came by sea."

"Ah, then perhaps we'd be better off to walk."

"I thought we were to be there by noon?"

"His Grace is never on time for such things. I swear one day he'll be late for his own burial."

"Then let us leave," said Natalia.

Once they arrived at the duke's estate, they were escorted into a small room and told to wait. Captain Marwen left them at that point, disappearing into the endless corridors making up the place, leaving Athgar and Natalia alone in the room.

"What do you make of this?" asked Athgar, staring at a large portrait of a man astride a magnificent horse, sword in hand.

"Must be one of his ancestors," she mused. "The clothing is dated, and the people in the background wear archaic armour."

"How long ago, would you say?"

"At least two centuries would be my guess."

THE AUDIENCE | 81

"How old is Reinwick?"

"I don't know the exact year, but I believe it was founded soon after the downfall of the Old Kingdom."

"You mean Therengia."

"I do, although now that we're using that name for ourselves, we're better off to use the local terminology for our historical predecessors."

"I didn't think the Old Kingdom was this far north?"

"It probably wasn't, but the warfare that accompanied its downfall spread across the Continent. They say scarcely a single realm was left untouched."

"So why a duchy, as opposed to a kingdom?" said Athgar.

"I have no answer for you."

"Could it be due to size?"

"There are smaller kingdoms elsewhere. If I had to guess, I'd say they were probably part of a larger country, then broke off at some point, opting for self-rule."

"Is that rare?"

"No," replied Natalia. "There are dozens of duchies. Remember Holstead? That's a duchy, as was its neighbour, Krieghoff."

"Yes, that's right. Does that mean they were once a single kingdom?"

"I'm not sure. From what Kargen told us, they went to war shortly after the destruction of Ord-Kurgad. Who knows, they may now be under a single ruler."

"And in that case, would the former Duke of Krieghoff proclaim himself king?"

"He might. There's been a tendency for the Petty Kingdoms to flex their muscles these last few years by expanding their kingdoms."

"Could the same be true here?"

"It's possible," said Natalia, "and something we might want to bring up with His Grace when we finally meet him."

A woman opened the door. "Lord Athgar? Lady Natalia?"

"That's us," they both answered.

"If you'll come with me, I'll take you to His Grace, Duke Wilfhelm."

"And you are?" asked Natalia.

"Enid, a member of His Grace's household."

"Then lead on, Enid, and we shall follow."

Once out the door, they headed down a long corridor, passing several side passages, which led Athgar to conclude this place was like a giant maze. Finally, they arrived at a closed set of ornately carved double doors.

"His Grace is inside," said Enid.

"Is he alone?" asked Athgar.

"He was when last I left him, but people come and go at odd times here, so I cannot guarantee such is still the case." She opened a door, then stepped through.

"Your visitors are here, Your Grace."

"Visitors?" came an elderly voice.

"Yes, Lord Athgar and Lady Natalia. Temple Captain Leona sent them?"

"Ah, yes, of course. Well, don't just stand there. Send them in."

A waft of warm air greeted them as they entered. The duke sat before a blazing fire, a blanket on his legs and his feet on a footstool, sipping from a steaming cup.

"Tell me," said the duke, "have we met before?"

"No, Your Grace," answered Natalia.

"I see. To what do I owe this visit? Have you come seeking coins, perchance? Because if you have, you shall leave disappointed."

"No, Your Grace. We bring news, but I'm afraid it requires some explanation."

The duke took another sip, swirling it around his mouth before swallowing. "Very well, tell your tale. I always like a good story."

"I am a Water Mage by training; to be more specific, I trained in the city of Karslev. Have you heard of it?"

"It's in Ruzhina, isn't it?"

"It is, Your Grace. The Volstrum, the magical academy there, specializes in training people like me."

"And is Lord Athgar here also a student of this Volstrum?"

"No," said Athgar. "I was taught the use of Fire Magic by less-traditional methods."

The duke raised an eyebrow. "Fascinating. You must tell me more of your tale, Lord Athgar, but should we not let Lady Natalia finish hers first?"

"Of course."

Natalia cleared her throat. "During my time at this academy, I realized my objectives did not align with those of the Volstrum. To that end, I left Karslev to seek my own way in life. During my flight, I met Athgar, and we travelled for a while before settling down in the east."

"All well and good," said the duke, "but what has this to do with me?"

"I shall get to that in a moment, Your Grace, but before I go any further, I must reveal my full name, though I ask you not to pass judgement until I've had a chance to explain myself."

"I promise you shall have the opportunity to finish your tale."

"My full name is Natalia Stormwind."

The duke's eyes went wide. "That is not a name I typically allow within these halls. However, you've captured my interest. I warn you, though, that name is not well thought of here in Reinwick."

"And well I understand that. The truth is the Stormwind family has been the bane of my existence for some time. We explicitly came here, to Reinwick, because we heard you banished them from your court."

"So, you sought refuge? Understandable considering your background."

"There's more, Your Grace. They sent agents to kidnap our daughter, and that was too much, so we journeyed to Karslev to end things once and for all. I won't bore you with the details, but we uncovered a shocking truth during our time there. A truth that helps explain much of the discord within the Petty Kingdoms."

The duke sat up, his feet now planted firmly on the floor. "Go on."

"The Stormwinds, and their kin, the Sartellians, are the power behind the Halvarian Empire."

"But they have an emperor, surely?"

"They do," said Natalia, "but we believe he is merely a figurehead."

"And what evidence have you of this?"

"A letter from the hand of Illiana Stormwind herself."

"And she is?"

"Until her death, she was the head of the Stormwind family and my grandmother, though I only discovered the latter later in life."

"The problem is," added Athgar, "we have no way of authenticating the letter. No one else even knows of its existence."

"I believe you," insisted the duke. "As you say, it explains a great many things. I assume you heard about what happened back in ninety-seven?"

"You mean the Halvarian fleet's destruction and Larissa Stormwind's actions? Yes, we're quite familiar with them."

"At the time, I thought it the actions of one corrupt member of that illustrious family, but Temple Captain Charlaine convinced me to ban all of them. I see now it was the right thing to do. However, I didn't believe it proper to banish the Sartellians as well. After all, they didn't participate in the scheme."

"Have you any Sartellians in your court at present?" asked Athgar.

"No, but I know who does have them—the King of Andover. This also helps explain our current problems."

"Current, Your Grace?"

"Yes. The new King of Andover cast his eyes north and is now making threats."

"Is there anything we can do to help?"

The duke laughed. "Not unless you brought an army with you."

"An army, no, but there are other mages in our group. Like us, they're eager to break the family's hold over the Continent's courts."

"Mages would be useful in the coming war, but there's still some hope we might prevent such a catastrophe. I'm considering sending an emissary to the court of Andover to work out our differences."

"Perhaps," said Natalia, "we could accompany him? At the very least, we could scout out the forces of Andover while your representative tries diplomacy."

"Or perhaps," said Athgar, "Natalia could help him in his endeavours."

"How would a Water Mage aid with negotiations?" asked the duke.

"She is a trained battle mage and familiar with the family's tactics at court. At the very least, she could provide insight into what they're up to."

"I'm not sure I follow. This is Andover we're talking about, not just a Fire Mage."

"They would like you to think that," said Natalia, "but the truth is, the family's been manipulating events for decades, perhaps even centuries. They care little about disputes between Petty Kingdoms, unless it enhances the power they wield over others."

"Are you suggesting they're orchestrating all of this?"

"That's exactly what I'm saying, Your Grace. What do you suppose would be the outcome of a war between your two kingdoms?"

"A lot of death, to be sure. As to actual borders, I doubt things would change very much. Our landward frontier is small and easily defended. The only real threat to us is from the sea."

"And if a fleet did threaten? You'd be required to leave a great many men scattered all over the peninsula to repel possible landings."

"I admit I hadn't considered that, but Andover has no ships, at least none that could threaten us."

"Ah, but they undoubtedly have alliances," said Natalia.

"And that would help them, how?"

"I can answer that one," said Athgar. "Imagine Andover sends a large army to your border. You, in turn, send the bulk of your warriors to fight them, leaving your kingdom at the mercy of a seaborne invasion. They could cut off your lines of retreat or even assault your northern cities with little to oppose them."

"You've given me much to think on. I will confer with some of my advisors, but thank you for bringing this to my attention."

"And our offer?"

"I would ask you to keep this to yourselves for now, but I will send word once I make my decision."

"Thank you, Your Grace. We look forward to hearing from you."

THE VISITOR

AUTUMN 1108 SR

The duke's answer took two days to arrive, and when it did, a rotund individual with greying hair delivered it. Lady Yelena's servants led him into the gardens where Athgar and Natalia sat, enjoying an unseasonably warm day.

"Good day. My name is Lord Kurlan Stratmeyer." He was about to say more when he noticed Athgar's grey eyes. "I'm sorry. It seems I've mistaken you for someone else."

"No. I am Lady Natalia, and this is Lord Athgar."

"Is this a jest? Because if it is, I find it in extremely poor taste."

"I assure you, Lord, there is no mistake. Have you come from His Grace, the duke?"

"Yes, but he made no mention I'd be dealing with one of his ilk." He nodded towards Athgar.

"And does that in any way change the duke's decision?"

"I'm sure it would if he were aware of the heritage of the man he's looking to hire."

"Lord Athgar and I spoke with His Grace at great length some two days past, so he is intimately familiar with his ancestry. He took no offence at his appearance. Do you now disagree with his opinion?"

Lord Kurlan reddened. "No, that is to say… certainly not. My apologies, Lord Athgar. If the duke saw value in your services, I should at least show you the same courtesy."

"I shall choose to overlook your ill manners," said Athgar. He managed a quick wink at Natalia before continuing. "I assume you bring us news?"

"I do, indeed. I come directly from His Grace's presence, but in an unofficial capacity, lest his political opponents gain knowledge of what he proposes."

"So he can deny it, if pressed?"

"I see you understand our ways quite well. We might save some time if you tell me how much the duke has already explained to you."

"He is worried about Andover," said Natalia. "He intends to send an emissary to try to talk their king out of a war, but I get the impression he doesn't expect it to succeed."

"Yes," said Lord Kurlan. "You have the gist of it. King Volkard sired three sons, but only one survived long enough to inherit the Throne. Dagmar is, by all accounts, a headstrong individual who's had an axe to grind with us for years. Add to that the humiliation they endured at the hands of Erlingen, and you can understand why he wants to prove he's a force to be reckoned with."

"Erlingen?" said Athgar. "Stanislav mentioned that. Where does it lie?"

"It's Andover's southern neighbour. Some years ago, their king married off his niece to the Duke of Erlingen, but he tired of her. Rumour has it he arranged her death so he could take up with his new mistress. It caused quite a stir, so much so that King Volkard marched to war."

"And he lost?"

"That's putting it mildly. Not only did he face defeat on the field of battle, but he himself was also captured. His ransom alone nearly bankrupted the kingdom. Ever since, they've been building up their army, determined to show their neighbours they're not weak."

"And now they want to go to war to prove the point?"

"Well, let's just say the young king is eager to expunge his father's record."

"You say young," said Natalia. "Any idea how old King Dagmar is?"

"In his early twenties, I would imagine, though I cannot claim to be an expert in such things. The duke's son, Fernando, would likely know, but I'm afraid he's otherwise engaged at this precise moment."

"When did he come to the Throne?"

"Early last year. His father was ill for some time and finally passed as winter ended."

"I'm a little confused," said Athgar. "What precisely is to be our role in all of this?"

"His Grace hoped you and your companions would accompany his emissary and assist him in the performance of his duties."

"So we are to spy on his behalf?"

"Yes, I believe that would be the appropriate conclusion. His Grace would pay your expenses, but we need to discuss your fee."

"Our fee?" said Athgar.

"He means," said Natalia, "our payment for spying on his behalf, over and above travel and such."

"I'm not sure I could name a price."

"I could," she replied. "Quite easily, in fact."

Lord Kurlan shifted uncomfortably. "And that would be?"

"Not coins, if that's what you're thinking. Instead, we would seek a favour."

"What kind of favour?"

"One to be named later."

"What you ask is a tall order. I can't, in all honesty, say His Grace will agree to such terms."

"Then he is free to seek expertise elsewhere. I assume he has others fully conversant with the family's way of doing things?"

"I... believe I might be able to convince him to accept your terms."

"Good. Then we are ready and willing to leave whenever the duke deems it a suitable time."

"I shall convey your message to him in person."

"This emissary," said Athgar, "it isn't you, is it? Not that I mean any disrespect."

"Me? No, of course not. There are far more important things for me to attend to back home in Blunden."

"More important than preventing a war?"

The baron blushed. "I do not mean to imply your mission is not of importance: merely its chances of succeeding are slim. In my opinion, we are better served by preparing our defences."

"And yet you come here representing your duke."

"I do, but while I am entitled to my own opinions, I am still a loyal servant of His Grace."

"Perhaps you can give us a better idea of how many men the duke commands."

"Why in the name of the Saints would you need to know that?"

"If the chance of peace is slight, as you claim," said Natalia, "then it would serve us well to discover as much about the enemy as possible. A thorough understanding of your own forces will give us a better probability of assessing the threat the army of Andover presents."

"Or to pass such information on to our enemy? I think not. My pardon if I offend you, but your group is new to this land. From all accounts, you used to serve the family who very likely orchestrated this entire conflict."

"His Grace told you all we revealed to him?"

"He has. I want to believe you, I truly do, but I've seen nothing so far to indicate you've earned that trust."

"Then let us turn our attention to other matters. This emissary, any idea who it might be?"

"There are several His Grace could select, but as of this morning, he's still undecided. However, from what he tells me, he's eager to settle matters with Andover, so I suspect he will make his decision sooner rather than later. In the meantime, I suggest you and your companions be ready to travel. Once he's chosen his man, he'll want him on the road before the colder weather sets in."

"Will we travel by horse?" asked Natalia.

"No. Carriage, I imagine, or perhaps I should say carriages since there are six of you. Even then, he'll probably assign an escort to ensure your safety."

"What kind of escort?"

"Horsemen, I would suspect."

"Knights?"

"Not likely," replied the baron. "He'll keep them close at hand in case war erupts. I hate to put it this way, but the entire expedition will, in all likelihood, be considered expendable."

"We should let you go," said Natalia. "Thank you for your visit, Lord Kurlan, and please convey to His Grace we are ready to ride at a moment's notice, providing he agrees to our terms, of course."

"I shall bear your message to him this very afternoon." He hesitated for a moment, struggling to find his words. "I... wish you well in this endeavour and will pray to the Saints for your success." He left them rather abruptly.

"What did you make of that?" asked Athgar.

"Lord Kurlan obviously doesn't agree with our mission."

"Our mission? Or our presence?"

"If I'm being honest, it could be either. He plainly has reservations about our involvement, while, at the same time, remains the duke's loyal servant."

"What was all that about a favour?"

Natalia smiled. "It's a powerful weapon if used properly."

"But a favour could be disavowed, couldn't it?"

"You must understand the mentality of the Petty Kingdoms. A favour is a highly coveted asset that can be used to cement alliances or even bring a kingdom into a war. No ruler in all the Continent would dare refuse to honour a favour; it would be their undoing."

"It carries that much weight?"

"It does," said Natalia. "You need to realize there are few guarantees when it comes to politics, and only two bear the risk of being ostracized if broken."

"Two?"

"Yes—marriage and favours."

"Is a man's word not good enough?"

"Amongst us Therengians, our word is our bond, but the people of the Continent are, by and large, less trustworthy and suspicious of strangers."

"Why is that?" asked Athgar.

"I'm afraid that's likely the result of the Old Kingdom. The Successor States, the precursor to the Petty Kingdoms, banded together to defeat your ancestors. Once they defeated that threat, they turned against one another. The concept of favours evolved out of that natural distrust. In the beginning, they were more of a strong promise, but then the Church of the Saints got involved. Now everyone is worried the Temple Knights might come after them if they break such an agreement."

"Which Temple Knights?"

"Take your pick," said Natalia. "Though I would wager most assume it would be the Cunars doing the enforcement."

"So the same Temple Knights who refuse to get involved with politics would enforce the breaking of a favour?"

"The term is confusing you. Think of it more as an oath, but one that expects something in return. Only the most desperate would agree to such terms."

"And you believe the duke will accept those terms?"

"He has little choice; he fears war. And honestly, if we die, he owes us nothing."

Athgar smiled. "You're quite clever. I would never have thought to ask for such a thing."

"Of course I'm clever. I chose you, didn't I?"

They returned to find the others inside, sitting around a table and nibbling away at a selection of fruit and cheese.

"Well?" said Stanislav. "How'd it go?"

"As expected," said Natalia. "Lord Kurlan was a little short on details, but I suppose that's only natural. Hopefully, whoever His Grace deigns to send will be able to provide more information."

"So he agreed to hire us?"

"He did, and to cover our expenses."

The mage hunter, about to pop some cheese into his mouth, suddenly halted. "We're potentially risking our lives just for expenses?"

"Not just expenses. Assuming His Grace agrees to our terms, he'll owe us a favour."

Stanislav smiled. "He must be desperate indeed to consider such an offer. What, precisely, did you have in mind for calling in the favour?"

"There are several possibilities. We could, for example, insist he recognizes Therengia as a kingdom."

"You think he would agree to that?"

"Why not?" said Natalia. "It's not as if a kingdom far to the east would be any threat to Reinwick. Who knows, he might even consider it an opportunity for a new alliance, one that would confound his enemies."

"What good would that do?" said Belgast. "It's not as if we could come to his aid if someone attacked him."

"It's not about that," she replied. "An ally could threaten an enemy's rear. In this case, it's not so much about Andover as his other neighbours."

"I'm not sure I follow," said Athgar.

"Currently, Reinwick has an agreement with Erlingen, the land lying south of Andover. Should Andover march north, Erlingen could respond, forcing them to send warriors to keep them at bay."

"Yes, but surely Therengia is a long way from threatening any of Reinwick's neighbours?"

"The Petty Kingdoms are a complex web of alliances and agreements. You must look at the whole Continent to truly appreciate them. In our case, defeating Novarsk has expanded our lands, which means more kingdoms on our borders. To counter that, we need contact with realms who can threaten those new neighbours, and the Duke of Reinwick may be the key allowing us to do just that."

"Yes," said Athgar, "but an alliance?"

"Think of it more as posturing. Should war come, we are too far away to lend any actual armies to assist them. Instead, it's a sign of their influence on the Continent. You can boil it down to a simple idea: the more friends you possess, the more powerful you are. At least, that's the perception."

"You mentioned Erlingen, but does the duke have any other allies?"

"Undoubtedly," said Natalia, "yet that's the only one I've heard tell of, likely because of its proximity to Andover."

"So let me get this straight," said Athgar. "If we ally with Reinwick, would that also make us allies with Erlingen?"

"That's the usual way of things."

"So the entire Continent can be divided into two camps?"

"More than two, actually," offered Stanislav. "Most of the Petty Kingdoms would love lots of allies, but the cold reality is they seldom have more than three or four, if they're lucky. If you had access to all the alliances on the Continent, you'd probably discover there were dozens of different factions."

"Factions?"

"Yes, groups of allied countries. I can think of no other word for them."

"I see there is much more for me to learn about being a ruler," said Athgar. "And here I thought a High Thane only worried about his own people."

"This is all part of that," said Natalia. "Securing peace from without helps keep your people safe."

"You mean our people. You're one of us now, remember?" He let his gaze drift across the rest of the group. "You're all Therengians now, assuming you want to be, of course."

"I should very much like to see Therengia," said Katrin. "I never really had a home."

"You had parents," said Galina.

"Yes, but my father disowned me when I failed at the Volstrum. And in any case, they never allowed me any freedom to make my own decisions. I was born a Stormwind; the only acceptable outcome for me was to graduate from the Volstrum and serve the family."

"Well, now you have the freedom to make your own decisions in life."

"Then I choose to be a Therengian."

"That's the spirit," said Natalia.

"As do I," said Galina. "Who knows, maybe one day we'll create a training academy of our own to rival the family."

"I like the sounds of that, but we'll make sure not to use it to corrupt the courts of the Petty Kingdoms."

"I can live with that."

Everyone stared at Stanislav.

"Don't look at me," replied the mage hunter. "I may not have grey eyes, but I'm already a Therengian. I live in Ebenstadt now, remember?"

"Ebenstadt?" said Galina. "I seem to recall that name. It was an independent city, wasn't it?"

"Yes," said Athgar. "The Temple Knights of Saint Cunar ran it, but after their crusade failed, they fled, leaving the place unprotected."

"So you captured it?"

"We did, but not in the way you think. Our daughter, Oswyn, was abducted, and her captor took her there. The only way to get her back was to besiege the place."

"Yes," added Natalia, "but the story gets even stranger. At the same time, Novarsk marched on the city to claim it as their own. Luckily, we breached Ebenstadt's walls before they did."

"I assume you rescued your daughter?"

"We did, although the abductor got away. She's who we fought on the way here to Reinwick."

"And now Novarsk is under your control."

"It is," said Athgar, "but that, too, was unintended. They marched into our lands to try to take what is ours. We defeated their invasion, turned around, and conquered them instead."

"And what will you do with the place, now that it's under your control?"

"That's an excellent question. I wish I had an answer. The truth is, we left it all in the hands of Kargen and Shaluhk."

"I recognize those names," said Katrin. "They're Orcs, aren't they?"

"They are, and I would trust no one more so than those two. I only hope they didn't run into any trouble in our absence."

"There will always be trouble," said Natalia, "but they can handle anything life throws at them. That reminds me: did you and Belgast ever discover the whereabouts of an Orc tribe?"

"We did," replied Belgast. "We met a Dwarf by the name of Barbek Stoutarm; he's smith to the Temple Knights of Saint Agnes."

"Yes," said Athgar. "He suggested we might find some in Andover, a group calling themselves the Ashwalkers. I hope while we're down there, we can make contact. It would be nice to get word home that we're still alive."

"You should've mentioned your discovery," said Natalia.

"Sorry, but with everything else going on around here, it completely slipped my mind. I must be getting old."

Stanislav laughed. "Old? What does that make me—ancient?"

INFLUENCE

AUTUMN 1108 SR

Lord Pavel Kolkov paced the halls of the Royal Palace, occasionally letting out a low growl.

"Calm yourself," advised Lord Valentyn. "Your anger will accomplish nothing."

"They cannot treat us this way. We are barons of Novarsk."

"Yes, and they, our conquerors."

"I would have thought you, of all people, would understand."

"Oh, I understand, but we must play the hand we're dealt. Besides, there are other ways to deal with people like them."

"Surely you're not suggesting we oust them?" asked Pavel.

"Only as a last resort. Instead, we must appeal to their baser instincts."

"They're Orcs," said Pavel. "What are we to do, offer them live sacrifices?"

"It's true they're not Human, but are they really so different? They communicate as we do, even speak our language. They must, therefore, share similar weaknesses."

"Such as?"

"Greed?"

"Surely you're not suggesting we bribe them?"

"Why ever not?" said Lord Valentyn. "We controlled the Queen of Novarsk well enough. Why not these savages?"

"I might remind you it was her idea to invade Therengia."

"You agreed to it."

"Only when pressured. From day one, I voiced my opposition, but to no avail. Eventually, I had to give in or lose my lands."

"Or your head," added his companion. "Rada was not one to listen to discontent."

"Is that what we've been reduced to?" asked Lord Pavel. "Discontented nobles?"

"Come now. We're far from that. Between us, we have more wealth than all the other barons combined. I see no reason we cannot continue living the life of luxury we've become accustomed to."

The door opened, revealing a sturdy fellow wearing a mail shirt. "Lord Pavel Kolkov?"

"That's me."

"Come with me, my lord. Chief Kargen will see you now."

"Good luck," said Lord Valentyn, "and remember what we talked about."

Lord Pavel entered one of the larger rooms in the Palace, warmed by a massive fireplace sitting against the far wall. Before it, stood the Orc chieftain, his back to the door, but upon hearing footsteps, the greenskin turned to gaze towards his visitor.

"Welcome," said Kargen. "No doubt you are wondering why I summoned you?"

"I assumed to discuss the running of Novarsk?"

"It was. Might I ask your thoughts?"

"Why would that even matter? You are the conquerors. Shall you not simply impose your will?"

"That is not our way."

"Then what is?" asked Pavel. "You've had us all on our toes since your arrival. Will you not now tell us what you have in mind?"

"We govern by consensus. Our leaders are chosen by the will of the people to lead them to prosperity and peace."

"Meaning what? You intend to abolish the nobility? That is not the way of the people of Novarsk."

"Then tell me," said the Orc, "what is 'your way'? Perhaps if I had a better understanding, I might see fit to keep things as they are."

Pavel straightened his back. "There are only two types of people: those who lead, and those who follow. You are clearly a leader; therefore, you should understand that followers must do what they're told, or society will break down."

"Break down?"

"Yes, cease to function properly."

"And how does one determine who is a leader rather than a follower?"

"Simple," said Pavel, warming to the topic. "It is a matter of birth. Nobles are, by their very nature, born to lead. You might say it's in their blood."

"And what is the purpose of followers?"

"Why, to serve the needs of the leaders."

"Permit me to make sure I understand what you are saying. You contend that the sole purpose of these people, let us call them commoners, is to satisfy the needs of the nobility?"

"Precisely."

"Without followers, you have no one to lead."

"I…" Pavel's words left him.

"You claim you lead because of your blood," said Kargen. "Yet the blood of nobles is no different from anyone else's, save for Orcs."

"Orcs?"

"Yes," said Kargen. "Our blood is black."

"How is that even possible?"

"You are asking the wrong person. Despite that, and the colour of our skin, I have come to realize Humans and Orcs share more characteristics than you might think."

"Such as?"

"We both value friendship, honesty, and the bonds of family."

"I did not expect this," said Pavel. "I always thought of Orcs as simple-minded savages."

"A belief I am learning is common throughout the Petty Kingdoms."

"Might I ask you a question?"

"Of course," said Kargen. "What would you like to know?"

"Why did the High Thane of Therengia send you to do his bidding?"

"He trusts me to act in the best interests of our people."

"But you must have your own ideas, surely?"

"I am at liberty to make my own decisions regarding the fate of Novarsk, subject only to the Thanes Council's approval."

"So you serve Human masters."

"No," said Kargen. "The Thanes Council consists of both Humans and Orcs. While our current High Thane is Human, he is also a member of my tribe, the Red Hand."

"How can that be? You are a chieftain. Would that not make him subservient to you?"

"You do not understand our ways. We rulers bear a sacred duty to care for the members of our tribe, village, or barony, even, to use your own terms. In that respect, we are servants of our people rather than the other way around."

"That is preposterous. Such a society would be doomed to failure."

"Yet," replied Kargen, "it has served my kind for generations."

"While it's true our traditions are different, surely our two peoples can learn to work together. Restore the monarchy to Novarsk, and we barons will ensure peace remains our greatest desire."

"I would do so if I believed I could trust your nobles. Unfortunately, history has taught us that, as a kingdom, your people are unreliable."

"I must object."

"And you are free to do so," said Kargen, "but the fact remains your queen launched an invasion of Therengia without provocation or warning. As a result of your desire to conquer us, you forced us to turn our efforts to removing your queen from her Throne, thus, bringing us to our current circumstances."

"Might I suggest an alternative solution?"

"By all means," replied Kargen.

"Occupying a kingdom like Novarsk can be an immense financial strain. Perhaps a donation of coins would go a long way to earning your trust?"

"How many coins are you referring to?"

"A thousand golden sovereigns?"

"And you think that sufficient to purchase your way out of your current predicament?"

"Then ten thousand. It's a princely sum, enough to set you up for the rest of your life."

"I already have what I need," said Kargen. "Your coins are useless to me."

"Useless? Surely you have expenses?"

"I am a hunter, Lord Pavel. What need have I for coins?"

"Wealth is the root of all power. With enough of it, you could find yourself a prize wife."

The Orc grinned. "I already have a bondmate. I doubt she would like the idea of being considered a prize to be purchased."

"I possess more gold than you could possibly imagine."

"And I more animal skins, but I doubt it is something you deem valuable. One's wealth is measured by the quality of their friends, not in how many things they accumulate."

"So you refuse the coins?"

"I have made that plain enough," said Kargen. "If there is anything else you wish to offer in the way of advice, I shall be pleased to hear it. Otherwise, I bid you a good day."

"You will regret this."

"Perhaps, but not likely. One must not stray from their true path, or the road becomes muddied."

"Is that some sort of Orc proverb?"

"No, it is the teaching of Saint Mathew."

"You worship the Saints?" said Lord Pavel.

"No, but such beliefs are not unknown in Therengia. There are even Temple Knights to help keep the peace."

"Temple Knights? Haven't they all fled the region?"

"I can assure you such is not the case. They have representation in Therengia, just as they do throughout the Petty Kingdoms."

"Don't all Therengians worship the god of death?"

"That is a commonly held misconception. Worship of the Old Gods is most common, but there is no god of death, nor do they sacrifice victims in any way in the name of religion."

"It appears we should learn more about you, just as you should learn more about us."

"On that, at least, we can agree."

Lord Valentyn turned as the door opened. "Pavel, back so soon? How did it go?"

"Not as I thought it would," replied his comrade.

"Meaning?"

"I had considered the Orc nothing but a brute, but the truth is he's knowledgeable, one might even say eloquent in his speech."

"Did you offer him coins?"

"I did," said Pavel, "but he refused. Said he had no use for gold. I'm afraid you'll need to find another way to bring him around."

"Nonsense. You obviously didn't offer enough."

"I offered ten thousand sovereigns!"

"Ten thousand?"

"Yes. He refused my first offer of a thousand. What else was I to do?"

"This requires a more deft hand."

"You think you can do better?"

"I could hardly do worse," said Valentyn.

"There's more."

"Go on."

"These Therengian leaders say they serve their people."

"Nonsense. Nobility rules—it's our destiny."

"That's what I told him," said Pavel, "but he was having none of it. Next thing I knew, he quoted Saint Mathew at me. I tell you, it quite unsettled me."

"Because he could quote a Saint?"

"Because he knew what they wrote. Don't you see? This is no savage brute, but an educated man, or maybe I should say creature?"

"You let him get to you, my friend," said Valentyn. "I shall not be so easily swayed."

"You say that now, but you haven't met the fellow."

At his words, the door opened, once more revealing the mailed warrior. "Lord Valentyn Sayenko? If you'll come with me, I'll take you to see Chief Kargen."

"Well, it seems I have no choice but to succeed where you failed, Pavel."

"He's not what he seems," said his comrade. "Listen to him. You might learn a thing or two."

"My days of listening to some foreigner who makes demands are done, my friend. It's time we seized the Crown for ourselves and chart our own destiny."

"My lord?" said the guard. "The chieftain awaits."

"Yes, yes, of course. Lead on, my fine fellow, but before you do, answer me a question, will you?"

"If I can."

"Why do you follow this green-skinned savage? Surely you would prefer to live under the rule of a Human?"

"But we do, Lord. Our rightful High Thane is Athgar, son of Rothgar. Chief Kargen is one of his most trusted allies."

"Allies, is it? Why would a man make an ally of an Orc?"

The guard frowned. "You do not understand them or our ways. Yes, the Orcs differ from us in appearance, but they hold many of the same values as Therengians."

"Therengians," spat out Lord Valentyn. "Don't make me laugh. The glory days of that ancient kingdom are long gone and with good reason. They were incapable of managing their own affairs, let alone those of others."

"The Old Kingdom stood for over five hundred years, far longer than any of the Petty Kingdoms."

The Baron of Krasnov waved off the remark. "Lead on, and I shall have words with this so-called chieftain of yours."

Kargen waited much as he had for Lord Pavel. He whirled around as the door opened, his eyes locking on those of his new visitor.

"Chieftain," said Lord Valentyn. "You wished to see me?"

"I did indeed. As you well know, I am talking with each baron of Novarsk, the idea being to enable me to consider the wishes of all when handing down judgement."

"Judgement? Who do you think you are, that you can just storm in here and decide the fate of a kingdom?"

"I might remind you we did not storm in here. We defeated your army and then conquered your realm to prevent such a thing from recurring.

However, in the spirit of friendship, I wish it to be known we harbour no ill will towards your people. Rather, we desire to reach a consensus on how our two lands might best live in peace and harmony."

"There will be no peace until you return our queen."

"That," said Kargen, "is not a topic open for discussion. Rada violated a peace agreement, and her actions have proven her to be untrustworthy."

"You have no right!"

"I have every right. Tell me, were we one of the Petty Kingdoms, would you be arguing so strenuously?"

"Ah, but that's the point, isn't it? You're not a Petty Kingdom. In fact, you're the very opposite."

"Would you care to explain what you mean?"

"Certainly," said Lord Valentyn. "The Petty Kingdoms evolved from the lands that defeated the Old Kingdom of Therengia. You've alienated yourself from civilized folk by announcing your intention to revive that ancient realm."

"Were it not for the Old Kingdom, your way of life would never exist. Many traditions you Humans hold so dear are remnants of our ancestors."

"Now, you're just making things up."

"I can assure you I am not."

"Then tell me," said the baron, "what precisely did we take from the Old Kingdom?"

"The Midwinter Feast, for one thing. It dates back to the early days of Therengia."

"Nonsense. It's a Church celebration in honour of the Saints."

"It is, now," said Kargen, "but before that, they celebrated the winter equinox, where thanks would be given for surviving the harsh weather."

"How would you know that?"

"Our scholars have unearthed much."

"But you live in the wilderness. How in the name of the Saints would you unearth anything other than dirt?"

"We are blessed by the presence of a scholar who brought much knowledge with him from the great city of Corassus. We have also uncovered several historical artifacts in Ebenstadt, including records the Temple Knights of Saint Cunar left behind in their haste to depart."

"You can't win. Eventually, the Petty Kingdoms will gather together and wipe you from the Continent."

"The Continent has more important things to worry about than a fledging realm on the far eastern border of the so-called civilized lands."

They stared at each other, each refusing to turn away. Finally, Lord Valentyn relented. "Very well. I concede Rada cannot reign here. To be honest with you, she was not one of our better rulers, but Novarsk needs one of their own. Someone who can command the respect of the other nobles."

"I assume you are suggesting yourself for such a position?"

"I hadn't considered that possibility," lied the lord, "but now that you suggest it, I suppose the idea has merit."

"Would there not be others with more compelling claims?"

"The Throne of Novarsk belongs to one who can hold it. I possess the largest number of warriors in the land. Give the Throne to me, and I shall ensure we trouble you no more."

"I wish I could believe you," said Kargen, "but your actions today reveal your true nature."

"What's that supposed to mean?"

"You are hungry for power and will stop at nothing to get your way. Were I to make you King of Novarsk, I have no doubt you would seek to ally yourselves with as many of the Petty Kingdoms as possible and invade us once more."

"You're making a big mistake."

"Perhaps," said Kargen, "but it is my mistake to make. You prosper as the Baron of Krasnov, but only at the expense of the people you rule. Or do I assume the famine and poverty I witnessed here in Halmund is limited to the capital?"

"You have no idea who you're dealing with."

"I have met your type before. You accumulate wealth and power at the expense of others, doing anything to succeed, regardless of who gets hurt. My duty here is clear. I must make a decision that benefits all the people of Novarsk, not only the nobility."

"The nobility ARE Novarsk!"

"We do not see things the same way, so I shall not keep you here any longer."

"And the Throne?" demanded Lord Valentyn.

"You will be informed when I render my verdict. In the meantime, I suggest you remain here in Halmund."

"Is that an order?"

"No," said Kargen. "Merely a suggestion. Should you feel the need to return to your ancestral lands, I shall do nothing to stop you. However, it might be in your best interests to remain here in the capital."

"Meaning?"

"News is best delivered in person so questions can be answered. I mean to render a verdict on the fate of your kingdom. Your absence would indicate to the rest of the nobles you lack interest in the outcome."

"You may see it that way, but others will view it as an act of defiance. Your days here are numbered, Orc. Heed my words." Valentyn stormed from the room, slamming the door shut behind him.

Harwath approached Kargen while he stared once more into the fire. Upon hearing his footsteps, the Orc chieftain turned.

"May I speak?" the fellow asked.

"By all means."

"I am grateful you gave me a second chance, even if it's only as a guard."

"You were led astray," said Kargen. "It is only proper I give you an opportunity for redemption."

Harwath stood there silently, deep in thought.

"Is there something else on your mind?" asked the chieftain.

"There is," said Harwath. "That one, Lord Valentyn, he's dangerous. He seeks to drive the Orcs and Therengians apart."

"Of that, I am well aware, yet there is little I can do. I must trust our people will be able to resist his attempts to divide us."

"Our occupation of Novarsk stretches us to the limit, Kargen. What if the baron raises arms against us?"

"I thank you for your candour, my friend, but we must take each day as it is presented to us. However, that does not mean we should sit back and do nothing. Keep your eyes and ears open and report anything you feel is of import."

"I will," said Harwath. "I promise."

THE MISSION

AUTUMN 1108 SR

They found themselves in a sitting room at the Duke's estate, once more summoned by a cryptic message that only indicated they should arrive with all haste. Athgar shuffled his feet as they awaited word that their host was ready to receive them.

"I don't like this," he muttered.

"Come now," replied Natalia. "It can't be that bad. It was a summons, not a warrant for our arrest."

"Perhaps, but why the hurry?"

"He wants the matter of Andover settled sooner rather than later. I suspect he's ready to see us on our way."

"What if asking for a favour was too much?"

"Then he'd just refuse our offer. He certainly wouldn't call us all the way here to say no."

The door opened, revealing a tall, well-attired man of about thirty years.

"Good day," he said, entering the room to look them over. "I assume you are Lord Athgar and Lady Natalia?"

"We are," said Athgar. "And who might you be?"

"Fernando Brondecker. His Grace, the duke, is my father."

"Are you here to bring us to see the duke?"

"Not at all. The truth is, I summoned you, not him."

"Why?" asked Natalia.

"I want to take my measure of you, as well as discuss the upcoming journey you volunteered your services for."

"Where would you like to start?"

"Please, sit. Let's begin with you, shall we? My father says you're a

Stormwind, yet you've distanced yourself from the rest of the family. Would you care to explain?"

"As I told the duke, I trained at the Volstrum, but when I discovered their true intentions, I wanted no part of it."

"Yes, my father indicated as much. It's these intentions that interest me. Can you elucidate?"

"Of course," said Natalia. "The Stormwinds have spread throughout the Petty Kingdoms like a plague, infiltrating the courts of kings and dukes to further their own agenda."

"Which is?"

"Our belief is they want to sow the seeds of disharmony and suspicion."

"To what end?"

"Athgar and I recently discovered the family is the power behind the Halvarian Empire. We believe they are keeping the rest of the Continent weak by inciting war between the various Petty Kingdoms. It also keeps their attention away from events to the west."

"What you say makes sense, from a certain point of view, but couldn't just the reverse be true?"

"The reverse?" said Athgar.

"Yes, couldn't they be working to unite the Petty Kingdoms against the common threat of the empire?"

"Their actions here indicate otherwise, or am I wrong in thinking Larissa Stormwind plotted against your father?"

"No, you are correct," said Fernando, "but how do I know you two aren't working towards the same end? After all, it's not as if we ever met before you came to Korvoran. For all we know, you made up the entire story about fleeing Ruzhina."

"Then why not simply refuse our offer?" asked Natalia. "You're the one in control here, or rather your father is. Nothing's forcing you to hire us."

"I never said I didn't believe you. It's just that some things don't quite add up. For example, you say this 'family' is behind the Halvarian Throne, yet how would they even accomplish such a feat? The empire predates the Stormwinds by centuries, doesn't it?"

"Yes, but I suspect their control over it is much more recent. After all, this isn't the first time they've tried such a tactic."

"You're suggesting they've interfered in other countries before?"

"Most definitely," said Natalia. "We suspect they might've been responsible for the eventual defeat of the Old Kingdom."

"Don't be silly," said Fernando. "The armies of the Successor States broke the back of Therengia."

"While that's true, it bears mentioning their success wouldn't have been possible without the chaos caused by political infighting."

"And you know this for certain?"

"No. We only suspect. The surviving records leading up to the dissolution of the Old Kingdom indicate a significant amount of internal strife. Most of that focused on mages who sought positions of influence in the king's court. Does that sound familiar?"

"Think about it for a moment," added Athgar. "The Old Kingdom was the pre-eminent military power on the Continent. Do you truly believe a bunch of upstart kingdoms could defeat them without help?"

"I'd choose my words carefully, if I were you. Those very same upstarts later became the Petty Kingdoms."

"I meant no offence, but you must admit it's a pretty compelling argument."

"But if that's the case," said Fernando, "why break up the kingdom? Wouldn't they be better served to take over what they coveted?"

"That was their original intention," said Natalia, "but somewhere along the line, something went wrong."

"Like what?"

"I don't know. Perhaps the Therengian people weren't easily fooled, or the family was simply inexperienced in how to proceed. Either option is a possibility. If we put our minds together, I'm sure we could come up with at least another half-dozen reasons why it might have failed."

"So, you're suggesting they used Therengia as a dry run for Halvaria?"

"In a sense, yes. They took what they learned, made changes, then carried out their revised plan in the west. I suspect the empire was an easier target."

"What makes you say that?"

"If what we've heard is true, it has a single leader and a monolithic rule. All they'd need to do is get the ear of the emperor, and then they could do what they wanted."

"Would that work in the Old Kingdom?"

"No," said Athgar. "Therengian rule is built on accountability, or rather, it was."

"Yes," agreed Natalia. "Their system was all about delegating responsibility to the person most qualified to make decisions, the exact opposite of what we suspect the empire uses."

"Very well," said Fernando. "I shall concede the point concerning the demise of Therengia. It does, however, bring up our current circumstances. If what you say is true, then there's likely a Stormwind at the court of Andover pushing for war."

"Or a Sartellian," replied Natalia. "The two families are inextricably linked. They are, in essence, two parts of the same whole."

"That makes your task all the more important. My father wants you to help his man negotiate peace with Andover. On the other hand, I want more, and I'm willing to pay for it."

"What is it you're looking for?" asked Athgar.

"I wish you to uncover who's the power behind the Throne. If it happens to be a member of this family of yours, then so much the better. If you break their hold over King Dagmar of Andover, then I truly believe we can achieve a lasting peace."

"Your father mentioned at least one Sartellian in their court."

"Unfortunately, my father listens to all sorts of idle gossip. I won't deny it's a possibility, particularly after your own revelations, but the likelihood his information is correct is slim. There may even be a third party, perhaps another Petty Kingdom, planting the seeds of distrust between our two kingdoms."

"You don't necessarily believe the family is involved, yet you suspect your other neighbours are? Might I ask what fuels this suspicion?"

"I'm not sure how much you know about the area, but Eidolon and Abelard are our two biggest trade rivals. Strangely enough, they are also the two biggest markets for our goods, but both are eager to be the dominant power in the region. Should Andover and Reinwick go to war, their influence will only grow. So, your visit to Andover might not involve the Stormwinds unless they're the ones pushing the other kingdoms to get involved."

"This just became so much more complicated," muttered Athgar. "I preferred it when the family was all we needed to deal with."

"No one ever said the game of politics was easy," said Fernando. "The fact of the matter is it can get pretty nasty sometimes. To that end, you must watch yourselves while outside of Reinwick. I wouldn't put it past any of our rivals to try an outright assassination attempt."

"We shall be careful," said Natalia.

"Good. Now, where did I put those coins?" He ran his hands along his belt. "Brandis? Where are you, you old rogue?"

The door opened, revealing an elderly servant. "I'm here, Lord."

"Where is that gold?"

"Here, Lord." He produced a small bag of coins, holding it out for his master to take.

"Don't give it to me," said Fernando. "It's these two who'll need it."

"Lord?"

"They are undertaking a mission under my employ. At least I hope they are?" He turned to his guests, and Athgar held out his hand.

"But he's a grey-eye, my lord. Are you sure this is wise?"

"Come now, Brandis. I think I'm a better judge of character than you, wouldn't you say?"

"Yes. Of course, Lord." He handed over the purse.

Athgar felt the weight of it. "This is most generous, Lord Fernando."

"I consider it an investment," replied the duke's son. "There's plenty more where that came from should you prove as good as you talk."

"We shall endeavour to find out who is behind this war," said Natalia, "regardless of whether it's the family or someone else."

"Excellent. In that case, I'll leave Brandis here to show you out. Good day, Lady Natalia, and to you, Lord Athgar. Let us hope when we meet again, you return in triumph."

Later, as they walked back to their home away from home, Athgar felt full of doubt. "What if he's right, and the family isn't involved?"

"They must be," Natalia replied. "One way or the other, they're not going to sit back and accept their expulsion from Reinwick. They'll want revenge for the slight."

"But it's been a decade. Surely they would have acted by now?"

"Not so. This type of planning takes years and likely involves coordinating actions across multiple realms."

"Do you believe there is some truth to his speculations that Eidolon and Abelard might be involved?"

"I think it's highly likely, don't you? Given what we know about how they operate, it wouldn't surprise me if even more players were involved in the grand scheme of things."

"So, what do we do now?"

"Simple," said Natalia. "We continue on as we were. Nothing we learned today changes what we need to do. In fact, it makes our success even more imperative. The family must be stopped—plain and simple."

"Easier said than done. If the family truly has that much power in Andover, couldn't they arrest us as soon as we arrive?"

"No. They'd consider us foreign emissaries. Arresting us would end any chance of them returning to influence here in Korvoran."

"I hadn't thought of that, but then again, it wouldn't be the first time someone targeted us on the streets of a city."

"That's why it's important we get introduced at court. After that, any action would come as an insult to King Dagmar, which is the last thing the family wants to do."

"And yet, it would work towards our aims. Not that I'm suggesting we attempt it."

"You won't be there anyway," said Natalia.

"I won't?"

"No. You and Belgast need to find those Orcs, remember?"

"And how do you propose I do that without raising suspicion?"

"We'll figure out something. Perhaps Belgast can decide to visit a distant relative. Saints know he has enough of them."

"Yes, and I could go to keep him company. That's an excellent idea, although I don't much fancy the thought of you going on alone."

"I won't be alone. Stanislav will be there to watch my back, not to mention Katrin and Galina."

"And the duke's men," said Athgar. "Don't forget, he's sending an escort."

She slowed before coming to rest at the door to a bakery.

"Smells delicious," said Athgar. "Did you want to go inside?"

"No. What I'd really like is to know why three men are following us?"

He resisted the temptation to look. "Are you sure?"

"Yes. I recognize at least one of them from the time they followed Katrin and me to the docks."

"Are you up to a confrontation?"

"No," she replied. "Though my physical strength has returned, my magic is still relatively weak. Added to that is the fact that we've just earned the duke's trust. I don't want to jeopardize that by creating a scene."

"I've plenty of magic to spare. I doubt three men would prove a problem."

"And what would you do, kill them? People already look down on you because of your heritage. It wouldn't take much to turn them against you entirely."

"I'm not sure what you're suggesting. A mob?"

"I fear it's a distinct possibility. I'm unsure what they'd make of a Therengian wielding Fire Magic."

Athgar risked a look over his shoulder. "Then we must lose them."

"I'm open to suggestions in that regard."

"Remember Draybourne?"

"I could hardly forget, but the last thing I want to do is injure you, and besides, my magic is weak, remember?"

"I'm not suggesting you use it, merely that we draw them into an alley."

"Why?"

"I'll throw up a wall of fire to prevent them from following."

"They'll just return to the street, surely?"

"Most likely," said Athgar, "but by then, we'll have made our escape."

"You need to be careful you don't set fire to any buildings."

"I thought of that already. I can cast so there's a slight gap on either side, and just to be safe, we'll seek an alleyway between stone buildings."

"What if we find some Temple Knights instead?" suggested Natalia. "That worked well last time."

"That's certainly another option, but I'd really like a better look at them. You say you recognized one from your earlier encounter?"

"Yes, a middle-aged fellow with a scruffy brown beard. I only saw him from a distance, but his manner was unmistakable."

"Manner?"

"He walked with a slight limp and wore baggy clothes, although I suspect that was to conceal a weapon."

They continued down the street, mingling with the townsfolk. Athgar cast his eyes back and forth, noticing all the wooden buildings in this part of the city. "Are there no quarries in Reinwick?"

"Stone requires a greater skill," replied Natalia. "That likely means it's limited to those with plenty of coins to spare."

"That hardly helps us."

"Wait. I have another idea. We're not that far from the Agnesite Commandery. I doubt they would follow us in there."

"No, but there's a good chance they'll simply wait outside and watch the place."

"Even better. It will let us get eyes on them."

"How?"

"Simple," she replied. "There are windows on the second floor."

"Windows?"

"Yes, we can observe them from there."

"Assuming they let us inside. I might remind you I'm not a woman. I don't think I'd be allowed in a building dedicated to protecting them."

"Let me worry about that."

"I suppose it's worth a try, but if they deny us entry, we'll do it my way, agreed?"

"Very well, although I don't think it'll come to that."

They reached a crossroads and turned right, heading eastward. The sounds of seagulls neared as Athgar recognized the stench of the sea.

"I miss the forest," he said.

"You'll see another soon enough."

"What makes you say that?"

"We're going to Andover, remember? And you and I both know how much Orcs love the woods. What was the name of that tribe?"

"The Ashwalkers."

She smiled. "I would say that's a good omen, wouldn't you? It likely means they have masters of fire. You ought to fit right in."

"I'll just be happy to get word back to Kargen and Shaluhk. I hope Oswyn hasn't been too much of a bother."

"And I'm sure she's grown since we last saw her." Natalia wiped her eyes.

Athgar took her hand. "We'll see her again. I promise."

As they rounded a corner, the commandery came into view. Natalia sped up, heading directly for the two Temple Knights standing watch at the main gate.

"Have you returned to see the captain?" asked the taller one.

"We have, though I'm afraid we have no appointment." She lowered her voice. "A trio of men are once again pursuing us, although we know not their intentions."

The knight turned to her companion. "Take them inside, then send word to Captain Leona. She'll want to hear about it."

The door led down a large alley into the centre courtyard where sister knights practiced. The two mages' unexpected arrival interrupted their routine, causing all to stare.

"Lady Natalia," called Sister Felicity. "I'm surprised to see you here."

"Good day, Sister. I hope we're not interrupting?"

"Not at all. Is there a problem?"

"There is. A trio of men are following us."

"The same group from the docks?"

"One of them is, but I'm not sure about the others."

"We thought," said Athgar, "that we might get a view of them from an upper window? It would be useful to have a better look at them."

The knight turned to one of her charges. "Carry on with the training, Sister Ava." She returned her attention to the visitors. "Let's go and have a look, shall we?"

"Should we not clear it with your captain?" replied Natalia.

"You'd have a hard time; she's not here."

"Shall I wait here?" asked Athgar.

"Why would you do something like that?"

"I thought you only allowed women in the commandery?"

"You're under escort. I'm sure the captain won't mind."

"Are you always so lax with the rules?"

"Actually," explained Felicity, "that's a misconception. There's no such decree; even if they were, you're accompanying me. Shall we proceed?"

"By all means, but perhaps you should go first. After all, I don't know the way."

They soon looked down on the trio, who seemed oblivious to their observation.

"Shall I send out some sisters to chat with them?" asked Felicity.

"No," said Natalia. "The family might have sent them, and at this point, I'd prefer to avoid entanglements."

"Do you perceive them as a threat?"

"I'm beginning to get the impression they're more interested in knowing what we're up to. Saints know, they've had more than one opportunity to attack us, if that's what they truly wanted."

"I must confess, I've not seen them before," said Felicity.

"And why would you have? You couldn't possibly know everyone in Korvoran."

"True, but we've watched Lady Yelena's estate since your arrival there."

"You're keeping an eye on us?" said Athgar. "Don't you trust us?"

"It's not you we don't trust; it's whoever's looking for you. We've been on guard ever since Larissa Stormwind was driven from Reinwick."

"But you don't recognize those men?"

"No, and that's what bothers me. We've identified several people sympathetic to the Stormwind cause, but none of them match those fellows down there. It appears you enticed a new group out into the open."

THE DUKE'S MAN

AUTUMN 1108 SR

B elgast entered the room. "It appears we have company."
"Anyone we know?" asked Athgar.

"Yes, Captain Marwen. You remember him? The one who escorted you two to the duke's estate?"

"Oh, him. You'd think the duke would at least send a baron."

"Come now," said Natalia. "I know all this waiting is getting to everybody, but can we at least attempt to be civil?"

"Sorry," Athgar replied. "I'd like to get going. I'm tired of sitting around here all day long." He shifted his gaze to the Dwarf. "So, where is the good captain?"

"Stanislav is chatting with him," said Belgast, "but he should be along presently. Ah, here he is now." He waited for a moment, but nothing happened. "Well, that's embarrassing. It appears my statement was ill-timed." He quickly stepped aside as voices approached.

"They're all in here," said Stanislav. Moments later, Captain Marwen finally made his appearance.

"Greetings, all. I come on behalf of His Grace, the duke."

"To what end?" asked Belgast.

"The duke chose me to travel to the court of King Dagmar as an emissary. I understand you will all be accompanying me?"

"Not quite all," said Natalia. "Athgar and Belgast will only travel with us part of the way."

"Are you sure that's wise, my lady? Andover is a dangerous land for men of your husband's nature."

"I'm aware of their attitude towards Therengians," said Athgar.

"As am I," added Belgast, "but there is a business matter to attend to that shall require Athgar's presence. We won't use the main roads, so we should be fine."

"It's your choice," said the captain, "but if I were in your shoes, I would remain here in Reinwick. The rest of you, I'm sure, will prove most useful at court."

"I assume," said Natalia, "that Lord Fernando has talked with you?"

"He has indeed, my lady. My understanding is while I negotiate with the king's representative, you and your associates will deal with any outside influences."

"Outside influences," said Athgar. "What a pleasant way of describing a family of conniving—"

"Let's not bore our new friend with family matters at this time," said Natalia. "I'm sure he has a lot on his mind at present. Might I ask, Captain, how many men we'll be taking?"

"There are a dozen armed men to keep us safe on the road. I took the liberty of organizing three carriages, which will result in less crowding as we travel and more flexibility once we arrive in Zienholtz."

"Is that their capital?" asked Galina.

"Indeed, it is, ma'am. It's said to be a place of great beauty, not unlike yourself, if I may be permitted to observe."

Galina blushed. "It seems there is a gifted courtier amongst us. Tell me, Captain, are all military men in Reinwick so blessed?"

"I cannot speak for them all, madam, nor can I claim such for myself under normal circumstances, but on occasion, I find myself overwhelmed by the moment. I hope you have not taken offence?"

"Not at all, though I must confess it's not something I've encountered before."

"I find that hard to believe. Surely men are throwing themselves at you?"

Belgast cleared his throat. "I hate to interrupt this thing you two have going on, but there are important matters to discuss."

"Yes, of course," said Captain Marwen. "What, in particular, would you like to know?"

"Well, for one thing, when can we expect to depart?"

"Early tomorrow morning, if you're ready. We can delay that a day or two if you've other things to look after?"

"No," said Natalia. "Tomorrow will be fine."

"How long a trip is it?" asked Katrin.

"It's around seventy miles, give or take a few. With any luck, we shall be there in three days."

"I should think we could do better than that," said Belgast. "A Dwarf could easily make that in two, and afoot, no less."

"While we could make faster time, I prefer not to exhaust the horses. In addition, we must consider the ladies' frail constitution."

"Frail? You honestly believe they'll fall apart?"

"The roads are rough," explained Captain Marwen, "and those riding in the carriages will shake around quite a bit. Of course, we could ride horses instead, but that precludes us from carrying much in the way of luggage."

"Luggage? What's all this nonsense?"

The captain sighed. "We are going to court, Sir Dwarf, which means we must dress in our finest garb."

"But our party has only the shirts on our backs... or dresses, for the women-folk."

"In that case, we shall delay our departure for a few days. I shall have a dressmaker visit you with strict instructions as to our time frame."

"My pardon," said Natalia, "but are you suggesting a seamstress could fashion clothes for all of us in only two days?"

"A single seamstress, no, but she will not be acting alone. I will harness the power of the duke's court to speed things up. Your current attire will suit the trip, but we must look our best upon arrival."

"And how many outfits do we require?"

"I should think at least a dozen. Now, before you get upset, let me clear something up. The seamstress will make each of you two outfits; the rest we'll arrange once we're in Zienholtz. As for you two"—he looked at Athgar and then Belgast—"I can only assume you're already equipped for your own journey."

"Quite," said Athgar.

"Good. Then I'm afraid I must leave you, for there is much to arrange."

"And the seamstress?" asked Galina.

"She shall, I'm sure, present herself to you this very morning. In the meantime, I suggest you consider what you would like in terms of courtly attire."

"Which is?" asked Katrin.

"Don't worry," said Natalia. "Galina and I learned all about courtly fashion back at the Volstrum."

The days flew by, and then the carriages arrived, along with their escort. Captain Marwen rode in the front carriage, leaving Athgar and Natalia to take the second. The rest were to ride in the third despite the Dwarf's grumblings. He'd have preferred to walk, but the ladies wore shoes—not precisely the type of footwear best suited to such things.

In the end, Belgast refused to bow to pressure and climbed up inside the wagon with Athgar and Natalia. His actions caught the attention of Captain Marwen.

"Are you lost, Sir Dwarf?"

Belgast's stubbornness grew. "Not at all, Captain. Why?"

"You are in the wrong carriage."

He peered out the window, making a show of looking down at the carriage's exterior. "Why? Is there a difference between them?"

"You know full well I assigned you to the third carriage. Why do you insist on not taking your rightful place?"

"Why does it matter?"

"Lady Natalia and Lord Athgar are riding in this one, making it unsuitable for one of your social standing."

"Are you saying I'm not good enough to be here?"

"I think," said Natalia, "that he prefers to ride with us."

"Yes," added Athgar, "and it's only fitting, all things considered. He is a Dwarven lord after all."

Captain Marwen's mouth hung open for a moment before he collected his wits. "What nonsense is this?"

"It's true. I swear. He served King Haglarith."

"Who is?" demanded the captain.

"The King of Kragen-Tor. By our standards, he'd rank as a baron, at least, if not higher."

Marwen eyed the Dwarf suspiciously. "I'll have to take your word on that. Very well, you may remain with Lady Natalia and Lord Athgar."

"I knew you'd see reason," said Belgast.

The captain closed the door before making his way to the front of the entourage, where he gave the command to move. Moments later, the escort began advancing, their horses' hooves echoing on the cobblestones. The carriage rolled forward and then settled into a steady pace.

"I don't like that fellow," said Belgast. "He's too full of himself."

"He's only doing his job," explained Natalia. "Court etiquette is important in this part of the Continent, and he's a man who wants to improve his standing."

"He's a captain," said Athgar. "How much higher can he go? They only have one rank above that, don't they?"

"Yes, that of commander. I doubt it's a military rank he seeks, though. More likely, it's a title."

"Reinwick's a small country, isn't it? What title can he possibly hope to receive?"

"I imagine the duke promised him a knighthood should this mission prove successful."

"And does that grant land?"

Natalia smiled. "I see you've learned something from our scholars. Yes, some knights receive land. In fact, we even call them landed knights, but the title is not hereditary."

"But the lands are?"

"I would assume so, but there are a lot of Petty Kingdoms, and I can't keep track of all of their customs in that regard."

"Then how does the family do so?"

"I would assume they keep records of such things. Before a Volstrum graduate travels to their first assignment, they must learn all about their destination and the customs of all the neighbouring realms."

"So," said Athgar, "what you're saying is any family member in Andover is going to know all about the region?"

"Exactly."

"And how will you counter that?"

"I've a few tricks up my sleeve."

"How?" said Belgast. "Your sleeves are cut tight?" He chuckled at his jest.

"The family," explained Natalia, "is very tight-lipped when it comes to its own inner troubles. They will only inform the most powerful of our escape, so there's a good chance whoever they've placed in Zienholtz has never heard of us."

"Could you use that to your advantage?" asked Athgar.

"Possibly. The Stormwind name alone would likely carry a great amount of influence, but first, I need to ensure there are no other Stormwinds, before revealing my connections."

"And the others?"

"Galina stands a good chance of being recognized, especially if any recent graduates are at court. She was one of the Volstrum's instructors, not the kind of person you can easily forget."

"What about Katrin?"

"She'll be fine," said Natalia. "They struck her name from all records. The chance of anyone recognizing her is slim. They'll likely just assume she is one of Galina's staff."

"The Stormwinds employ assistants?"

"Of course. How else could they devote so much of their time to winning influence?"

"And how many might we expect to run across?"

"That depends on how important the family member is. At the very least, I think half a dozen, maybe double that if they're more powerful. The Sartellians follow the same principles."

"And we tell their power levels from their rings, correct?"

"Yes," said Natalia. "The magerite embedded in their jewellery grows darker as the mage's power increases, though it's not always in the form of a ring."

"Then you must avoid showing yours until you're ready to announce yourself."

"Yes." She stared at her ring. "It's strange to think this very ring led us to Karslev in the first place. Perhaps we'd be better off if we hadn't discovered the secret it kept hidden for all those years?"

"Nonsense. We couldn't let them try to abduct Oswyn and get away with it."

Her eyes lifted, although she was close to tears. "Do you think you'll be able to get word back to Shaluhk?"

"If there are Orcs out there, we'll find them."

"Aye," agreed Belgast, "and how hard can it be? Trust me, between your husband's hunting skill and my flair for diplomacy, we've got it all in the forge."

They stared at him in confusion.

"Sorry," said the Dwarf. "Did you not understand me?"

"I assume you meant all in the bag?" said Athgar.

"Why would I put everything into a bag?"

"You tell me. It makes more sense than putting things into a forge."

The Dwarf chuckled. "You Humans have such strange sayings."

They crossed into Andover late in the day, passing through hills that formed the border between the two realms. No signposts alerted them of the fact, but as they rolled into the courtyard of a roadside inn, a stable hand rushed forward to greet them.

"Welcome to Andover," he said. "You must be tired after traversing the hills."

"Aye," said Belgast, "and then some. I'll never understand why they don't put more padding on those carriage seats." He hopped down, rubbing his backside as he stretched.

The sight of the Dwarf left the stable hand speechless. All he did was stand there, staring.

"What's the matter? Never seen one of the mountain folk before?"

"My pardon, sir, but no, I haven't. Of course, I've heard of Dwarves, but I never knew of any in these parts."

"Well, get your fill, my young lad. It's likely to be some time before another Dwarf passes through this region."

"Young lad? I'm twenty-three."

Belgast shrugged. "What do I know? You Humans all look alike to me."

Athgar stepped from the carriage, then held his hand up to guide Natalia down the steps. Surprised only a moment ago by the Dwarf, the stable hand was doubly so at the appearance of a Therengian.

"Is there a problem?" said Belgast.

"No, sir. I mean, Mr. Dwarf, sir. Not at all."

"Good. Then be about your business."

Captain Marwen, meanwhile, exited his carriage and came towards them. "How is everyone doing?"

"Fine," replied Natalia. "The ride was much smoother than I expected."

"Yes, the roads have been well-kept of late, though I'm not sure if that's good news or bad."

"Why would you say that?" asked Athgar.

"A well-maintained road makes it easier to march an army, while an ill-equipped one… well, you see my point."

"So, you believe they made the road better to facilitate an invasion?"

"We cannot dismiss the possibility. Of course, it works both ways, for good roads also make it easier for the army of Reinwick to march."

"Let's hope we can avoid any marching at all," said Natalia. "Remember, our task here in Andover is to prevent war, not to encourage it."

Captain Marwen bowed. "You are right, of course, my lady. I shall endeavour to bear your words in mind, going forward." He cast his gaze around the courtyard. "If you'll show yourselves inside, I'll check on the others."

Athgar watched as he wandered back to the third carriage. "What do you make of him?"

"He's harmless," said Belgast.

"Not quite," piped in Natalia. "He may be a smooth talker, but don't let that fool you. In the long run, I fear the good captain might be more interested in making a name for himself than carrying out the duke's wishes."

"But isn't it in his best interest to do precisely that?"

"The politics of court make for strange bedfellows. One can never quite be certain on which side of the bed a person sleeps."

"Well," said Athgar, "I know which side I sleep on."

"As do I, and that's what makes us strong, but let us not make the same assumption of our host. It could be our undoing."

"Surely you don't believe he'll work against us?"

"He'll do whatever he needs to get the credit he feels he deserves."

"And how do you counter someone like that?"

"By convincing him we do not need such rewards. Do that, and we'll keep him happy."

"You know what they say," added Belgast. "Keep the client happy, and you'll reap more coins."

"Says who?" asked Athgar.

"The smiths guild, that's who."

"Say, was that some sort of secret handshake I saw you give Master Barbek?"

"It was," said the Dwarf. "What of it? It got us information on the Orcs, didn't it?"

"Admittedly, yes, but I must wonder at what point it becomes a problem for us."

"Problem? In what way?"

"Should the guild's needs take a different course from our desires, where would you stand?"

"Are you suggesting my loyalty is in question?"

"Not at the moment," said Athgar, "but there are many things in motion, and it's difficult to track all of them."

"What things?"

"Well, we never discovered who was following us. If the family is on our trail, it could jeopardize our entire mission. We're also operating in a foreign court, while at the same time, concealing our true identities."

"But we're going to look for Orcs," said Belgast, "not to court."

"Yes, but Natalia and the others are, and what if they get to court, and someone recognizes them?"

Natalia placed a hand on her husband's shoulder. "Calm yourself," she soothed. "Getting all worked up will only serve our enemies. We've known Belgast for years, and he's not the sort of fellow who betrays his friends."

Athgar stared at the ground. "You're right, of course. I just don't like us separating, that's all. Sorry for doubting you, Belgast."

"I can't say I disagree with your logic," admitted the Dwarf, "but I thank you all the same for your sincerity. I cannot conceive of a situation where the guild's needs would conflict with your own objectives, but I will give you a promise: should I find myself in such a quandary, I'll immediately bring it to your attention."

"Thank you. That's all I can ask."

"Shall we go inside?" asked Natalia. "I don't know about you, but I could use some food."

"Food?" called out the Dwarf. "Why didn't you say so?" He pushed past them, disappearing into the inn.

UNREST

AUTUMN 1108 SR

K argen stood, looking through the Palace windows to where all was quiet in the streets, yet he felt uneasy. Soft footfalls approached, and then Shaluhk wrapped her arms around him from behind.

"What troubles you, bondmate mine?" she asked in their native tongue.

"I sense trouble brewing."

"What kind of trouble?"

He shrugged. *"I wish I knew. I am not normally one to fret over decisions, yet I feel it might have been a mistake to come here."*

"In what way?"

"I put you and Agar at risk."

Shaluhk chuckled. *"Agar and Oswyn are always getting into mischief. What matters if it is here or in Runewald?"*

"I am serious. Danger is coming. It is as if the very air is thick with it." He turned to face her. *"Tell me, am I now so fearful of making a decision, I see threats where there are none?"*

"Never have I doubted your choices in all the time I have known you. You came to Halmund because you knew only here could we settle the matter of Novarsk once and for all. As for your concern, it is well justified."

"Then please enlighten me."

"Your meeting with Lord Valentyn was not all you hoped for. Thus, it is only natural you suspect he will move against us, likely with help from fellow conspirators."

"You have given words to my fear," said Kargen. *"How do we deal with this?"*

"The Thane Guard is still some days away, but Harwath commands the local

garrison. Alert his warriors and double the guard. That, at least, will give us warning."

"*And when they come for us?*"

"*We put down the uprising,*" said Shaluhk, "*as quickly as possible. The barons do not speak on the people's behalf.*"

"*How do you know?*"

"*You saw them with your own eyes. Can you honestly believe those starving people would rise up against us?*"

"*Desperate people are prone to desperate acts.*"

"*Send word to Harwath to be vigilant, then come to bed. The night grows chilly, and I would have you warm me.*"

Kargen jerked awake. He strained, trying to ascertain what had disturbed his slumber. Hearing shouts in the distance, he stood abruptly, his movement waking Shaluhk.

"*What is it?*" she asked.

"*Fighting,*" he replied. "*Someone is assaulting the Palace.*" He buckled on his belt, tucking in his trusty axe before grabbing his bow and quiver. Meanwhile, Shaluhk wrapped herself in furs and then grabbed her long knife.

"*Mother?*" She turned to see Agar peering in the doorway.

"*What is happening?*" the youngling asked.

"*It would appear the people of Novarsk are assaulting the Palace. Grab your axe and protect Oswyn and Skora.*"

He nodded before disappearing back into the hallway. Kargen moved to the window, throwing open the shutters to reveal the glint of steel and dozens of torches below. Whoever it was that had breached the outer courtyard now flooded towards the front door, flinging curses at the men of Therengia, who formed a thin line to hold back the enemy.

"*Come,*" said Shaluhk. "*We must act quickly if we are to put these men in their place.*" She rushed from the room, Kargen following, his great strides soon catching up to her.

The main entrance to the Palace consisted of a large, two-storey room with a balcony overlooking the marbled floors. They rushed up there. Kargen strung his bow as his Therengian warriors backed into the room below, the surging mob pushing against them.

Even as he nocked an arrow, Shaluhk cast. Ghostly images materialized beneath the balcony, Orc warriors of old pulled from the spirit realm to do her bidding. They moved forward, extending the Therengian's line on either side. Any other warriors would've broken at the sight, but those of Runewald had practiced this very tactic, assisted by the tribe's shamans.

The mob rushed in, slowing as they noticed the ghostly warriors. Shaluhk waited until they almost filled the room before giving the command to attack. The warriors of the past surged forward, their Therengian counterparts joining them. Not expecting a disciplined response, the mob fell back, then panicked as the two sides made contact.

The fight was bloody but effective. Kargen saw few signs of injury amongst his own troops, but the counterattack against the invaders devastated them. Dozens went down under spears and axes before they broke, fleeing in all directions to avoid death at the hands of their conquerors.

Kargen and Shaluhk watched their own warriors maintain their formation, advancing into the courtyard with little opposition. "*Come,*" he said. "*Let us go down and see the results of this attack.*"

Harwath met them at the bottom of the stairs. "Five wounded, my lord, with no losses," he said in the language of Humans. "I fear the enemy did not fare as well."

"Your estimate of their dead and wounded?"

"At a quick guess, I'd say at least a dozen dead, maybe three times that wounded, though their comrades carried them away. Shall we pursue them into the city?"

"No. Let us count ourselves lucky we came through this relatively unscathed. Good work, Captain. I shall be sure to mention your success to the High Thane upon his return."

They entered the courtyard, and Shaluhk knelt by a body. "This man is no commoner; see his armour?"

Kargen stared down. "He wears mail, a great expense for someone with a modest income."

"Yes, and look at this man. He is a warrior, not a shopkeeper. Likely this was at the urging of one or more of the barons."

"Agreed, yet they wear no colours or coat of arms to identify the lords they serve. Which ones do we blame for this attack?"

"It is a difficult situation in which we find ourselves. Come morning, you, Harwath, and a dozen warriors should go out amongst the townsfolk."

"To what end?"

"To discover all you can about this night's events. I do not believe the common folk support such an attack, for to do so would, in their minds, result in reprisals. Also, I suspect there is no love lost for their nobles. We saw first-hand how their leaders treat them. Now let us discover if they are willing to name those responsible for oppressing them."

"And if they do not?"

"Then we are no worse off than we are right now."

"You are wise beyond your years," said Kargen.

"Of course! I am a shaman with the knowledge of our Ancestors to guide me."

The previous night's violence had left many fearing for their lives, and the streets of Halmund were now quiet. Kargen made his way through the city on foot, Harwath and his men trailing him at a respectful distance.

Most of the townsfolk fled the area upon their approach, but one man, a baker, rolled his cart towards them, the smell of fresh bread filling the air.

Kargen halted, not used to such displays. "What have you there?" he asked the man in the Human tongue.

"Bread, fresh from the ovens."

"I shall take two." The Orc passed over some coins.

"You gave me too much, sir. I'm afraid I cannot make change."

"Then keep it, and tell me what you know of last night's events. I promise you there will be no repercussions."

"You mean the riot?" said the baker. "We all heard about it."

"But you did not participate?"

"You wouldn't catch me within three blocks of a fight like that. No, sir, that was a job for soldiers, and we all know which ones, don't we?" He spat on the ground.

Kargen, unused to such an action, stared back. "I presume you are ill-disposed towards the nobility of Novarsk?"

"Ill-disposed? I suppose that's one way of putting it. Outright hate would be a better description, but I'll deny I said anything of the sort if they ask."

"Tell me, why is it you hate them?"

"Wouldn't you? They tax us to no end, particularly us merchants. Then war comes along, and they expect us to take up arms for a mere pittance. And where does that leave the common man, I ask you? I'll tell you where— dead on the battlefield, that's where. It wouldn't be so bad if they properly equipped us, but no, they save their coins for other, more important things, like living a life of debauchery. The cursed nobility are the worst thing to happen to poor folk like me. A plague on them; that's what I say."

"And how do you see us Therengians?"

The man sneered. "I won't talk ill of you, not with a dozen warriors nearby, but I've yet to see anything from you lot that sets you apart from our own leaders."

"I can assure you nothing could be further from the truth."

"I wish I could believe that, but if there's one thing I've learned in life, it's to judge a man by his actions, not his words. I suppose the same could be said of Orcs."

"Do you fear me?"

"Fear? No, but I worry for what you represent."

"You intrigue me," said Kargen. "Please, explain what you mean."

"I have a family," the fellow continued, "and while I'm still free to go about my business, I wonder what my son's future will look like under foreign rule."

"Could it be any worse than it is now?"

"I could be dead! We've heard of other conquerors who killed any who opposed them."

"I assure you," said Kargen, "that is not our intention here in Novarsk. Think of us as liberators rather than conquerors."

"And you think that makes you different from everyone else?"

"We did not desire to invade your land—that was a direct consequence of your queen attacking us. We are generally a peaceful race; all we wish is to let our people live in peace and harmony."

"And yet here you are."

"We can accomplish little until we locate the perpetrators of this rebellion," said Kargen.

"Little is not the same thing as nothing."

The Orc chieftain stared back. "You are correct. As you say, deeds are worth more than mere words. I shall endeavour to show the good people of Halmund they can prosper under our rule."

"So that's it, then? We are to be forever part of your empire?"

"Our rule here is only meant to be temporary."

"And yet," said the baker, "you want us to return to our old way of life, where we are taxed beyond all reasonable measures and treated like cattle."

"Answer me this. What do you want from life?"

"The ability to support my family by making an honest day's living."

"That is something your people and mine have in common. You have given me much to think about. I thank you for it."

Kargen waved his guards forward and continued on. His interaction with the baker garnered considerable attention from the locals, so much so that more entered the street. Before he knew it, a press of people encircled him, offering their opinions on what ailed the kingdom.

By the time Kargen returned to the Palace, it was late in the evening. He slipped into his room as quietly as possible, but the precaution proved unnecessary, for Shaluhk was still awake.

"*Was your mission a success?*" she asked, using their native tongue as she always did when it was only the two of them.

"*It was,*" he replied, sitting down beside her.

She handed him a bowl of porridge. "*It has grown cold, but it will still fill your belly.*"

He grabbed a spoon and dug in, enjoying the taste despite its tepid nature.

Shaluhk let him finish his meal before continuing the conversation. "*What did you learn today?*"

"*That the people of Novarsk harbour no love for their queen or their barons.*"

"*According to Nat-Alia, such indifference towards their rulers is common.*"

"*It is more than that,*" said Kargen. "*There is a large divide between ruler and ruled, much larger than there should be. These people have been mistreated and harbour great resentment towards those responsible.*"

"*Yet they have not resisted such treatment.*"

"*Can you blame them? The barons of Novarsk have many warriors at their disposal. The common folk would never stand a chance against such might.*"

"*Surely they are not all bad?*"

"*I only spoke to people here in the capital, but I fear the mistreatment at the hands of their nobles is widespread.*"

"*You also spoke to the barons,*" said Shaluhk. "*What was your impression of them?*"

"*They are nervous, as you would expect of someone defeated in war, but there is more; there is also fear.*"

"*They are not afraid of us. The uprising demonstrates that.*"

"*It is not us they fear,*" said Kargen. "*It is their country's future and whether or not they will be part of it.*"

"*Fear I can well understand, but surely they must realize the futility of attacking us here, in the Palace?*"

"*That attack was meant to scare us, nothing more. They would have sent more men if they truly wanted to seize the building.*"

"*Then they miscalculated,*" said Shaluhk, "*for there is little an Orc fears.*"

"*Still, it leaves me with a difficult choice. To do nothing in response to this uprising would be to encourage disobedience in the future. I must act with a firm hand, but against whom?*"

"*The barons, obviously.*"

"*But which ones? There is no evidence to suggest who was behind this attack.*"

"*I do not envy you your task,*" said Shaluhk. "*Has Harwath heard anything useful?*"

"*Not as yet, but at least he has some good news.*"

"*Which is?*"

"*The merchants of Halmund are more than willing to accept Therengian coins for their goods. Perhaps, in time, they will come to confide in us and reveal something that may be useful."*

Shaluhk smiled. *"There is more good news."*

"Oh? Care to enlighten me?"

"While you were with the commoners, our hunters collected the dead. We stored their arms and armour within the very walls of this building."

"How does that help us?" asked Kargen. *"We have plenty of weapons for our warriors."*

"True, but I have spent some time with our Dwarven smiths and learned something quite valuable."

"Which is?"

"Weapon smiths invariably leave a mark when making their goods. It serves as a way to acknowledge their skill and receive recognition."

"And?"

"The weapons below, that our attackers used," said Shaluhk, *"bear marks of that nature."*

"So we can identify who equipped them?"

"In time. We discovered the maker's marks but not to whom they belong. To find that, we must visit those employed by the barons."

"Then it appears our next step is laid out before us. We have some travelling to do."

"Not so fast, bondmate mine. If we begin this undertaking, our enemy might hear of it."

"What of it?" said Kargen. *"It is not as if they could make these people disappear."*

"True, but they could deny the marks were theirs, which would end our search. There are other, less intrusive ways of getting the information we need."

Kargen grinned. *"I should have known you would not bring up the matter without having a solution. Very well, tell me your idea."*

"We send people to each of the barons' lands to purchase a weapon. In that way, we can obtain samples of the various smiths' marks."

"A brilliant plan, but it has one tiny problem. No smith of Novarsk would forge a blade for a Human of Therengian descent or an Orc."

"Then we find others to send in our place. Surely there must be someone in Halmund willing to take on the burden for the right amount."

"Also an excellent idea," said Kargen. *"I shall have Harwath begin making enquiries at once. With any luck, someone will be ready to travel before the ten-day is done."*

"Yes," said Shaluhk, *"and you can finally put this entire matter to rest."*

"Not quite. This is but the first step. Once we identify those who rose against us, we must take action."

"*At the very least, you should arrest those who planned it.*"

"*That might prove difficult,*" said Kargen. "*I doubt they would go willingly into captivity. Quite the reverse, in fact. They would likely head back to their keeps to wait things out, necessitating an army to bring them to justice. That alone is not an insurmountable feat, but the more barons involved, the more complicated it grows. We can hardly arrest them all.*"

"*Agreed,*" said Shaluhk, "*but we must deal with each problem as it confronts us. Yes, they may all be against us, but more likely, only a few were involved.*"

"*What makes you so sure?*"

"*The attack was of insufficient numbers to achieve its objective, yet, if each baron sent only two dozen men, they could have overwhelmed us.*"

"*We would still outnumber them,*" said Kargen.

"*True, but our strength is spread throughout the city, while they could concentrate theirs.*"

"*That will no longer be a problem once the Thane Guard arrives. In the meantime, Laruhk will bring the tuskers into the city. Perhaps the sight of them will serve to keep our enemies at bay.*"

ON THE ROAD

AUTUMN 1108 SR

The diplomatic entourage continued their journey to Zienholtz the next day, the terrain growing rougher when they entered the hills. As the sun reached its zenith, they halted where a trail crossed the main road.

Captain Marwen soon opened the door to the second carriage. "This is it, Lord Athgar, the road westward. My men will get your things down."

"I have all I need, thank you." The Therengian looked at the Dwarf. "Ready?"

"As ready as I'll ever be." Belgast exited the carriage, then made a big display of stretching his legs. "Finally. My feet back on solid ground!"

Athgar was about to follow, but Natalia grabbed his hand. "Please be careful. It's dangerous out there."

"I'm well aware. Trust me. I have no intention of putting my life at risk." He leaned in and kissed her, savouring the moment. "I'll see you back in Korvoran. I promise."

"Go before I decide to give up this hopeless quest and join you."

"Hopeless? I would hardly call things hopeless."

"Really? We're going to the court of King Dagmar, who we believe is in league with the family. A family, I might add, that's been causing trouble for centuries. What chance do we stand against that?"

"Ah, but we have the one thing they don't—you!" She smiled, and he felt the better for it. "Farewell, my love. I'll see you back in Korvoran. Look for me in three weeks."

"You think that will be enough time?"

"If we haven't found them by then, we likely won't. In any case, if we discover something that might delay us, I'll try to send word."

She nodded as he climbed from the carriage, too worried for his safety to speak.

"Take care, my lord," said Captain Marwen, "and watch yourself on the road in these parts. King Dagmar doesn't like Therengians. If he discovers your presence, you won't live long."

"I sincerely hope that wasn't meant to bolster our confidence, Captain," said Athgar.

"This is no idle joke. If his men find you, they'll waste no time in stringing you up."

"Don't worry," said Belgast. "I'll keep an eye on him." His gaze drifted to Athgar. "Let's get going, shall we?"

They headed westward, following the trail as it wound farther into the hills.

Captain Marwen shook his head. "It's a fool's errand."

"Not so," said Natalia. "If anyone is playing the fools, it's us."

"He's trekking across hostile territory looking for people who might not even be out there, and you call us fools?"

"Athgar is well-equipped to survive in the wilderness, and Belgast is no slouch. I would wager their chance of success exceeds our own."

"If you feel we are likely to fail, why did you agree to accompany me?"

"We are dedicated to breaking the influence of the family. We cannot simply back down when things get difficult."

"But you risk capture, don't you? I can't imagine that would make Lord Athgar happy."

"My husband is not my keeper, nor I, his. We each walk our own path in life, even if we often tread the same trail. You may rest assured that I, and my companions, will do all we can to aid you in your mission, regardless of my personal feelings on the matter."

"In that case, I shall climb back into my carriage, and we'll be on our way."

Athgar topped the rise, then looked eastward. Belgast was only a few paces behind him but moving much slower, necessitating frequent stops on Athgar's part. He knew it wouldn't last, for Dwarves can march for much longer without rest. Doubtless, their positions would be reversed by the time the sun set.

"Anything interesting down there?" asked his companion.

"No. I hoped I could see the carriages from here, but the ground is too uneven in these parts."

"They're long gone by now, anyway."

Athgar turned his attention westward once more. The trail was washed out in places, evidence of its infrequent use and the effects of rain. Not that he required a trail to navigate, for the sun was the only guide he needed to head west.

"What do you think they'll be like?" asked Belgast.

"Who? The Orcs?"

"No, the Prior of Korvoran! Of course, the Orcs."

"I imagine they'll be similar to the Red Hand—both tribes use Fire Magic."

"Meaning?"

"There are shamans in all Orc tribes, but most have a tradition of a particular type of magic. The Red Hand has masters of flame, or they did before Artoch died. I'm the only one left now."

"Just out of curiosity," said Belgast, "why are they called the Red Hand? It's not as if their hands aren't the same colour as the rest of the tribes."

"When the tribe goes to war, they dye their hands red to symbolize their association with fire. I thought you'd know that by now."

"I'm far too busy doing other things. Now, tell me, is there some special way of greeting a new tribe?"

"Had I my torc, I could simply show it to them, but I'm afraid that's back home. I am fluent in Orc, though, so that should help."

"So, the idea is to find them, then introduce ourselves?"

"Yes. Why? How else would you do it?"

"I'm a simple merchant. What would I know?"

"Come now," said Athgar. "You're anything but simple. In any event, there's nothing for you to worry about. Orcs and Dwarves get along just fine. If anything, it's me who should be worried, especially here in Andover."

"Meaning?"

"If King Dagmar's men execute Therengians on the spot, I can't imagine what they'd do to an Orc."

"I suppose that means they'll live deep in the woods. You know what else lives in those parts? Nothing good!"

"It's not as bad as all that. When was the last time anything threatened us in the wilderness?"

"Do you truly have such a short memory? Need I mention water drakes?"

"That was on a river," replied Athgar.

"And what about those spiky creatures that attacked us on the road to Caerhaven?"

"You mean the thornlings? You worry too much."

"It's hard not to when travelling with the likes of you. They should call you danger; you attract it often enough."

"I would say the city is much more dangerous. Anytime we go to a so-called 'civilized' town, people try to kill us."

"Well," said the Dwarf, "I can't argue with you on that one." He walked a few more steps. "On the other hand, perhaps I can. We were in Korvoran, and no one tried to kill us."

"Did you forget the men who chased us into Barbek's shop? And the trio who followed Natalia and me?"

"Very well, you made your point. What I'd like to know, though, is how much farther we have to travel?"

"Hard to say, exactly. The innkeeper reckoned the forest's edge was two days by foot, but I doubt the Orcs will live on the fringes. We'll probably need to travel much deeper into the woods to spot any signs of them."

"And you're confident you can find them?"

"I'm very familiar with Orc hunting practices. If they're nearby, I'll find them."

"And if they're not?"

"Then we'll wander around the forest for weeks on end."

"Weeks?" said Belgast. "You can't be serious? How would we survive?"

"I have a bow," said Athgar, "and I can read tracks as well as the next fellow. Fear not, my friend, we shan't starve."

"Maybe I should have gone with the others."

"It's not that bad, is it?"

"You tell me? What do we have to look forward to other than tall trees and damp moss?"

"I'm told it's common practice to set up taverns where trails head into the forest."

"Ah," said the Dwarf. "Now you have my attention." He was about to say more but halted unexpectedly, looking over his shoulder.

"Something wrong?"

"Did you hear that?"

"Hear what?" asked Athgar.

"Hooves, or so I thought. Best we get off the path and take cover."

They turned off the trail, taking refuge behind some bushes and waited, both straining to hear more. Athgar was about to give up and started to get to his feet when a horseman appeared atop the hill they'd recently vacated.

"Ah," whispered Belgast. "I was right. It is horses."

"Yes, but how many?"

They watched as the lone rider waved at someone behind him.

Moments later, more horsemen appeared, and they continued down the hill, a dozen men, all told.

"Who are they?" whispered Athgar.

"Likely king's men, patrolling the road, looking for bandits."

"That's a large group just for keeping the roads safe."

Belgast shrugged, although it was difficult to notice while he lay prone behind a bush. "Maybe they're on their way to a new assignment?"

The riders came closer and then halted, only a stone's throw from the duo's place of concealment.

Athgar, realizing he held his breath, tried to relax. He'd made a name for himself as a hunter, even tracked down dangerous game, but the sight of a dozen armed men reminded him this was something else entirely. Here, his grey eyes would likely result in execution. He considered himself a brave man and knew he could fight. With his magic added into the mix, he could handle three or four opponents, but a dozen? Even with Belgast's help, he couldn't conceive of a victory against such odds.

His muscles tensed, his hand going to his axe, ready to draw it forth. One of the riders regaled the others with a story, and the rest broke into laughter. Moments later, they urged their horses onward, resuming their westward journey.

Once they were out of sight, Belgast stood. "I'm getting too old for this."

"As am I," added Athgar. "And now we must contend with an enemy ahead of us."

"Perhaps we should turn around?"

"No, we can't. I need to get word back home; they'll be worried sick about us."

"Then what do you propose we do? If we continue, we risk encountering those fellows."

"We could leave the road?"

"That's a terrible idea," said Belgast. "The road is the only thing leading us to our target."

"Then we continue and remain vigilant. With any luck, that lot will be miles away by the time the sun sets."

By late afternoon they left the hills, replacing the scenery with fields of wild grass and trees. To the Dwarf, it was nothing exceptional, but Athgar looked on in wonder, so much so that he slowed his pace.

"What's the matter?" grumbled Belgast.

"I've never seen grass that high."

"And I've never seen a dragon. What of it?"

"That grass could be used to thatch roofs."

"Once again, what of it? We don't live here, my friend. Surely you're not suggesting we harvest it and take it all the way back home?"

"No, of course not, but there's something about this place." Athgar stepped off the trail, moving a dozen steps or so into the field of grass. "I've seen this type of grass before, though not at this height. We used it in Athelwald." He began following the edge of the field after an idea suddenly struck him.

"What in blazes are you doing?" called out Belgast.

"This is no accident."

"Grass does grow in the wilderness, you know."

"In a field this size?"

"Surely you're not suggesting someone came out into the middle of nowhere to plant grass?"

Athgar waited for the Dwarf to catch up. "That's precisely what I'm suggesting, only it was likely a long time ago."

"So, what are we looking for?"

"I'll know it when I see it."

"That doesn't exactly inspire me with confidence."

They continued to a nearby forest, where some ruins came into sight.

"There! What did I tell you?" said Athgar. "It's a village."

"Yes," said Belgast. "One that somebody burned to the ground. How long ago do you reckon it was destroyed?"

They moved closer. "Hard to say for sure, but my best guess would be at least ten years."

"And what makes you say that?"

Athgar pointed. "There's a small field over yonder that's overgrown with weeds."

"And?"

"You don't fence in a field of weeds. They likely used it for growing crops. Let's go take a look, shall we?"

"At weeds? Have you lost your wits?"

Athgar hopped over what was left of the fence and knelt, using his knife to cut away at something.

Belgast, preferring his wilderness less crowded, remained at the fence. "Find anything useful?"

"I'll tell you in a moment." Athgar rummaged around, then held his hand up triumphantly, an onion dangling from his fingers. "I told you there were crops here at some point in the past."

"That means someone attacked the place before harvest," said the Dwarf, "but who would do this? Bandits?"

"Bandits would steal, but why torch the place? No, I suspect this was the work of King Dagmar's men. How long has he been King of Andover?"

"Saints, if I know, but they say he's not too different from his father. What am I missing here?"

"This was a Therengian village."

"Are you certain? Didn't the Crown eradicate all descendants of the Old Kingdom?"

"I'm sure that was their aim, but look around you. This place wouldn't be visible from the road."

"Still? A Therengian village? Right in the middle of Andover? Wouldn't someone report it to the Crown?"

"The king's men can't be everywhere, and chances are the locals turned a blind eye. Remember, the nobles fear the Old Kingdom's return, not the farmers, and I suspect we're miles from the next village."

"Is it a Human custom to ignore the presence of an enemy in your land?"

"A village's land only extends so far, and the average farmer cares little for anything farther than an afternoon stroll. You might call it a live-and-let-live attitude."

"And you know this, how?"

"You forget," said Athgar. "I spent time in Ebenstadt. Deep down, Humans are much the same; we all want to live in peace and get on with our lives."

"Except for the nobles, it would seem."

"Agreed. Tonfer Garul told me that, at its height, the Old Kingdom was quite prosperous. He described it as a Golden Age."

"How is it you know so much about all of this?"

"Since becoming High Thane, I've come to realize it's important to honour the past. Don't you know the history of your own home?"

"Of course I do," replied Belgast. He paused a moment. "Ah, I understand what you're trying to say. Well played, my friend." Athgar tossed him the onion, and the Dwarf held it. "This would go nicely in a soup."

"Why don't you look in the ruins? You might find us a pot or something. I doubt that's the kind of thing a king's soldier would want to plunder."

"And what will you do?"

"I'll dig around here some more. There's likely to be more food hiding in amongst the weeds."

"We have rations," said Belgast.

"True, but the Gods have seen fit to guide us here. It would be a shame to waste such a bounty."

"It wasn't the Gods, it was your insatiable curiosity, but I'll admit the idea of fresh food is causing my belly to rumble in appreciation."

. . .

Their search proved fruitful. And as darkness invaded, they huddled around a fire they'd built in the ruins of one of the houses. The structure had no roof, but the walls sufficed to keep the evening breeze at bay, while the clear skies held no threat of rain.

Belgast had found a small pot which they used to gather water at a nearby stream. They tossed in the onions, along with an odd assortment of carrots, turnips, and even some potatoes. Athgar scoured the area, finding some wild herbs to help add an extra bit of flavour, and then they sat, watching it boil by the fire's light.

"This reminds me of my youth," said Athgar.

"You were a farmer?"

"No, a bowyer, but I took care of my sister, Ethwyn, which meant I needed to cook."

"I thought Skora looked after you both?"

"She helped, but it still fell to me to provide most meals."

"You miss her, don't you? Your sister, I mean."

"I do, though I cannot forgive her for what she did. I suppose it matters little now that she's dead, but it would've been nice to have her in my life again."

"You have your own family now."

"True, yet there's still a part of me that yearns for the simpler life of my youth. In those days, I had little to concern myself with other than food. What about you? Do you miss the days of your youth?"

"Me?" Belgast laughed. "You forget how old I am. My youth passed many, many years ago." He stared at the flames. "I'll admit I have some fond memories of those days, but I enjoy the life I have now, even if I am in the middle of this Gods' forsaken country."

"Don't tell me you enjoy the danger?"

"Danger? No, but I do enjoy the mystery of it all. They say a Dwarf is never as happy as when he's on a quest, and finding these Orcs would certainly qualify as a big one."

"That it would." Athgar leaned forward, peering into the pot and sniffing. "Not much longer now."

"Tell me," said Belgast, "if you could live your life all over again, would you do anything differently?"

"No. Everything that's happened to me, good or bad, ultimately led me to Natalia, and I wouldn't change that for anything."

ANDOVER

AUTUMN 1108 SR

Natalia poked her head out the window as the carriage rolled to a stop. "Is something wrong?"

"Not at all, my lady," replied the driver. "We're merely stopping to water the horses."

She climbed out, luxuriating in the sun's warmth. "How much farther, do you think?"

"We shall enter the city of Zienholtz before dark, my lady." He busied himself with fetching a bucket and then went off in search of a stream.

Galina wandered over. "I don't understand why we brought three carriages. Surely two would have sufficed?"

"Take another look," said Natalia, pointing. "Captain Marwen needed two just for his own belongings, though what he's got in those chests is beyond me."

"He looks to be a man who likes his creature comforts."

"Is that a hint of a smile I see? Don't tell me you're enamoured of the fellow?"

"Of course not," said Galina, although the sudden flush to her cheeks spoke otherwise.

"What are you two up to?" called out Katrin.

"We were just chatting about Galina's interest in our host," said Natalia.

"As I suspected."

"Come now," said Galina. "You're imagining things."

"If you say so."

"Where's Stanislav?" asked Natalia. "You haven't lost him, have you?"

"No. He had to answer a call of nature. Don't worry. He won't go far."

Katrin looked westward. "You don't suppose Athgar and Belgast found the Orcs yet, do you?"

"After only a day of travel? I doubt they got very far; the great forest is likely still days away. Even then, they'll have hundreds of miles of wilderness to search."

"Do you honestly believe they'll succeed?"

"Don't underestimate Athgar," said Natalia. "If the Ashwalkers are there, he'll find them."

"And then what?"

"They'll contact Shaluhk and send word of everything that's transpired."

"How do you know they'll be willing or even able to do that?"

"I've lived amongst the Orcs for some time now and understand their ways. They're always friendly towards those they perceive as brothers. Athgar is a member of the Red Hand, so they'll welcome him as one of their own. Each tribe usually has at least one shaman, possibly more. They use their magic to regularly keep in touch with other tribes."

"And you know this, how?"

"My tribe-sister, Shaluhk, has contacted dozens of tribes scattered all over the Continent, some even far to the west."

"Tribe-sister?" said Galina. "Are you telling me you actually live with the Orcs in a primitive hut back in Runewald?"

"It isn't a palace, I'll grant you, but it's far more than just a hut; it's my home. I wouldn't trade it for all the elegance of the richest courts."

"From what you told us of Runewald," said Katrin, "it sounds quite nice."

"And yet," said Galina, "there is something to be said for the finer trappings of civilization." She sighed. "I suppose I should resign myself to living the simple life."

"At least the family won't be telling us what to do." Katrin paused a moment, thinking things through. "How, exactly, does the family communicate over great distances?"

"I'm not sure," said Natalia. "Perhaps Galina could tell us more."

The older Water Mage was busy watching Captain Marwen.

"Galina?" Natalia tapped her on the arm. "Are you listening?"

"Sorry. What was that?"

"Katrin wants to know how the family communicates over long distances."

"It's an advanced spell which requires specialized preparation. I learned it myself when I became a mistress at the Volstrum."

"What type of preparation?"

"They take a pair of bowls made from rare materials, place them close together, then cast a ritual to establish a link between them. It's a variation on the spell magic pool that allows one to see and hear what's reflected in the companion bowl. Unfortunately, it has limited usefulness."

"Why so?" asked Katrin. "I would think it quite useful, especially considering how scattered the family is."

"Ah, but there is no way of notifying the recipient that the spell is being cast."

"So you would need to arrange a specific time to be in front of the bowls?"

"Either that or someone is always there, watching the bowl. Of course, the mages of the family are far too busy for such pursuits. The Sartellians, on the other hand, have a similar spell that employs a conjured fire, and I've heard they can use it anywhere. Yet one more difference between the family's two branches."

"I could see how that would be better," said Natalia.

"I can teach it to you if you like. The magic pool spell, that is."

"I'll take you up on that offer, though now is not the time to consider such things. We must, instead, concentrate on preparing ourselves for the court of King Dagmar."

"And what of your own strength?" asked Galina. "Have you recovered from your ordeal?"

"I feel stronger than I have in weeks, but I doubt I could cast another maelstrom anytime soon. More importantly, how are we to behave at Dagmar's court? I would suggest you take the lead in that regard."

"But you've dealt with rulers before, haven't you?"

"There's no court in Therengia, and the meetings of the thanes and chieftains are far less formal than here in the midst of the Petty Kingdoms. Any idea what we can expect?"

"Let me think on that a moment," said Galina. "For one thing, our interactions are likely to be far more formal. Only the ruler's closest advisors meet in private, meaning any audience will probably be in the presence of others."

"And how do we behave?" asked Katrin.

"Speak little, and only offer opinions if you have something to back them up. Assuming the family has representatives there, they'll be looking to trip us up at any opportunity."

"And if the family IS there, will we be in danger?"

"I doubt it, at least not directly. No member of the court would take any action without the king's blessing. They may realize we're not true Stormwinds, but they wouldn't dare admit that to outsiders, especially not Dagmar. It would cause them to lose face."

"I agree," said Natalia, "but they will employ every means at their disposal to discredit us and our mission here. On the other hand, if the Stormwinds are NOT at court, we may be able to use that to our advantage."

"How?" asked Galina.

"If we present ourselves as true representatives of the family, we can infer that any information presented to the king is out of date."

"But wouldn't a Sartellian know all about us?"

"Not unless they were in the upper echelons of power. Remember, like the Stormwinds, their mages are all over the courts of the Continent. They would trust very few with such information for fear it might get leaked."

"So you're saying we're an embarrassment to the entire family?"

"Precisely," said Natalia. "But in this case, it works to our advantage. Of course, it's still a gamble. We don't know how important Andover is in the grand scheme of things. On the one hand, they might consider it their top priority to get back at Reinwick, but they may also have already washed their hands of the entire affair."

"In that case," said Galina, "we must proceed carefully. I suggest we hold off on revealing our true identities until absolutely necessary, and even then, we limit such knowledge to only a select few."

"Here comes Stanislav," said Katrin. "Perhaps he knows something that might be of use?"

The three ladies turned to face the newcomer, who slowed at their attention. "Did I miss something?"

"We wondered if you could shed any light on what we can expect in Zienholtz," said Natalia. "You've travelled the region, haven't you?"

"Not for some years, and definitely before Dagmar's rule, but if he's anything like his father, he shouldn't be too difficult to manage."

"Meaning?"

"King Volkard was a vain man," said Stanislav. "I suspect flattery will get you far more influence over his son than accusations. And he'll likely prefer to believe all ideas came from his own head rather than from one of his advisors. It's a simple enough tactic I've used successfully over the years. Then again, I only visited the court to pay my respects, not try to diffuse a potential war. Have you discussed any of this with Captain Marwen?"

"Our objectives are not necessarily in line with the good captain's. In any case, we want to show a united front."

"The captain certainly believes peace is obtainable. Your best bet is to focus on that aspect whenever dealing with him."

"And the family?" asked Katrin.

"We want them out of Andover's court," said Natalia, "but such an objective could well work against us. Captain Marwen wants peace; I doubt he cares one whit about who's at Dagmar's court."

"Then we shall heed your advice," said Galina. "For the moment, let us concentrate on peace. Then, once we are more familiar with what we're up against, we can work towards our true objective."

"How much do we truly know about Marwen?" asked Stanislav.

"Why?" said Galina. "What are you suggesting?"

"Only that it might be a good idea to learn more about the fellow. He seems to have taken an interest in you, Galina. Perhaps you should ride with him the rest of the way?"

"That's hardly proper."

"Proper? We're outcasts from Ruzhina. I don't believe now is the time to consider what's proper, do you? Saints alive, we're only asking you to engage the fellow in conversation, not bed him. Not that we'd hold anything against you if you did so."

Galina turned beet red.

"I think she gets the idea," said Katrin. "Perhaps our time might be better spent by changing the subject?"

"To what?" said Stanislav.

"I don't know, anything? How about that tree over yonder? It's awfully green, don't you think?"

They eventually continued on their way. It delighted Captain Marwen to accept Galina's offer to accompany him in the lead carriage. Stanislav rode along with Natalia and Katrin, leaving the third one empty of passengers.

Off in the distance, a dark-grey stone wall encircled Zienholtz, while the gleaming white spires of its temples towered over the city. The carriages slowed to a stop as they arrived at the gate.

A couple of guards approached the carriages, one insisting Natalia open the door to allow an inspection of its contents. He made only a cursory inspection before waving them through.

The streets here were not as narrow as those in Korvoran, for there was no coast to follow. Instead, the city was a collection of square blocks, each of uniform distance, evidence of its careful planning.

They rode through a merchant district before the area opened into carefully cultured gardens and trimmed trees. Shortly thereafter, they crossed over a river and into the Palace grounds. The building itself was smaller than the Duke of Reinwick's, yet its red stone caught the light of the dying sun, giving the appearance of a place glowing with energy.

Numerous carriages waited in front, evidence the king's court was in session. Whether it was for the business of state or entertainment was yet to be determined.

Natalia watched with interest as Captain Marwen's carriage rolled up to the door, and a trio of servants stepped forth, one with a carved wooden step stool. The captain exited, then put his arm out, guiding Galina down. The carriage rolled forward, and then the next was ready to unload its passengers.

"Shall I go first?" offered Stanislav.

"If you would be so kind," said Natalia.

The mage hunter waited until the servants opened the door, then stepped down, taking in his surroundings, before offering his arm to Natalia. Katrin followed, and a stiff individual who appeared unable or unwilling to talk conducted them inside.

"Impressive," said Stanislav. "It appears we arrived in the middle of a celebration of some sort."

"Where is our captain?" asked Natalia.

"Already inside, along with Galina."

"Excuse me, madam?" This came from a servant dressed all in gold. "Are you the Lady Natalia?"

"I am."

"I was tasked with conducting you to the herald. He is to announce your arrival. I'm told it was Captain Marwen's idea?"

"Of course. Lead on."

The servant led them through the central doorway, down a side corridor, and then up a set of stairs.

"Where are we going, precisely?" asked Natalia.

"His Majesty likes a grand entrance. The herald announces all nobles as they descend the main staircase into the great hall."

They arrived at another hallway packed with the wealthy elite, each awaiting their turn to enter the celebration. Much to her surprise, the servant brought Natalia to the head of the line, where a tall man with thinning hair waited.

"There must be some kind of mistake," she said.

"Not at all, my lady. Seldom are we blessed with the presence of one of your august standing."

Before she could reply, the door was flung open, and the servant whispered something to the fellow on the other side.

"After you, madam."

As she stepped through, a booming voice rang out, "Lady Natalia Stormwind."

Panic surged through her. They'd intended to hide their association with the family, but it appeared Captain Marwen harboured no intention of keeping their secret. Realizing their ruse was up, she grasped the magerite ring hanging from her neck and slipped it on her finger.

All eyes were on her as she reached the bottom of the stairs, and then more than a dozen people surged forward, each eager to make her acquaintance.

They introduced themselves so fast that she couldn't remember their names, except for one who waited until the last and then stepped forward, her eyes flickering to Natalia's ring.

"Greetings, Lady Natalia. My name is Lady Ria Sartellian. I was unaware the Stormwinds intended on sending a representative to Zienholtz."

"Just as they did not inform me of the presence of any Sartellians. It appears both families have much to answer for." Natalia let her gaze wander over her counterpart, finally noting the dark red brooch pinned to the neck of her dress. Judging by the colour, Ria was a most powerful mage, yet her age suggested she was new to the ways of court. "You are a recent graduate of Korascajan, I presume?"

"I have that honour, yes. Yourself?"

"It's been a few years since I completed my studies at the Volstrum. Since then, I've travelled the Continent, working to further the family's aims." She hoped her bluff was sufficient to avoid further questioning, but it appeared luck was not on her side.

"Then you haven't been assigned to court service?"

"Only in special cases. You might say I act in an advisory capacity, travelling where I'm needed most. In fact, I came here directly from Karslev on a very important mission."

Ria locked eyes with her for a moment, then politely curtsied. "Then I hope I can be of assistance to you during your stay in Andover."

A wave of relief flooded over Natalia, but she kept her composure. "Your offer is graciously received. I shall have my people contact you if there is anything I require." She watched the Fire Mage disappear back into the crowd. Someone touched her elbow, and she turned to see Katrin.

"Galina and Stanislav are over there," said Katrin, pointing off to the side of the room.

"And Captain Marwen?"

"Waiting to be introduced to His Majesty." She lowered her voice. "I thought we weren't going to announce our family name?"

"That's what I intended, but it appears the good captain beat us to it."

"Are you sure it was him?"

"Who else knew? It's not as if one of the coachmen came in and spoke to the herald."

Katrin glanced around the room. "Well, it wasn't all bad. No one's rushing forward to arrest you."

"No, but my arrival has brought out a member of the family, a woman by the name of Ria Sartellian. We need to keep an eye on her."

"Anyone else of note to watch for?"

Natalia chuckled. "I only just arrived. Give it some time."

Katrin led her across the room to where the others waited, but before they could say anything, Captain Marwen appeared out of nowhere.

"I have news," he announced. "His Majesty, King Dagmar, wants to meet you."

"All of us?" said Natalia.

"No, my lady, only you. Your name piqued his interest, although whether or not that bodes favourably remains to be seen. In any event, I would suggest we delay no longer; he's not known as a patient man."

"Then lead on, and I shall do my best to impress him." She turned to her companions. "Stay close and be ready for anything. If things go amiss, we may well find ourselves in the middle of a hostile mob."

The captain grabbed her elbow in an effort to speed her along. Natalia was having none of it, coming to a halt and raising her voice. "Remove yourself, Captain. It is not your place to lay hands on a Stormwind!"

The man backed off, duly chastised, but Natalia noticed the king watching the exchange with keen interest. She stepped closer, then bowed at the waist. It was a calculated gamble, for they expected women to curtsy, not bow. She knew, however, that those with power would never demean themselves in such a fashion.

"Your Majesty," she said. "I bring you greetings from Ruzhina."

PLOTS

AUTUMN 1108 SR

A servant ushered Lord Pavel into the room. "You wanted to see me, Valentyn?"

"Indeed," replied his host. "I hoped we might discuss the matter of these foreigners occupying our soil."

"There is little to discuss unless you're proposing we take more direct action?"

Valentyn smiled.

"Surely you jest?" said Pavel. "We don't have the men."

"Ah, but we could have, if we were careful."

"Would you care to explain that remark?"

"It's not how many we have that's important; it's how we use them."

"No. I'm sorry, but I'm still not understanding. Are you proposing we take up arms against the Therengians or not?"

"I am doing precisely that," said Valentyn, "but not in the way others might. I propose we wage a war of economics."

"And how would that work?"

"We begin by setting up groups of warriors to harass their supply wagons. In essence, we make the cost of travelling the roads expensive."

"It won't work," said Pavel. "They'll only assign more warriors to guard travellers."

"And that, my friend, is exactly what we want. Don't you see? The more they put on the road, the less they have to maintain the peace in the cities of Novarsk. That's when we move into the second phase of our plan."

"Which is?"

"We begin by attacking their city garrisons. No doubt, with enough provocation, our populace will rise up and join us in the fight."

Lord Pavel shook his head. "It won't work. Saints know you're a brilliant tactician, Valentyn, but even you must realize the futility of the matter. The common folk despise us!"

"Then it is imperative we persuade them."

"How? Do you mean to purchase their loyalty? Or would you use force? Such a move would only serve to deplete what few men remain. No, the time for such action has passed."

"Then what would you have us do? Surrender? It is not in our nature."

"Perhaps there is another way."

"Go on," said Valentyn. "I'm listening."

"What's the one thing we have that they don't?"

"Knowledge of the area?"

"That's a suitable answer," said Pavel, "but not what I was looking for. No, I refer to our keeps."

"How do they help us?"

"Have you noticed how the Therengians equip themselves?"

"With weapons and armour, if that's what you mean."

"True, but their armour pales compared to ours. They also lack one crucial element—siege weapons."

Lord Valentyn smiled. "Ah, I see what you're getting at. You're proposing we trick them into assaulting our keeps. That's a marvellous idea! We'll grind them into the dirt! Wherever did you come up with that?"

"While reading the accounts of the recent war. The Therengians and their Orc allies excel at using the wilderness to their advantage, but a siege lets us fight on our terms."

"Still, it's a bit risky. There's always the possibility they'll try to starve us out."

"Ah, but we can prepare for that by stocking up on food. We'll also strip our lands of anything they might use against us."

"That's a bit of a gamble," said Valentyn, "and it would cause us hardship afterwards. After all, we still need to house our workers."

"I'm not suggesting we destroy their homes, merely scour the area of any food that might feed the enemy."

"And if they bring food in from Halmund?"

"I hadn't considered that."

"No, I don't suppose you had." Valentyn wandered over to the fire, staring into its flames. A log collapsed, sending sparks flying up the chimney, and he suddenly smiled. "I have it!"

"Care to elaborate?"

He turned to face his guest. "We do as you say—lure them into attacking my keep. Then, when their attention is on the siege, you shall march into their rear. My own men will sally forth, and together we'll crush, them like the insects they are."

"It's an interesting idea, but how do you propose I move my entire army without being noticed?"

Valentyn waved away the objection. "Don't worry me with trivial matters. I will look after everything. I promise you."

"Easy to say, not so easy to do. I hate to admit it, but these are experienced military commanders we're dealing with. We won't easily fool them."

"An Orc leads them, for Saint's sake. Surely, if we appeal to his baser instincts, we can draw him into our trap."

"Do not let his rough exterior fool you," warned Pavel. "Their chieftain has a sharp mind."

"Then I shall take care to lay the necessary groundwork this very day."

"And how do you intend to do that?"

"By planting the spark and allowing his own people to fan it into flames."

"Now you're just talking in riddles."

Valentyn chuckled. "Fear not, my friend. Everything is under control."

"Meaning?"

"I will go to the Palace this very day and once more talk to this Orc who rules over us."

"And?" pressed Pavel.

"I'll pressure him to restore the nobility to their rightful place."

"He'll never agree to that."

"Of course not. That's precisely the point. Don't you see? I need only hint we will rise up if he doesn't appease us, giving him no room to negotiate. Just promise me that when the time comes, you'll be able to march to my aid. The last thing I want is to be trapped in my keep with no hope of escape."

"I shall be there. I promise."

"Good," said Valentyn. "Now, you best leave me alone with my thoughts. There are details to work out. I'll contact you later once I've visited the Palace."

"Assuming he doesn't clap you in irons. You're leaving us very little wiggle room here, Valentyn. If this plan of yours fails, it will be the death of us all."

"Then so be it. If we cannot live as free men, what's the point?"

.   .   .

Kargen tossed another stick into the fireplace. "*It is chilly,*" he complained in his native tongue. "*Winter will soon be upon us, and we are still stuck in this miserable Palace. I wish Athgar were here.*"

"*Ah,*" said Shaluhk. "*Now we get to the heart of it.*"

"*I am not suited to this. Athgar is far better at dealing with Humans than I.*"

"*Yet he trusted you to rule in his absence above all others. Would you now doubt his wisdom?*"

"*It is not his wisdom I doubt; it is my own.*"

"*Come now,*" she soothed. "*You are Kargen, Chieftain of the Red Hand, the leader who brought our tribe to a new home and helped fight off the invaders who threatened our way of life. Can you honestly sit there and tell me you are incapable of dealing with a small group of Humans?*"

"*They are barons!*"

"*They are still men. Take away their titles, and they are not so different from our Therengian friends. To believe otherwise is to give them too much power.*"

"*Men with warriors,*" corrected Kargen. "*And therein lies the problem.*"

"*A problem that is not insurmountable. I contacted the other shamans, and they agreed to send more hunters. The Thane Guard will be here by the end of the tenday, not to mention the fyrds of both Runewald and Bradon. We shall be ready if they choose to fight our occupation of their land.*"

A knock demanded their attention.

"Who is there?" called out Shaluhk in the Human tongue.

"Harwath," came the reply. "Lord Valentyn is here to see Kargen."

"It appears the wolf has entered the den."

"No," said Kargen. "This lord is more viper than wolf." He raised his voice. "Very well, Harwath. Let him in."

Lord Valentyn Sayenko swept into the room, his footsteps echoing on the marble floor. He paused as his gaze befell the two Orcs but did not bow, only nodded his head in recognition. "Chief Kargen. I hope I'm not disturbing you?"

"I am here to serve the people of Novarsk."

The baron's eyes flicked to Shaluhk.

"You may talk freely," said Kargen. "Shaluhk and I speak with one mind. Was there something, in particular, you wanted to discuss with me?"

"Indeed. In fact, you might say I came to offer you an olive branch of sorts."

"An olive branch? I am afraid I do not understand what you mean?"

"A peace offering. A method of resolving our differences and bringing our two people closer together."

"Why the change of heart?" asked Shaluhk.

"I admit I let my emotions get the better of me on my last visit, but I assure you I only wish to better the lives of the people of Novarsk. To that end, I have a proposition for you."

"Then speak," said Kargen, "and I will consider your words."

"I realize there has been violence of late, and while I abhor such tactics, I understand where the hatred comes from. The people of this fair kingdom have spoken, and their voice is clear. Give them back their rulers."

"I will not release Queen Rada. Her unprovoked war cost both our realms dearly."

"Quite so, and on that, we agree. Rather, I refer to the nobility. Restoring their rights and privileges will go a long way to placating those who rose against you. Refuse, and I fear there will be more violence."

"Are you suggesting outright rebellion?"

Valentyn shrugged. "It is not beyond belief. A people, once roused, can commit unspeakable acts of violence. I shouldn't like to think of you, and yours caught up in the middle of such carnage."

"If I were of the opinion that the common folk of this country truly wanted that, then I would not hesitate. As it stands, I have reason to believe precisely the opposite."

Valentyn's cheeks flushed with anger. "They only want what we tell them to want."

"Ah, yes," said Kargen. "Lord Pavel expressed the same opinion some days ago. I am curious to know if this is a commonly held belief amongst you barons or simply ignorance on your part."

"I did not come here to be insulted."

"Then you must consider it an unexpected bonus," offered Shaluhk.

"How dare you speak this way to a baron of the realm!" he shouted at the shaman before turning back to Kargen. "Are you going to let your woman talk to me like that?"

"Unlike your fellow countrymen," replied Kargen, "we encourage others to speak their mind. Shaluhk is also a shaman of the Red Hand. Thus, her opinion holds great sway over my decisions." Kargen stepped closer until he smelled the stench of sweat on the Human. "Tell me, Lord Valentyn, why do you fear her words? Could they have a ring of truth to them? Are you so insecure in your position that you must resort to belittling others?"

The baron stared back, refusing to be intimidated. "I gave you fair warning, Orc. The people of Novarsk want their rulers. Failure to comply with their wishes could well result in open war." He paused a moment. "Or is that what you wish for? Another uprising, where you can slake your thirst for blood?"

Only Shaluhk's hand on his arm prevented Kargen from striking the baron down where he stood. "Begone!" he shouted. "And do not darken my door again!"

Lord Valentyn stepped back, then nodded slightly before he turned and left the room, his footsteps heavy.

"You must not let him get the better of you," Shaluhk said in their native tongue. *"He seeks to inflame your passions."*

"And he has succeeded, that much I freely admit, but I can no longer stand back and give him free rein. Something must be done, yet I am at a loss as to what that might be."

"You are not alone in this. Let us gather our allies and discuss the matter. Perhaps, then, we can come to a resolution which benefits us all?"

"I understand the need for privacy," said Wynfrith, "but of all the places we could meet, why here?"

Kargen looked around the forest, the trees disappearing into the darkness. "Both our people live in harmony with nature. Thus, it is only fitting we meet here to discuss the future of this land." His gaze turned to his new arrivals. "Zahruhl, thank you for answering Shaluhk's summons."

"It is my pleasure," replied the chieftain. "And a demonstration that the Stone Crushers stand with the rest of Therengia."

"As do the Cloud Hunters," added Grazuhk, "but like our brothers and sisters, we are eager to know why you need us in Novarsk. Have the Humans of this realm once more taken up arms?"

"No," said Kargen. "At least not yet, but I fear it will not be long before war strikes this land again."

"Tell us your thoughts," said Rugg, the master of earth. "We would share your burden."

"The barons of Novarsk seek to reclaim their power."

"Understandable, given the circumstances, but not something we can condone. To do so would invite more animosity between our two lands."

"On that," said Kargen, "we agree, yet it leaves us in a tough position. The logical action is to absorb this realm into our own and govern it as a province, as they did in the kingdom of old."

"Then why not do so?" asked Grazuhk. "Do we lack the hunters for such a task?"

"Our forces hold all the major cities, but the barons' keeps remain beyond our control."

"Then let us attack them," said Zahruhl, "and break their control over this land once and for all."

"There are too many. Such a campaign would spread our army too thin."

"Then we must take each in succession," said Raleth.

"One moment," said Wynfrith. "What of Queen Rada's cousin? Could we give him the Crown? Surely that would solve our problems?"

"I thought of that," said Shaluhk. "Unfortunately, Harwath's contacts confirmed he is the guest of Lord Valentyn."

"And," continued Wynfrith, "no doubt he's waiting to crown the lad king so he can rule in his stead."

"Is that a common occurrence in the Petty Kingdoms?"

"I have no idea. I imagine Natalia could tell you more, were she here, but that has no bearing on how we proceed. If this royal is a guest of Lord Valentyn, we should not count on his support."

"Then again," said Raleth, "it gives us the excuse we need to siege the baron's keep. What's he baron of again?"

"A place called Krasnov," said Kargen. "Near the border with Ostrova."

"We must tread carefully," warned Wynfrith. "If our warriors move too close to the border, Ostrova might see it as a provocation, and we can ill afford a war with our northern neighbour at this time."

"I doubt they would consider us a threat," said Raleth. "Of more concern is how we get into the keep? It's not like we have any siege weapons."

"We shall destroy the keep," said Rugg. "Let the Stone Crushers worry about how."

"Raleth," said Kargen. "Confer with our other captains. I want an estimate of how many warriors you think we need, but do not begin gathering them just yet. We may still be able to resolve our differences peacefully."

"Tell me," said Grazuhk, "what do the common folk of Novarsk think of all of this?"

"The few I spoke to despise the barons, but Harwath is better suited to talk of such things. He has been amongst them these past few days, learning more about their culture."

"It's true," added Harwath. "Queen Rada was a despot, even more despised than her father. The townsfolk blame her, and by extension her barons, for the higher taxes they had to shoulder to support the war. The merchants, in particular, were hard hit, many of their businesses failing."

"And the farmers?" asked Grazuhk.

"Feeding Rada's army was difficult, leaving little for everyone else. Now, there's a good chance many might starve before the coming of spring."

"What can we do to ease their suffering?"

"We could bring food from Therengia," offered Wynfrith. "Our harvest was plentiful this year, and there is much to spare. Unfortunately, the population of Novarsk is large, and I fear it won't be enough."

"I wonder..." said Raleth.

"If you have something to add," said Kargen, "please speak your mind."

"The concentration of wealth appears to lie with the barons. Would it not be likely they are also hoarding food stores?"

"From what I have seen of them, it would be highly likely. These nobles only seem concerned with preserving their own lives, not those of the folk around them."

"I shall make some discreet enquiries," said Harwath. "If they are hoarding food, I suspect people will be well aware of it."

"Even that might not be enough to stave off widespread famine," said Wynfrith. "Perhaps we should appeal to the neighbouring realms for help?"

"I shall send envoys," said Kargen, "but I would not expect much in the way of assistance. The Petty Kingdoms bear no love for Therengians and see Orcs as savages. Still, they may be willing to help their fellow Humans."

"Do we have any idea how Rada's neighbours felt about her?"

"None at all," offered Shaluhk. "I took the liberty of speaking with several servants at the Palace. Queen Rada had little to do with those bordering her lands other than us. The consensus was she despised them, though there is no evidence whether they reciprocated the feeling."

"If they hated her," said Grazuhk, "that might work to our advantage."

"How so?"

"With her gone, the way is open to reconciliation with Novarsk. Perhaps our defeat of Rada may finally bring the peace we have sought for so long?"

"Let us hope so," said Shaluhk. "For the alternative is a prolonged and bloody war."

AMBUSH

AUTUMN 1108 SR

C old winds embraced Athgar and Belgast as they greeted the morning sun.

"Winter will soon be upon us," noted the Dwarf, "and there's little I hate more than walking in the snow."

"Come now," said Athgar. "It's merely a cold snap, and I can use my Fire Magic to keep us comfortable. Shall I cast the spell of warmth now, or would you prefer to shiver for half the morning?"

"Now would be fine, if you would be so kind."

Athgar called on his inner spark. As the power flowed through him, he pointed at Belgast. There was no beam of light, no aura that enveloped his companion, yet he watched the Dwarf relax as the warmth settled into his bones.

"That's much better. Thank you."

He repeated the spell on himself, then started looking around.

"Did you lose something?" asked Belgast.

"Just taking one last look. It's not every day I get to see a village like this, even if it has been destroyed."

"You live in Runewald. Your entire home is similar to this."

"Yes, but Runewald doesn't have the history that this place does. Think of it; this used to be on the outskirts of the Old Kingdom."

"You don't know that. The Old Kingdom died five hundred years ago. This village is likely far newer."

"Why would you think that?"

"I know my history," said Belgast. "When the Successor States destroyed the old Therengia, they made it their business to tear down its cities brick by brick."

"But Therengians don't generally build with bricks."

"Timber by timber, then. The point is they destroyed anything reminding them of that once great power. Do you think they'd leave a village untouched? No, this was likely built long after those events. Not that it matters much to you and me. This place is only a ghost of its former self. In any case, it's high time we were on our way."

"I wonder how many other villages they destroyed?" mused Athgar.

"Too many to count, I'd warrant. The kings of Andover have not been kind to your people."

"Did the mountain folk suffer such treatment?"

"When we Dwarves first encountered Humans, there was much bloodshed, but in time, we came to tolerate each other. Of course, we didn't live in the same terrain you folk prefer, so there wasn't much in the way of competition. Eventually, they learned to value our skills, particularly our mastery of metalworking. You know, my people taught you Humans how to work iron, or at least that's the story."

Athgar made an exaggerated bow. "Well, on behalf of Humans everywhere, I thank you. Now, shall we continue westward? It's not like we'll find the Orcs in these parts."

"Lead on, my friend, and may Gundar watch over you."

As they topped a rise later the next day, dense woods spread out before them, stretching as far as the eye could see.

Belgast groaned. "There must be thousands of miles of wilderness down there. How in the name of the Gods are we to find the Ashwalkers?"

"Simple. We don't. We let them find us."

"That's all well and good, but where do we begin?"

"Well," said Athgar, thinking things through. "For a start, we still need to reach the edge of that forest. It appears there's a trail coming up from the south."

"Aye, and there's a building down there, a roadside inn by the look of it. At the very least, they should be able to provide us with some idea of what to expect in these parts."

"Yes, and they might even have heard rumours of something in the forest. That would give us someplace to start."

They made their way downhill, the trees growing more numerous, the bushes and shrubs thicker the farther they went. The inn, if that's what it was, was soon lost from sight, causing the Dwarf to curse.

"I'd give half my beard to see that inn again. I can't tell east from west."

Athgar peered up at the canopy of leaves overhead. "I can still see the sun. Don't worry. We're going in the right direction."

"I certainly hope so. I can't take much more of—"

At the Dwarf's sudden silence, Athgar wheeled around. "Belgast?"

The Dwarf lay prone on the forest floor. "I tripped on a blasted root. Don't worry. I'll be fine." He tried to stand, but his ankle wouldn't support his weight. "Give me a hand here, will you? I think I twisted my ankle."

"We'll rest awhile. The inn can wait."

"I'd prefer to rest indoors. At least, then, we'd have ale!"

"But you're injured?"

"I can hobble."

Athgar moved beside him, grabbing the Dwarf's arm to help steady the fellow, then led him forward, taking small steps.

"This is going to take a while," said Belgast. "Perhaps you're right. We should rest."

"Halt in the name of the King!" The shout echoed off the trees as a horseman emerged from the thick underbrush. Behind him came the sound of additional riders.

"Who are you?" he demanded.

"My name is Athgar, and this is Belgast Ridgehand."

"And what is your business in these parts?" More horsemen emerged from the woods.

"We are poor travellers seeking the great western woods."

The horseman approached, his eyes locking on those of Athgar. "You are a grey-eye," he said. "You have no business in Andover."

"We shall be happy to leave this place."

"I'm afraid it's too late for that. You are under arrest by order of King Dagmar."

"Come now," said Athgar. "We are no threat to you. Let us be on our way. I beg of you."

Over a dozen riders were now there, watching as their leader and three of his men dismounted.

"The penalty for trespassing for one such as you is death." He shifted his gaze to Belgast. "As for you, Master Dwarf, you're free to be on your way. I warn you, however. Interfere in the king's business, and it will go ill for you."

Belgast's hand went to the pick on his belt. "I see you're not familiar with Dwarven customs. We don't like threats."

"Seize them!" ordered the leader. Those on foot moved forward, ready to grab Athgar, but before they closed the distance, a green flame burst forth from the Therengian's hands.

"Stay back," warned Athgar. "I have no desire to hurt you, but come any closer, and I shall unleash my magic." He hoped a simple show of force would cause them to back off, but instead, to a man, they drew weapons.

"And just when I thought we were all going to get along," grumbled Belgast.

Athgar let a streak of flame erupt from his fingers as the warriors rushed forward. It lanced out, catching one of his attackers squarely on the chest, his surcoat bursting into flames. The man screamed out in fear, backing up and dropping his weapon in a vain attempt to smother the fire with his hands.

Belgast appeared at Athgar's side, pick at the ready, just as a sword struck out. A loud clang echoed off the trees as the pick stopped the blade.

Athgar sent another blast of fire at the one engaging Belgast, but it missed. Still, the enemy backed up, naked fear in his eyes. The last of the three attacked, drawing blood as he raked his sword across Athgar's thigh, who quickly drew his axe, readying for the next attack.

With a dozen warriors, the result looked like a foregone conclusion, yet Athgar had no option. He had to fight, or they would execute him—his only crime being born with grey eyes.

Then an arrow flew out of nowhere, piercing the enemy leader's throat. The man's eyes rolled up, and he collapsed, his breath coming in ragged gasps. Two more arrows flew in amongst the horsemen, knocking another from the saddle.

"Ambush!" one of them roared. "Withdraw!"

With the attack now blunted, the men desperately tried to avoid being picked off one by one. Athgar cast another fire streak, not designed to injure anyone but to frighten their horses.

A riderless mount rushed towards him, then veered off, heading deeper into the trees. By the time Athgar returned his attention to the clearing, the enemy had fled.

"Well now," said Belgast, still clutching his pick. "Looks like we found ourselves an ally or at least someone with whom we share a common enemy."

"Show yourselves," called out Athgar. "We mean you no harm. We seek only to thank our benefactors."

The leaves rustled, and then a man stepped out from behind cover. "I am Herulf."

"Aren't you one of the men who followed us back in Korvoran?"

"Aye, it was us, all right." He turned his head. "Come out and make yourself known." Two others joined him. "This is Lofwine and Osbert."

Athgar moved closer, then noted their eyes. "You're Therengian!"

"We are. Descendants of those who lived in the Old Kingdom."

"I thank you for coming to our rescue, but at the same time, I wonder why you were following us?"

"Our people noted your arrival in Korvoran. It's not often a Therengian arrives by boat, especially in the company of a mage hunter."

"You know Stanislav?"

"We know of him," said Herulf. "Our people made it our business to avoid men like him."

"Why?"

"Need you ask? They take away children and make them into agents of the Petty Kingdoms."

"To my knowledge, there are no Therengian children at the Volstrum."

"What about your sister?" asked Belgast.

"That's different," said Athgar. "The Sartellians took her."

"Ah, but it's the same family, isn't it? And look at your own situation."

"I'm not sure I follow."

"You're a master of flame, Athgar, as is your sister. I put it to you that such magic is more common amongst Therengians."

"There's no evidence to support that."

"Isn't there?" said the Dwarf. "Think about it for a moment. We know the Old Kingdom had their own mages, yet they were a landlocked country. I hardly think Water Mages would develop there."

"The Dwarf makes sense," said Herulf. "There are tales of our ancestors having such powers, and you've demonstrated an aptitude for fire. You're not from this region of the Continent, so where are you from?"

"I was born far to the east, in a village called Athelwald, but I call Runewald my home now."

"And are there other Therengians there?"

"There's an entire country of them," said Athgar. "In a place we call Therengia."

"So, the rumours are true. The Old Kingdom has returned!"

"Well, maybe not the Old Kingdom itself, but a new incarnation of it."

"Why did you come west?"

"It couldn't be helped," said Athgar. "We came to break the grip of a powerful group of mages called the Stormwinds."

"Reinwick has no Stormwinds. Not anymore."

"Yes. That's one of the reasons we travelled there in the first place. We intended to use it as a position from which to spread out and tell people about the family's duplicity."

"And why would a Therengian help those who oppress his own kind?"

"By helping others, we show how our people can be powerful allies instead of enemies. I know it's a lot to absorb, but I assure you, the entire safety of the Continent is at stake, whether or not you're a Therengian."

"What you say makes sense, but I wonder why you came to Andover. Do you not realize the danger you put yourself in?"

"I had no choice. I need to find the Ashwalkers."

"Who are?"

"A tribe of Orcs," said Athgar. "You may not know this, but there's always been a strong bond between our people and the Orcs. It is presently so in the east, just as it was in the Old Kingdom."

"But what are these western Orcs to you? Surely they are too far removed from your lands to be useful."

"They possess magic. Magic with which they can communicate over long distances. I hope to use that to communicate with those back home."

"And then?"

"That largely depends on what happens here. The rest of my group are on their way to Zienholtz in an attempt to prevent a war."

"And who are they to you?" asked Herulf. "They're not even Therengian."

"One of them is my wife, Natalia. The others are my friends. Where I'm from, we do not judge a person by the colour of their eyes. Now, it's my turn to ask a question. Why did you follow us? Surely we're nothing to you?"

"For generations, stories of the rebirth of the Old Kingdom floated around. They even foretold of one who would come and lead us to a better life."

"Such stories are nonsense," said Belgast. "You should know better than to listen to children's tales."

Herulf kept his gaze on Athgar. "And yet you came to us, not only one of our own, but a Fire Mage as well. What could be more auspicious?"

"What would you have me do?" asked Athgar.

"Let us serve you, Lord, and you can show us a way to a better life."

"I am no Saint."

"But you come with tidings from the east. Therengia is reborn, and with it, the hope of thousands of our people."

Athgar was torn. He was on an important mission to get word back to Kargen and Shaluhk, yet the man's pleas could not be easily ignored.

"I can promise you nothing," he said at last, "but if you help us with our quest here, I promise to speak to the duke on your behalf. Whether or not that will do any good, I cannot say."

Herulf glanced at his companions. "Then we are in agreement, Lord."

"My name is Athgar, not 'Lord.'"

"And yet you are now our leader. It is only proper we use the correct form of address." His gaze wandered to the bodies. "We shall see to the dead, Lord. You might consider searching for a horse while we are so engaged. By my reckoning, there should be a couple wandering loose hereabouts."

They dragged the bodies into the woods, covering them with bracken. The horses, still spooked from the fight, proved too difficult to locate. Athgar felt it wiser to continue rather than waste more time on a fruitless search.

They reached the inn as darkness fell, the soft light in its windows inviting after their ordeal. Belgast went in first to ensure none of the king's men were present. He soon reappeared at the doorway, waving them over.

The roaring fire warmed them, and they were the only guests. They took a seat as a middle-aged woman emerged from a back room.

"It's late to be out at the Drake," she said.

"The Drake?" said Athgar.

She pointed to a sign hanging on one wall.

"I would've thought a place like this would be busy this time of year," said Belgast. "What with the harvest being in and all."

"Aye," the woman replied, "and well it would be if it wasn't for the king's calling."

"The what?"

"The king's calling. He's sent word for all men of fighting age to gather in the villages."

"And the nearest village is?" said Athgar.

"Blackwing."

"Strange name for a village," grumbled the Dwarf.

"It's named after a bird," the woman replied. "Now, are you just going to sit there warming yourselves or order something to drink?"

"Drink, of course. What do you recommend?"

"We have a nice ale, or mead, if you prefer."

"Mead will be fine. Thank you."

Her gaze swept the table. "And the rest of you?"

"Ale," said Herulf.

"Yes," Athgar agreed. "Ale for all of us."

She disappeared into the back room.

"Well?" said the Dwarf. "What do you think?"

"It sounds like King Dagmar has already decided to go to war."

"No. That's not what I meant."

"Then what?"

"Do you believe that woman knows anything about the Orcs?"

"Wait for her to return, then we'll see."

They waited patiently. Their host soon reappeared carrying a tray loaded with pots of ale and the Dwarf's mead.

Athgar tossed some coins on the table, then, when the woman moved to retrieve them, he spoke. "Might I know your name?" he asked.

"Edna," she replied.

"Tell me, Edna. Have you heard any tales of the woods in these parts?"

"Tales?"

"Yes, you know—ghost stories, tales of monsters, that sort of thing. Anything to entertain a group of weary travellers?"

"I don't know about no monsters, but the fairy lights been acting up of late."

"Fairy lights, you say? You must tell us more." Athgar placed another coin on the table. "I have more, if need be. Please, share what you know."

"The woods in these parts is dark," she said, "and folk don't wander into them at night."

"Because of wild animals?"

"No. There be worse things than animals out there. Only one man ever come back out of those woods alive, and he wasn't quite himself afterwards."

"Are you saying he lost his mind?" asked Belgast.

"Aye, his mind and an arm. He claimed savages abducted him, but his story made little sense."

"In what way?"

"He said strange lights shot up out of the ground and lured him into captivity."

"I've never heard such a thing," said Athgar.

"Nor had anyone here, but the rumours persist. They say some nights, a streak of flame will shoot skyward, warning all to stay away. I'm not one to put much faith in ghost stories, but I wouldn't go more than three steps into a place with that kind of reputation."

THE KING

AUTUMN 1108 SR

As far as kings go, King Dagmar was relatively young. He'd not been meant for the Throne, but the death of his two older brothers sealed his fate. After the passing of his father, the late King Volkard, his only real family left was his older sister, Viktoria, who seldom set foot in the Palace, preferring to remain at her country estate.

Before him, bowed a woman only a bit older than himself. At first glance, she was little more than a pale foreigner with black hair, but her name spoke volumes, for she was a Stormwind.

"Greetings, Lady Natalia," said the king. "This is your first visit to Andover, is it not?"

"It is, Your Majesty."

"Are you to become a permanent fixture here at my court?"

"I am only here for a short time, Majesty, to consult with my cousins, the Sartellians."

"Ah, that explains it, then. You're here to see Lady Ria. I hope she hasn't got herself into trouble on my account?"

"Not at all. It's merely a formality, a visit to catch up on all that's been happening here and around the Continent at large."

"Fascinating," said the king. "You know, I take a strong interest in events myself. Perhaps you could see your way to having dinner with me tomorrow night. It would be marvellous to catch up on what's been unfolding of late."

"I shall certainly give it some consideration, Your Majesty, but I must warn you, I have a very tight schedule."

His voice grew frosty. "Too busy for a king?" He noted the mild look of distress and smiled. There were times when the use of absolute power was so satisfying.

"I shall endeavour to ensure it is a priority, sire."

"Good. Then I will inform my chef to create something special. I presume you're from Ruzhina?"

"Indeed."

"Excellent. I shall see what I can do to make your stay with us most satisfying. I hear they consider grilled moonfish a delicacy in Karslev."

"Indeed, it is, although my tastes run more to venison."

"Perfect," said the king. "That, we have in abundance."

"Your Majesty is too kind."

"Not at all. It is the least we can do for a distinguished guest such as yourself. Now, you must excuse me. I need to speak with my chamberlain."

With the dismissal, the woman retreated, only turning her back when she was ten paces distant. He watched her walk across the room, his thoughts elsewhere.

"Majesty?"

He turned at the interruption. "Yes? What is it?"

"The emissary from Abelard is here, Your Majesty, and wishes a private word."

"Abelard, you say? Wonderful. It's about time we heard from that backwater kingdom. Lead on, my good man, and let's see if our sowing allows us to reap a bountiful harvest."

Natalia returned to her companions.

"How did it go?" asked Galina.

"Fine, I think. He invited me to dine with him tomorrow evening."

"I'd be careful if I were you," said Stanislav. "The king is used to getting his way."

"I doubt even he would try something untoward with a Stormwind. In any case, I could hardly refuse him. We're trying to get on his good side, remember?"

"Men like that don't have a good side."

"Perhaps," said Galina, "but we still need to discover what the family's doing in Andover. The friendly ear of the king could go a long way to helping with that. I'm not suggesting you do anything that would compromise your principles, Natalia, but you might consider a little flattery. Men like that."

"I'm not about to flirt with King Dagmar. I'm a married woman, and happily so, I'll have you know."

"May I make a suggestion?" said Katrin.

"By all means," replied Natalia.

"It's not uncommon for attendants to accompany powerful women. Might I suggest I fulfill that role for you in the king's presence?"

"That's an outstanding idea."

"Yes," said Galina. "I'm surprised you remembered that after your poor showing at the Volstrum."

Katrin reddened.

Natalia locked eyes with Galina. "That was uncalled for."

"I apologize. I did not intend to offend. I was merely stating Katrin's education was incomplete."

"Her magical training was, to be sure, but we all undertook the same lessons in etiquette and courtly manners before our respective unleashing ceremonies."

"So, what's our next move?" asked Stanislav. "Confront that Sartellian woman?"

"No, at least not yet. She's already expressed an interest in our presence here at court. It would better serve our interests if she came to us."

"Why would you think that?"

"She believes me superior to her in terms of power. She might see it as unusual for us to seek her out."

"So, we just wait?"

"We can do more than just wait," replied Natalia. "I suggest we move around and mingle with the guests. Even mindless gossip could reveal something of value if we dig deep enough."

"So that's it?" said Galina. "We just wander around and talk to people?"

"I was going to suggest someone sticks close to Captain Marwen. It would be handy to know what he's up to. Does anyone care to volunteer?" They all looked at Galina.

"I'll do it," she replied, "but only because someone has to."

"Your sacrifice is duly noted," said Stanislav. Galina wandered away, looking for the good captain.

"I'm off in search of a drink," said Katrin.

"Don't go too far. We don't want to lose you." He watched her disappear into the crowd. "What was that all about, do you think?"

"What, specifically, are you referring to?" asked Natalia.

"That remark from Galina. Is there something going on we don't know about?"

"Like what, for instance?"

The mage hunter shrugged. "Galina was rude to Katrin. That doesn't seem like her, at least not the woman we've travelled with of late."

"Galina was an instructor at the Volstrum. As such, the presence of one of the Disgraced is difficult to accept."

"But we travelled all the way here together. Surely that accounts for something?"

"It does," said Natalia, "but old habits die hard. Chances are she's not even aware of the insult."

"And you believe that's all there is to it?" Stanislav shook his head. "No, there's something else. I feel it—a growing rot that has to do with her association with the captain. I shall see if I can get to the bottom of it."

"Good idea," said Natalia. "Talk to Katrin first, but let's not interrupt Galina while she's shadowing Captain Marwen. The last thing we want is the entire court witnessing an argument."

"How well do you know Galina?"

"We were in the same year at the Volstrum, but we didn't socialize, if that's what you're asking. She's a high-born and one of the girls who conspired to put magebane in my food, along with Oksana and Svetlana. Katrin did, too, although she later apologized."

"And you feel we can trust Galina?"

"She helped us fight off the family back in Karslev."

"I wish that made me feel better."

"Galina holds no love for the family. That we know first-hand, and she actively worked to thwart Marakhova's influence. How much more proof do you need?"

"I'll bear that in mind going forward." He looked around the room, taking it all in. "This is well out of my comfort zone."

"As it is mine," said Natalia.

"But you trained for this, didn't you?"

"I did, but that's a far cry from enjoying it. I'd prefer to be back in Runewald, sitting around the fire with friends, but there's work to do. If we can't break the influence of the family, we'll never get any peace."

"What do you think the odds are of actually accomplishing that?"

"Low," said Natalia, "but at least we're doing something other than waiting for them to make the next move."

"And what do you think our next move will be?"

Her gaze wandered around the room. "I shall arrange to bump into Ria Sartellian. She's currently of the belief I'm here at the family's behest. I intend on encouraging her to continue thinking so."

"The objective being?"

"To find out what they're plotting."

"I must say, you fall into the role well. Perhaps too well, if I'm being honest."

She smiled. "Don't worry. I'm in no danger of turning to their cause. I shall put on the face others expect, but only in public. You have my word."

"What do you want me to do?"

"You were a bounty hunter for a few months in Ebenstadt, weren't you?"

"I was, though most of them are unpleasant fellows. Why?"

"Bounty hunters came after me back in Draybourne, which tells me the family employs them. That being the case, it might be worth our while to learn what they've been up to of late. I get the impression you'd be much more comfortable on the streets of Zienholtz than here amongst the nobles of Andover."

"That's a splendid idea," said Stanislav, "but I don't want to leave you here alone in a nest of vipers."

"I'll be fine. You'd best get going, though."

He bowed. "I shall be delighted to accommodate your wishes, my lady."

As the evening wore on, Natalia had fleeting glimpses of Galina hanging off the arm of Captain Marwen, while Ria Sartellian proved impossible to find. She soon concluded the Fire Mage must have left the Palace entirely. Katrin finally reappeared, a smug look of satisfaction on her face.

"What are you smiling at?" asked Natalia.

"It's amazing what you overhear in a place like this."

"Oh? Are you going to share, or do you prefer to keep me in suspense?"

"I heard," said Katrin, "a certain court mage left in a huff, upset her superiors didn't see fit to warn her of your arrival. What I'm wondering is, does that work for us or against us?"

"If I'm being honest, it could be either. We must tread carefully. I shall reach out to her tomorrow and see if I can't arrange a meeting to try to smooth things over."

"And if she warns her superiors?"

"That primarily depends on how skilled she is with Fire Magic," said Natalia. "If she's powerful enough, there's the distinct possibility she can communicate over long distances. And if that's the case, our deception will be revealed sooner rather than later."

"How much sooner?"

"I would say as early as tomorrow morning, possibly even this evening, although I doubt they'd take any direct action."

"And if Ria is not powerful enough?"

"I imagine she'll send a message the old-fashioned way, by courier, and we'll be long gone by the time it reaches Karslev."

"Did her magerite ring give you any indication of her power?"

"She wore a brooch, but it was awfully dark."

"So, powerful, then?"

"I'm afraid so," said Natalia. "Which likely means time is of the essence."

"If I recall correctly, family protocol calls for her to defer to the more powerful mage."

"That is the practice, but things get a little more complicated where Sartellians and Stormwinds are concerned. We may find she insists on carrying on with her assigned mission instead of co-operating with me. In the end, it matters little, as long as we determine what they're up to."

"And how does that help us, exactly?"

"Our objective is to thwart their plans. We can hardly do that if we are ignorant of what those are."

Katrin lowered her voice. "And how, precisely, do we do that? We can't just override her orders, can we?"

"That's hard to say without knowing what those plans entail."

"And if you had to guess?"

"You've wandered amongst the guests," said Natalia. "What's the main topic of conversation, other than the Fire Mage being upset?"

"War, without a doubt. Do you think that's what Ria is up to?"

"I don't believe it would have taken much to encourage Dagmar to march his army, but there's got to be more to it."

"What makes you say that?"

"Reinwick and Andover appear well-matched. I can't see the king marching north without something to guarantee victory, can you?"

"How does one guarantee victory? A plot at the Reinwick court, perhaps?"

"No," said Natalia. "The duke has no family members amongst his advisors. It has to be something else, but I'm just not seeing it. Then again, we only just arrived."

"Perhaps a good night's sleep will help?"

"It certainly couldn't hurt. Do you know where we'll be staying?"

"Now, that," said Katrin, "I can answer. According to the good Captain Marwen, we'll be guests of His Majesty."

"Meaning?"

"The king arranged rooms for us here at the Palace. In the east wing, to be exact. Apparently, that's where all the important guests stay."

"Then let's retire, shall we?" suggested Natalia.

"Should I let Galina know?"

"Perhaps it would be best if we leave her alone for now. She looks happy entertaining Captain Marwen."

"Then I'll find someone to show us to our new lodgings."

Katrin soon returned with a servant in tow, who led them from the festivities and through the Palace's immense halls.

"You're up on the third floor," he announced.

"Third?" said Katrin. "Just how many floors are there?"

"Four, although I suppose five, if you include the lower level."

The journey to their quarters was long, but the way was easy enough to remember. However, seeing the king's warriors standing on guard in the hallway surprised them.

Natalia slowed. "Where are Captain Marwen's men?"

"Billeted in town," replied the servant. "It wouldn't be right to allow foreign troops in the Palace. In their absence, His Majesty instructed the utmost care be taken to guarantee your safety, Lady Stormwind; hence, the guards."

"And does that make me a guest or a prisoner?"

"A guest, most assuredly. Rest assured, you are free to leave your quarters anytime, my lady."

"And if I do, will guards accompany me?"

"Of course. How else can they ensure your safety?"

"How indeed," said Natalia.

The servant halted at an ornately carved door and knocked, then waited. A tall, thin fellow opened it. "Yes?"

"This is Lady Stormwind."

"Good evening, madam. My name is Deveral, and I have the honour of performing the duties of head servant during your stay here at the Palace."

"Head servant? Do you mean to imply there are more?"

"Indeed. His Majesty insisted on only the best for such a prestigious visitor."

"How many are there?" asked Katrin.

"Seven," the fellow replied. "In addition to two lady's maids, there are a pair of housemaids and someone to look after Your Ladyship's garments."

"By my count, you're missing one," said Natalia.

"That would be Greta, the youngest. Her job is to carry any messages that might be required."

"Messages?"

"Yes. Notes to the cook, requests for an audience; anything your heart desires."

"And this is normal for guests?"

"Only the most important ones," replied Deveral.

"In other words," said Natalia, "a way of ensuring the king is privy to any communications."

The head servant merely smiled. "Would you care to examine your quarters, madam?"

"Most certainly."

He swung the door open the rest of the way, revealing a large room adorned with luxurious furnishings. The remaining servants lined up to one side, looking straight ahead as if they were statues, all except for a young girl who stared at Natalia, her mouth agape.

"Greta," snapped Deveral. "Eyes to the front."

"We can dispense with the introductions," said Natalia, "but we would appreciate a quick explanation of the layout.

He pointed at a few doors. "Over there is the largest suite with a dressing room, leading into a bedroom, with a large, four-post bed. The next three doors are other guest rooms, smaller and without dedicated dressing rooms."

"And the door to the right?"

"An office, a place of refuge where you might seek some privacy to write letters or discuss matters of a private nature. Of course, you're welcome to do all that out here, in the main room."

"And where do the servants stay?"

"Elsewhere in the Palace, but young Greta will always be at your beck and call. As such, she'll sleep outside the door."

"In the hallway?"

"Naturally? Where else could such an individual sleep and still be available at all times?"

"I doubt I shall need a messenger late at night."

"Perhaps not, but one can never predict when a messenger might be required. The king strongly believes a person of import, such as yourself, should have a courier available at all hours."

"And how long will you be gracing us with your presence?" asked Natalia.

"From sun-up until you retire for the evening."

"And if I don't wish you to be present?"

"You may ask for another head servant, madam, in which case I shall make the arrangements myself."

"And if I prefer not to have any servants at all?"

He stared back, clearly at a loss for words.

"Thank you," said Natalia. "You may leave us."

"But madam, I—"

"We're retiring for the night. I trust we will see you tomorrow morning?"

He bowed reverentially. "Of course, my lady."

"As for the rest of you," she said. "You may also resume your duties on the morrow. I am capable of undressing myself."

They filed out, although with solemn faces. Greta trailed along at the tail end, then sat down in the hallway, her back to the wall.

"Good night, madam," said Deveral as he closed the door behind him.

Natalia waited until the footsteps receded, then turned to Katrin. "Please fetch me a blanket."

"Why? Are you cold?"

"No, but I imagine young Greta might appreciate it."

Katrin retrieved a blanket from her room, handing it to Natalia, who then opened the door and peered into the hallway.

"This is for you," she said as she knelt and lay the blanket over the young girl's legs.

Greta's eyes widened in disbelief. "Thank you, my lady."

"Rest easy. I shall not be needing you this evening."

TROUBLE IN NOVARSK

AUTUMN 1108 SR

Weyland looked out onto the streets of Halmund. As a Therengian, he'd spent most of his life in Runewald, but the recent war had taken him far afield. First was Ebenstadt, the great free city now part of the new Therengian Kingdom. Next, he was here, in Novarsk, staring at cobblestone streets and strange-looking buildings that appeared too massive to support their own weight.

Outside the iron gates, the commoners of Halmund went about their business, ignoring, for the most part, the occupying army. Thus, it was with some surprise Weyland spotted a mail-clad warrior heading directly for the gate, but his weapons remained sheathed, indicating he intended no threat.

"Greetings," the warrior called out. "My name is Sir Yarren of Lorodka, in service to Lord Valentyn, Baron of Krasnov, who has tasked me with delivering a message."

"What manner of message?"

"My pardon," replied the knight, reaching into his belt, pulling forth a folded and sealed letter. "I am charged with delivering this to the brute who sits in yonder Palace."

"You mean Kargen?" replied Weyland. "He's a chieftain, and you should address him as such."

The knight stared back, unsure how to respond.

"If you intend to deliver your message," continued Weyland, "I suggest you try being a little more diplomatic."

"Who are you to tell me how to behave?" said Sir Yarren. "I am a Knight of the Mailed Fist."

"And I am a member of the Thane Guard. Right now, my choice alone determines whether you can carry out your assigned duty. Will you apologize for your behaviour and meet Kargen, our chief, or do you hold fast to your beliefs, forcing you to slink back to your master, your letter undelivered?"

"You wouldn't dare!"

Weyland glared back.

The knight visibly swallowed as he contemplated his answer. Finally, he calmed. "I apologize if I offended you."

"There," said Weyland. "That wasn't so hard, was it?"

"Will you now take me to your chieftain?"

"That is not my duty."

"But you said you would take me to see him."

"No, I said I had the choice to allow you to deliver your message or not. It is my duty to bring you first to my captain. If he approves it, you will be permitted an audience with Kargen."

"Then lead on, guardsman, for the message I bear is urgent."

Weyland called over another warrior to replace him at the gate, then led Sir Yarren into the Palace, where Captain Raleth sat at a table issuing orders and receiving reports.

At their approach, the captain looked up. "Who's this?"

"A messenger," said Weyland. "Sir Yarren of Lorodka with a letter from Lord Valentyn."

Raleth looked over the newcomer. "Sir Yarren, you say?"

"Yes," said the knight. "Of the Order of the Mailed Fist."

"Who knighted you?"

"I beg your pardon?"

"Unless I'm mistaken, it's common in orders of chivalry for someone of consequence to induct you into the order. Is this not true?"

"It is," said Sir Yarren, "but I'm surprised you'd be familiar with our customs."

"Our warmaster is aware of many aspects of the Petty Kingdoms, particularly those of our foes."

"Warmaster?"

"I believe you would refer to her as a general."

"Your general is a woman?"

"Yes. Why? Does that surprise you? Was not your own ruler a queen?"

"Rada was most assuredly queen, but she hardly led the army herself. That's why we have generals."

"Then it might surprise you to know our warmaster is also a Stormwind."

The knight's eyes went wide. "A Stormwind, you say?"

Raleth smiled. "I see you recognize the name."

"I had no idea you'd gained such recognition. You must be a powerful kingdom indeed to have a mage of such renown at your court. At least, I assume you have a court?"

"We do, though it might not look like the court Rada held."

"As fascinating as that is," said Sir Yarren, "the fact remains I have a message to deliver."

"Give it to me, and I'll ensure it is placed into the chieftain's hands."

"I cannot do that, for I swore to deliver it in person. Will you take me to see him?"

"No," said Raleth. "I'm much too busy for such things, but I will allow Weyland here to escort you in my stead."

"Are you sure, Captain?" asked Weyland. "I am but a guard."

"Even a guard has the right to be in the presence of his thane. You know the way?"

"I do."

"Then take this knight to see the acting High Thane, but keep your eyes on him. I trust him not."

Wynfrith stared down at what passed for a map of Novarsk. It was a poor rendering, as such things went, with no indication of scale or even which edge represented north. "Is this the best we could do?"

"I am afraid so," said Shaluhk. "This was taken directly from the queen's council chamber and bears the Royal Mapmaker's mark."

"I assumed a realm as powerful as this would put a greater effort into making this more accurate. According to this, we should have marched an extra week to reach Halmund, and this river here"—she stabbed down with a finger—"runs into the mountains rather than out of them. Have these people no pride in their work?"

"The question," added Kargen, "is whether it accurately represents the baron's lands."

"Difficult to say. We could set off for Krasnov and end up in the middle of nowhere!"

A knock drew their attention.

"Come," said Kargen.

The door opened, revealing the guard Weyland, along with a visitor.

"Greetings," said the knight, stepping into the room and bowing to Wynfrith. "I am Sir Yarren of Larodka," he said. "I come bearing a message from my lord, Valentyn Sayenko, Baron of Krasnov."

"It is not me you should talk to," replied the Thane of Bradon, "is it Kargen."

The visitor's gaze flicked to the Orc, then back. "And who is to read him the message?"

"Why do you assume he cannot read?"

"Everyone knows the Orcs don't use a written language. They are incapable of literacy."

"You presume too much," said Shaluhk. "While it is true Orcs have no written language of their own, we of the eastern tribes use the common tongue of Humans to send dispatches." She held out her hand.

Sir Yarren withdrew the letter from his belt and handed it over. The shaman, in turn, passed it to Kargen, who broke the seal and perused its contents.

The room fell silent while the Orc chieftain finished reading. He handed it to Shaluhk before turning to face their visitor. "Are you aware of this message's contents?"

"I am, and I am ready to take whatever punishment you deem fit."

"Punishment? I am afraid you need to explain that to me."

"It is common amongst the Petty Kingdoms for the bearer of bad news to be executed. I only hope I can do so in a stoic manner."

"What a barbaric practice," said Shaluhk.

"Agreed," added Kargen. "And they call us savages."

"It is a sacrifice I am willing to make," continued Yarren. "I am not afraid to give my life in service to my lord."

"Then you are a fool," said Wynfrith. "Fighting for a cause is honourable, but dying for one man's ego serves no purpose."

Shaluhk held out the letter to Wynfrith, but the Thane of Bradon showed no interest in taking it. "I am not one for flowery words. Perhaps you might summarize its contents?"

"By all means," said Shaluhk. "It is an ultimatum. It claims the people of Novarsk do not recognize Therengia's right to rule over their land. It goes on to say that if we do not vacate the territory immediately, they shall consider a state of war to exist again between our two peoples and act accordingly."

"Do they not understand that we defeated their army?"

"Apparently not."

"And what gives Lord Valentyn such new-found confidence?"

"It is not only Lord Valentyn," said Shaluhk. "All the barons of Novarsk put their names to this."

Wynfrith looked at Kargen. "You are acting High Thane. Will you give in to these demands?"

"No, of course not," he replied. "While the barons assembled their forces, so, too, did we."

"We have you outnumbered," said Sir Yarren. "You cannot hope to win."

"We are in precisely the same situation as we were at the start of the war. You had us outnumbered then, and it made little difference."

"How much time have we?" asked Wynfrith.

Kargen consulted the message. "They generously decided to give us two days to quit the capital." His gaze fell on the knight. "If your masters put their efforts into bettering the lives of common folk rather than suppressing them, they would yield a far more successful hunt. Instead, they spend vast amounts equipping and fielding large armies with which to oppress their own people. I am sure I speak for the High Thane when I say under Therengian rule, this behaviour will no longer be tolerated."

"And where is this High Thane of yours? Does he even exist, or is he merely an invention to placate your enemies? Who truly rules in Therengia?"

Kargen moved closer, his breath menacing the knight. "Let there be no doubt. Athgar, son of Rothgar, rules Therengia, and were he here today, he would refuse these demands just as I do."

"Yet he refuses to show his face. Is the man a coward?"

"If you knew him, you would not question his bravery or his decisions. As I act in his name, I refuse your master's demands. Since the baron is so intent on fomenting rebellion, you may inform him we have stripped him of his title and forfeited his lands. He is a baron no longer."

"You possess no authority to do that," said Sir Yarren. "Only the ruler of Novarsk can make such a judgement."

"Answer me this," said Kargen. "Who currently occupies the Royal Palace in Halmund, this very building?"

The fire went out of the knight's eyes. "You do."

"Then I have precisely the authority I require for such a measure. By his own hand, Lord Valentyn condemns himself." He turned to the guard. "Weyland, escort this man from the premises."

"I shall not forget this," said Sir Yarren. "Nor will His Lordship look kindly upon this decision."

"Nor would I expect him to, but there are consequences to a person's actions, even for a baron."

"This way," said Weyland. "Your audience is at an end."

Weyland led Sir Yarren back through the Palace in silence. Only as they arrived at the main entrance did the knight finally speak.

"You're making a terrible mistake."

"You are the ones threatening rebellion," said Weyland. "We defeated your army once; we can do so again."

"Ah, but this time we are fighting in our home territory."

"You lost at Heronwood, and we captured your queen. Are you suggesting the village magically transported to another kingdom?"

"Rada was a fool. Lord Valentyn—" He cut himself off.

"Is what? An even bigger fool?"

Sir Yarren halted, wheeling to face the guardsman. "You fooled us at Heronwood, I'll give you that, but you have no idea who you're dealing with now. Your little army of misfits won't be able to use the same trick twice."

"We don't need tricks to defeat the likes of you."

"Really?" The knight poked Weyland in the chest. "That chain shirt of yours won't stand up to the men of Krasnov. You won't be dealing with a peasant levy next time but a highly trained army of professional warriors."

"More professional than Temple Knights?"

The statement caught the fellow off guard. "What are you talking about?"

"When you get back to Krasnov, I suggest you ask someone about what you people call the Battle of the Wilderness. I think you'll find it quite illuminating."

"Bah. You're just trying to get into my head. Well, it won't work."

"It matters not whether you believe me, but it is the truth. On that battlefield, the Temple Knights of Saint Cunar sent everything they had at us. I should know—I was there."

Seeds of doubt crept into the knight's thoughts. "What happened?"

"They died to a man, and let me tell you, there were hundreds of them."

"You took no prisoners?"

"They gave no quarter nor asked for any in return. We offered them the opportunity to surrender, but they chose to die with their swords in their hands rather than dishonour their vows. Is that the fate you want for your fellow countrymen?"

"How can you be so sure it won't be us who defeats you?"

"I have faith in my leaders."

"As do I," said Sir Yarren, "but faith alone will not win battles. It takes skill at arms, which we have in abundance."

"Yet not in such numbers as to be able to defeat us, it appears, or are you now trying to claim you held back your best warriors at Heronwood?"

"You impress me," said the knight. "Though the same cannot be said of your chieftain." He shook his head. "If only you could see things as I do. Imagine the army we could field if you Therengians would only throw off the shackles of your masters and join with us. It would be like the great kingdom of old."

"You perceive us as under the thumb of our rulers because of how you choose to rule your land. In Therengia, the thanes serve the people, not the other way around. I serve not out of a sense of fear but of pride and honour."

"Traits we of Novarsk share. Come now, you are a warrior. Is it not right that we should be set above others? Those like us are born to fight; it is in our blood. You of all people should recognize that."

"You think I fight because I'm born to it? Nothing could be further from the truth. I am a simple man by nature, born to work the fields of my home. I only stand here a warrior because of men like you. Had your queen not invaded our soil, I would be back in Runewald, reaping my harvest. Instead, I am forced to take up arms and leave such work to others."

"What of it? Harvesting is women's work."

"Women's work, is it? Then I imagine it would surprise you to know many of our warriors are women."

"Come now," said Yarren. "I appreciate a good jest when I hear it, but that pushes credibility a little too far, don't you think?"

"It's true. I swear it. Furthermore, I would put any of those women against your own so-called warriors and expect them to be victorious. However, I must warn you, Therengian women can be brutal on the battle-field and are not known for their mercy."

"That subject would benefit from further discussion, I'm sure, but I fear the next time we meet, it shall be on the opposite sides of a battlefield. I would wish you well, but in truth, I hope your army is utterly destroyed, its warriors left as food for ravens."

"Then there is no more to speak of," said Weyland, "other than to part ways." He paused, taking in the full measure of the knight. "The next time I see you, it will be to end your life."

Yarren chuckled. "You are welcome to try, my friend, but many have attempted that very thing only to end up in the Afterlife." He walked through the gate and never looked back.

"Trouble?" came the voice of Raleth.

"Are all knights so haughty?"

"My experience with such things is limited. The few I met proved humble, but then again, they were Temple Knights of Saint Mathew or Saint Agnes. As for the Knights of the Mailed Fist, they serve lords who think highly of themselves. Small wonder, then, that their servants think the same."

"He seems very confident of his abilities."

"With good reason. He has likely spent a lifetime preparing for war. To think otherwise would, in his mind, be an admission that he'd wasted all those years. I might not know any of them personally, but I know what it is to understand the mind of an enemy."

"Can we truly defeat them?"

"They are not the first we've faced who claimed to be invincible, nor, I fear, will they be the last."

"You speak of the Cunars?"

"I do. We defeated them at Ord-Kurgad, yet the order would have us think otherwise. As for Sir Yarren's order? Well, we beat them once; we can do so again."

"But our warmaster is not amongst us!"

"I might remind you, Kargen's hunters won the day when they flanked the enemy and captured Queen Rada. Do not underestimate our acting High Thane. That is our enemy's job, and the more they discount his abilities, the greater the advantage we shall have."

"So, we must fight them again?"

"Yes," said Raleth, "but this time, we'll give them a defeat from which they can never recover."

ASHWALKERS

AUTUMN 1108 SR

A mist clung to the trees as Athgar and Belgast made their way into the great forest, with the three Therengians they'd recently met trailing behind. Occasionally, a streak of light pierced the dense canopy, burning off the tendrils of white that obstructed their view.

By mid-morning, the mist had cleared, yet the humidity clung to them like a leech. It appeared summer wanted one last gasp before the icy winds of winter descended upon the land.

There was no trail to speak of nor any sign of Orcs that Belgast could see, but he trusted Athgar not to lead them astray.

At noon, they stopped by a stream to rest, the cloying air covering everyone in sweat. Trying to find a bit of relief, Osbert removed his tunic, dipping it in the stream and then using it to wipe his face. Lofwine, less energetic, flopped down on the ground, finding a nice patch of shade to avoid the sun.

Herulf took half a dozen steps to find a place to relieve himself but suddenly stopped. "Lord," he called out. "I found something."

Athgar moved closer. "What is it?"

"I'm not sure. A hunter's mark, perhaps?"

Athgar knelt, pulling away a small seedling to expose the tree behind. "That's no hunter's mark, at least not a Human one. That's an Orc rune. It appears we've entered the Ashwalkers' hunting grounds."

"Are you sure?"

"There can be no doubt it's Orcish in nature, although I cannot confirm which tribe. It's unlikely two such tribes would hunt in the same region, though."

"They do back in Therengia," said Belgast.

"Yes, but according to Kargen, that's the exception, not the rule. Tribes rarely cross into each other's territories."

"Why's that?" asked Herulf. "Are they hostile to one another?"

"Not at all, but they are very aware of overhunting an area."

"Overhunting?"

"Yes. They are careful not to hunt too much game in one region for fear it will affect future hunts. Think about it for a moment: the last thing you'd want is to kill all the deer in the area. How would future generations eat?"

"But surely there are enough deer for everyone?"

"We Humans hunt little since we adopted the practice of raising livestock. On the other hand, the Orcs' entire way of life is based around hunting. In a sense, it is the very backbone of their existence."

"And they can strip an area of all its meat?"

"I presume you've never met an Orc," said Athgar. "They are larger than Humans and require more meat to sustain them."

"How much larger?" asked Lofwine, peering up from his place of repose.

"In height, they are much like us, but broader of shoulder and thicker of chest. Of course, they vary in size, same as we do, so I'm talking in generalities here."

"And is it true they eat the flesh of Humans?" asked Osbert.

Athgar laughed. "You've been listening to too many children's tales. To answer your question, no, they do not. I should also point out they eat things other than meat. Shaluhk, for example, makes a delicious porridge."

"Shaluhk?" said Herulf.

"Orc Shaman of the Red Hand."

The Therengian archer stared down at the mark. "Perhaps I should find somewhere else to relieve myself?"

"Probably a good idea," said Athgar.

The fellow moved deeper into the woods. Moments later came a popping sound, and then a streak of fire shot up into the air, rising high enough to penetrate the canopy of leaves.

"What was that?" shouted Osbert.

"Stay here," said Athgar, his senses immediately on the alert. "Herulf," he called out. "Can you hear me?"

"I'm all right," came the reply. "I've set off a trap, I think."

Athgar moved through the forest, taking his time, carefully watching his step. He soon found Herulf standing on a fallen log, too afraid to move for fear of triggering another trap.

The location where the flames erupted was easy to spot, for all around it was singed greenery. Athgar moved closer, stopping to investigate. "This is the work of magic," he said. "Though what spell they used is beyond my understanding."

"But you're a Fire Mage," said Herulf. "Are you suggesting this is some other type of magic?"

"No, it's Fire Magic, all right, just not a spell with which I'm familiar. I imagine it acts like some sort of sentry to warn them when someone is in their territory."

"You mean it's not supposed to kill? You could have surprised me. That flame shot up past the highest tree."

"If they meant to hurt you, you'd already be dead. We've obviously entered their territory. The question now is, in which direction do we head?" He looked again at the singed plant life, then cast his gaze around the area. "We're close to that stream. I imagine that marks the border of their hunting grounds. I suggest we go west. What do you think?"

"I am more than willing to follow your lead, Lord, but in future, I'll not wander as far from camp when nature calls."

"That would probably be for the best," replied Athgar.

As they proceeded through the forest, the day grew hotter, the trees thicker, and the underbrush more restrictive. By late afternoon, they were using their axes to cut a path through the plants obstructing their way.

Athgar had just cleared one when he noticed all noise in the woods suddenly stopped. He halted, twisting his head left and right, attempting to spot anything that might indicate what was happening.

Belgast, noting his companion's actions, moved up. "Problem?" he said, keeping his voice low.

"We're being watched."

"By what? An animal? You're not about to tell me there's a bear to fight, are you?"

In answer, Athgar called out in Orcish. "*We mean you no harm. I am Athgar of the Red Hand.*"

The reply came quickly. "*How is it that a torkul knows our tongue?*"

"*I am tribe brother to Kargen, Chief of the Red Hand. I myself am a master of flame, taught by the great master himself, Artoch.*"

An Orc emerged from behind a tree. "*I am Zhogral, hunter of the Ashwalkers. Why have you come here?*"

"*I come seeking a shaman.*"

"*Are you injured?*"

"*No, but I need to contact Shaluhk of the Red Hand. Long has it been since I set foot in the woods of my home, and I would know how my brothers and sisters fare.*"

"*Who travels in your company?*"

"The Dwarf, Belgast Ridgehand, along with three of my own people: Herulf, Lofwine, and Osbert."

Zhogral moved closer, soon joined by half a dozen others who appeared from the woods.

"Follow me, Athgar, master of flame, and I shall take you to meet our chieftain, Rugal." The Orc turned and moved off swiftly, forcing the rest to catch up.

"Where are we going?" called out Herulf.

"To meet their chief," replied Athgar.

The Ashwalkers, being a wandering people, lived in a camp instead of a village—a collection of lean-tos and tents, primarily constructed of branches and the skins of animals.

Zhogral led them past several younglings gathered about a fire, tossing a small ball of flame back and forth. The scene fascinated Athgar.

"What are they doing?" he asked.

"You must ask our own master of flame, Marag. Only she can explain the ways of her pupils."

"How many flame wielders do you have?"

"Six, if you include the younglings we just passed. Of those, three are reckoned as masters, but none rival the power of Marag herself."

The Ashwalkers took a keen interest in the newcomers, a few even drawing closer for a better view. Athgar welcomed their enquiries, answering questions as he walked, but the other Therengians looked decidedly uncomfortable with being in such close quarters with so many Orcs. They finally halted before a large Orc, a golden torc hanging from his neck.

"I am Rugal," he announced loudly in his native tongue. *"Chieftain of the Ashwalkers."*

"Greetings, Rugal. I am Athgar, son of Rothgar, master of flame and member of the Red Hand."

The Orc stared back, his manner giving no clue about his disposition. After a moment, he looked at Zhogral.

"The others look to this Human as their leader," said the hunter.

"And these others, do they have names?"

"The Dwarf is named Belgast. The torkul are Herulf, Lofwine, and Osbert."

The chieftain broke into a grin. *"It has been ages since we welcomed another tribe to our home. Come, sit, and we shall drink of the milk of life."*

"What did he say?" asked Herulf.

"He invited us for a drink," said Belgast.

"Ah, now that's what I call hospitality!"

· · ·

That evening they all sat around a fire.

"*This,*" said Rugal, indicating the Orc next to him, "*is Marag, our master of flame.*"

"*Greetings,*" she replied. "*It is an honour to meet such a rare individual. A torkul who can wield fire. Did I hear Orcs taught you?*"

"*Indeed,*" replied Athgar. "*My master was an elder named Artoch and was the last master of flame amongst the Red Hand until I came along. However, the same can not be said of the Ashwalkers, for it appears you are blessed with many.*"

"*We are fortunate in that regard. Perhaps, on the morrow, you would like to meet the others? I am sure they would enjoy the chance to get another tribe's perspective on things.*"

"*I would enjoy that very much. Thank you.*"

"*Now,*" said the chieftain. "*As to our shaman, he will join us shortly. In the meantime, can you tell us more about our distant cousins to the east?*"

"*The Orcs of that region formed a confederation with my people,*" said Athgar, "*in a land called Therengia. Perhaps you've heard of it?*"

"*I have, though only as a reference to the kingdom of old. Tell me, how many tribes are part of this confederation?*"

"*Four, at present. Along with the Red Hand are the Stone Crushers, the Black Axe, and the Cloud Hunters. We do, however, have room for plenty more, should they appear.*"

"*I am told it was thus in the kingdom of old as well.*"

"*It was,*" said Athgar, "*or so our scholars informed us.*"

"*And how did this confederation come about?*"

"*Borne out of necessity. The east was a refuge for my people after the growth of the Petty Kingdoms drove them into the wilderness.*"

The chieftain nodded. "*I am familiar with the threat. Our own Ancestors came here to evade the very same menace, though it appears our territory is shrinking. The Humans hereabouts do not tolerate those of our persuasion amongst them, so we continue to move deeper into the forest we now call home. The Ashwalkers became a wandering people, constantly on the move to avoid conflict with Humans.*"

"*Am I interrupting?*"

Everyone looked up at the tall Orc, his skin darker green than most, his hair tinged with grey, yet he stood proud, as one of fewer seasons.

"*Ah,*" said Rugal. "*Vagrath is here at last. Come, my friend. Join us, and we shall partake of the milk of life.*"

The shaman sat, reaching behind his chieftain to retrieve a wooden bowl and what looked like a wineskin. From this, he poured a milky liquid into the bowl, filling it almost to the brim. "*Let us now drink of the milk of life.*" He lifted the bowl and took a sip before passing it to Rugal. The chieftain, in turn, did likewise, handing it to his right.

Marag eventually gave it to Athgar, but before drinking, he looked at his Therengian brothers. "Take only a sip," he warned in the Human tongue. "The milk of life can be strong." He then took his own measure of the milky-white substance. He had participated in this ceremony many times before, for the Red Hand used it to celebrate any occasion of significance. However, he wasn't prepared for its impact on him this day.

It had barely touched his lips when his body started to shake. Someone took the bowl from his grasp as he fell backwards, his vision blurring. He saw himself running through the woods, axe in hand, into a battle, though whom he fought was impossible to comprehend. He emerged into a field, where a large army stood before him. The scene suddenly shifted, and he stood amongst a group of Orcs. One of them uttered the words of power, producing a ball of flame hovering over their hand. Moments later, they tossed it to the next, the ball growing in intensity as this new Orc added to the flames' power. It moved to a third, and then the ball was tossed his way. He caught it, feeling the heat as his own magic brought it to an intensity he wouldn't have imagined possible.

His eyes snapped open. Belgast stared down at him. "For Gundar's sake, Athgar. You had us worried there for a moment."

"What happened?"

"You passed out after you took a sip of milk."

Vagrath loomed into view, moving close to stare into his eyes. "*He had a vision,*" the shaman announced.

"*I did,*" said Athgar, replying in the tongue of the Orcs. "*How did you know?*"

The shaman chuckled. "*You are not the first to receive such a blessing. Tell us, what did you see?*"

"*There was a battle,*" he replied. "*Though I couldn't make out who we were fighting.*"

"*And?*"

"*A group of Orcs tossing a ball of fire. They threw it to me, and I made it even hotter.*"

The shaman looked at Marag. "*What do you make of that?*"

"*It appears,*" mused the master of flame, "*that the time has finally come to make a stand.*"

Rugal stood, searching out a nearby hunter. "*Zhogral, gather all the hunters. Tell them the moment to move is nigh.*"

"*I don't understand,*" said Athgar. "*What's happening?*"

"*The time is coming when we must fight for our very existence. Your vision has told us that.*"

"*But wasn't it only a dream?*"

"*So some would have you believe. In truth, the milk of life links us to the Ancestors. They are who send such visions into our minds, though whether they are warnings or a prophecy of what is to come is a matter for some discussion.*"

"*But couldn't you head farther west?*"

"*These woods are not infinite. Should we move farther west, we risk conflict with the Human realm of Burgemont. No. Our time of wandering has come to an end. Like many of our folk, we need to find a permanent home, a village where we can prosper.*"

"*Agreed,*" said Rugal. "*But where? The vision speaks of battle but does not tell us where we will find it.*"

"*The only conflict I'm aware of,*" said Athgar, "*is the impending war between Reinwick and Andover, two Human realms lying to your east. Could that be what I saw in my vision?*"

"*It would seem the logical conclusion.*"

"*But why would the Ashwalkers concern themselves with a Human conflict?*"

They all looked at Vagrath, their faces hopeful.

"*I know not the answer to this riddle,*" said the shaman, "*but perhaps the answer has yet to reveal itself.*"

"*Perhaps,*" said Marag. "*In the meantime, we should rest. A good night's sleep would not go amiss.*"

"*Agreed,*" replied Vagrath. "*I shall show our guests where they can lie down.*"

"*A moment, Athgar,*" said Marag. "*I would have words.*" She waited until everyone left before continuing. "*It is no accident you came to us in our time of need. The Ancestors must have heard our pleas for help.*"

"*Surely you're not suggesting I was fated to find you? I'm only looking for a way to contact my family.*"

"*Then does your presence here not serve us both? Let us make a pact, Athgar, son of Rothgar. I will arrange for Vagrath to send a message to your family, but you, in return, will learn the ways of the Ashwalkers. I sense great power within you. It is now time you learned how to harness it properly.*"

"*But I already know how to harness my inner spark.*"

Marag smiled, showing her ivory teeth. "*There is more to harnessing your spark than simply producing flames. You saw the younglings playing with a ball of fire, yes?*"

"*I did, but what has that to do with anything? Surely you're not suggesting the younglings are to play a part in this war?*"

"*No, never that. It is a difficult thing to explain, especially to an outsider. Come, and instead, I will show you."* She led Athgar through the camp, stopping by a smaller fire near its periphery. *"This is Snaga, one of our masters of flame."*

"Greetings to you," said Athgar.

"And you," replied the elderly Orc.

Marag continued, *"Snaga here, like me, is an Ashwalker."*

"Aren't you all?" asked Athgar.

"Perhaps I should clarify. It is because of us, the clan bears the name Ashwalker. Snaga, myself, and all our masters of flame can pass through fire without taking damage. Naturally, it requires preparation, but that is part of our training."

"Are you suggesting I'm going to learn to walk through a bonfire?"

"Not at present, but maybe a demonstration might help explain what you saw in your vision?"

"Very well."

Marag conjured a ball of fire only a hand's span in diameter, floating right above her hand. She nodded to Snaga, who made a similar gesture, and waited. Marag tossed the flame to her companion, and Athgar watched it grow in intensity.

"What you are seeing," she explained, *"is a feat known as the fire chain. As we pass the fire to each Ashwalker in turn, they add their own power to it. In this way, we create a much more powerful result without straining any single caster."*

Snaga tossed it back, and the ball grew hotter.

"As you can see," she continued, *"it does not grow in size, but its heat increases with each passing. Were we to do this enough times, it would be hot enough to melt iron."*

"And you allow younglings to play with this spell?"

"Fear not. They are performing a lesser spell that produces only light, not heat. However, it serves as a useful training exercise. Now, are you ready to unleash the full power of your inner spark?"

"I am."

"Then let us begin."

OUTMANOEUVRED

AUTUMN 1108 SR

"Have we heard from Galina?" asked Natalia. "I haven't seen her yet today."

"She's out walking with Captain Marwen," said Katrin. "That seems to be her new morning ritual."

"Yes. I noticed that." She looked across the room to where Stanislav was choosing nuggets from a selection of cheese. "Stanislav? Your thoughts?"

The mage hunter glanced at the servants before answering. "Regarding?"

"Captain Marwen and Galina?"

He pursed his lips as he thought about a response. "They make a handsome couple," he finally said grudgingly.

"And as to the captain's intentions?"

"From all that I could discover, they are honourable. In fact, he's gone out of his way to be courteous and respectful these last few days."

Natalia returned her attention to Katrin. "And has Ria Sartellian indicated she wanted to meet with us?"

"Her aide said she was out of the capital for a few days but promised a visit would be a priority upon her return." She paused, reluctant to say more.

"And?" said Natalia.

"I'm afraid His Majesty, the king, cancelled dinner arrangements yet again."

"That's the third time this week. Have we somehow insulted him?"

"If I may?" interjected Deveral. "The king is known to have a weak disposition."

"Are you suggesting he's ill?"

"Not ill so much as indisposed. On such occasions, he tends to remain in bed for most of the day. It's his stomach, you see. It troubles him."

"Has he seen a physician?"

"Several, but they all claim the same thing, blaming it on his diet."

"Has he considered changing it?"

"Let's just say His Majesty can be a force of nature when required."

"Meaning he won't listen to them."

"Precisely."

"It appears we once again find ourselves with little to do." Natalia turned to Stanislav once more. "Any more news from the city?"

"None, I'm afraid. I made some enquiries, but I don't expect any replies for another day or two."

"A pity."

A knock on the door drew everyone's attention. Deveral quickly moved to open it, revealing none other than Ria Sartellian herself.

"Is Natalia Stormwind available?" she asked.

"One moment, and I shall see." Deveral closed the door before he turned to face the room. "It is Lady Ria, madam. Shall I admit her?"

"Yes, of course."

He opened the door, then bid the Fire Mage to enter.

"Come in," said Natalia. "Can we fetch you something to drink?"

"No, thank you," said Ria.

"We'll use the study. That way, we'll have some privacy. Katrin, I would like you to keep an eye on the servants and ensure they don't wander too close to the door."

"Yes, mistress."

"Good. Now, if you'll follow me, Ria, we'll get to work."

Natalia led her visitor into the side room, then closed the door and took a seat.

"I'm sorry to have taken so long to meet with you," said Ria, "but I was out of the city."

"So I heard. I trust all is well?"

"As well as can be expected when coordinating something of this complexity."

"And you are convinced everything will go according to the plans already set into motion?"

"To be honest, it's an unnecessary complication. Dagmar's forces are more than sufficient to ensure victory without all this additional bother, but you know how the family can be. Ultimately, we will defeat Reinwick and put our advisors back into the duke's court."

"I suppose the problem," said Natalia, "is whether or not the duke will still have a court. Dagmar could well insist on placing the entire region under his rule."

Ria shrugged. "It matters little in the long term. We would still have his ear and control of the northern waters. It wouldn't take us long to be rid of the Holy Fleet. Why? Do you not favour war?"

"I'm not convinced it's the best way to achieve our goals. Sometimes the threat is more effective than the action itself."

"An interesting observation, but I doubt the duke will welcome us back with open arms. We can thank the blasted Temple Knights for that. Don't get me wrong; threats have their uses. That's how we get the job done ninety percent of the time, but there comes the point where we must push for war."

"You've obviously given this a lot of thought," said Natalia. "But my superiors are not convinced."

"You mean to call it off?"

"I am here to gather information only. It is not my decision whether or not this plan proceeds. To that end, I need more details. For example, how do the numbers stack up?"

"Dagmar has worked diligently to increase the size of his army. His father's death ended the restrictions Erlingen imposed after Andover's attempted invasion, and he's eager to see his forces put to the test."

"I understand enthusiasm, but what is your honest evaluation of his army's capabilities? Can they defeat Reinwick?"

"I've been asking this question for months."

"And your answer?"

"If the two armies faced off in the field," said Ria, "I would say Dagmar has a clear advantage in terms of numbers. Of course, there's the matter of morale, a difficult thing to account for even in the best of times. However, I think that in this instance, Andover also has the advantage there."

"What makes you so confident?"

"Reinwick is their traditional rival, and their warriors are eager to erase the shame of their defeat under King Volkard. None of this matters much in the long run, as it's doubtful Reinwick will be able to field its entire army."

Natalia smiled. "I assume that explains your absence from the capital?"

"It does. We've arranged the full support of his allies. Come next spring, Reinwick will be under our complete control once more. Now, as to whether that's under Duke Wilfhelm or King Dagmar remains to be seen."

"You appear to have everything under your control. Might I ask how long it took you to devise this plan?"

"I've been working on it for nigh on five years. The letter from Korascajan, which started the process, arrived back in oh-three, but they only spoke in grand terms, leaving the specifics up to me."

"And the timetable? Was that yours?"

"They gave me seven years to complete the assignment, but with a bit of luck, I'll finish in less than six."

"I'm impressed," said Natalia, "but I must admit to some concerns. Dagmar appears to be the weak link in all of this. What if he changes his mind? After all, if he lost, it could well be the end of Andover. I doubt another military defeat would go unpunished by his neighbours."

"The king's lived with the shame of his father's defeat for years. I don't think we could dissuade him from war even if we wanted to. Not only does he favour the plan, but I convinced him it was one of his own devising. He'll march; the only question is when."

"You don't have a date in mind?"

"Oh, we have several," said Ria, "but there are outside influences with whom we must coordinate."

"And when will those be settled?"

"By month's end, assuming all goes to plan."

"And if it doesn't?"

"Then we shall push back our plans for a month."

"Are you suggesting a winter campaign?"

"I am."

"You realize that goes against all conventional wisdom?"

"The cold weather affects both sides, but Dagmar has Fire Mages to back him up, while Duke Wilfhelm has none."

"Are you suggesting the family will take direct action in battle? That's almost unheard of."

"I admit it surprised me, too, but we cannot accept our losses in Reinwick. We must show everyone our power, not only in terms of influence but also in our military might. The moment for more overt action is at hand."

They sat in silence for a time.

"I assume you approve of the plan?" said Ria.

"I shall take some time to digest it before making my final recommendation, but my initial opinion is that it has merit. I will be certain to mention your thoroughness to those higher up."

"Thank you. That means a lot to me. I shan't keep you any longer. I'm sure you'd like some time to consider everything I told you."

"Yes," said Natalia. "And thank you for being so candid."

She escorted her guest out of the office, then let Deveral show her the door. She waited until Ria left before continuing. "Katrin, Stanislav? If you have a moment, I'd like a word."

They both made their way into the study. Natalia ensured the door was closed, then took a seat.

"Well?" said Stanislav. "Did you learn anything?"

"Plenty, but I can't be sure how much of it's true."

"You suspect she's lying to you?"

"I'm not sure, but she left out a lot of details."

"Such as?"

"She hinted at an ally but never named who it was. I would not expect such things from another member of the family."

"Really?" said Stanislav. "The family even plots against itself. I imagine she fears you taking the credit for all her hard work. I bet she's holding back the details to ensure she can claim it as her own."

"Could she be feeding us false information?" asked Katrin.

"To what end?" said the mage hunter.

"Natalia said Ria was powerful. If she's contacted Korascajan, or even Karslev, wouldn't she know your true purpose here?"

"But if that were the case, why reveal anything at all? Wouldn't it be better to simply capture her?"

"They can't," said Katrin. "We're under the king's protection. Such an overt act would ruin any chance of co-operation from King Dagmar."

"So, they feed us false information instead?"

"We should confirm the information she presented," said Natalia.

"And how do we do that?" asked Stanislav.

"Armies march on their stomachs, and you can't move hundreds or thousands of warriors without a significant amount of wagons and supplies. If there's an army preparing for a campaign, there'll be evidence of it."

"And if we find these wagons?"

"We count them. It won't give us their exact army strength, but it will provide an educated guess."

"Anything else?" asked Katrin.

"Yes. Ria hinted they had at least one ally lined up, but we need to discover whom."

"The logical choice would be Eidolon," said Stanislav. "The only other kingdoms that could send troops across the border without antagonizing their own neighbours would be Langwal or Burgemont, and they'd both need to march through a thick forest."

"That makes sense, but how big an army would Eidolon be willing to supply?"

"Enough to guarantee victory," offered Katrin, "but your guess is as good as mine."

"So, how do we counter that threat?" asked Stanislav.

"We tell the duke to muster every man he can and send them south. I don't suppose the Temple Knights would condescend to help?"

"I wouldn't count on it," said Natalia. "They're sworn to neutrality."

"So that's it?" said Katrin. "We return to Reinwick and report what we discovered?"

"Stanislav still has yet to confirm some numbers, and we are also waiting on Captain Marwen, but other than that, it would appear we're done."

"Is it only me," said Stanislav, "or did all this seem just a little too easy?"

"What are you suggesting?" asked Natalia.

"Perhaps I'm just getting old, but Ria Sartellian only met you a few days ago, and now she tells you all about the plan to defeat Reinwick?"

"Natalia outranks her," offered Katrin, "and you know what a stickler for protocols the family is."

"I'm still not convinced."

"Even if your suspicions are warranted," said Natalia, "what could we possibly do about it?"

"Not much, admittedly."

Gregori Stormwind looked up from his desk as Ria Sartellian entered his study. The interruption was annoying, to say the least, and to add insult to injury, she'd not even knocked. Rather than lose his temper, he took a breath and finished his letter. He slowed his pace, deliberately choosing to make her wait. She shuffled her feet as he signed his name.

"Yes?" He looked up from his work with feigned surprise. "Ah, Ria. I trust all went according to plan?"

"I did as you asked, Master Gregori, but I don't know whether or not she believed me."

"That matters little in the long run. We presented her with information she cannot ignore, for doing so could cause the loss of Reinwick."

"I still don't understand why she's here, in the north."

"Nor do I, but then again, I gave up trying to keep track of her where-abouts some time ago."

"You taught her at the Volstrum, didn't you?"

"In a manner of speaking, yes. I helped tutor her and another student, but they later banished that one."

"Why do we not simply arrest her?" asked Ria.

"For one thing, we're not in Ruzhina. The family is powerful; never forget that, but even we have our limitations. Also, there is the matter of appearances. Were we to take such a bold move, it would come to light that there are malcontents within our family, doing grievous damage to our reputation."

"And so, we let her have the run of the place? Is that not dangerous in and of itself?"

"Fear not," said Gregori. "The matter is well in hand."

"And will you ever reveal yourself?"

"Not for the present. For this scheme to work, Natalia must think her ruse has succeeded. You already gained her trust; the trick now will be to reveal, by subtle hints, that which we want her to believe."

"And you don't think she'll catch on?"

"She may suspect we're up to something, and of course, we are. In that sense, there is nothing to hide, but it's imperative she thinks Eidolon is coming to Dagmar's aid."

"Then why not name them?"

Gregori sighed. Talking to Ria was akin to carrying on a conversation with a child. "Natalia must come to her own conclusions regarding our allies. To be blatant about such things will only arouse her suspicions. Even now, she may have doubts, making it all the more important you do all you can to set her mind at ease."

"And how do you propose I do that?"

"By the careful application of diplomacy."

Ria stared back, clearly out of her depth. "And how do I do that?"

"Did they teach you nothing in Korascajan?" He waited for a response, but as none was forthcoming, he continued. "We shall not speak directly of such things. Instead, we'll hint of matters by spreading rumours."

"So, I am to be the source of gossip now?"

"Do not be so quick to dismiss the usefulness of such a tactic. The careful manipulation of facts has toppled many seats of power."

"Just out of curiosity, what would we have done had it not been Natalia Stormwind Reinwick sent?"

"Let us not dwell on what could have happened; instead, concentrate on the here and now. The plan to take Reinwick has been long in the making, and I'm confident there is nothing Natalia, or anyone else, for that matter, can do to disrupt it. Her presence here, while unexpected, only serves to benefit our cause, rather than hamper it."

"And if she learns the truth?"

"What is the truth, except for what we make it?" Gregori stared down at his letter, hoping she would take it as a sign he was done with her.

Ria, however, had other ideas. "So, I am to start rumours concerning the involvement of Eidolon?"

He looked up in irritation. "Have I not made that plain enough for you? Yes. You are to talk to your contacts at court and let slip Eidolon is set to offer its considerable assistance in the coming campaign."

"Do we not risk incurring their king's wrath?"

"Their king has no representation at the court of King Dagmar. Now, stop worrying, and be about your business."

"Yes, Lord." Ria bowed before quickly turning and fleeing.

Gregori stood, making his way to the fireplace, where a roaring fire warmed the room. He leaned on the mantel, his mind elsewhere.

Natalia Stormwind was a resourceful woman. How else could she elude the family for so long? Her presence at the court of Reinwick troubled him. Why was she there, and more importantly, how had she evaded the family's agents? He'd dismissed her unexpected appearance to the upstart Sartellian, yet he must admit to a certain admiration for Natalia's accomplishments. She'd infiltrated Stormwind manor, a feat unto itself, then she'd torched the place, burning it to the ground in her escape. Some back in Karslev felt it best to give her a wide berth, but he was not amongst them. Like their new matriarch, Marakhova, Gregori knew of the raw power residing in their wayward student.

Their mistake was sending someone to kidnap her daughter. A foolish endeavour, and one that had roused the motherly instincts of a powerful mage. Now, they'd paid the price, and Stormwind manor was nothing but burned wood and hollowed-out stone. It would take a far more subtle approach to best her this time, and Gregori knew he was the one to do it.

He returned to his seat, staring down at the letter once more. He'd addressed it to Marakhova Stormwind, and within, it revealed Natalia's presence in Dagmar's court. He could have used his magic to notify the matriarch directly but feared that might result in a heavy-handed response that would likely jeopardize all his work in Andover. Better, he thought, to rely on more conventional methods of communication, allowing him time to bring his plan to fruition.

NEWS

AUTUMN 1108 SR

Shaluhk's hurried footsteps announced her arrival in the room where Kargen consulted with Wynfrith, Raleth, and the other Orc leaders, causing them to pause their discussion.

"You look pleased with yourself," said Kargen in the Human tongue. "Have you good news?"

"As a matter of fact, I do. Vagrath, the Ashwalkers' shaman, contacted me."

"I am not familiar with that tribe," said Grazuhk.

"It lies to the west, close to the Great Northern Sea."

"And what is the nature of this contact?"

"I received word Athgar and Nat-Alia are safe. They fled Karslev, sailing west to escape their enemies, eventually landing in a place called Reinwick. The ruler there has welcomed them, but it is a land on the brink of war."

"As are we," said Kargen.

"I passed that on to him. He asked me to inform you he approves of all the steps you have taken so far and continues to trust in your judgement."

"Any idea when they will return?"

"Not as yet. They are struggling to break the family's hold over the Continent, and I suspect this war he spoke of has something to do with that."

"And Nat-Alia?"

"They were temporarily parted, but he reports she is safe and unharmed. I passed along our own best wishes, with our thanks to Vagrath for allowing us to make contact."

"Are the Ashwalkers masters of fire?"

"They are," said Shaluhk. "And Athgar has accepted their offer to increase his knowledge of his inner spark."

"Good," said Grazuhk. "Perhaps when he returns, he can begin training an apprentice. That is the correct Human term, is it not, Wynfrith?"

"It most certainly is," replied the Thane of Bradon. "If Athgar truly has increased his mastery of fire, it will benefit us all."

"This is good news," offered Zahruhl, "and it is reassuring that our High Thane agrees with our actions so far, but we must still contend with this threat. The barons of Novarsk need to be dealt with once and for all."

"Agreed," said Kargen. "That is one of the reasons I wanted you all here today. As we discussed earlier, Lord Valentyn looks to be the one leading the disaffected nobles. I, therefore, propose we focus on capturing or destroying his keep in Krasnov." His gaze swept the room, finally resting on Raleth. "Some days ago, I asked for an assessment of how many warriors we could assemble. Have you the numbers?"

"Yes, I have," replied the captain. "I estimate Lord Valentyn's forces to be close to four hundred warriors."

"Might I ask how you came about that number?"

"Primarily through speaking with Royal Administrators and Wynfrith. He started the invasion with more, but reports indicate he took losses during the campaign."

"And the other barons?"

"None have as many as he does. As to composition, I possess no detailed information on how many horsemen they now have, although they appear to be lacking in archers, the bulk of which we destroyed at Heronwood. I expect them to have recovered to a certain degree, but it takes time to train a skilled archer."

"They used crossbows at Heronwood," said Wynfrith, "but there are reports their stocks are now at an all-time low."

"Good," said Kargen. "Archers are the one thing we possess in abundance. However, their horsemen, particularly their knights, are of more concern to us. The man who delivered the ultimatum, Sir Yarren, was a Knight of the Mailed Fist. Do we have access to any records about that order?"

"We do," said Shaluhk, "and I spent much of my time looking through them. From what I can gather, they number around a hundred or so, but the Crown saw fit to disperse them amongst the barons, primarily to offset the expense."

"That fits with what I learned," said Harwath. "I've spoken with men of the new levy we raised. Many of them were conscripted to serve in Rada's army. The consensus seems to be that the barons might only be able to field one hundred or so knights. Having said that, they lost a lot of horses during the campaign, so many may need to fight afoot."

"I would expect no less," said Rugg, "particularly as we will be conducting a siege. That raises an interesting question, however. Is it likely they will have horses in their keep?"

"I have no idea," replied Kargen. He looked around the group. "Anyone have anything to say in that regard?" Blank faces stared back from most of them, except Raleth.

"I suspect they'll deploy them early on," said Raleth. "A horse needs a lot of food, and if Lord Valentyn thinks a siege is imminent, he won't want the extra mouths to feed."

"Meaning?"

"He'll likely use them during our initial approach."

"And then?"

"He might disperse them or send the horses off and have his knights man the garrison; it's difficult to say. We don't use keeps, so this is all new to us."

"And what of our own numbers?" asked Wynfrith. "We still need to garrison the cities."

"I've taken that into account," said Raleth, "and I can safely say we could put together an expedition of eight hundred without compromising our situation here, in Halmund."

"And its composition?"

"Two hundred foot, taken from the fyrds of Runewald and Bradon, along with the Thane Guard. There are also two hundred Therengian archers, and the same number of Orcs ready to melee, plus a further two hundred hunters, fifty of which are armed with warbows. Naturally, that's not including shamans and mages."

"And you believe that enough to capture a keep?"

"The most dangerous part of this expedition will be marching to Krasnov. If Valentyn has time to prepare, we could find ourselves subject to attacks by small bands of raiders."

"Not with my hunters acting as a screen," said Grazuhk. "You worry about getting us there, and I will make sure the enemy keeps their distance."

"And how will you do that?"

"Rotuk, our master of air, will call upon his airborne friends to watch out for danger. There is very little that escapes the notice of a hawk."

"And what of our tuskers?" asked Kargen.

"I thought it best to keep them here, in Halmund," replied Raleth. "They are of little use in a siege, and their presence will deter any attack on our garrison."

"You did well. What do we know about the baron's keep?"

"I'm told it is a square keep, which I assume refers to its general shape, but we know very little beyond that. We shall revise our plans once it's within sight."

"Who will command the garrison in your absence?" asked Rugg.

"That is for Kargen to decide."

"I have given that much thought," said Kargen, "and decided to leave Wynfrith here to rule in my stead."

"Me?" she replied. "Why would you choose me?"

"You are an experienced thane and understand Athgar's wishes as well as I. You are also someone I trust not to succumb to the barons' bribes or threats should they make another attempt at negotiating."

"Then I shall do all I can to preserve the peace here in the capital. Speaking of which, what are you leaving me in terms of warriors?"

"Rather a mixed bunch," said Kargen. "Harwath is best suited to explain the details."

Harwath cleared his throat. "As I mentioned earlier, I have, at Kargen's behest, begun training a local force of warriors. You might compare them to a fyrd, yet service is not mandatory. They have rudimentary weapons at present, little more than spears and shields, but I have hopes that with further training, we could improve their equipment, even give them some armour, if we can spare it."

Raleth smiled. "Well done, Brother, but I doubt they would be much of a threat to our enemies."

"They don't need to be. Their primary purpose is to free up our people so you can carry on your attack on Krasnov."

"I'm curious how you convinced them to serve us?"

"I allowed them to select their own captains, men they know will look after their best interests. I also promised them a voice in the rule of their province under Therengian law."

"You promised them much, perhaps too much. You may well be arming our next adversary."

"I think not," said Harwath. "These people want a say in how they're ruled, same as us."

"But they are the conquered ones!" insisted Raleth.

"Harwath speaks wisely," said Shaluhk. "We shall never find peace if we treat others as a conquered people. Rather, we must accept them into our lands with open arms."

"We did that with the barons, and they turned against us."

"True, but the barons are not the general populous. Harwath's decision to train a levy was not made lightly, nor without Kargen's blessing. You would do well to remember that."

"My apologies," said Raleth. "I grow weary of war, and the thought of yet more battles frustrates me."

"As it does all of us. Peace will come in time, but we must be patient."

"What about the neighbouring realms?" asked Wynfrith. "I seem to recall some fear that Ostrova might take offence to our presence near their border. That is where Krasnov lies, isn't it?"

"It is," said Kargen. "We sent a messenger to assure their king we have no intentions of crossing into their land, but we have yet to receive a reply."

"Quite reasonable," added Shaluhk, "considering the distance involved. We also sent word to Zalista to negotiate a lasting peace with them, but once again, the distances involved make it too early for any predictions."

"As usual, the shamans will keep us updated on the campaign's progress. I shall accompany the army, along with Shaluhk, while Laghul remains here, with Wynfrith." Kargen's gaze swept the room. "Are there any questions?"

He waited, but all remained silent. "As you can all see," he continued, "we are working to ensure not only the success of this coming campaign but the future of Therengia. I thank all of you for your contributions."

Two days later, the army was on the move.

Weyland halted, taking a moment to catch his breath. Beside him, the rest of the Thane Guard waded across a stream while hunters of the Red Hand kept watch. The advance north had proceeded at a fast pace, and Weyland's feet were sore. All he really wanted to do right now was lay down and soak his feet in the cool water, but he knew there were still many miles left to travel.

He entered the stream, soon waist deep in its frigid waters. His breath came in brief gasps, and then a hand grabbed him under the arm and pulled him forward. He looked up to see Hilwyth grinning.

"Cold, isn't it?" she said.

"Yes, Captain."

"Don't stop. It'll only get worse."

He felt the mud suck at his boots, and then the stream grew shallower, allowing him to pull himself from the water. He looked behind him, where others were already crossing in his wake.

"Keep going," said Hilwyth with a grin, "or you'll make us look bad." He pushed on, knowing he and his companions formed the backbone of the army.

Here, the terrain was not so different from Therengia, at least in the flatter regions. Back in Runewald, tall pines surrounded the village, but here, ash, elm, and oak took their place.

Weyland had always considered himself just a farmer, but still, he'd not wasted his time in Novarsk. When he wasn't guarding, he wandered the city of Halmund, finding particular comfort in the artisans' section, where he discovered a fascination for bows and their construction. He'd made himself a promise he would learn all he could once he returned home, intending to become a bowyer.

The thought caused him to smile, for the High Thane himself was a maker of bows. Weyland imagined himself living a life of comfort, with hunters lined up to purchase his creations and a loving wife fawning over him.

A twig snapped to his left, interrupting his thoughts. A trio of Orcs ran towards some woods, axes in hand. An arrow took one in the shoulder, but the Cloud Hunter kept running forward, letting out a blood-curdling challenge.

Weyland veered left, following in their wake. The Thane Guard was armed with a Therengian short sword and a war axe. The sword proved little use against heavily armoured opponents, but the axe, a one-handed weapon, was effective at splitting mail. He slowed as he approached the treeline, taking a moment to unsling the shield from his back.

The sounds of melee echoed off the trees, guiding him to the conflict. He advanced cautiously through the thick underbrush, axe in hand, ready to take the fight to the enemy. He wanted to rush forward, screaming out defiance, but endless weeks of training reinforced the need for discipline.

The first sign of any fighting was an Orc with his spear raised high for a toss, but before he could let loose, an arrow took the unfortunate hunter in the chest, and he fell to the forest floor.

Weyland altered course, heading directly for the poor soul, but as he approached, he saw the Orc waving him on, even as he pulled the arrow out, sending black blood splashing onto the ground.

A rustle ahead alerted Weyland to danger, and he raised his shield in time to block the attack. His opponent, clad in chain links, pulled his sword back for another strike, but the Therengian was faster, bashing out with his shield, using its edge to smash into the mailed chest. His opponent, now off balance, couldn't attack, so Weyland immediately followed with an over-head axe strike into the fellow's chest, breaking links and sinking into flesh.

As Weyland's foe fell, he finished him off with an efficient blow to the neck. He took a moment to catch his breath while the shouts and screams of men and Orcs echoed off the trees.

An Orc hunter appeared beside him, drawing one of the Red Hand's mighty warbows. He let loose with an arrow, and it struck a man in the middle of his chest, sinking in deeply. Weyland moved up, passing the poor fool even before he hit the forest floor.

As someone burst out from behind a tree, the Therengian raised his axe, but it was only Hilwyth, her axe dripping blood, her mail shirt soaked in it, yet she appeared unhurt.

"They're on the run," she said. "Hold your position here." She let out a loud whistle. "To me!" she shouted. "To me!"

Warriors and hunters alike converged on their location. She quickly organized a line, then spread it out. "Advance slowly," she commanded. "There's a field to the west, and we need to drive them back into the open. Weyland, take command of this end and keep the pace steady. We don't want it breaking up." She was gone in a flash, but he still heard her calling out orders.

Weyland took a moment to alternate members of the Thane Guard with the bow-armed hunters, the better to allow them to react should a counter-attack come their way.

They advanced slowly, maintaining the line. Ahead, the sounds of feet running through the forest, of scabbards slapping against armour, alerted him that the enemy would soon be within sight.

Then, as sunlight filtered through gaps in the trees, a field appeared before them. A dozen of the enemy hurried across the wild grass, heading towards a group formed in line. Weyland slowed, seeking out Hilwyth.

The enemy skirmishers, having completed their bid for safety, fell in behind the line of their warriors.

"Halt!" ordered Weyland. "Nock arrows and loose in your own time." He saw the look of confusion, then repeated the order in Orcish.

A ragged volley of arrows flew forth, felling two, but the enemy remained in place. Weyland stepped from the woods and ordered his archers to reform their line.

Behind the enemy line, someone of import looked out over his men, his horse providing a height advantage. Weyland's gaze locked with the fellow, and recognition dawned. Sir Yarren of Larodka had come to take vengeance in the name of his master.

The Therengian line grew as more warriors emerged, battle-hardened and ready to fight. Sir Yarren watched with interest but didn't take the bait. Instead, he held up his sword in salute, then turned his men around and marched away.

Weyland ordered another volley, but to little effect. He considered running after the enemy, but Hilwyth finally arrived to take command.

"By the Gods, but that was clever," she said.

He stared back. "Clever?"

"Somehow, he got past our scouts, not to mention the Cloud Hunters' magic."

"That was Sir Yarren. A knight in service to Lord Valentyn."

"You know him?"

"Yes," said Weyland. "I met him back in Halmund. I told him the next time I saw him, I'd kill him. He said the same."

"Well, it appears your prediction was a little premature. Don't worry, though. We'll be in Krasnov soon enough, and there'll be plenty of fighting for everyone. You'll get your chance to see him again."

TRIAL BY FIRE

AUTUMN 1108 SR

B elgast turned to Athgar. "Are you sure you want to go through with this?"

"It is the culmination of my training. I can hardly refuse."

"Training, I understand, but this? You must be mad!"

Athgar fell silent as Marag smeared the ash on his cheeks. "*Your quest for knowledge is nearly complete,*" said the master of flame in the language of her people. "*You have only to pass this one final test before unlocking your true potential.*" She paused in front of him, staring intensely into his eyes. "*Are you prepared to finish the journey you began under Artoch's guidance?*"

The mention of his tutor caught him by surprise. The old Orc was the first to identify Athgar's capacity for Fire Magic. 'Touched by fire' had been Artoch's expression, and it somehow felt fitting that Marag, another master of flame, complete his journey. He brought his mind back from the past and then focused on her face. "*I am ready.*"

"*Snaga will lead the way,*" she replied. "*Then you will proceed through the inferno. I will greet you on the other side.*"

He nodded, then turned to Belgast. The Dwarf was a stalwart companion and appeared worried, but Athgar knew this was something he had to do. He was excited by the prospect of growing in power, of mastering his manipulation of fire, yet at the same time, fear nearly overcame him. Natalia once told him Fire Mages were often consumed by their magic, the lure of the flame difficult to resist.

Athgar tried to brush off his worries but to little avail. The Orcs had achieved a high level of competency with their magic, yet he'd never heard of a master of flame succumbing to its lure. He, of course, was Human, and he wondered if that wasn't the fatal flaw. Would he burst into flames as he passed through the wall of fire?

The logical part of his mind said no, for the spell of shielding protected him from harm. The emotional side of him, however, told him otherwise. In some places, it was considered folly to even attempt to harness the most powerful of the elements, an ancient superstition, no doubt, but one that still nagged at him.

Snaga moved up to stand before him. "*Come*," said the Orc. "*It is time.*" He began casting, the words of power coming easily to the elder's practiced mind.

Behind him, Marag fed the wall of flame, assisted by the younger masters-in-training. They each produced a ball of fire which they then passed to Marag. She, in turn, fed them to the great barrier through which the initiate, Athgar, would pass.

At a word from his chieftain, Zhogral stepped forward, a haunch of meat stuck to the end of his spear, which he poked into the flames only for it to sizzle and blacken from the intense heat. He quickly withdrew the weapon, the metal tip drooping.

Snaga divested himself of his clothes save for a loincloth. He took a moment to stare at the wall of heat before slowly stepping forward.

Athgar watched the old Orc draw closer to the flames. The heat's intensity was painfully obvious, yet the master of flame didn't flinch. Instead, he stepped directly into the wall and stood there amid the flames for the count of ten before emerging out the other side. His hair, what little there was, smoked, and sweat covered him, but his smile left no doubt he emerged unscathed.

Snaga looked directly at Athgar and nodded. Athgar called on his inner spark and let it grow. This time, however, instead of releasing it in the form of fire, he held it in check, feeling its protective blanket settle over him.

He turned to Belgast. "Here," he said. "Look after my axe and bow. I shouldn't like to need to replace them."

"And yourself?" said the Dwarf. "Be careful, my friend. Mess this up, and Natalia will never forgive me."

"It's not you who will shoulder the blame if this goes awry."

"Maybe, but I'll be the one bearing the bad news."

Athgar's gaze flicked to the wall of fire.

"Aren't you going to strip?" asked Belgast.

"It's not a very useful spell if I have to take off all my clothes to use it."

"Are you sure of that? Snaga didn't think so."

"I am. Don't worry. This will all be over soon."

Like Snaga, he slowly advanced, his gaze glued to his target. The intense flames reminded him of a smith's furnace, and the heat assailed him, but it was not the intensity of a forge but that of the sun on a terribly hot day. He resisted the urge to close his eyes, halting a hand's breadth short of the flames. Reason told him his spell would protect him, yet the fire threatened to overwhelm him. The image of Athelwald burning suddenly struck him, and his heart began pounding. His mind screamed in protestation, but he ignored it, stepping forward to let the flames engulf him.

It was a strange sensation, for as they licked at his clothes, he felt the currents flowing around him like water, yet the fire never touched him. He paused, mentally counting to ten as Snaga had done.

One - His body warmed, and he imagined himself lying in the sun.

Two - The blistering heat soaked him in sweat.

Three - He held up his hands, staring at them, but saw no sign of burns.

Four - His eyes wandered to his tunic. It, too, was now soaked in sweat, but the material kept the fire at bay.

Five - A flame loomed close to his eyes, causing him to pull back involuntarily.

Six - He focused his mind, ignoring the flames, looking beyond them.

Seven - The tribe watched with intense interest, and he noted Marag's nod of approval.

Eight - The heat grew more extreme, and his inner spark strained to keep it at bay.

Nine - He poured the last of his reserves into his protective bubble.

Ten - He stepped from the flames, emerging into the cool evening air. The wall of fire vanished behind him, the area falling dark.

Athgar closed his eyes and took a deep breath. His energy reserves were low, and he realized he'd come very near to outstaying his welcome amongst the flames.

Marag stepped close, placing her hands on his shoulders. "*It is done,*" she said. "*You are an Ashwalker now. Come, it is time to celebrate.*"

A cheer erupted from the tribe, followed by a familiar thumping sound as fists pounded the ground.

Belgast plopped himself down by the fire. "That mead is heady stuff," he said. "I'd love to know how they make it."

"Perhaps another time," said Athgar. "We accomplished our aim here. It's time to return to Korvoran."

"It was not that long ago that we parted ways with Natalia and the others. They're probably still at Dagmar's court."

"Nevertheless, we must return. War looms, and we must do our part to help stave off invasion."

"*We shall join you when you travel north,*" said Rugal.

"*I'm sorry,*" said the Dwarf, quickly switching to Orcish. "*Are you suggesting your entire tribe will accompany us back to Reinwick? I doubt the duke would be inclined to welcome you.*"

"*That is understandable,*" said the chieftain. "*But Vagrath has consulted the Ancestors. The time for action is upon us. No more will we be a wandering clan. We will now settle down and create a lasting home.*"

"*And where would that home be?*" said Athgar. "*I'm not familiar with the area, but it seems to me the ruler of Reinwick might not like the idea of you settling so close to his borders.*"

"*That is where you come in.*"

"*Me? I possess little influence over the duke.*"

"*Are you not the High Thane of Therengia?*"

"*I am, but that means nothing here, amid the Petty Kingdoms.*"

"*You underestimate your power of persuasion. You speak of war, yes?*"

"*I do,*" said Athgar. "*Between Andover and Reinwick.*"

"*Then the duke would likely look favourably on the possibility of allies, would he not?*"

"*I suppose he would if that's how I presented it to him, but are you sure that's what you want? Going to war will inevitably result in a loss of hunters. Are you willing to make that sacrifice?*"

Rugal paused, thinking things through. "*It is worth the risk to secure our future.*" He turned to his shaman. "*What think you, Vagrath? Have you consulted the Ancestors?*"

"*I have, my chieftain. The time to act is upon us. If we do not, we risk dwindling as a people until the name Ashwalker is lost forever.*"

The chieftain looked at Athgar. "*There, you see? We have little option in the matter. According to our Ancestors, if we are to survive as a tribe, we must go north, following in your wake.*"

Athgar felt the weight of responsibility fall heavily across his shoulders. "*In that case,*" he said, "*I shall do all I can to convince the duke of your good intentions.*"

Rugal nodded his head. "*That is all I can ask. Now, as to the manner of your return. Zhogral?*"

The Orc hunter looked up from where he ate. "*Yes, my chieftain?*"

"*The tribe moves north, to the very edge of the great forest, where it meets the great sea. You shall lead the way, and ensure Athgar reaches his destination. Is that clear?*"

"*It is.*"

"Good. Take Gharog with you."

"Gharog? To what end?"

Rugal sighed. *"She is a shaman in training. Her presence will allow you to notify the rest of the tribe of any developments."* He shook his head, then turned to Athgar. *"You must excuse Zhogral's behaviour. He is uncomfortable around Gharog."*

"Why is that? Does he fear her magic?"

The chieftain chuckled. *"No. Only her attention. Gharog has taken a keen interest in him. It would not surprise me if they were bonded by next spring."*

"And is that a good thing?"

"I believe so. Zhogral can sometimes be a little headstrong. A bonding with Gharog would smooth out his rough edges. Tell me, Athgar, are you bonded?"

"I am, and quite happily so. My bondmate is Natalia Stormwind, a Water Mage of exceptional power, although I suppose you might call her a master of water."

"And has the union been blessed with offspring?"

"It has indeed, a daughter named Oswyn, though she is back in Therengia."

"Oswyn, you say? How appropriate that your youngling be called 'Orc friend'. Did you pick the name yourself?"

"No. The Ancestors chose it in the tradition of the Red Hand."

They set out the next morning. Athgar expected the Ashwalkers to take days to pack up their belongings, but the tribe, used to a life of wandering, was ready by first light.

Zhogral led the way, Gharog beside him, while Athgar, Belgast, and the three Therengians followed. During Athgar's training, Herulf, Lofwine, and Osbert stuck near the Dwarf. But now, having lived amongst the Orcs for some time, they'd grown accustomed to their presence. Indeed, Herulf even learned a few words of their language, although his comrades appeared less inclined to do so.

The forest grew thinner as they headed northward, the green canopy finally offering glimpses of the sun. At noon they halted, enjoying a rest in a woodland clearing while the hunters filled waterskins, allowing Athgar some time to lie down for a moment of rest—at least that's what he thought. It seemed, however, his companions had other ideas.

"I never imagined an entire tribe could move so quickly," noted Herulf. "We must've covered over ten miles today."

"That's all right for you lot," said Belgast, "but I've got shorter legs. If I keep up this pace, I'll have no feet left by dark."

Lofwine looked up from where he lay. "Are you suggesting we're continuing on? Aren't we done for the day?"

"Hardly," said Athgar. "Did you forget how far we came into Andover?"

"Of course not, but I didn't think we'd be in such a hurry to return. It's not as if the Orcs have a reason to go so fast."

"You don't understand Orcs. They don't take half measures when they make their minds up to do something."

Osbert groaned. "How long will they keep this pace?"

"Till we reach the border."

"That would be the Thornwood," said Herulf. "They say it's impenetrable."

"I doubt that," said Athgar. "No forest is that thick, particularly if one has the will to explore it. I don't think it would intimidate the Ashwalkers."

"So that's it? They'll just march into the Thornwood and claim it as their own? I can't imagine the duke liking that."

"I doubt he would even notice, considering the war about to erupt. In any case, I'll make my plea on their behalf as soon as we're back in Korvoran."

"And what of us?" said Herulf. "Are you to abandon us now that your quest is done?"

"No. I shall plead your case to the duke, just as I will the Orcs."

"It will take more than words to sway the duke."

"Perhaps, but I must at least try." Athgar paused a moment as an idea struck him. "How many Therengians are in Reinwick, would you say?"

"Hundreds, perhaps even thousands. Several hundred are in the vicinity of Korvoran, mostly in the country or living rough in the oak forests to the west. Many hire on to cut trees for shipbuilding."

"Why is that?"

"It's one of the few jobs we're allowed to hold. Apparently, our rustic nature fits in well with their idea of what a woodsman is supposed to be like."

"So, they see us as simple folk, fit only for manual labour?"

"That's about the size of it," said Herulf.

"Anything else I should know?"

"We're not allowed to bear arms, though an axe is acceptable as a tool. After all, we need to chop down trees with something."

"And the duke's army?"

"We're forbidden to join the army though they still expect us to take part in the levy. Have you such a thing back in Therengia?"

"We have a fyrd, if that's what you mean, but we train them. What of you? You're pretty handy with that bow. Have you any formal training?"

"No. I learned that from my father. If the duke knew I carried a bow, I'd likely be arrested." He stared at it. "And this isn't even a warbow. Back home, we had the large Therengian bows. Are you familiar with them?"

"I would hope so," said Athgar. "I make them."

"You're a bowyer?"

"I am. At least, I was. Recent events keep me from taking up my old profession. I even helped the Red Hand make their own version of the warbow."

"Meaning?"

"The warbows we Therengians favour are the height of a man. They require a lot of strength, so our archers must constantly train with them. On the other hand, the Orcs are stronger than us by a significant degree. They can use a bow with a heavier draw weight, so I modified the design to fit their frame."

"Are they powerful?"

"I'll say. They can punch an arrow through plate armour under the right conditions, though naturally, they'd need special arrows for the occasion."

"And you gave them such weapons?" said Osbert. "Are you sure that was wise?"

"I have nothing to fear from Orcs," said Athgar, "nor should you. They are the traditional allies of Therengia and form an important part of our new realm."

"Still, what if they rose up against you?"

"Would you expect your fellow Therengians to rise up against you?"

"No," said Herulf. "Of course not."

"Then understand this. In the east, Therengians and Orcs are one people. Our respective strengths complement each other, a lesson I hope one day to be accepted here."

"You are wise, Athgar," said Herulf. "Are you sure you're not a descendant of Aeldred?"

"I thank you for the compliment, but I am content to rule as thane rather than king."

"You're a thane?"

"Yes, the High Thane of Therengia. Did I not mention that?"

Belgast looked around the small group standing there, their mouths agape. "Apparently not, if their faces are any indication."

Herulf rose to a kneeling position. "Lord," he said. "I swear to serve you to my dying day." He reached out, hitting Osbert on the leg, who then followed suit, as did Lofwine, kneeling beside his comrades. Each pledging a life of service.

"I thank you for the oath," said Athgar, "but I'm a long way from Runewald and have little sway here in these parts."

"Yet you are on a grand quest, Lord," said Osbert. "Let us help you on this endeavour. It is the stuff of legends."

"Legends? Hardly that, and our chance of success is slim."

"True, Lord, but a burden shared is easier to carry."

"He's got you there," said Belgast, "but isn't that a quote from Saint Mathew?"

"Is it?" said Athgar. "I wouldn't know, but regardless of who said it first, it's a valid point. Very well, I accept your service." He saw the look of wonder in their eyes.

"Are we done yet?" asked the Dwarf. "Because the Ashwalkers are getting ready to move again."

LAST CHANCE FOR PEACE

AUTUMN 1108 SR

Deveral's silky-smooth voice interrupted her thoughts. "A letter from His Majesty has arrived for you, madam."

Natalia took the note, breaking the seal.

"News?" said Katrin.

"It appears King Dagmar finally made a decision. I am to dine with him this evening." She turned to Deveral. "You may inform His Majesty I graciously accept."

"Very well, madam. I'm sure he'll be pleased to hear it."

He scribbled a note, then handed it to Greta. The young girl opened the door and tore down the hallway, narrowly avoiding a collision with Galina, who was just returning.

"Did I miss something important?" she asked.

"You did," said Stanislav. "The king finally agreed to a meeting."

"And is that good news or bad?"

"That depends on your point of view."

"Before we say anything we regret, it might be prudent to adjourn to the study?"

"An excellent precaution," said Natalia.

They crowded into the room, and Katrin shut the door.

"Well?" said Galina.

"This may be our last chance to sway him from the temptation of war," said Natalia. "But before we get into that, I need to know what we've discovered so far. We'll start with you, Stanislav. Found anything of interest?"

"I have," replied the mage hunter, "though I wish it were better news. I confirmed the king has called out the levy, and his barons are concentrating their forces here in Zienholtz. I also made a few enquiries, and the cartwrights are very busy. If numbers are any indication, I'd say Reinwick is in for quite the invasion."

"Any idea of their strength?"

"I'm afraid that's not my specialty. I tried to gain access to their camp, but the guards were too alert for such antics."

"And your other contacts?"

"You mean the bounty hunters? They're all concentrating on deserters, a common contract when the army is massing. As for foreign contacts, I found none."

Natalia turned to Galina. "You've been spending time with Captain Marwen. Any encouraging news?"

"No, in fact, quite the opposite. He's been frustrated at every turn. The king's advisors listen to his pleas but take no action, nor make any promises. At this point, I think he's ready to give up and return to Reinwick."

"How is he taking it?"

"Not well," replied Galina. "He pinned his hope for advancement on this mission. Now he has nothing to show for his actions but defeat."

"He's still a captain," said Stanislav. "Is that really so bad?"

"He hoped for a title, or at least a knighthood, something to recognize his efforts."

"Well," said Natalia, "he might not have succeeded here in Zienholtz, but he'll still get his chance to make a name for himself in battle. Has he fought before?"

"We haven't talked of such things, but I get the impression his career thus far has been peaceful. As to his leadership potential, I spent a lot of time with him, but I saw nothing to indicate what he would be like in front of his men."

"Do we know who commands the duke's army?" asked Katrin.

"I would assume the duke," said Galina. "He has a general but no real military organization other than each baron leading their own men. It's also noteworthy that when Halvaria threatened Reinwick ten years ago, he let the Temple Knights deal with it rather than commit his own warriors."

"I would say that puts us in a precarious situation," noted Natalia. "If we can't convince King Dagmar to give up the war, our entire enterprise will have been for naught. The family will be back into the court of Reinwick, and the north will be at the empire's mercy once more."

"Our chances of success are slim and only getting worse. Rumour is Eidolon will join Dagmar's army, giving him an even greater advantage."

"Have we heard any more on that?" She looked at Katrin for an answer.

"Nothing that adds to what Galina already told us. Talk at court is that Andover has itself a powerful ally, one that can easily destroy Reinwick, and the consensus is its Eidolon. That's not exactly welcome news, but if it's true, we can make a few generalizations."

"Such as?" asked Natalia.

"The most logical approach would be for Eidolon to march its army directly to Zienholtz. In fact, there's a direct road between the two capitals."

"Well, they're not here yet," said Stanislav. "I saw no foreign flags flying over that encampment. That means we still have a little time."

"Yes," said Natalia, "but how much?"

"Do you believe you can get anything from the king?"

"You mean like peace?" said Natalia. "I doubt it. It's not as if I can simply say, 'Oh, by the way, I need you to ban the family from your court and not invade Reinwick. Do that, and I'd be ever so grateful!' He'd probably arrest me on the spot."

"No. I mean, can you learn more about the size of his army? If he's anything like his father, he'll like to brag about how many warriors he has. That, at least, would give us a better idea of what we're up against."

"I can definitely give it a try, but if the family has discovered our true identities, it's possible this entire dinner is nothing but an elaborate trap."

"Nonsense," said Stanislav. "We're virtual prisoners here at the Palace. If the king wanted us arrested, we'd already be in the dungeons."

"What of Captain Marwen's plans?"

"Has he not seen fit to talk to you?" said Galina.

"We've seen neither hide nor hair of him since our arrival. If it wasn't for you, we'd have no idea what he's been up to."

"I have a feeling we'll be on our way back to Reinwick by week's end. He sees little reason to remain here in Zienholtz when he's rebuffed at every turn."

"Then it appears I'm our last hope."

To say the dining hall in King Dagmar's Palace was opulent was an understatement—the red marble fireplace, the shadowbark table, and the gold-laced silverware combined to create an elegant experience.

Even though she was the only one invited to dine, Natalia was seated at the far end of the long table. When the king entered, she stood as he sat at the opposite end. Servants scurried forward, pouring wine and bringing plates filled with delicacies. Apparently, the king's appetite for food was just as extravagant as his decorations.

"I remember offering you moonfish," said the king, "but then you said you preferred venison. I've taken the liberty of supplying both, in case you changed your mind."

"Your Majesty is too kind."

He sipped his wine and smiled. "A fine vintage. Tell me, do you consider yourself an expert in such things?"

"I am a battle mage, Majesty. My tastes run more towards understanding strategy and tactics."

"But you had wine back at the Volstrum, surely?"

"Of course, and I still appreciate a fine vintage. It just isn't a priority for me."

He took another small sip. "You can tell a lot about a person by what they eat. Take you, for example."

"Me, Majesty? I've yet to eat anything."

"True, but your preference for venison tells me you are a down-to-earth woman at heart. If I had to guess, I'd say you'd be perfectly happy settling down with a landowner of some sort. No, not a landowner, a hunter, someone who has mastery over nature. Am I close?"

The accuracy of his statement surprised Natalia. Was he privy to her true identity? She must watch her words carefully. "And what of yourself? I see a broad range of delicacies before you. What does that say of your own character?"

He chuckled. "I see there's a clever mind beneath that pale exterior." His gaze swept over the table. "Like my appetite, I am a complex individual, driven to try new things in the hopes of bettering myself. I am never satisfied with how things are. Rather, I seek to win glory and honour."

"And you feel this war with Reinwick will bring you precisely that?"

"Don't you? After all, your family has assured me my plan will work. Why, if it hadn't been for the assistance of your brother mage, Andover might have languished after my father's failure."

"My brother mage?" said Natalia. "Surely you mean sister?"

"I'm sorry, is Gregori not your brother? I thought all Stormwinds were related, and you do bear a slight resemblance to him? Cousin, perhaps?"

At the mention of his name, panic threatened to overwhelm her. Gregori Stormwind was an instructor during her years at the Volstrum and had even tutored her and Katrin. There was no possible way he wouldn't recognize her, yet she'd not seen the man. Was he abroad, gathering allies? She needed time to process this new information, but the king waited for a response.

"The family is considerably large," she finally replied, "but he is, I believe, a distant cousin."

"Then why the delay in answering?"

"As I said, the family is quite extensive, so I was trying to calculate how distant a relative he actually is. Not that it matters, but I assumed you would wish an accurate reply."

The answer appeared to mollify the king. "Have you enjoyed your stay in Zienholtz?"

"I regret I've been far too busy to take advantage of it. My aides, however, speak of their admiration of its architecture. This Palace, for example, is a wonder to behold. Wherever did they get the red stone for the walls?"

"If I'm being honest, I have no idea. My tastes run more to the martial than the design. I suppose that's something we have in common, considering your chosen profession. Tell me, how does one become a Water Mage? Is it a family profession, or can anyone join the academy in Karslev?"

"There is a rigorous screening process," said Natalia. "They permit only those with true potential to learn the Volstrum's secrets."

"But there are other academies, surely?"

"Of course. Korascajan is one such example, and there are many smaller schools scattered throughout the Petty Kingdoms, but none can claim the same prestige as the Volstrum."

"And why is that, if you don't mind me asking?"

"The Stormwinds have spent generations perfecting the art of Water Magic, just as the Sartellians did with Fire Magic."

"Yet the family has no Air Mages? Or Earth? Or does it?"

"The elements of air and water are less useful in battle. In addition, most Earth Mages are more rustic in nature, so the family has wisely chosen not to expend its energies on such things."

"And that," said the king, "is precisely why the Stormwinds and Sartellians are so successful. Why, courts all over the Continent are fighting amongst themselves to acquire your services, and here I am, blessed by no less than three."

"Three?"

"Yes. Ria, Gregori, and yourself. Why? Did I miss someone?"

"Not at all, Majesty, but I'm afraid my position here is only temporary."

"And what, precisely, is your reason for visiting us in Andover?"

"They sent me to make sure all is in readiness."

"No doubt you speak of war preparations. You may rest assured, Natalia, all is well in hand."

"My concern is with the numbers. We've had reports of late indicating Reinwick has increased the size of its army."

"That's news to me," said Dagmar, "but I doubt it'll make much difference. At last count, we have a clear majority, and that's not even including our allies. Fear not. We will crush the army of Reinwick and restore the honour of your family name to the Continent." He emptied his cup, then held it out for more. A servant dutifully came forward, urn in hand, to refill it.

"And," said Natalia, "might I enquire about your own goals, once you secure victory?"

"I'm not sure what you're asking?"

"Will you appoint your own Duke of Reinwick or absorb it into Andover?"

"Perhaps both. I've often thought a duke belongs beneath a king, haven't you? That would enlarge my coffers while keeping me from the headache of actually ruling over a conquered territory."

"That makes perfect sense," said Natalia. "Though I am curious about the reason for the animosity between your two realms. I'm led to believe it's existed for years, maybe even decades."

"It all has to do with Erlingen, if you must know. The Duke of Erlingen married my first cousin, but she died under questionable circumstances. At the time, the duke had taken up with a woman from Reinwick, and it was rumoured my cousin's death was by design. My father was incensed, so much so that he assembled his army and marched across the border. Unfortunately, the invasion was unsuccessful, and he had the added indignity of being captured, leading to a ransom that nearly bankrupted the kingdom."

He sipped some more wine. "The terms of my father's release terminated when he died, so you can understand I'm eager to avenge his name."

"But why Reinwick? Why not Erlingen? They're the ones who defeated him."

"Ah, but Reinwick is richer, by far. It's all that sea trade, you see. And I can always turn south once I've filled my coffers, then Andover would become the dominant force in the northern Petty Kingdoms."

"While I understand the lure of power, I'm afraid further expansion would likely end in disaster. Reinwick has allies, Your Majesty, and while you might defeat Lord Wilfhelm, by the time you can turn south, his allies will have mustered their forces. A quick war is to your advantage, while a long one becomes a burden."

"You are remarkably candid for a Stormwind. I thought you'd be more supportive of a great northern power."

"And I am," said Natalia, "but we must not let reason give way to passion. There is opportunity, and then there is danger; going to war is treading the fine line between the two."

"I like you," said the king. "You are very plain-spoken when it comes to advice. I wish more of my advisors were of a similar mind. Tell me, in your estimation, what do you think of my chances of success?"

"Against Reinwick, or both it and Erlingen?"

"Just Reinwick."

"That would largely depend on your forces. It is one thing to claim superior numbers, but we must also examine the quality and mix of warriors. How large would you say your army is?"

"My father fielded close to three thousand men when he marched south. I've mustered three and a half, not including our allies, of course."

Natalia felt the familiar sense of panic rising. She fought to maintain her calm. "Three and a half thousand! An impressive feat, Your Majesty, but I wonder how much of that consists of knights or professional footmen."

"You must have no fear on that account. Thanks to you Stormwinds, I've recruited knights from all over the Continent."

"Foreigners? Are you sure you can trust them?"

"There is always a certain element of risk when it comes to such things, but these are knights we're talking about, not mercenaries. They'll do their part, don't you worry. When it's all said and done, there'll be riches galore and ransoms by the bucketful to fill the coffers of even the humblest of knights."

"It would seem you have things well in hand."

"True," said Dagmar, "but I must, in all humility, thank the Stormwinds for providing their influence regarding recruiting. Had it not been for your cousin, Gregori, I would never even attempt this campaign."

"I thought it was your plan?"

"Well, yes, it was. The idea was floating around for years, but his arrival solidified the details. You know it was his idea to recruit knights from all over the Continent? I'm also told he's a master strategist, although I suppose the same could be said for any member of the Stormwinds. What of you? Will you accompany the army when it marches?"

"I'm afraid not," said Natalia. "The family requires my presence elsewhere, but I shall take a great interest in the campaign. I assume it will start shortly?"

"Indeed. We begin marching on the feast of Saint Agnes. Rather fitting when you think about it, at least from the Stormwind point of view."

"I'm afraid I don't see the connection."

"The Temple Knights of Saint Agnes drove your family from the duke's court."

"I assume Gregori chose the date?"

"He did. Said he had a flair for the dramatic. To be honest, I doubt it makes any difference whatsoever, but it has to start sometime, and better sooner, before winter sets in."

"And so, you settled for a late fall campaign. A risky venture, especially if the weather turns."

"Don't worry. There won't be much marching involved. I fully expect the duke will advance into Andover to face off against us. Better to fight on foreign soil than to risk the enemy capturing your capital."

"And you're not worried about Zienholtz?"

"Not in the least. Even if he could march all the way here, he'd still be outnumbered. Of course, if he were smart, he'd surrender before the battle begins. At least that way, he'd avoid a blood-bath." He drained his cup once again. "Not that I'd expect him to give up without a fight. In fact, I look forward to giving his army a really good thrashing."

SIEGE

AUTUMN 1108 SR

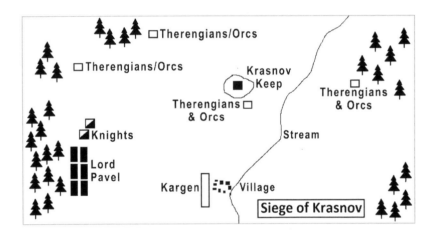

Siege of Krasnov

K argen halted as he cleared the trees, taking in the view. Ahead of him marched his army, heading towards a group of buildings that constituted the village of Krasnov.

It wasn't much to look at, consisting of maybe a dozen buildings clustered near a stream, yet not so different from Runewald. Surrounding the village, fields sat empty, for they'd brought in the harvest some time ago.

"*It is quiet,*" he said in his native tongue. "*Too quiet.*"

"*Yes,*" agreed Shaluhk. "*And there is no smoke. I think they have emptied the place of its villagers.*"

"*And of its livestock, it would seem.*"

Raleth appeared at his side. "We are ready to advance on your command."

"I do not trust the silence," said Kargen, quickly switching to the common tongue of Humans. "Have Kragor take the warbows westward and clear that group of trees of anything dangerous. Once they are done, they are to proceed eastward into the village."

"And the rest?"

"Hold here until we know those buildings are safe."

"You suspect a trap?"

"Valentyn's war band has already demonstrated its capacity to surprise us. Let us not be fooled a second time."

Raleth ran off, calling out orders.

Kargen once more focused his attention on the village, then let his gaze follow the stream as it led to a prominent mound, upon which sat Valentyn's keep.

Rectangular in shape, it was an impressive sight, dominating the area and reminding all those below who the master of this land truly was.

"*Interesting, yet, at the same time, foolish,*" came an Orcish voice.

Kargen turned in surprise to see Rugg.

"*Foolish?*"

"*Yes,*" continued the master of earth. "*True, it is an impressive structure, but the hill it sits upon is a weak spot when it comes to the magic of the earth.*"

"*How so?*"

The old Orc grinned. "*The weight of all that stone will be tremendous. Were the dirt beneath it shifted, I would imagine its own weight would prove its downfall.*"

"*But you would need to get within arrow range to perform such a feat, would you not?*"

"*You understand our ways well. We would indeed require close access to that mound. Can our hunters keep their bowmen at bay?*"

"*That is difficult to assess. The defenders have a nice stone wall to hide behind, while we have none.*"

"*Yet,*" added Rugg.

"*Are you proposing we construct our own?*"

"*You forget, us Stone Crushers can manipulate dirt, even form it into stone. It would be a time-consuming process, to be sure, but would provide us with some protection as we strive to undermine that monstrosity.*"

"I will bear that in mind," said Kargen. "First, though, we must take possession of the village. Once that is done, we shall encircle the keep, cutting off all communication with the outside."

"*Have we enough people for that?*"

"It will stretch us to our limit, but I believe so. That keep has only one way out, and watching a door is not difficult, even from a distance. The question is whether or not he has secreted away any warriors in the woods hereabouts."

"There is also the matter of the villagers," offered Shaluhk. *"It is not likely the baron pulled them into the keep. Such an act would strain his stores of food."*

"Agreed," said Kargen, *"and from what I have seen of Lord Valentyn, he has little time for those of common birth. That means they are probably out there, somewhere, struggling to survive."*

"You should send Hilwyth out looking for them," said Shaluhk. *"She has an inviting manner. Perhaps she can convince them we mean no harm."*

"No harm?" said Rugg. *"We come with an army to destroy Lord Valentyn's keep. I should say that is the very definition of harm."*

"We are here to destroy the baron, that is true, but that does not have to be at the expense of the villagers."

"Shaluhk is correct," said Kargen, *"and Hilwyth is well-spoken. Perhaps she can convince them to come out from hiding."*

"Assuming they are still here," said Rugg. *"In any event, it is of little consequence to me."*

Kargen focused once more on the distant keep. *"That is the real prize here. If we bring down those stone walls, we will break Lord Valentyn's power. Can you assure me of success?"*

"I can, though it will take some time."

"You have three ten-days. After that, our food stores will be exhausted."

"Then we had best get started."

The woods had proven bare of any resistance, and now Kragor's hunters crossed open fields, heading towards the buildings that stood eerily silent.

"Remain alert," he called out.

His hunters slowed, their arrows nocked but not drawn. Grundak led the way, with the others following single file. Kragor watched as they reached the outermost building and then entered the village, disappearing from sight.

Moments later, an Orc yelled out, and the sound of fighting drifted towards him. He ordered the rest of his hunters to rush in, then slung his bow, drawing an axe in its stead.

He cleared the first building, only to witness a scene from the Underworld unfolding before his very eyes. Dozens of men converged on the central clearing in the middle of the village, where Grundak and his hunters had formed a rough circle. The enemy would soon swarm them. Kragor ordered a charge, then screamed out a challenge and rushed in, throwing all caution to the wind.

The enemy, intent on overwhelming the small scouting force, suddenly faced the prospect of a full engagement. Sword met axe with a great clash, and then the battle was on.

Kragor took down one with his first swing, his axe biting deep into the man's shoulder. He ignored the scream, pushing his foe aside and forcing his way forward.

Arrows peppered the crowd, and more Humans went down. He briefly glimpsed someone in metal armour directing the attack, but then a pair of warriors loomed before him, forcing him to fight for his life.

A blade dug into his bicep, black blood flowing down his arm. The rage built, and his axe took a Human in the face, getting stuck. His enemy fell, threatening to take the Orc's weapon with him. Kragor held on, using all his strength to pull it free.

A blade dug into his back, and he screamed as his legs gave out, no longer under his control. He fell heavily, then rolled over, ready to meet his death. A Human loomed over him, prepared for a fatal strike, but it never came. Someone yelled something in the Human tongue, then the baron's men broke off the fight, fleeing north. Moments later, Grundak's face appeared, along with the smell of smoke.

"They torched the village," the hunter said.

Kragor grunted back.

"Are you badly injured?"

"I cannot feel my legs."

"I shall send for a shaman."

"What of the Humans?"

"They are retreating," said Grundak. "They hit us hard, then withdrew, leaving us in confusion. It seems the baron's men still have a few surprises left for us."

Kargen watched the village burn.

"They are masters of deception," said Raleth. "What will they do next?"

"Have you secured the village?"

"What's left of it. Shaluhk is looking after the wounded, but we have taken casualties."

"Kragor?"

"Badly injured, but he should make a full recovery, thanks to your bond-mate's magic."

"That is good," said Kargen, "but he will probably require much rest. I must appoint a new leader of the warbows. Perhaps I shall lead them myself?"

"You can't," replied Raleth. "We need you here."

"I am not used to commanding from afar. I would prefer to be amongst my tribe, leading by example."

"Your expertise is required to lead the entire army."

Kargen let out a sigh. "You are right, but the losses of our people weigh heavily upon me."

"Our losses were light, relatively speaking."

"Even the death of one hunter is too much. Perhaps we would have been better off letting the barons have this wretched country?"

"And have them invade us again in a few years? No, Kargen. You did the right thing, and your guilt over the loss of your fellow tribemates reveals your true quality."

"And what quality is that?"

"Compassion," said Raleth. "A trait you share with Athgar."

Kargen grunted. "I shall take that as a compliment. I wish he were here. I could use his support, not to mention Nat-Alia's expertise. No doubt, such trickery would not have fooled her."

"I doubt even Natalia could predict such a tactic. In any event, it's over and done with. All that remains is to clear the area surrounding the keep. There are no more hiding places, not if they hope to take refuge behind those walls."

They gathered that evening in the ruins of the village, its burned timbers looming over them like the warped bones of some long-dead creature.

"Have we secured the perimeter?" asked Kargen.

"We have," replied Hilwyth. "We also located some villagers…" Her voice trailed off.

"You have more to say?"

"They were driven from their homes by order of Lord Valentyn. He wanted nothing left to aid us in our endeavours."

"And the cattle?" asked Kargen.

"Slaughtered and taken inside the keep. Some of the townsfolk even tried to gain entry but were refused. Most took to the wilderness, fearing we would butcher them."

"We do not kill innocents!"

"We know this," said Hilwyth, "but that's not what they were told. You must remember, the only outside news they receive comes from the baron."

"He's used that to warp their minds," added Raleth. "It will take a lot of work to convince them otherwise."

"Feed them," said Shaluhk.

"But we have limited stores."

"Then we shall make do. It is more important to win over the people than defeat the baron."

Raleth stared back. "You can't possibly mean that. Our entire purpose in coming here was to destroy Valentyn's army."

"What matters who rules if no one is left to rule over?"

Raleth stood there, his anger threatening to boil to the surface. Hilwyth calmed him, placing her hand on her husband's forearm. "She's right," she said. "We cannot allow these people to starve. When we defeated Queen Rada, we took it upon ourselves to rule in her stead, a task that carries a heavy burden—one we can ill-afford to ignore."

He turned to face his wife, ready to argue but saw only compassion. "You're right. The entire point of what we're trying to do here is to give these people a better life. We cannot do that by letting them starve."

"It is a difficult situation we are in," said Shaluhk, "but the Ancestors will guide us."

"You consulted them?"

"I have, though our situation is something they have not experienced for centuries."

"Are you suggesting they know how to assault a keep?"

"You forget, our Ancestors fought alongside the Old Kingdom. There is much to be learned from their experiences." She turned to Rugg. "How long will it take you to bring down the keep's walls?"

"We do not know how much dirt we must remove to cause the collapse, which is one of our problems. We must also get close enough to wield our magic. At the moment, their arrows would pick off our masters of earth before they could even cast their first spell."

"The plan," said Kargen, "is to send a group of hunters to the base of that hill under cover of darkness, accompanied by Rugg, who will assess the best place to base the eventual attack. Once complete, they will mark the area, then return to report their findings."

"And then?" asked Raleth.

"A digging party will advance to the marked area and create a shallow ditch, piling the dirt up so Rugg and the other masters can turn it into a stone wall."

"That will be dangerous. It's likely the defenders will rain arrows down on them."

"That is expected," said Kargen. "To counter that, we must use archers of our own. It is not a perfect solution, but it is better than accepting the inevitable losses."

"The Runewald fyrd volunteers to do the digging," said Hilwyth. "They are farmers, for the most part, used to performing manual labour."

"I accept their offer," said Kargen. "Anything anyone else would like to add?"

"How about a diversion?" asked Raleth. "An attack on their gate would draw their attention quite nicely."

"I assume you are volunteering to lead it?"

"I am."

"Then I approve, but remember, it is a diversion only. We can ill-afford losses this early in the attack."

"Understood."

"Shaluhk, I would like you to take charge of the villagers. We should also look at finding them some shelter. The leaves have changed, and winter's icy winds will soon be upon us."

"I shall help her," said Grazuhk. "My Cloud Hunters are used to living in the wild and making camps."

"Then it is settled," said Kargen. "Now, each to your duties. We have a busy night before us."

Hilwyth crouched. Ahead of her, a group of Orc hunters made their way north in the dark. The ground here was open, for someone had cleared the trees years ago, the better to spot any who might seek to attack the keep.

She waited for the customary call and then moved her warriors up another hundred paces. The Orcs, in response, held, their eyes glued on the keep. Once in place, she raised her hand, signalling they'd completed their movement. It was an odd sensation, giving a signal in the dark, but on a cloudless night like this, she knew from experience the Orc's night vision allowed them to see her.

All went quiet. The next part of the advance would be the most danger-ous, for they would be well within the range of the defenders' arrows. She looked left and right. The Runewald fyrd was almost prone, so determined were they to remain hidden. A third of them clutched hoes and shovels. They would dig the ditch while the rest stood guard, ready to repel any counterattack the enemy might attempt.

She briefly wondered if other leaders felt as she did before a battle. Did the champions of the Petty Kingdoms worry about their fate, or were they so used to death that they laughed in its face?

Panic threatened to overwhelm her. She would die here, in this gods' forsaken country, never again to set foot in Runewald. The desire to flee turned her blood cold, but then the sound of fighting drifted to her ears— Raleth's attack on the gate had started. Hilwyth's sense of duty took hold, and she waved her warriors forward.

The Thane Guard advanced up the steps that led to the keep. It was a steep climb, for the stairs began at the bottom of the hill. He ordered shields to be placed above heads, overlapping to give them some protection from arrows.

The warriors crouched as they awkwardly took the stairs one at a time. Arrows thudding into shields, sounding like hail. One slipped through a flaw in their defence and sank into a shoulder. Luckily, the man's mail saved him, but the arrow hung there, entangled in the chain links, a sign of the ferocity of the volleys.

Raleth's legs ached from the climb, his back from the forced crouch, and his left arm from holding his shield aloft. He wondered if there was any muscle left in his body that wasn't sore.

They were halfway up the hill when the volleys quieted. Raleth felt something was about to happen, but for the life of him, he couldn't imagine what.

"Shield wall!" he called out.

The warriors spread out, no small feat, considering the incline. Ahead, the moon behind the tower bathed the entrance in shadows, but Raleth swore he saw movement.

"Hold fast," he said. "They're coming!"

The sound of footsteps on stone came towards them, and then the enemy left the shadows. There were at least a dozen of them, all knights in the plate armour they so prized. Their leader led his men down the stairs, rushing into the fight without taking time to coordinate their attack.

The knights hit the wall of shields with a loud crash. Weapons struck out, splintering at least one shield and driving back the Therengians. Raleth tried to push his way to the front of the line, but in the dark and on uneven ground, all he managed was to hold his position.

The press of warriors grew, those in the back pushing forward to give strength to the front. Blood flew freely, some spraying onto his face as an axe dug into the neck of one of his men. The fellow collapsed, his body sliding downhill, knocking two others from their feet.

The enemy, eager to take advantage of their misfortune, gave a yell, increasing the attack's ferocity.

Raleth spotted a knight looming closer and smashed his axe into the fellow, digging into the man's pauldron but failing to penetrate the thick metal plates. He followed that up by rushing forward and striking again. This time his weapon hit his foe's helmet, but it, too, did not penetrate. He tried to pull it free, only to find it lodged between the helmet and visor. Another tug released it, twisting the helmet and leaving his enemy temporarily blind.

Other Therengians swarmed the poor fool, and he fell to the ground. The sounds of axes ringing on the metal plates accompanied his screams of agony.

Raleth looked around, seeking another target, but the enemy was withdrawing up the stairs to the safety of their keep. As difficult as it was to make out details in the dark, it appeared half a dozen of his warriors had fallen. He ordered them gathered, then withdrew as more arrows rained down on them.

COUNCIL OF WAR

AUTUMN 1108 SR

"I'm afraid I must leave you," said Athgar, still using the Orcish tongue. "*Beyond those farms is the city of Korvoran, and I doubt the soldiers there would look kindly upon you.*"

"*Understandable,*" said Zhogral. "*We will linger here awhile and await word.*"

"*How will we eat?*" said Gharog. "*To hunt the fat cows of these farms would be to invite retribution.*"

"*There is plenty of food in these woods, and the Humans are easy enough to avoid, should it prove necessary.*"

"*I shall get back to you as soon as possible,*" said Athgar. "*Farewell, my friend, and may the Ancestors look kindly upon you. You, too, Gharog.*"

The shaman in training turned a darker shade of green. "*You honour us, Ashwalker.*"

"What did they say?" asked Herulf.

"They are wishing us well," said Athgar. "Now, we'd best be on our way if we want to reach Korvoran by nightfall."

"Allow me to lead, Lord. I know this area well."

"Is this where you live?"

"No, not anymore, but I grew up here. My home lies north of Korvoran now, thanks to the efforts of Lord Wilfhelm. When our presence came to his attention, he became alarmed, claiming we were a threat to the realm's security. I suppose, to his mind, a community of Therengians living so close to the border could aid an invasion. Apparently, it never occurred to him that Andover executes us on sight."

"So, he just moved all of you?"

"Moving us all wouldn't have been so bad, but the duke went to the trouble of spreading us out over a large swath of land between Korvoran and Herenstadt, mixing us in with the local population to dilute our presence. They tore families apart, separating children from their parents, and for what? We were no threat to him!"

"They took your children?"

"Aye, to be sent to work on farms. They thought they could work the culture out from them."

"I'm sorry," said Athgar. "I knew they feared the rebirth of the Old Kingdom, but I had no idea they went to such extremes."

"It is not your fault, Lord. The blame rests firmly on the duke's shoulders."

"Then you may rest assured, once I'm back at his court, I will do all I can to bring the plight of your people... our people, to his attention."

"I doubt it'll do any good."

"We shall see," said Athgar.

They entered the city of Korvoran, where word of the impending war weighed heavily on everyone, with groups gathering in the streets to discuss the matter. Athgar avoided these assemblies, for the most part, but they were greeted with suspicious looks wherever they went.

The discussions became more passionate the farther they travelled into the city; it didn't take long for the blame to fall on the grey-eyed quartet and their Dwarf companion. Athgar turned westward, heading towards the duke's estate, but soon people started following them.

Herulf looked around nervously. "I don't like the looks of this, Lord."

"They're nervous," said Athgar, "and want someone to blame for their ills. Ignore them. We will be at the duke's estate soon enough."

A small stone hit him in the back. He halted, turning to meet his attacker. A half-dozen men were yelling at him, raising their voices to gird their fellows into action.

"We are not your enemy," said Athgar. "Go home and look to your families."

One individual stepped forward, clutching a cudgel and looking like he knew how to use it.

"Begone, I say!" Athgar raised his hand, conjuring a flame, then kept it floating there, a display of power rather than an overt threat. It had the desired effect. Eyes went wide, and then, one by one, the townsfolk left. Only the man with the cudgel remained, and then he appeared to rethink his position. He backed up a few steps before he turned and strolled down the street as if it were just another ordinary day.

Herulf let out a sigh of relief. "You see what we have to deal with? We might not be under penalty of death here, like in Andover, but they blame us for everything."

"Let's see if we can change that, shall we? Though perhaps not today, when an invasion threatens the kingdom."

The streets grew wider before the duke's estate came into view. Guards watched them approach, and then one of them ran into the building, presumably to warn others.

"I am Athgar, son of Rothgar, here to see His Grace, the duke." He noted the hesitation in the guards, then realized his companions were still armed. "These men are sworn to my service," he added, "but will lay down their arms in order to gain entry."

The guards moved forward to disarm them before leading them into the building.

"This way," ordered a guard. "His Grace is presently consulting with his advisors." They halted at a door. "Wait here."

Athgar waited as one of their guides entered the room. Moments later, he returned, waving them in.

"Lord Athgar," called out Lord Fernando. "So glad you could make it."

"Where is your wife?" asked the duke. "Have we any word from Zienholtz?"

"Not at present, Your Grace," replied Athgar. "I'd hoped to find her here, amongst your advisors." He looked around, taking in the faces of those present. They were mostly old men, though he recognized Temple Captain Leona amongst the group.

The duke grunted before returning his attention to the table before him. Athgar moved closer to look at the crudely drawn map of the area. Small painted stones sat upon it, though to what end he wasn't sure.

"I say we move the bulk of the army here," said an older, white-haired individual who sported a large moustache. He moved several stones, and then Athgar noted the small symbols painted on them. Clearly, they represented warriors, either foot, horse, or bow; at least, that's what he assumed.

"Yes," said the duke. "We all know your opinion on the matter, General, but do we move the entire army? That would leave our home undefended, wouldn't it?"

"It would," replied the general, "but the threat comes from the south. To hold back now would be to court disaster. We must send everything we have and smash their army before it has a chance to organize."

The duke turned to his son. "What do you think, Fernando?"

"I'm interested to hear what news Lord Athgar brings."

All eyes fell on Athgar.

"I've heard nothing of the enemy's strength, if that's what you're asking," he said, "although I learned they have called the levy to assemble. If Andover is to march, it will be soon. I do, however, have some good news."

"Which is?" said the duke.

"I may have found us an ally."

"An ally, you say? Has Burgemont decided to come to our aid, or Erlingen, perhaps?"

"No, Your Grace, but I received a pledge of aid from Rugal, Chieftain of the Ashwalkers."

"Ashwalkers?"

"A tribe of Orcs, Your Grace. They come seeking a home in exchange for their help. I thought maybe the Thornwood?"

The room exploded with shouts of disdain.

"Orcs?" said the duke. "We stand on the edge of ruin, and you bring me Orcs? By the Saints, I thought you smarter than that! We need real allies, not green-skinned savages!"

"The Orcs are valuable allies, Your Grace. I've worked with their kind many times and always found them to be stalwart companions."

"Get him out of here! By the Saints, I should string him up for his insubordination."

"Lord Athgar," said Fernando, "might I have a word in private?"

They stepped out of the room, the duke's son leading the way. "You must excuse my father. He's rather set in his ways."

"His lands are in peril," said Athgar. "I would think he'd be grateful for any help offered."

"And he should, to be sure, but he's exceedingly stubborn, always has been."

"Then what am I to do? Simply tell the Orcs to go home?"

"How many warriors have they at their disposal?"

"The Orcs don't have warriors; they have hunters, and they're the best skirmishers on the entire Continent. The Ashwalkers also have Fire Mages, which would greatly benefit your father's army, not to mention their shamans."

"Shamans? Priests of some long-forgotten god?"

"You would know them better as Life Mages, something I understand is rare amongst the Petty Kingdoms. Would you refuse their healing magic simply because their beliefs differ from your own?"

"I admit," said Fernando, "I know little of the Orcs, but I can see the benefit they would bring to this campaign. Talk to this chieftain, Rugal, and tell him that if he comes to our aid, we shall give the Ashwalkers the Thornwood to call their own."

"And your father will accept this agreement?"

"My father is an old man, and sooner or later, I shall inherit the seat of power. If my father does not honour my promise, I will, once I become duke. You have my word on it."

"And in the meantime?"

Lord Fernando shrugged. "What my father doesn't know won't hurt him. The truth is there is little reason for someone to journey into the Thornwood. Should the Orcs take up residence there, I doubt anyone would even notice."

"And if they do?"

"I shall be sure to intercept any such message heading my father's way. In time, I believe I can convince him of the benefits, but this impending invasion consumes him right now."

"And so," said Athgar, "we help him behind his back?"

"Let's be clear, shall we? I will do everything in my power to save Reinwick. If that means giving away a portion of our border to secure our safety, then so be it."

"There is, perhaps, more we can do."

"I'm listening."

"Within the borders of Reinwick are many who would help but are banned from taking up arms."

"You speak of those descended from the Old Kingdom."

"I do," said Athgar, "and I believe they could make the difference between victory and defeat. Let them join your army. They can fight as well as any other."

"That, I fear, would be a step too far. My father might overlook the Orcs, for he would see them as a relatively distant and unseen threat. Therengians, however, are another story entirely."

"He accepted my help readily enough."

"True, but you came here with your wife, and the Stormwinds' power is known throughout the Petty Kingdoms. Who are you compared to her?"

Athgar found his anger building. "I am Athgar, son of Rothgar, master of flame and High Thane of Therengia."

Lord Fernando stared back, at a loss for words. He finally closed his mouth and found his wits. "High Thane? Are you telling me you're the ruler of Therengia?"

"I am. And Natalia Stormwind is our warmaster. You would be wise to seek her advice when it comes time to go into battle."

"I shall. I promise. Might I ask where a High Thane sits in relation to a noble? Are you a king, for example, or are you more like a duke?"

"The position of High Thane is not hereditary; a council consisting of all the thanes of the realm selects its occupant. He, or she, also serves at the will of the people, with a solemn oath to serve them. At least, that's the intention."

"And no one ever tries to use the position to their advantage?"

"We are a young realm, but we follow the ideals our ancestors laid down. Yes, there is the possibility that a ruler might seek to take advantage, but if that happened, the Thanes Council would remove him from the position and appoint someone new."

"And you work with Orcs?"

"Yes," said Athgar. "Our ruling council includes the chieftains and shamans of each tribe along with the thanes."

"Each tribe? Are you saying there's more than one?"

"There are four at the moment, but it's possible more have sought to join us since Natalia and I left home."

"I am sorry, Lord. Had I known of your true identity, I would have taken steps to treat you accordingly."

"I hid my identity because I feared what may happen should it be discovered."

"Then why reveal it now? Aren't you worried we might arrest you?"

"The thought had struck me, but I sense you are a man of your word, Lord. I reveal all to you now to impress upon you the need for strong action. The descendants of the Old Kingdom can be of immense benefit to you, should you allow them that option."

Lord Fernando nodded. "I understand you, Lord, or do I call you Your Majesty?"

"How about you just call me Athgar?"

"I can do that, providing you call me Fernando. Let me offer you the hand of friendship."

Athgar grasped his hand in a firm grip. "A great distance separates our lands, yet I see a bright future for us both."

"How so?"

"Therengia needs recognition, while Reinwick needs allies."

"And that's your price for helping us? Simple recognition?"

"Is that too high a price?"

"Not at all. The fact is, this new kingdom of yours is far too distant to be seen as a threat to Reinwick. I'm sure even my father would recognize the advantages of such an exchange. Of course, this is all dependent on us defeating Andover."

"Then arm the descendants."

Fernando stared back, deep in thought. "My father would never allow it. There is, however, an alternative."

"Which is?"

"Are you familiar with the concept of a levy?"

"Of course. We have the same idea back home but call it a fyrd."

"Every man between the age of fifteen and sixty is expected to take up arms should the levy be called upon. Normally, everyone equips themselves based on their income, but each village must keep a store of arms as spares. Therengians, or rather descendants of the Old Kingdom, may not be given any of those, but I could argue the need, for the kingdom's defence outweighs such a restriction. I shall ensure word is spread that they are to be armed when we raise the levy."

"And when will that be?"

"As soon as we receive word that Andover is marching."

"Why wait?" asked Athgar.

"The levy only serves for thirty days. Call it too soon, and we would find it deserting us before the battle."

"And will this levy march with your father's army?"

"Unlikely. They'll be used as garrison troops to free up the rest to head south. Most likely, they wouldn't even fight, but at least it would allow them to do their part."

"And when the war is over?"

"I cannot promise my father will make amends," said Fernando, "but I will do all I can to improve their lot in life. I promise. We are not so different, you and I."

"In what way?"

"We both care for our people."

"Do we?" said Athgar. "You have a strange way of showing it. Your people openly mock those with grey eyes, yet you do nothing to discourage it. And all this even though the Old Kingdom died off over five hundred years ago."

"You are from the east, so I will excuse your ignorance of our heritage. The truth is the Petty Kingdoms have feared the return of the Old Kingdom for centuries."

"I understand that; what I don't understand is why. What is it about Therengia you fear so much?"

"Everything about your culture threatens our way of life; don't you see? Imagine a continent ruled by those chosen by the masses. It would be utter chaos. And where would that leave people like me? I know it's selfish, but we nobles wish to preserve our way of life. It has served us for centuries and should continue to do so."

Athgar shook his head. "Therengia is no threat to you. We are a peaceful people, intent on bettering the lives of all who choose to live amongst us."

"And yet we hear you conquered a Petty Kingdom. Novarsk, wasn't it?"

"It's true, I'll not deny it, but you must know the full story. Following the rebirth of Therengia, warriors from all across the Continent came east, eager to see us destroyed. We defeated them, but then the Queen of Novarsk, thinking us weakened, launched an invasion of her own."

"I had no idea," said Fernando. "Then again, I suppose I only heard one side of the story, the one that painted you as the villains of the campaign. It shows what can happen when one takes a narrow view of events."

"And now?"

"I think you are earnest in your desire for peace, but that being the case, I fear you've come to the wrong place. I still hope Captain Marwen's diplomatic efforts might prove successful, but at the same time, I'm a realist. Andover will invade, perhaps not today or this week, but war is coming, and there is little we can do to prevent it. Having accepted that, I must do all I can to ensure the survival of Reinwick, and if that means giving land to the Orcs and arming your people, then I shall do so to accomplish precisely that."

"Thank you," said Athgar. "And I, in turn, will do all within my power to bring you victory. I only wish Natalia were here to lend her aid."

FLIGHT

AUTUMN 1108 SR

Stanislav popped a piece of cheese into his mouth. "Delicious," he said. "I'm getting quite used to all this pampering."

"Don't get too comfortable," warned Natalia, staring out a window. "We can't stay here forever."

He sighed. "It's just as well. If I stayed, I'd just keep eating, and then where would I be?"

"Lying in a coma, most likely, the result of eating too much cheese."

"Come now, can a person ever have too much cheese?"

She was about to respond with a retort, but a knock interrupted her thoughts. Deveral quickly answered the door, revealing young Greta, note in hand.

"From the king," she said.

"Give it here, then," snapped the servant.

"I'm to deliver it to Lady Natalia in person."

"Then don't just stand there. Come in, for Saint's sake."

The girl crossed the room, coming to a halt by Natalia's side, but her gaze darted back to Deveral.

Natalia took the note and broke the seal, perusing its contents. "It appears His Majesty has once again invited me to join him for dinner."

"Tonight?" said Stanislav. "That's short notice, isn't it?"

She opened her mouth to respond but then noticed Greta shifting back and forth, a sure sign of nervousness. The young girl met her gaze before glancing apprehensively again at Deveral.

"I suppose I should send a reply," said Natalia. "I will adjourn to the study." She moved towards the room, then paused, looking back at her messenger. "Come, Greta. You can wait in here for my response." She waited as the young girl entered the room, then followed her, closing the door behind them.

"Is something wrong?" Natalia asked.

Greta merely nodded, too terrified to speak.

"Come now," soothed Natalia. "Whatever it is, you can tell me." She knelt, taking the young girl's hands in hers. "We're not here to hurt you."

"It's the king. He means to kill you."

The words shook Natalia to the core. "How would you know that?"

"When I was summoned to take that letter, I overheard him talking with the other mage."

"Ria Sartellian?"

"That's the one. They said all of you had to die. He plans to do it tonight when you show up for dinner."

"And you're sure of this?"

The girl nodded her head emphatically.

Natalia moved to the door, opening it a crack. "Stanislav, I require you and Katrin in here to help me pick out a suitable gift for King Dagmar. You, too, Galina."

They all filed in and gathered around her.

"Is something wrong?" asked Katrin.

"Yes, there is," Natalia replied. "It appears the king wants us all dead. According to Greta, he plans to kill us this evening."

"And you trust this girl?" said Galina.

"There is no reason not to. She risked severe punishment bringing us this news. What has she to gain by lying?"

Stanislav looked around the room as if trying to see through the walls. "I shouldn't need to remind you of our current predicament. There are guards everywhere, and the only protection we can call on is the captain's escort, and they're miles away."

"We're hardly defenceless," replied Natalia. "I might remind you we have three Stormwinds at our disposal, not to mention a seasoned mage hunter."

"Seasoned? Is that your way of saying I'm old?"

"Never mind him," said Katrin. "How do we get out of here?"

"We have a little time," said Natalia. "But we can't afford to waste it. Stanislav, you must get into the city. Find the escort, if you can, but whether or not you're successful, I need you to acquire us some horses."

"We're not taking the carriages?"

"Those will be in the possession of the Palace stable hands. It's also the first place they'll expect us to go should we try to escape."

"I'm afraid that's going to be expensive. With the army massing, the price of mounts will have gone up considerably."

Natalia dug through the writing desk, pulling forth a purse. "This is what Lord Fernando gave us. Use all of it, if necessary, but get us those horses."

"Even if I have to steal them?"

She smiled. "I shall leave that to your discretion."

"And where will I go once I have said mounts?"

"I would suggest outside the north gate," said Katrin. "That's the way we entered the city. If you remember, there was an old tavern about half a mile down the road."

"I remember now: the Watering Hole, wasn't it? We never did go there. Captain Marwen was in too much of a hurry to get to the Palace."

"Speaking of the captain, what do we do about him?"

"We can't leave him here," said Galina. "They'll kill him."

"Then go and find him," said Natalia. "Tell him I need to consult with him before my dinner with the king. Whatever you do, say nothing of what we've learned."

"And once we're all together?"

"She could use the frozen arch spell," said Katrin. "Like she did back in Karslev."

"That would save us," said Galina, "but then we'd be at the family's mercy. The spell only works with known magic circles, remember?"

"I know a way," said Greta.

They all turned to her in surprise.

"The servants' stairs are nearby," she continued. "There's a hidden door down the hallway."

"We'd still need to get past all those guards outside our door," said Katrin. "I doubt they'd let us have free rein to wander the Palace grounds without an escort."

"Then we'll have to fight," said Galina. "Unless Natalia has another way of getting us out of here? I don't suppose you learned some new spell from that ancient tome of magic we liberated from the Volstrum?"

"Nothing that would help us here, I'm afraid. We'll have to rely on good old-fashioned battle magic." Natalia opened the drawer to the desk, withdrew some paper, and then dipped a quill, holding it ready for use. "Now, Greta," she began, "how about you tell us everything you can remember about the servants' quarters?"

.   .   .

Greta poked her head into the hallway. The guards noted her presence but remained in place. She carefully closed the door.

"They're still out there and still wide awake."

"I would expect no less," said Natalia. "Now, I want you to leave us."

Tears welled up in the girl's eyes. "But I want to go with you."

"Surely you have family who will miss you?"

"No. They died years ago, and the Palace servants yell at me."

"It's far too dangerous for you to accompany us."

"I'll take care of her," said Katrin. "I know what it's like to be alone. I won't allow Greta to suffer as I did."

"Very well, but I must insist we do things my way." Natalia knelt, putting her head at the young girl's level. "I need you to wander down the hall and enter the servants' stairwell. We'll follow along shortly, but it's important they don't know you're expecting us. Do you understand?"

"I do."

"Good. Then off you go, just as if you were delivering a message."

Greta stepped out into the hall, and then her footsteps receded. Natalia closed the door, putting her back against it and taking a deep breath.

"Are you sure this is wise?" said Captain Marwen.

"Escaping?"

"No, putting our faith in a little girl. For all we know, she could be working against us."

"Would you prefer to enter a room full of Dagmar's warriors?"

He paused before finally relenting. "No, I suppose not."

"Everyone know what you're supposed to do?"

They all nodded.

"Good, then let's begin." She turned to face the door, taking a moment to work up her courage. Natalia had seen her fair share of battles, but there was no army on which to rely here. She would have only her own magic to save them. No, she thought, that's not entirely correct. Galina is a powerful mage in her own right, and Katrin had already mastered several spells. Still, the numbers were stacked against them, for the Palace was crawling with the king's soldiers, and the most inconvenient ones were those standing watch outside their door.

She opened the door and spoke as if continuing with a conversation. "And see that my clothes are laid out for me come morning." She stepped into the hall, with Katrin at her side.

Meanwhile, Captain Marwen turned his attention to the servants. "Remember, one word of this to anyone, and you'll feel my wrath! Galina here has placed a spell on each of you. Try to reveal our secret, and you will instantly die." He noted their look of fear. It would keep them quiet for now, but it wouldn't matter anymore by the time they escaped. He turned once more to Deveral, who sat tied to a chair, his mouth gagged. "As for you, you can tell your king the next time we see him, we'll be hunting for his head."

"Are we done?" said Galina. "I only ask because Natalia and Katrin are already halfway down the hallway."

"Of course, my apologies, my lady." He offered his arm, then they stepped through the doorway, the manoeuvre made even more cumbersome by his gallant offer.

Natalia kept chatting away, but in her head, she counted the columns that decorated the corridor. She came to a halt, then looked at Katrin and nodded. Katrin stepped to the side, pressing a wall section that produced a click. A doorway appeared, revealing a narrow set of stairs.

"You there!" called a guard. "That area's forbidden." He moved from his position, his hand going to the hilt of his sword.

Natalia threw out one arm, calling forth her power and sending a shard of ice flying down the hallway, striking her intended target full in the chest, shattering against his breastplate and knocking him to the floor.

His comrade, standing against the opposite wall, took three steps before Katrin's bolt of ice struck his leg, making a metallic noise as it hit. The fellow's leg went out from under him, and he fell, screaming in pain.

"Go!" shouted Natalia.

Katrin entered the stairwell while Natalia watched those behind them. Now on full alert, the rest of the guards ran down the hallway, swords in hand, intent on slaying the two women. What they hadn't counted on, however, was the delayed exit of Galina and Captain Marwen.

Galina knelt, touching her hand to the floor. Ice formed, then spread out in front of her, down the hallway, freezing all it contacted. The guards, intent only on their prey, took no notice until the floor suddenly became icy beneath their feet.

One of the king's knights, more aware of his surroundings, slowed his pace before he turned, noting the presence of these two interlopers. "Hah!" he cried out, making his way towards Galina.

Captain Marwen stepped forward, his sword ready to take on this new threat. Natalia knelt, mimicking Galina's actions, but this time a thick layer of ice exploded, rushing down the hallway, gripping boots as the magic grew.

Almost all the guards now struggled to free their feet, their enemy forgotten in a wild moment of panic. A clash of swords echoed down the hall, and the last guard's weapon flew off to one side. The sword wielder threw up his arms, begging for quarter, but Captain Marwen and Galina were already past him, moving slowly to avoid slipping on the ice.

"That was impressive," said the captain. "But it won't take them long to recover."

"Let me worry about that," said Natalia. She guided them into the stairwell and then turned back to the concealed door, raising her arms and calling forth more words of power. Ice built up, jamming the door shut as the frozen portal spell took hold. Down the stairs she fled, following the echoing footsteps of her companions.

Greta led them, turning abruptly at intersections and through doors hidden inside panels. As they raced through the corridors, Natalia struggled to keep her bearings. Shouts of alarm echoed throughout while the sound of running feet was their constant companion. Eventually, a thick wooden door appeared before them, and Greta pushed it open, revealing the Palace gardens.

"This way," she called out before running down a pathway. Trees and bushes obscured their view of the path ahead until the high metal fence surrounding the grounds finally came into view, and they turned and ran parallel to it.

"The gate is just down here," said Greta, skidding to a stop.

Before them stood the back gate, a tall, imposing metal monstrosity that looked like someone had pulled it straight from the Underworld. Strange metal heads adorned it, twisted into a mockery of Human faces with sharp, pointed teeth and enlarged eyes.

A dozen guards stood before it, their weapons drawn, their shields held ready. The only saving grace was that they had not yet seen the escaping prisoners.

Katrin grabbed Greta, pulling her back out of the way, while Galina looked at Natalia. "What do we do now? We can't possibly take on that many."

"I'm not afraid to fight," said Captain Marwen.

"Nor I," added Natalia, "and I'm sure we could defeat them ,given enough time, but I fear any confrontation will only bring more."

"But we must get to the other side of this fence," said Katrin.

Natalia moved closer to the wall, peering past its metal bars to the grounds beyond.

"Can we climb it?" asked Katrin.

"You tell me. The fence is topped with points, not to mention being well over our heads. They'd spot us long before we reached the top, and I doubt any of us could cast spells while holding on to those bars."

"This is so frustrating. We're so close!"

Natalia glanced towards the gate, then settled on a course of action. "Watch the gate," she said. "I need time to cast." She closed her eyes and dug deep inside her. Athgar taught her to harness her inner spark, but for her, a pool of water enveloped her soul, bringing her peace and tranquillity. She calmed her nerves, letting the feeling spread and then pulled the power forth. The air before her grew cold, two ice pillars forming, increasing until they were taller than her, then the tops joined, forming an arch. She kept casting, now focusing on a distant spot.

"What are you doing?" called out Galina. "We can't go back to the Volstrum! They'll kill us on sight!"

Natalia blocked out all sounds, concentrating on the field beyond. More ice appeared, and then a second arch on the other side of the fence. Natalia released her spell and felt the two arches connect.

"Go," she shouted, pushing Katrin and Greta through the closest arch.

Captain Marwen soon followed, but Galina, wide-eyed, stared in wonder. "How did you do that?"

"I'll explain it later," said Natalia, then took the woman's hand, pulling through the arch. They emerged in the field beyond, and Natalia quickly dismissed the spell. Both arches collapsed, breaking into chunks of ice no larger than a fist.

Alerted by the sound, the guards rushed to the gate, but they had locked it to prevent the prisoner's escape. They struggled to produce a key, but by the time they did, the Reinwick delegation had already fled into the woods.

Stanislav paced nervously. It was late, far later than he'd intended to remain here at the Watering Hole, and he was starting to garner attention. He'd even moved the horses off the road, the better to conceal their presence, but a lone stranger wandering back and forth on the road would likely arouse suspicion in even the most easygoing of folks.

He heard them well before he saw them and held his breath. Did they all survive? Moments later, they came into view, and he resumed breathing.

"By the Saints, you had me worried there. I see everyone made it out all right?" Stanislav's gaze fell on Greta. "You brought the child?"

"She helped us," said Katrin. "And we agreed to take her."

"I know, but it's likely to be dangerous, and I only managed to get five horses."

"Please don't send me back!" pleaded the young girl.

"Hush," said Katrin. "No one is sending you back. You're one of us now."

"The escort?" said Captain Marwen.

"Under arrest, I'm afraid," replied Stanislav. "They even seized their mounts."

"But you said you had horses?"

"And I do, but I had to resort to my wiles to get them."

"Your wiles?"

"He means he stole them," said Natalia. "Don't worry about it, Captain. The important thing is we're all together again. I don't know about you, but I'd much prefer to discuss this on the road. Where are these horses you mentioned?"

"Over here." Stanislav led them into the trees, where they soon mounted and were ready to ride. Greta sat before Katrin, looking like she was enjoying a grand adventure, an expression that appeared to irritate the captain.

"Does she not realize the danger?" he retorted.

"Ignore the nasty knight," said Katrin. "He's upset because his mission failed."

"Need I remind you it was your mission as well?"

"Of that, I'm fully aware, but unlike you, I don't owe fealty to the duke, nor do I hold rank in his army. Now, unless you want us to condemn your actions in front of His Grace, I suggest you adopt a more civilized tone in our company."

He reddened slightly before turning towards Natalia.

"Don't look at me," she added. "I'm with Katrin on this one."

COUNTERATTACK

AUTUMN 1108 SR

As the day wore on, Kargen wondered if this entire campaign wasn't a colossal waste of time. Rugg and his masters of earth had spent the last few days consolidating their position, but so far, they'd done little to bring down the keep.

The problem wasn't their magic but their precarious situation. Without a forward bastion to help protect them, they would soon fall prey to the unending hail of arrows. Kargen suspected there were far more arrows in the keep than in all the rest of Novarsk, a thought that did little to ease his mind.

The nightly raids carried out by Lord Valentyn's knights added to his troubles. Kragor's recovery had proved timely, and although he wasn't entirely back to normal, he could at least direct the deployment of his archers. The next time the enemy knights emerged intent on raiding, they were met with a series of deadly volleys. They quickly retreated to the safety of their walls but left three of their comrades behind, their bodies lying cold on the ground.

The weather had chilled considerably, and the first bite of winter frost was upon them. Kargen awoke to ice in his hair, the surprise doing little to soothe his ragged nerves. Shaluhk did her best to reassure him, but delay after delay had overwhelmed him. He'd been the chieftain of the Red Hand for five years, but running an entire country was much more complicated

Oswyn rushed past, her wooden axe in hand, growling like an Orc, and he smiled. Agar would undoubtedly be behind her as they ran through the camp with wild abandon. Today, however, she surprised him when she halted, looked westward, pointing.

Kargen followed her gaze and then caught his breath. To the west, a swarm of birds fled the safety of the woods, a sure sign something was on the move. For a moment, he wondered if Ostrova had decided to take advantage of the situation and invade, but something told him otherwise. To invade a country like Novarsk was no small feat, requiring an immense army. From his estimation, whatever had disturbed those birds was smaller, likely the forces of another baron.

His advance party, guarding Rugg and his companions, was sufficiently large enough to dissuade any attacks from the keep, but this new threat was an entirely different matter.

"To arms!" he called out, in both the Human and Orcish tongues.

Men and women rushed to grab weapons while hunters formed a thin skirmish line. Off to the west, the Cloud Hunters withdrew from their positions in the woods. Whoever approached took great pains to flush out any skirmishers who threatened them.

"Any indication of numbers?" Grazuhk asked in the Human tongue.

"Not at present," Kargen replied. "They are still behind that western wood, but I imagine it will not be long before we see them emerge." He stared west as if doing so would somehow magically reveal the enemy.

A group of Therengian warriors rushed past, forming a line. Kargen acted decisively. "Send word for all our sentries to pull back to the village. It could go badly if the enemy hits us before we concentrate our forces." He noticed movement off to his right. "Agar, fetch Oswyn. Danger threatens."

The youngling grabbed his tribe-sister's hand, pulling her back towards Kargen's position. "Are we in danger, Father?"

"There is always danger where the unknown is concerned. We shall know more when our enemy reveals itself." He spotted Raleth running towards him. "Form your men just west of the village, archers to the flanks."

"Aye, Kargen." Raleth called out the orders, and the army of Therengia started moving into position.

In theory, Kargen's forces numbered some eight hundred souls, enough to hold off any relief attempt. Unfortunately, he'd dispersed them, the better to watch for any attempted flight on the part of those they sieged. Their scattered positions presented a problem, something that quickly dawned on the Orc chieftain.

The enemy emerged from the trees, revealing their numbers and loyalties, for the flag of Novarsk flew proudly amongst its ranks. Kargen strained to make out a second flag.

"Who is that?" he asked.

"It is blue," said Agar, "with a yellow dragon upon it."

"The standard of Lord Pavel," said Grazuhk. "I remember seeing it at Heronwood."

"Why did we receive no word of its approach?" asked Kargen.

"The woods are thick in these parts, making detection difficult, even with the aid of our magic. They are also likely familiar with the area and used it to their advantage."

"Will we beat them, Father?"

Kargen looked down at his son. "We must trust in the power of our axes." He paused, struggling to count them.

"It seems our enemy has once again taken us by surprise," said Grazuhk. "Lord Valentyn has the cunning of a fox."

"Even a fox can be caught if the trap is properly laid. Sound the horns."

It started as a single call, an echo of an age long past when Therengian warriors campaigned across the Continent. Three blasts came forth, and then the answers as the rest of his army responded.

"We must hold them here," said Kargen. "Our army will come to our aid, but we must hold back the enemy until they can mass."

Agar pointed. "Look, Father. Horses!"

A line of riders appeared to the north of the enemy line, the sun glinting off their armour leaving no doubt as to who they were.

"Knights!" growled Grazuhk.

"We have beaten them before," said Kargen. "We shall do so again." His gaze went to his own forces, but he needn't have worried, for they'd seen the threat and planted their spears to counter them.

Kargen wanted to tell Agar to take Oswyn and run, but nowhere was safe. The village was in ruins, and the only place of safety was far to the rear. If they ran now, there was a good chance the knights would cut them down.

The enemy advanced, taking their time and keeping their formation. Clearly, Lord Pavel had been planning this for some time.

Therengians and Orcs ran from all over the area, but they were still too far away to be of immediate assistance. Those working on the keep might be able to return in time, but a quick glance in their direction revealed they were holding in place. Kargen tried to think why they would not come to assist but quickly gave up, concentrating on what he had at hand.

Lord Pavel's troops were primarily footmen, formed into a solid line, anchored in the south by archers, while the knights took the north. These troops were soon within reach of the Therengian archers, and the volleys began, longbows and warbows working in unison, making the air thick with arrows.

The baron's archers were overwhelmed by the defender's ferocity, their meagre bows outdistanced. Panic set in quickly, causing them to flee westward, back towards the safety of the trees.

In the centre, the footmen kept advancing, their swords and axes ready to deal death and destruction to those who would destroy their ally.

To the north was the greatest danger, for the knights were picking up speed. Kargen was sure they were about to launch their charge when, for some reason, they slowed, many turning around to face north. It only took a moment to recognize the horn sounding. Some of Therengia's warriors had come from the north and now threatened Lord Pavel's flank. The horsemen appeared disorganized, milling about in a mob until they finally moved off to meet this new threat.

As soon as he saw they'd committed to the manoeuvre, Kargen ordered his archers to close up, concentrating instead on the advancing footmen.

With a crash, the two lines met, and the battle soon became a screaming match as the men of Novarsk tried to break the Therengian shield wall.

To Kargen, it was as if two giant serpents writhed around, each seeking to gain the upper hand, and he pushed aside all thought of the knights as he concentrated on watching the struggle before him. Shaluhk moved up beside him, readying her magic, her intense stare brooking no interference.

The Bradon fyrd, outmatched by their opponents, lost their resolve when the enemy cut down half a dozen men, opening a gap in their line. The baron's men, emboldened by this unexpected development, fought with renewed vigour, widening the gap.

Shaluhk completed her spell, and the spirits of Orcs, long dead, appeared before her. She pointed, and they surged forward, yelling out a challenge in the language of the ancients.

Kargen's army, used to such tactics, did not flinch, but to the common soldier of the enemy, such things were beyond understanding. Lord Pavel's line wavered, and Kargen rushed forward, axe in hand, ready to join the fight.

"Therengia!" he called out, the chant picked up by those near him. The enemy line grew closer, with other warriors falling in behind him. Kargen followed the spirits straight into the enemy footmen, carving a wide path. He had the briefest view of a surging mass following him before he was in amongst the enemy.

His axe dug into a mailed sleeve, splitting chain links. His opponent, overwhelmed by the sudden development, could only look back in horror as blood soaked his arm.

Kargen struck again, hitting the side of the fellow's helmet and splitting it. Down went the lifeless body, and then he was barrelling into another footman.

An arrow sank into the man on his left, just as an Orc on his right rammed a spear into a mailed chest. The stench of death hung in the air as his blood-caked axe swung back and forth. He was Kargen, Chief of the Red Hand, and he would see his foes struck down this day!

An enemy spear took him in the leg, and the limb collapsed beneath him. As he stumbled, he swung again, cutting into a wrist, eliciting a horrible crunching noise as the bones shattered from the blow's force.

The enemy spear pulled back, then plunged forward again, this time into his stomach. Black blood welled up, and he tasted it bubbling in his throat. He grabbed the spear's shaft with what little strength he had left and yanked it free. The enemy footmen screamed at the green monstrosity standing before him and fled.

Kargen felt his strength leaving him and dropped to his knees, blood clogging his throat while he fought to breathe. All around him, his warriors pushed back the enemy. He closed his eyes, ready to join the Ancestors, knowing he'd brought his people victory.

"Over here. Over here!" a voice called out.

Kargen fell onto his back, but the blood filling his throat threatened to drown him. He rolled onto his side, but the pain in his chest made even breathing painful.

A vision came to him. A small figure stood before him, axe in hand. Was this one of the Old Gods sent to welcome him to the spirit world of the Ancestors? He tried to make out what they were saying, and then things shifted into focus.

Agar knelt at his side, his hands pressed to his father's wound. A shadow fell over him, and he looked up to see Shaluhk.

"Hold still," she said, "and I will use my magic."

Words of power drifted from her mouth as her hands glowed. Kargen's eyes wandered past her, and he watched in horror as an enemy footman approached. Somehow the fellow must have avoided dying in the assault, and now, spying a prime target, he stalked towards her, sword in hand.

Kargen tried to warn her, but the blood choked off his words. The weapon rose, ready for the killing blow. Agar, seeing the danger, rushed forward. It was nearly impossible for an Orc as young as him to take down an experienced warrior, so he did the only thing he could, swinging his axe in a wide arc and smashing it into the fellow's ankle.

The steel blade sank into the boot, slicing through both leather and skin, and the fellow toppled, the pain of the blow stealing the breath from his lungs.

Shaluhk's spell took hold, the magic flowing into Kargen, his laboured breathing eased, the pain in his chest receding. Shaluhk looked down at him, tears in her eyes, oblivious to the threat looming behind her.

The warrior rose, swinging his sword to drive Agar away just as Kargen's axe sailed through the air to take him squarely in the face.

The youngling stepped forward to peer down at the man. "I think he is dead." The body twitched. "Not quite." Agar brought his own axe down onto the man's neck. "There. That's better."

"What have we here?" came Raleth's voice. "Has young Agar blooded himself?"

"The kill is my father's. I only helped him along to the Afterlife."

The captain of the Thane Guard turned to Kargen. "He's a bit young to be fighting, isn't he?"

"He is five," defended Kargen, "but by the reckoning of Humans, he is closer to ten in size."

"Even so, an impressive accomplishment."

Kargen walked over to the body and grabbed the handle of his axe. He was about to remove it when a thought struck him. "Agar," he said. "Withdraw the axe. You have earned it."

"But it is yours, Father."

"It has served me well for many years. I now pass it to you."

"I am humbled, Father."

"Kargen!" called out Raleth, pointing to the northwest.

The Knights of the Mailed Fist, having finished off a group of Therengians to the north, had turned around and were now approaching. Raleth barked out orders, and the weary warriors of the fyrd once more formed into a line. Orc hunters spread out on either side, their bows ready to pepper the advancing horsemen.

"Listen!" called out Oswyn. "Rumble!"

Kargen turned, having forgotten about the young Human. She looked towards the keep and pointed, her eyes full of wonder. It started with a vibration of the ground, and then the rumble, so easily detected by younger ears, grew in intensity.

Everybody turned as dust rose from the base of Krasnov Keep. From this distance, it was difficult to tell precisely what had happened, but Kargen had no doubt that Rugg had finally completed his objective. Individual stones broke loose, and then an entire wall section fell away from the keep, striking the hillside before it slid downward, sending a giant plume of dust and dirt flying into the air.

"By the Gods," said Raleth. "I never thought to see such a sight."

"You knew they were attempting to collapse the wall," said Shaluhk.

"True, but I never imagined it would be so effective."

"You should place more trust in our masters of earth."

"I shall never doubt their abilities again."

"Father?" said Agar. "What does a white flag mean?"

Kargen broke into a grin as he spotted the small piece of cloth flying above the keep. "It means they have had enough." He turned his attention back to the approaching knights. They'd come to a halt, and soon thereafter, a white flag appeared on the tip of a spear. Two riders came forth, one wearing an elaborate surcoat.

"Come, Shaluhk," said Kargen. "It is time we end this."

They walked out to greet the horsemen. Kargen immediately recognized Lord Pavel, for the baron had removed his helm. His companion was younger, though there was a resemblance.

The baron dismounted, then moved closer and knelt. "I surrender to you, Lord Kargen. You wield magic far more powerful than anything at our disposal." He offered his sword, hilt first.

"What is he doing?" asked Agar.

Shaluhk turned to her son. "I do not remember inviting you to this discussion."

"Let him stay," said Kargen. "It will serve him well to learn how civilized folk end wars." He shifted his gaze to Lord Pavel before turning back to Agar. "He is surrendering to us. Take his sword."

Agar stepped forward, showing no fear. Lord Pavel handed him his weapon but remained in a kneeling position. "What would you do with us, Lord Kargen?"

"Your men will surrender their mounts and their weapons. I would have you pledge never to take up arms against us, but you did that at Heronwood and then broke your word."

"I accept that my life is forfeit," said the baron, "but I plead on behalf of my men. Spare their lives. I beg of you."

"I shall spare your life but hereby strip you of your lands and title."

"And my men?"

"Free to return to their homes and families, provided they never again take up arms against us."

"And what is to become of me, Lord?"

"That is for the Thanes Council to decide. In the meantime, you shall be put in irons." He turned to Shaluhk. "Is that the correct term?"

"It is," she replied.

"With your permission," said the baron, "I will surrender myself to your custody and let my son command the men to lay down their arms."

"Very well," said Kargen. "But my hunters will watch you closely. Any sign of trickery, and they shall unleash their warbows, and I should not have to tell you how effective they are against knights."

"A moment with my son, my lord?"

Kargen spared a glance at Agar, understanding the connection of blood. "Very well."

Lord Pavel rose, stepping towards his son and embracing him. "Do as they say, Oleg. My sins are not yours."

"But Father, these foreigners seek to rule our land."

"Which is their right, by conquest. Learn from them, and hopefully, together, you can bring a brighter future to this land. Saints know we haven't served our people well. You must do better."

"I will, Father. I promise."

They embraced once more, then the younger lord handed over his horse into the care of Kargen's warriors and walked back to the knights. For a moment, the Orc chieftain feared treachery, but then, to a man, they all climbed out of the saddle and tossed their weapons to the ground. The rebellion was over.

MARCHING TO WAR

AUTUMN 1108 SR

Gregori Stormwind rode behind King Dagmar as he inspected his army. The day was warm, unusual for this late in the season, and His Majesty kept calling it a good omen. Gregori smiled and nodded his head, anything to let the fool think he controlled these events.

The king turned unexpectedly, looking him directly in the eyes. "Did they manage to escape all right?"

"Indeed, Your Majesty. All went exactly as we predicted it would."

"Exactly?"

"Well, the details varied slightly from our original intent, but the result was the same."

"And they believe Eidolon is marching to our aid?"

"They do, Majesty. Now, all that remains is to lure them farther into Andover. Once that's accomplished, Abelard's ships can land unopposed."

King Dagmar laughed. "I must admit, Gregori, I was a little skeptical when you first suggested this twist, but it's worked out magnificently. I shall be sure to speak favourably to your superiors."

Gregori bowed. "Your Majesty is too generous."

Lord Fernando looked up as someone entered the tent.

"Lady Natalia, I didn't know you had returned."

"And yet you've already assembled the army?"

"It couldn't be helped. Your husband informed us Andover had called the levy to assemble. That could only mean war was upon us."

"Athgar is here?"

"He was, but I'm afraid he returned south to gather the Orcs."

Relief flooded through her. "Then he found them."

"Yes, a tribe called the Ashwalkers. Apparently, they possess an affinity for Fire Magic."

"And he's bringing them here?"

"Well, I say here, but the truth is by the time he returns, we'll likely be in Andover."

"You mean to cross the border?"

"If we want any hope of defeating their army, we need room to manoeuvre, and staying on our side of the border restricts us to tight quarters. I assume you're not bringing an offer of peace from King Dagmar?"

"I'm afraid not. We did, however, learn more about the enemy army. Perhaps we should bring it to the duke's attention?"

"My father is indisposed at present. Tell me what you know, and we'll see if we need to adjust our strategy."

"I'm afraid it's not good. By our estimation, the enemy army has mustered some three and a half thousand, not including allies."

"Allies? Are you telling me there are more coming?"

"Unfortunately, yes. We have no idea of the additional numbers, but Eidolon has seen fit to throw their lot in with Dagmar. What of your own forces?"

"It appears they outnumbered us even before we knew of these allies of theirs. This will require much thought. I understand you are the Warmaster of Therengia. I don't suppose you'd be willing to lend us your expertise?"

"Athgar told you that?"

"He did. He even insisted we heed your advice. It seems you have quite a few battles under your belt."

"It's true, but for me to lead, I must have full control over your army." She glanced at the table where he'd arranged small painted stones. "Is this an accurate representation?"

"Of our location, yes, of our numbers, no." He pointed as he talked. "These are our footmen. We divided them into three commands, four if you include my father's reserve. Within each group, we added supporting archers and horsemen."

"How many men have you?"

"Each group numbers seven hundred, with the duke's reserve at only three hundred, although half of those are knights."

"And horse?"

"It varies. My own group has close to one hundred knights and some professional horsemen. The bulk of each formation, however, is footmen."

"You appear a little weak in archers."

"We are, I shan't deny it. It comes from being a country that looks primarily to the sea for its security. Should we mass the horse together, do you think?"

"No. Cavalry is there to take advantage of any weakness in the enemy's line. We won't know ahead of time where such an opportunity will present itself. We may need them to counter the threat of enemy horse."

"These allies you spoke of earlier. Any idea when they'd be arriving?"

"I imagine they would march directly to Zienholtz and join Dagmar's army. Why? What are you thinking?"

"If we marched straight for their capital, we might be able to hit them before they merge. It would at least give us a fighting chance."

"They'd still badly outnumber you," said Natalia. "It would be better to take a defensive position in the hills that make up your border."

"No," said Fernando. "That would let Andover and their allies come at us at full strength. There'd be less room to manoeuvre, but with that many men, they wouldn't need to; they could send everything they've got straight at us. Better to be in the open countryside, where our horsemen have the freedom to move."

"Any idea how many hunters the Ashwalkers will bring?"

"No, though, as I said, they have some Fire Mages."

"That will help immensely," said Natalia, "especially considering what we're up against."

"Why? What is it you're not telling me?"

"I suspect Dagmar's army will have a few mages of its own."

"Fire?"

"Yes," she replied, "and possibly water as well. It seems the family has a vested interest in defeating Reinwick, even to the point of committing some of its own mages."

Lord Fernando paled. "What hope have we against such power?"

"A mage cannot destroy an army. Yes, a spell can kill an individual, even two or three, if the caster is powerful enough, but what is that compared to the thousands on the field of battle?"

"Are you suggesting such power is useless? I've a hard time accepting that. You yourself are a battle mage. Does that mean nothing?"

"Battle magic is about concentrating one's power to achieve maximum results."

"Meaning?"

"An army wins or loses based on morale. Break the will to fight, and defeat is assured."

"So, the right spell, at the right time, can make all the difference?"

She smiled. "Congratulations. You've grasped something some Volstrum students never seem to master."

"And does your training include countering other mages?"

"It does, along with more traditional tactics and strategy."

Lord Fernando looked down at the coloured stones. "Am I wasting my time here? Clearly, we're outnumbered. Would we be better off retreating to Korvoran and waiting for a siege instead?"

"Marching to defeat Dagmar before he can join with his allies is a gamble, but one worth pursuing. The danger is we arrive too late and find them already united with the army of Eidolon."

"And if we manage to surprise them, can we defeat Andover? They will still outnumber us."

"It's true they outnumber us, even without their allies, but it wouldn't be the first time I've seen inferior numbers win through to victory."

He picked up a stone, staring down at the symbol painted on its top. "Win or lose, it will be a bloodbath."

"War is seldom without casualties, but if you don't face them now, they will only grow stronger."

"Yes, but is it the right choice?"

"Only you can make that decision, unless you mean to take it to your father?"

"I can't," replied Fernando. "The truth of the matter is he's grown despondent ever since my mother's death. He leans on me more and more every day; a decision like this would likely break him."

"Meaning?"

"He'll follow whatever I suggest."

"You have a general. Couldn't he possess some valuable insight?"

"General? The man has never fought a battle, let alone won one."

"But he leads the army, doesn't he? He must have some mastery of tactics?"

"He's an old friend of my father's and should have retired years ago. When I saw him this morning, he was ready to withdraw the entire army back to the safety of Korvoran."

"And he commands?"

"My father commands but keeping him focused these days is a constant challenge, especially when others give contrary advice."

"How soon can you march?"

"We need two more days to assemble the rest of the army. In the meantime, I'll send the cavalry south to watch for any signs of the enemy."

"How far south?"

"I was going to ask you that same question."

"If I were you," said Natalia, "I'd organize them into groups of twelve. Send them as far into Andover as you can, but give them strict orders not to engage. Ideally, they should withdraw at the first sign of the enemy. Our intention here is to find out where they are, not test their warriors' quality."

"I shall do as you ask. Anything else you'd recommend?"

"Not yet, but I want to examine those who have already assembled."

"The numbers are listed here, somewhere."

"No doubt, but it isn't quantity I'm interested in, it's quality, and I must see that for myself."

"Shall I assemble them all for your inspection?"

"No, there are far more pressing issues to keep you busy. I'll find you once I've made my assessment."

Two days later, the army, broken into four brigades, marched. The general headed out first, having the honour of leading the advance. Lord Fernando's brigade came next, followed by the duke's cousin, the Baron of Herenstadt, and then finally the duke himself, who commanded the Royal Reserve.

Natalia walked amongst them all, chatting with captains and warriors alike. The results had been promising, for they were, for the most part, well trained and highly motivated. Only the third brigade left cause for concern as it consisted of primarily local levies, poorly armed and wearing only rudimentary armour. She would have to ponder how to best employ them in battle.

The duke was in fine form as they approached the border, even going so far as to address the army before they crossed into Andover. From Natalia's perspective, the speech was uninspiring, yet it invoked confidence in the warriors of Reinwick, so much so that they travelled another five miles that evening, despite the need for rest.

Unfortunately, their enthusiasm did not last. She was used to the Therengian Army and its warriors, hardened to the march. On the other hand, the duke's men were used to a sedentary life and barely managed ten miles a day. She kept her gaze to the west, hoping to see Athgar and the Ashwalkers.

Once they cleared the hills that demarked the border, the army picked up a bit of speed. The terrain here was much flatter, but eventually, they'd need to travel through the hills where she'd said goodbye to Athgar

The advance now slowed as General Koch had neglected to organize enough supplies to keep the men fed. They fell to raiding farms, a time-consuming practice that turned the local populace against them even more.

Natalia was wondering if they'd ever reach their destination, when a patrol returned with news from the south. The army of King Dagmar had assembled outside of Zienholtz and was preparing to march. There was no news of allies, and word soon spread through the camp that Fernando's strategy had succeeded. Morale rose significantly as the ponderous brigades began preparing for battle.

The duke slammed his fist onto the table, causing the coloured stones to jump slightly. "By the Saints, we have them!"

"I would urge caution," said Lord Fernando. "Even without their allies, they still outnumber us, and the army of Eidolon could be anywhere."

"True," added General Koch. "The last thing we need is for them to show up on our flank."

"Send riders to the east," said Natalia. "If they're close, it will be difficult to conceal them."

"Any word on the savages?"

"They are Orcs," she bit back. "And no, not as yet, but they would need time to gather food before they marched."

"I doubt they'll be of much use, anyway."

"They will arrive. Athgar will make sure of it."

"I admire your faith in your husband, Lady Stormwind, although I fear it is misplaced. They are not professional soldiers, my dear, and are unused to the rigours of a long march."

"First of all," said Natalia, "Orcs often hunt for days at a time, covering much greater distances than the army of Reinwick has so far. Secondly, I am not your 'dear'. I am Lady Natalia Stormwind, Warmaster of Therengia, not some lady of the court. Should you insult me again, I will demonstrate the effectiveness of my magic upon you."

The general fell silent, his face pale.

"Our riders report there is a village up ahead," said Lord Fernando. "I hoped we might send a small garrison to it."

"That would be Ebenhof," said Natalia. "We passed it on our way to Zienholtz."

"Is it worth defending?"

"No, but if memory serves, there's an area north of it that might be a good place to make a stand."

"Then I'll send horsemen to the village with orders to pull back as soon as they spot the enemy. That should at least give us some warning of their approach."

"How will we form up?" asked the duke.

"That largely depends on the terrain," replied his son. He turned to Natalia. "You said you observed the area?"

"Only from a distance, but if I recall, there's a large pond we might use to our advantage. I need to see it up close to perform any further assessment."

"I suggest we halt the army here, Father, until we look for ourselves."

"And if we make a stand there," asked the duke, "how shall we deploy the men?" His attention turned to General Koch.

"I would place myself on the eastern flank, with Lord Fernando on the west. Lord Egon's brigade will take the centre, with your own forces behind, Your Grace, so they can deploy as needed."

"Yes, that sounds reasonable enough. Where shall you place yourself, Lady Natalia?"

"In whatever position presents the best view of the surrounding area."

A hue and cry went up outside the tent just before they heard a horse reining in. Moments later, Sister Felicity entered the tent, her scarlet surcoat caked in dust and dirt.

"What's this?" called out the duke.

"I come from Korvoran with grave news," the Temple Knight replied. "The *Vigilant* has sighted a large fleet assembling off the coast of Abelard. Captain Grazynia fears it may be an invasion fleet bound for Reinwick."

"Nonsense," said the duke. "Why would Abelard do such a thing?"

Natalia swore as the pieces of the puzzle fell into place. "We've been deceived," she said. "It was never about Eidolon. Dagmar wanted to bait us into entering Andover so they could land unopposed."

The duke paled. "We are doomed!"

"No. Not yet, we're not." She ran to the entrance, then called outside. Katrin, Galina, and Stanislav were there in moments, ready to do whatever was needed.

The mage hunter's gaze fell on the knight. "This can't be good."

"It's not," said Natalia. "Dagmar tricked us. The army of Reinwick is here, in Andover, and now a fleet threatens their shores."

"What do you need us to do?" asked Galina.

"Return to Korvoran. Organize the merchant ships there into a makeshift fleet. Our only hope is to keep the invasion from reaching land."

"Should we withdraw the army back to Korvoran?" asked Fernando.

"I'm afraid it's too late for that," said Natalia. "Any attempt to retreat will be met with swift retaliation. We must prepare to make a stand here."

"I should never have trusted you," shouted the duke. "You led us to disaster!"

"They've drawn us into a trap, but we can still turn it to our advantage."

"How? There are no troops left in Reinwick, at least none worth the name."

"That's not entirely true," said Lord Fernando. "Before he left, Lord Athgar told me the descendants of the Old Kingdom were willing to fight if we gave them certain concessions."

"Are you mad? We can't arm Therengians. They'll turn against us!"

"Would you prefer to surrender all of Reinwick?"

"Please!" shouted Stanislav. "Now is not the time for arguing."

"And what would you have me do?" said the duke. "We are quite literally trapped between a rock and a hard place."

"Send your general to take command of what's left of the levy and organize a defence."

"Are you mad? We're about to face the army of Andover. I need him here."

"Then send me."

"You? You're just an old man. What can you possibly hope to accomplish?"

"Give me the authority to release weapons to the populace. We'll seal up Korvoran and hold them off until your return."

All in the tent fell silent, watching the duke as he stared at the mage hunter, desperation in his eyes. "Very well. I will empower you to act in my stead."

"Are you sure that's wise?" said the general. "We don't even know this fellow? He could be working for the enemy?"

"I trust him with my life," said Natalia. "Stanislav has always been a stalwart companion. He would never betray us."

"Let us hope you are right," said General Koch, "or we may all end up on the end of a spear."

THE ENEMY APPROACHES

AUTUMN 1108 SR

Galina watched as a dozen men marched past, making their way towards the merchant ships. They were armed with spears and axes, even a few carrying shields, but the terror on their faces was enough to tell her they would be of little use.

"This is hopeless," said Katrin. "An enemy fleet is bearing down on us. Do you truly believe so few ships will be able to stop them?"

"Likely not," Galina replied, "but we can't give up all hope. These men may make little difference in the long run, but you and I are Water Mages. If we can't slow down a fleet of ships, then we should give up our magic."

Katrin was about to argue the point but caught sight of a mounted knight coming their way, the scarlet surcoat standing out against the dock workers' muted colours.

"Captain Leona," Katrina called out. "I'm surprised you're down here."

"I thought I'd come to see how things are going."

"I don't suppose your knights would be willing to lend a hand?"

"They would, but I'm afraid they're not here. In their absence, I can at least offer my expertise. Naturally, I'm forbidden to fight for Reinwick, but that doesn't mean I can't suggest how you might proceed."

"Won't that upset your superiors?"

"That's a risk I'm willing to take."

"And the other orders?"

"I know the Mathewites are setting up hospices to treat the injured."

"And the Cunars?" asked Katrin. "There is a detachment of them here, isn't there?"

"There is, but I wouldn't be looking to them for help if I were you."

"Do I detect a note of displeasure in your voice?"

"Let's just say our two orders came to an understanding here in Reinwick."

"An understanding? Why would that even be necessary?"

"I'm afraid I'm not at liberty to discuss such matters with outsiders."

"You said your knights weren't here," said Galina. "Might I ask where they are?"

"They are on an exercise. They left port two days ago."

"I find it strange they should leave port after we receive news of an impending invasion, especially when you ordered the news brought to us in the first place."

Captain Leona shrugged. "These are dangerous times, and my order must be prepared to fight at a moment's notice. The only way to do that is to constantly hone our skills."

"You couldn't have picked a worse time. Thanks to the Stormwinds, there's an enemy fleet bearing down on us, carrying Saints know how many warriors."

"Stormwinds, you say?"

"Yes," said Galina, "not to mention the Sartellians, who are just as bad."

"I assume that means they'll have mages?"

"You would know better than us. Your ship first spotted them." Galina looked over the harbour. "I see the *Vigilant* is no longer in port."

"It is not."

"So, she'll sit out this battle as well. Have you no shame?"

"No, they don't," said Katrin. "They can simply sail back after the war and take up residence once more in their commandery. That's what the Church does, isn't it?" She glared at Leona.

"Might you at least have a suggestion as to how we could proceed?" asked Galina.

"If I were defending Korvoran," said Leona, "the first thing I'd do is block off the entrance to the harbour."

"And our fleet?"

"The duke's fleet will be helpless against Abelard's ships. I'd keep them here, or better yet, send them scattering to the four winds. And those men?" She nodded at a few lounging by one of the ships. "I'd suggest you'd be better to use them to defend the docks in case the enemy lands."

"You think they'd attack us here?"

"I doubt it," said Leona. "More likely, they'll land farther north. The beaches there make excellent places for a landfall."

"But we're Water Mages. Are you suggesting we just stand by and watch?"

"No, of course not." Leona cast her gaze around the docks. "Find yourself the fastest boat you can and sail up the coast. The Holy Fleet will meet you there."

"Isn't your order forbidden to interfere in secular matters?"

"We are, but nothing says we can't undertake a training exercise now and again."

"So that's all it is? A bluff?"

Captain Leona lowered her voice. "The time for sitting on the fence has come to an end. No longer can we be bound by rules set by those in distant parts."

"But won't you be held responsible for interfering?"

"Oh, I think we're well past that stage."

Katrin looked at Galina. "It appears there is hope after all." She turned back to Leona, but the captain had already resumed her ride along the dock.

"What do you think that was all about?" asked Katrin.

"I have no idea, but let's not look a gift horse in the mouth. Help is coming. That's the important thing, even if it might be a little late."

"And in the meantime?"

"We do as she suggested. Now, let's talk to these ship's captains and see how to go about blocking up the mouth of the harbour."

Natalia watched as what seemed like an endless stream of enemy soldiers poured onto the field. It was late in the day, and they'd taken up a position opposite the army of Reinwick. There'd already been a skirmish at Ebenhof, but the duke's men fell back in good order. The village now sat squarely in the middle of the Andover line, King Dagmar's flag flying prominently from the bell tower.

General Koch commanded Reinwick's eastern flank, the large pond forming a safe anchor point. Lord Egon, the Baron of Herenstadt, commanded the centre while Lord Fernando led the western flank.

The custom in Reinwick was to place the bowmen behind the footmen in a piecemeal fashion. To Natalia's mind, this was a mistake. Her experience told her it was best to use such warriors in large formations, but then again, Therengia prized archers. In contrast, Reinwick used them as a necessary element of an army, being neither decisive nor particularly well-respected. The knights considered bowmen cowardly, an attitude Natalia struggled to understand.

A road divided the field into east and west, and it soon became apparent the enemy was determined to advance on either side. To her left, the stream and pond would funnel the forces of Andover straight into the general's position. On her right, the enemy had formed a large column, led by a thin line of footmen, with archers on each flank. It was a classic approach, one Natalia remembered well from her studies in the Volstrum.

Either of these assaults could prove decisive, but she was more concerned about Dagmar's reserve. According to their scouts, there were close to three hundred knights in the village of Ebenhof, not to mention the king's personal footmen. That reserve alone numbered almost as much as Fernando's entire command. She knew the battle would be entering its last stage once Dagmar committed his reserve. The trick was knowing precisely when and where they would use it.

She wondered if they might end up fighting in the dark, but then the ponderous legions of Andover halted. Natalia had read of such things before, for it was often the case that two opposing armies would line up the night before the battle, but she could scarcely believe it was truly happening.

As the light faded, hundreds of fires burst into life, the warriors going through the small rituals that superstition told them would spare their lives in battle.

Natalia relaxed. There would be no battle this evening. The greater the delay, the greater the chance Athgar would join them. She wondered where he was and wished she was there with him, hearing the familiar sounds of the Orcish language and taking comfort in them. Even though two thousand souls surrounded her, she'd never felt more alone.

Although a native of Ilea, Admiral Graziano had served the King of Abelard for decades. He was the first to support the invasion of Reinwick, a chance to show off the navy he'd spent years perfecting. Now boasting more than two dozen warships, it was the strongest fleet in the north.

The thought made him look astern, but the merchant ships packed with the king's warriors followed in the *Ardent's* wake, surrounded by the protective screen of the rest of his warships.

He looked off to the west, where the sun, now close to the horizon, reminded him they would soon need to anchor. The thought of checking his navigator's calculations entered his head, but then a lookout called out that he'd sighted land.

The admiral smiled. It'd been quite a feat, getting all these ships across the Great Northern Sea without being spotted. He'd taken the fleet north to accomplish this, shadowing the Five Sisters' southernmost coast. There, he'd lain in wait for five days, biding his time for the arrival of the dispatch boat, which would send them on the way to their final destination.

Graziano moved to the bow, squinting to make out details and widened his smile. He'd tasked his navigator with plotting a course to land them between Korvoran and Herenstadt, a difficult job, considering they must approach from the sea. The man had objected, for it was far safer to follow the coast from the north, but the admiral knew their best chance of success lay in the ability to land unobserved. With their target now in sight, they would anchor the ships, sending in the king's warriors first thing tomorrow morning. After that, it would be simple to march them to the Reinwick capital and seize control of the countryside, especially considering the duke had stripped the land of its warriors to support his campaign in Andover.

The admiral was quite pleased with himself, for little could stop this enterprise now. He would return home to Abelard covered in glory, the greatest admiral to ever sail the Great Northern Sea.

A shout of warning interrupted his thoughts. He moved to the port side, worry replacing his previous confidence.

"Ship off the port bow," the lookout yelled, but try as he might, the admiral could see naught of it.

A splash from the bow indicated they'd dropped their anchor. The *Ardent* swung slightly to port, and a distant vessel came into view.

Graziano had spent a lifetime at sea and instantly recognized the ship, a simple fishing boat hugging the coast. A sigh of relief escaped his lips, and he turned to his captain. "Ignore it," he said. "It's harmless."

"But sir, they could take word of our presence to the duke."

"And do what? All his warriors are off in Andover! Mark my words, friend. Tomorrow we shall land our men unopposed and march on Korvoran. By this time tomorrow night, we'll be dining at the duke's estate."

Athgar looked up at the stars. Gundar's forge was low to the south, portending great change. Behind him, the Ashwalkers stretched out on the ground, closing their eyes in sleep as the masters of fire set their sentinels.

He smiled. The spell that first alerted him to the Ashwalkers' presence was now quite familiar to him, yet he still felt uneasy. It had always been the Red Hand's habit to post hunters when resting, the better to warn of an impending attack. These Orcs, however, trusted in their magic, and with good reason. A single fire sentinel could be seen at a great distance, giving ample warning of any approach.

A chilly wind blew in from the north, and he shivered, longing for the warm embrace of Natalia. He looked eastward. Somewhere over there lay two armies, ready to fight to the death to establish dominance. It was a tale as old as time, and he shook his head. Would Humans never learn?

The Old Kingdom had lasted for more than five hundred years, but Athgar had to wonder if it, too, suffered from endless wars like its successors, the Petty Kingdoms. Was the Continent doomed to forever be fighting amongst its own people?

His mind drifted back to Runewald. He knew Oswyn was safe; he had Vagrath to thank for that, but at the same time, Shaluhk informed him there were problems in Novarsk. Would he and Natalia eventually return home only to find their land conquered by enemies? Dark thoughts entered his mind, scenes of fire and death, and despite his best efforts, he couldn't shake the feeling of dread.

"You are thinking of home?"

He looked up to see Marag. *"I am,"* he replied, slipping into the language of the Orcs, *"although I can't help but feel apprehensive."*

"That is to be expected," she replied, taking a seat, *"but you left your home in the care of Kargen, Chieftain of the Red Hand, did you not?"*

"I did, and I trust him with my life. Shaluhk, too, yet, still I worry."

"That is only natural where younglings are concerned. Your daughter will become an adult one day, yet your concern for her safety will remain. It has always been so for parents and will probably continue to be thus forever more."

"Do you have younglings?"

"I do, a daughter."

"And is she an adult now?"

"She is."

"And does she handle herself well?"

"You tell me," said Marag. *"You have travelled with her."*

"I have?"

"Of course. My daughter is Gharog."

"Gharog? But she's a shaman. Surely a daughter of yours should be a master of flame?"

"She takes after her father, Vagrath."

Athgar looked at her with raised eyebrows. *"Vagrath is your bondmate? I had no idea!"*

"And why would you? It is not our way to announce such things to visitors. I would have thought you, as a Red Hand, would understand this."

"My apologies. I meant no offence. I am merely used to the openness of Kargen and Shaluhk."

"That is only fitting, considering your close friendship. I know this bondmate of yours, Nat-Alia, is a master of water, with great power, but what is she like as a person?"

"She brings a smile to my face at the mere thought of her." He nodded east-

ward. "*She's over there, somewhere, getting ready to go into battle. If the duke is smart, he'll heed her advice.*"

"*Why is that?*"

"*She was trained as a battle mage.*"

"*That is something I am not familiar with,*" said Marag. "*What does a battle mage do?*"

"*She can use her magic to benefit the army, but she also has extensive training in strategy and tactics. They highly prize such folk in the courts of men.*"

"*And how is it you, a Therengian, met such a powerful mage?*"

He laughed. "*She tried to kill me, actually.*"

Marag's eyes went wide. "*Kill you?*"

"*All due to a misunderstanding, I assure you. I saw a group of men following her and feared for her safety, not knowing she could deal with them by herself. One of her spells caught me by surprise, badly injuring me.*"

"*I assume she realized her mistake?*"

"*She did. She took me back to the place where she was staying and nursed me back to health. That was, oh, let's see... five years ago.*"

"*And now you have a youngling of your own. Oswyn is her name, is it not?*"

"*It is.*"

"*Perhaps one day she will grow up to be a* master of flame, *like her father?*"

"*Funny you should say that.*"

"*Why? Surely you are not suggesting she already has an affinity for fire?*"

"*Natalia did so at a very early age, though she seldom speaks of it.*"

"*And what of yourself? Did you manifest in your youth?*"

"*Not at all. A great tragedy triggered my inner spark.*"

Marag nodded. "*I have heard of others whose powers were unlocked in this manner. It was fortunate you found someone to help you control yours, else the consequences might have proven fatal.*"

"*And for that, I am eternally thankful to my mentor, Artoch.*"

Vagrath approached. "*I hope I am not interrupting?*"

"*Not at all,*" said Marag. "*Come, sit with us beneath the stars.*" She took his hand, guiding him to a place beside her. "*What has you wandering around this night?*"

"*I wish I could say I was seeking you, but the truth is I have consulted the Ancestors about tomorrow's battle.*"

"*And?*"

"*They have taken an intense interest in the newest member of our tribe.*" He looked at Athgar.

"*And what did they say?*" the Therengian replied. "*Good news, I hope?*"

Vagrath chuckled. "*You likely know as well as I that they speak in riddles. They do, however, have some advice.*"

"Which is?"

"When the time comes, you must meet fire with fire."

"What's that supposed to mean?"

The shaman shrugged. *"I have no idea. I am only their messenger. I assume you have dealt with the Ancestors before?"*

"Shaluhk has consulted them on numerous occasions."

"And have they ever led you astray?"

"No," said Athgar. *"I can't say they have."*

"Then you must heed their words."

"Meet fire with fire," said Marag. *"Do you think they might have Fire Mages amongst the enemy?"*

"It is possible," replied Athgar. *"We suspect the family is behind this war, which could well mean the Sartellians are involved."*

"Then you must seek them out tomorrow."

"I don't know if I could take on a Sartellian again."

"You will not be alone," said Marag, *"for we walk with you."*

TERMS

AUTUMN 1108 SR

Kargen stared at the ruins of Krasnov Keep. One entire corner had collapsed, creating an immense pile of rocks and stones that people now dug through, hoping to find survivors. The garrison had surrendered soon after Rugg and the others worked their magic, bringing the news that Lord Valentyn was amongst those buried beneath the rubble.

"A fitting end to a tyrant," said Hilwyth. "The villagers all hated him."

"Yet he was the most powerful of all the barons of Novarsk," mused Shaluhk. "I do not understand the Petty Kingdoms' ways."

"Nor do I," said Kargen, "but once news spreads of what has happened here, I doubt much will be left in the way of resistance. The rebellion is effectively over, crushed beneath the walls of Valentyn's keep."

"What shall we do now?"

"Remain here and assist in the recovery of the bodies."

"We also need to help these villagers," said Hilwyth. "Their homes were burned to the ground."

"I already sent hunters to fell trees. I hope we can build enough shelters before the first snow of winter descends upon us."

"Then they had best be quick," said Shaluhk, "for cold winds already blow in from the north." She noted the approach of Raleth. "Here comes your captain. No doubt he has more work to add to your woes."

Kargen sighed. "Win or lose, after the battle is always a difficult time. Why should yesterday's fight be any different?" He turned to face the Thane Guard's leader. "You have news, Captain?"

"I do, Chieftain. Amongst those who surrendered is Sir Yarren." He turned, waving forward a pair of guards with a prisoner between them. "He is responsible for the raids on our army." Raleth waited until the knight stood before Kargen, then forced the fellow to his knees. "You should beg for mercy for all the lives you cost us."

"I was only doing my duty," Sir Yarren retorted. "Would you do any less?"

The captain made to slap the fellow, but Kargen intervened.

"Stay your hand, Raleth." He moved closer, kneeling to look the knight in the eyes. "Do you consider yourself an honourable man, Sir Knight?"

Yarren did not flinch. "I do, my lord."

"And will you take an oath to never again raise your sword against Therengia?"

"I do. I solemnly swear."

"Surely you're not going to let him walk away?" said Raleth.

"Walk away? No," said Kargen. "I have something else in mind for this errant knight." His gaze drifted to Raleth before returning to the prisoner. "I will give you a chance to redeem yourself, Sir Yarren. You will serve a year in our army under the supervision of one of our captains. Do so honourably, and you will be released from all further punishment. Do you accept my offer?"

"Yes," said the knight. "With all my heart. I shall prove to you I am a man of my word."

"Who will you entrust with his service?" asked Shaluhk.

Raleth smiled. "I know the perfect person for such a task." He turned and whispered to a guard, who then left, his eyes darting around, searching for his target.

"I will be faithful to my pledge," insisted Sir Yarren.

"So you have said," replied Kargen, "but I do not judge a man by their words alone. Rather, it is their actions that have the greatest meaning. I see a strong sense of duty in you, but you must use it for your people's betterment instead of the profit of the nobles."

"And what is to happen to the barons?"

"That largely depends on how they react to yesterday's events. They already broke their word by rising against us, so at the very least, they shall lose their right to maintain warriors."

"And their lands?" added the knight.

"They may keep them for now, but should they fail to recognize our rule over Novarsk, they will be forfeit."

"You mean to stay?"

"I see no other choice," said Kargen. "We did not want war with Novarsk, but in her greed, your queen invaded our home. We defeated her and came here with peaceful intentions, but again, we were thwarted, this time by the barons. It is clear to me the entire ruling class of this land is determined to destroy us, and I will not permit that to happen. From this day forth, Novarsk is a province of Therengia."

"And what does that mean, precisely?"

"I shall appoint a provincial governor to rule over this land. They, in turn, will appoint other men and women to rule over each region."

"But you said the barons could keep their lands?"

"As long as the barons heed the local administrators' wishes, they are free to go about their lives. All of this will, of necessity, require time. To that end, I hope some of these same barons may be willing to assist in these duties. Who knows, they might even prove worthy of continuing in these positions more permanently."

"And what of my fellow knights?" asked Sir Yarren.

"Those who wish it will become part of the army of Therengia."

"And those who don't?"

"Are free to leave Novarsk, providing they swear to never take up arms against us."

"Ah, here we are," said Raleth. "Just the person I was looking for."

All eyes turned to Weyland, who was making his way towards them. "You wanted me, Captain?" He was about to say more, but the sight of Sir Yarren broke his concentration. "What is he doing here?"

"This knight," explained Shaluhk, "has agreed to serve for one year in the army of Therengia. It will be your duty to watch over him, ensuring he behaves during that time."

"Why me?" said Weyland. "I took an oath to kill him."

"An oath that is no longer valid."

"Still, I'm hardly the best person to keep an eye on a prisoner."

"He is not a prisoner," corrected Kargen. "He has sworn to serve faithfully."

"And how is it you chose me for this burden?"

"You've served us well," said Raleth, "and since Novarsk is now a province of Therengia, we need to raise additional companies of warriors. As a seasoned member of the Thane Guard, I decided to make you the captain of your own band."

"We call them companies," said Sir Yarren.

"Company?" said Kargen. "Where have I heard that term before?"

"Our cousins to the west use it," said Shaluhk. "In the land of Merceria."

"Very well," said Kargen, "then companies they shall be called from this day forth." He chuckled.

"Something amuses you, bondmate mine?"

"It just occurred to me our army is getting complicated in its structure.

First, we had hunters, then fyrds, then tuskers. Now, we are adding knights to the mix. I wonder what Nat-Alia would think of such things?"

"I am sure she would be pleased with the results."

"Who rules the knights?" asked Raleth. "Or rather, who did?"

"That would be the Knight Commander," said Sir Yarren. "Lord Taras Kirilov, Baron of Yusenka."

"Do we know him?"

"I met the baron back in Halmund," said Kargen. "He was a quiet fellow and quite short, if I recall correctly."

"That's him," said Yarren, "although he takes easy offence at the mention of his height, or lack thereof."

"And do you believe he will agree to our terms?"

"If he's allowed to keep his position as Knight Commander, then yes. The order is more important to him than any loyalty to the Crown of Novarsk."

"I suggest we keep a close eye on the order," said Raleth. "The last thing we need right now is a group of disgruntled knights plotting against us."

"I agree," said Kargen. "I shall leave it to you to find someone suitable for such a task. Consider them as an advisor to the Order of the Mailed Fist."

"And to whom will they report?"

"The acting governor, Wynfrith."

"A good choice," said Shaluhk.

"I hope she agrees to take on the position in a more permanent capacity, but there is much to settle before we worry about that."

Weyland walked down the hill, Sir Yarren far behind him.

"Slow down," called out the knight. "I can't keep up."

The warrior wheeled on his captive. "I didn't ask for this."

"Nor did I, my friend, but fate has thrown us together yet again."

"I should kill you where you stand."

Sir Yarren spread his arms wide. "Then go ahead. I shan't stop you."

"How can you be so cheerful when facing a year of servitude?"

"Servitude? Is that what you think it is?"

"What else would it be?"

"Service in your army is a golden opportunity, my friend."

"Hardly that, and I'm not your friend."

"Comrade, then," said the knight. "Come, let us bury the past."

"You fought for Lord Valentyn."

"What of it? Did you not serve Kargen? We are all soldiers in the end, sworn to serve those who rule. You believe you're better than me because you won the war, but the truth is that's only a matter of perspective."

"I am a plain-spoken man," said Weyland, "not used to the ways of the Petty Kingdoms. You confuse me with your grand speech."

"Then let me make it simple. I trained all my life for honour and glory. It matters not who I serve so long as my actions are honest and honourable. I seek not to conquer or oppress but to serve a master worthy of my trust."

"And was Lord Valentyn such a man?"

"I thought he was, but now that I see the results of his actions, I believe I was wrong. Look, I know I'm no Saint, but deep down, I want to do the right thing. If that means serving the Thane of Therengia, then so be it."

"High Thane," said Weyland. "You can't even get his title right."

"Then teach me, and I, in turn, will educate you in the ways of the Petty Kingdoms. It's not all bad, you know."

"I am far too busy for such things."

"Let me ease your burden. You have your own company now and need to learn how to lead people, something I've been doing for years."

"I'll admit there is much to learn, but our ways are not yours."

"A fact of which I'm fully aware. However, I am willing to learn more about this new kingdom, or realm, or whatever it is you're calling it."

"So you can use that knowledge against us?"

"No, so I can better serve this ruler of yours… of ours."

"Very well. Where do you want to start?"

Sir Yarren smiled. "That's the spirit! Why don't you start by telling me about this High Thane of yours."

"His name is Athgar, and he originally hailed from a place called Athelwald."

"Has he a last name?"

"Not as you would understand it. He sometimes goes by Athgar, son of Rothgar, or simply Athgar of Athelwald, but disdains any use of honorifics such as majesty or sire."

"And from where does the tradition of High Thane originate? Didn't the Old Kingdom have kings?"

"It did. They offered him the Crown, but he refused it, taking the more humble title of High Thane instead."

"Remarkable," said Sir Yarren. "That must be the only time I've ever heard of a man refusing a kingship. He shows great humility. He's not a Temple Knight by chance?"

"No," said Weyland. "He worships the Old Gods as most of us do."

The knight paled. "Please tell me I'm not expected to give up my beliefs?"

"You may rest assured your religion is your own business. There are

Temple Knights of Saint Mathew within our lands, and our warmaster worships the Saints herself."

"Warmaster? But isn't Kargen the warmaster?"

"Kargen is the Chieftain of the Red Hand and a great friend to Athgar and Natalia."

"How great a friend?"

"They are both members of his tribe, if you must know."

"Doesn't that result in a conflict of interest?"

"How?" asked Weyland.

"If Athgar rules the land, how can he be subservient to an Orc chieftain?"

"Being a member of a tribe is not being subservient."

"But the tribe members serve the chieftain, surely?"

"You have it the wrong way around. It is the chief who serves the tribe. After all, they chose him to be their leader."

"I find the very idea of choosing one's leader to be most unsettling. Not that it's wrong, you understand, but my entire life, I've been told nobles were born to rule."

"Therengians also choose their own leaders," said Weyland. "It's a tradition going back centuries."

"But everyone knows they had kings."

"They did, but thanes ruled the villages of the Old Kingdom, much as they do now, and thanes are chosen by the will of the people."

Sir Yarren shook his head. "I can see I have much to learn."

"And I, much to teach."

"Let's start with something simpler then, shall we? I note you wear a chain shirt and helm. Am I to adopt similar garb in service to your High Thane?"

"I have no idea. I only just found out I will command a company."

"I can hardly go about in plate armour when those around me are wearing mail links."

"So, you would voluntarily give up your armour?"

"If I am to be a member of your company, then I shall arm and equip myself as one of them. I note you have both sword and axe; have you a preference when it comes to battle?"

"The axe is the fyrd's traditional weapon, well... that and the spear, but I'm a member of the Thane Guard, or at least I was. Now that I have my own command, I don't know what I am."

"And what do I call you? Captain?"

"That is the common practice, or sir, if need be."

"Then, sir, it will be. And if someone asks me who my captain is, do you have a last name?"

"No. I am simply Weyland of Runewald."

"Does that mean I call you Captain Runewald? It seems there would be numerous like-named individuals, assuming it's a fair-sized village."

Weyland laughed. "No, Captain Weyland will do nicely. Now, speaking of companies, I must bid farewell to my comrades in the Thane Guard."

"And what of me? Shall I accompany you?"

"I suppose you should if only to give weight to my claims of a new command."

Shaluhk looked up from the fire to see Kargen smiling at her, prompting a smile of her own.

"*Have you news?*" he asked in their native tongue.

"*I do. While you were off seeing to matters here, I used my magic to contact Vagrath, shaman of the Ashwalkers.*"

"*And?*"

"*I told him of events here, and he promised to pass them on to Athgar.*"

"*There is more,*" said Kargen. "*I know that look.*"

"*They are about to see battle. From what I learned, the enemy clearly outnumbers them.*"

"*Have you any news of Nat-Alia?*"

"*Athgar believes her to be with the army of Reinwick, but he has had no direct contact for some time.*"

"*And the Ashwalkers?*"

"*They may well prove the deciding factor in this conflict. Though small in numbers, they count many masters of flame as members of the tribe. There is more.*"

"*Go on.*"

"*They taught Athgar mastery of the flame.*"

Kargen knitted his brow. "*He is already a master of flame.*"

"*True, but they showed him things that have taken him far beyond Artoch's teachings.*"

"*Such as?*"

"*Vagrath declined to offer more. He is, after all, a shaman, not a master of flame, so the details may be beyond his comprehension.*"

Kargen chuckled. "*I thought shamans knew everything. Are you only now telling me they are fallible?*"

"*Tread carefully, bondmate mine. Are you suggesting I am somehow imperfect?*"

"*No, of course not—you complete me. I was merely suggesting no individual can know everything.*"

"*In that, we are in agreement. A shaman knows much when it comes to healing*" *or the spirit realm, but mastery of fire is a very different thing. Fire is the most destructive element and, as such, the most dangerous to wield. Nat-Alia once told me madness runs rampant amongst Human Fire Mages."*

"Meaning?"

"They become enamoured of their ability to control fire, forgetting it can consume them."

"Tell me, honestly, Shaluhk. Do you fear Athgar might succumb to such a temptation?"

"I would hope not, but he is a Human. I would be lying if I said it was not a possibility, even if a remote one."

Kargen shook his head. *"No, he learned well the lessons of Artoch. I think he will be fine."*

"Yet, at the Battle of Ord-Kurgad, he almost immolated himself. Had it not been for the efforts of Nat-Alia, he would have surely died."

"That is true. I will not deny it, but his mastery of magic has improved significantly since then."

"Also true, but we do not know what new spells the Ashwalkers taught him. If they are as powerful as Vagrath thinks, Athgar may inadvertently try to draw forth too much of his power."

"I understand your concern, but he and Nat-Alia are far removed from our presence. All we can do now is put our faith in his common sense and hope they are granted victory in the coming battle."

THE BATTLE BEGINS

AUTUMN 1108 SR

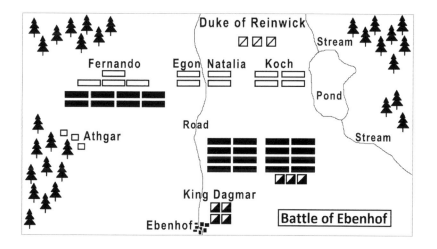

"The time to attack is nigh," said King Dagmar. "Order the left to advance."

"And the right, Your Majesty?"

"Hold them in place for now. I want to see how Duke Wilfhelm reacts."

The aide rode off, kicking up dirt in his haste to deliver the orders.

"They're keen," said the king. "I'll give them that."

"Your Majesty is too humble," said Ria Sartellian. "The men are eager to win you a victory."

"You know, I had my doubts about this entire enterprise, but your estimates of Reinwick's numbers proved quite accurate. It appears we didn't need the fleet of Abelard after all."

"I would caution you against making rash decisions, Majesty, particularly when we have yet to see the calibre of the opposing army."

"My dear," replied the king, "I am sending fourteen hundred men against their western flank. They have what, seven hundred or so? I think you overestimate their chances."

"They could still reinforce from their centre."

"In which case, we'll advance in the east. You worry too much."

"My apologies, Majesty, but it is my job to worry on your behalf. I might also remind you that Natalia Stormwind is out there, and she can make quite a difference on a battlefield."

"What is one person, even a mage, to an army of our size?" He noticed her scowl. "I readily admit she can do some damage, but our numbers will bring us victory in the end."

"Let us hope so," said Ria.

They watched as the morning mist burned off, revealing the army of Andover in all its splendour.

"Finally," said Dagmar, "after all these years, I shall restore my father's reputation."

The army began advancing as the king looked on in appreciation, but it quickly turned to confusion. "Why is my right moving up? I gave no such order!"

"They are merely tying down the eastern flank, Majesty. Don't worry. They shall remain well out of the range of any archers."

"Ah, yes. Perhaps I should move my reserve up? It would certainly give them something to think about. Who knows, it might even serve to convince them to surrender."

"Your Majesty is free to do as he pleases," said the mage, "but I suggest you wait and see how things develop from here, where you have a more commanding view."

"Yes, of course." As King Dagmar watched his men advance, he imagined a glorious victory, of parading through Korvoran, with Duke Wilfhelm in chains. He shook it off, trying to concentrate on the moment. "This is boring," he said. "We need something to liven it up a little."

"Liven it up?" said Ria. "We are attacking the enemy in great force. What else would you have us do?"

"A little magic certainly wouldn't go amiss. Perhaps some streaks of fire to put the fear of the Saints into the enemy?"

"Then, with your permission, Majesty, I shall join the attack."

"Splendid. I will be sure to include your name as a hero of this campaign. You will win everlasting fame."

She rode off as fast as she could to join the attack.

Lord Fernando tightened the grip on his reins. "Hold fast," he ordered. "Steady that line."

The enemy was coming straight for him, their footmen leading the attack. They were, in essence, armed and armoured much the same as his own men, but their numbers were more than he'd anticipated.

The lead elements of Andover struck the line first, then the point of contact increased as those on either side advanced. Soon it was a swirling mass of men, all thoughts of manoeuvre or tactics thrown to the wind. Those in the second rank moved up to take over from any who fell, but the enemy was everywhere.

Fernando looked west to where the edge of his formation stood. Thankfully, the enemy attacked head-on rather than enveloping a flank. He thanked the Saints his warriors on that side only had to endure a smattering of arrows. Upon his order, his footmen advanced, engaging some enemy archers on the westernmost portion of his position.

To his left, Lord Egon watched the fray with great interest. Part of him wished the baron would come to his aid but to do so would leave the east dangerously exposed. Instead, he turned his attention to the fight before him.

The duke's son had never commanded in battle, and though he was loathe to admit it, he found the entire experience both fascinating and terrifying. The clash of battle drowned out any sounds of the dying or wounded, and for that, he gave thanks.

The line wavered as the press of men began in earnest. He thought of committing his cavalry to push back the onslaught but knew he must wait until the decisive moment. All along the line, his men were dying, those of Andover climbing over the Reinwick dead to push farther north.

A streak of fire flashed by, and his heart quickened. Intellectually, Fernando knew the enemy likely had Fire Mages, but to see one amid such carnage made his blood run cold. He understood magic would do negligible damage against hundreds of men, yet that knowledge did little to quell his rising fear. He'd always considered himself a brave man, but the sight of fire tearing through his lines was almost too much to bear.

. . .

Athgar crouched, peering through the foliage to watch the battle raging beyond.

"*That doesn't look good,*" he said, being sure to speak in the tongue of the Orcs.

"*It appears they have a wielder of flame,*" said Marag.

"*Yes, and I can only imagine the effect that will have on the men of Reinwick. We must do something.*"

The Orc glanced behind them, where the Ashwalkers gathered. "*Remember the words of the Ancestors.*"

"*Meet fire with fire,*" he replied, rising to his feet. "*It's time we did just that.*"

A group of mounted warriors followed in the wake of the Andover advance, but he ignored them. They might try to intervene at some point, but he was confident their horses would balk at any order to advance against wielders of magical fire.

Athgar stepped from the woods, the tribe's hunters on either side. The masters of flame followed him, ready to do their part once they closed with the enemy. They'd emerged on the western portion of the battlefield, right behind the Andover column and in full view of the assault against Lord Fernando's men.

Athgar waited a moment, giving the Orcs time to form up before beginning the advance. The enemy horsemen, as expected, turned to face them, but a few well-placed fire streaks convinced them to keep their distance.

The enemy, concentrating on the Reinwickers to the north, failed to notice their presence at first. It wasn't until the Ashwalkers' bows began picking off targets that their attention shifted. They hastily repositioned their troops to form an opposing line. Judging by their actions, these were not the seasoned warriors of Andover but lightly armoured levies, with a smattering of professional soldiers mixed in to bolster their confidence. More importantly, the enemy Fire Mage who'd threatened Fernando's line now moved to thwart this attack from their rear.

Athgar smiled. Under normal circumstances, it would've been difficult to spot an enemy mage, at least until their magic flew forth, but the fact she was mounted and riding amongst footmen made identification easy. His gaze flicked left to where a small group of enemy archers were forming up.

"*I wonder,*" said Athgar, "*if you might take some of your archers and take care of that group over there?*"

Rugal grinned. "*I shall lead them myself.*"

Athgar slowed their pace, allowing the archers time to get into position. His initial impulse was to engage the rear of the enemy's forces, but with only the levy to oppose him, he thought of an alternative. He turned to Marag, Snaga, and the other masters of flame and nodded.

Ria pushed her way through the levy, determined to see for herself where a line of Orcs had emerged from the trees behind their advance. The Fire Mage cursed her luck but doubted that such savage brutes could withstand the power of a Sartellian.

A flicker of fire shot out from the greenskins, keeping the king's cavalry at bay, and she smiled. It seemed this would be the day to test her mettle against other casters. She dismounted, then stepped in front of the line, confident in her abilities.

The Orcs halted, and then a half dozen began walking directly towards her. She was shocked to see a Human leading them, but then everything fell into place.

"So," she called out, "you must be the Therengian, Athgar."

"That I am," he replied. "Surrender, and you shall be spared."

"You believe me a fool? I am Ria Sartellian, a Fire Mage of great power. Come no closer, or I shall unleash the full extent of my magic upon you."

He moved closer, both arms held out from his sides. "You must do what you think best."

She stared back, disbelief clouding her judgement. Was this fellow a fool? Did he honestly believe she wouldn't kill him? She raised her hands, ready to cast. "Begone, I say, or I shall burn you to ashes."

"You are welcome to try," he said, "but I warn you, I will not be the one to perish—it will be you." He began gesticulating in preparation for a spell.

Ria thrust out her hands, letting loose with a streak of fire that flew through the air, hitting the fool directly in the chest. She laughed as the power flowed through her, feeding a flame so great it would consume all it touched.

"Is that all you can do?" called out Athgar.

Her mouth fell open, for the man appeared untouched. She redoubled her efforts, bracing herself against the tremendous magic she was unleashing. For a moment, she wondered if her aim was off, but the more she stared, the more she became convinced she'd engulfed him in the magical flame.

With her arms aching, a tightness grew within her chest, indicating she was reaching the limits of her power. Still, this strange mage kept coming, ignoring her magic as if it were only a nuisance.

Years of training in Korascajan had taught her no one could withstand the formidable might of a Sartellian, yet this lowly Therengian was somehow immune to her magic.

He drew closer, and then she noticed the sweat glistening on his brow.

Clearly, he was now feeling the heat; only a moment or two longer, and he would succumb! She dug deeper, pulling forth every ounce of energy she could muster and throwing it at him. Blood seeped from her nose, and her ears grew damp as she used up the very last of her energy reserves. Still, she continued, drawing on her own flesh to power her magic.

The heat broke through as Athgar's spell of resistance waned. The edge of his tunic glowed with embers, his face growing warm as if under a scorching sun. He concentrated on the enemy Fire Mage, moving ever closer. Had the warriors been so inclined, they could easily run forward and kill him, but no one dared approach the streak of flame engulfing him.

He held up his arms, preparing to cast and noted his sleeves were smouldering, the smoke billowing upward and causing his eyes to water. The enemy mage maintained the spell far longer than he'd expected, and he feared he'd sealed his own fate.

Flames engulfed his hair, and then Marag was beside him, casting a spell to extinguish the fire. The enemy mage was close now, blood streaming from her eyes, ears, and nose. A final scream erupted from her mouth, and then her skin split open, flames erupting to consume her flesh.

Athgar had seen this before, back in Ord-Kurgad, and even almost died from the same thing—self immolation. Fire was a fickle ally. Artoch, his old mentor, always said it would consume those who didn't respect it.

The enemy mage burst into a fireball, falling to her knees. She pitched forward, her body still alight, greasy black smoke trailing into the air.

The men of the Andover levy, unused to seeing such things, broke, dropping their weapons and fleeing. Many ran directly into their own countrymen, throwing the entire attack into confusion.

Athgar let loose with some magic of his own, sending streaks of fire overhead, not to kill but to urge them on their way. The entire enemy attack on Fernando's brigade fell apart.

The tribe resumed their advance, but there was little to oppose them. Athgar saw horsemen coming from the north, but as they approached, he realized they were knights of Reinwick, breaking through the enemy line. Shortly thereafter, a small group rode towards him, bearing the banner of Lord Fernando.

"Lord Athgar," said the duke's son. "Your arrival couldn't have come at a better time."

"I'm pleased I could help. Is this all they had?"

"I wish it were so. Unfortunately, it is but a third of their army. I'm afraid the main battle will be fought farther east."

"Natalia?"

"She is well and in the centre of our army. Shall I have someone take you to her?"

"Yes, if you would be so kind."

King Dagmar frowned. The attack in the west had failed miserably. He scanned the area for Ria Sartellian, but she must have perished; either that or the enemy captured her.

"Ah, well. We'll have to do this the old-fashioned way." He turned his attention to one of his aides. "Tell the right to advance and make contact."

The aide paled. "But, sire, we did that to the west and failed."

"True, but this time, while they're busy fighting, I shall take the reserve and circle around that pond. We'll be in amongst their rear before they know it!"

Far to the north, Admiral Graziano stared out at the shoreline. He'd sailed the fleet of Abelard into Reinwick waters without opposition, picking a spot between Korvoran and Herenstadt, on a flat stretch of coastline that was ideally suited to landings of this nature. Now the *Ardent*, his flagship, lay at anchor, standing guard over the merchant ships carrying the king's warriors. He watched as ship's boats crammed with soldiers rowed ashore.

The day was chilly, with a strong northerly wind promising an early winter, yet nothing could dampen his enthusiasm today. Thirty years ago, the king had recruited him to reinvigorate the fleet of Abelard. This was the culmination of that storied career—one that would ensure his place in the history of the Petty Kingdoms.

The first of the men disembarked, wading through the surf to form up on the beach. By his estimation, it would take most of the morning to get the men ashore. Then he would march them to the Reinwick capital and capture it. The operation should take a day or two, and then the whole kingdom would be at his mercy.

He smiled. The admiral had distrusted the plan when he first heard it, but recent reports indicated the entire Reinwick Army had marched south, leaving the land undefended.

A yell from the shore drew his attention to some trees where a small group of men had emerged and were now forming up into a thin line. He strained to make out whose colours they wore, but all he could see were brown and green surcoats, garments typical of the peasant class.

Those of his own men already ashore moved to intercept these newcomers, but they loosed arrows from bows taller than they were. The effect was quite pronounced, for a dozen of his men went down. An irritation, to be sure, but the admiral knew he had more than enough men to take care of this annoyance.

"Get the rest of them into the boats," he called out.

The order was repeated to the other ships, and more men swarmed into boats. As he watched, the admiral felt a surge of pride, but a "Sail, ho!" from the crow's nest commanded his attention. A fleet was bearing down on them at full sail.

An aide appeared at his side. "My lord, the enemy approaches! We are undone!"

Admiral Graziano refused to be intimidated. "Calm yourself," he said, allowing himself time to focus. The lead ship was much smaller than the *Ardent*, hardly a threat. Then he beheld the pennant flying from its mast and felt relief.

"It's a Holy Fleet," he said. "They will not interfere. The Church does not intervene in secular matters."

"But, Lord, they are at full sail!"

"It is but a bluff, nothing more, a manoeuvre meant to distract us. Ignore them!"

The lead ship approached, then turned to come alongside, revealing Temple Knights cramming its decks, their scarlet surcoats bright in the early morning sun. The admiral heard a loud crash as a great grapnel smashed into the railings, and then the Temple Ship began winching the *Ardent* in for boarding.

THE BATTLE CONCLUDES

AUTUMN 1108 SR

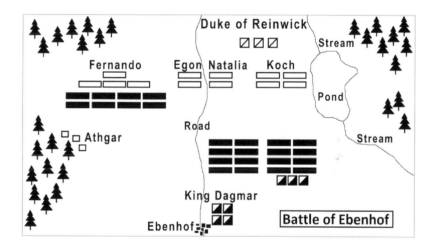

A thgar smiled as he spotted Natalia sitting atop a horse, looking east to where something commanded her attention.

"Something wrong?" he called out.

Her eyes lit up as she turned. "Athgar!"

He ran towards her as she dismounted, embracing her even as her feet hit the ground. Moments later, they were kissing, all thoughts of their surroundings thrown to the wind.

"Ahem," said General Koch. "There is a battle to win, you know."

"My pardon," said Natalia, "but I haven't seen my husband for some time."

Athgar chuckled, then noted the look of concern on the man's face. "What were you looking at?"

"The enemy is advancing," he replied, "pinning us in place with a mass of foot while his cavalry heads around that pond."

"Have we no reserves?"

"His Grace is taking his knights to intercept, but they badly outnumber us."

"I'm afraid I've failed," said Natalia. "I urged the duke to march into a trap."

"A trap?"

"While they pin us down here, a fleet is sailing for Reinwick."

"Then we must beat them at their own game."

"I'm open to suggestions."

Athgar scanned the water. "I assume, since it's on your flank, that the pond isn't shallow enough to cross?"

"Correct," she replied. "Why? What is it you're thinking?"

"To get to us, they must round the northern end, crossing the stream that flows north. Can you cast a smaller version of the maelstrom spell?"

"That only affects water. How can that help us?"

"I had hoped you could spin it fast enough to rise into the air."

"I have something similar called vortex. It creates a small waterspout."

"Can you cast it close to the land?"

"I can, though once again, I don't see why I'd want to?"

He stared into her eyes. "Do you trust me?"

"With all my heart."

He looked over his shoulder. The masters of flame were making their way towards him, drawing looks from all the men of Reinwick.

"I brought some friends," he continued, "and a new spell I'm dying to try."

"A new spell? You HAVE been busy."

"I require your horsemen, General."

"I may need them," Koch replied.

"If we can't stop Dagmar's flanking manoeuvre, a few extra horses won't make any difference."

The general, to his credit, remained silent for only a moment. "Very well. Take them and pray to whoever you worship for success."

King Dagmar's knights rushed along the pond's eastern shore. The Duke of Reinwick, having seen the threat, responded by leading his own knights in a desperate bid to buy time for the rest of the army. They met with a thunderous crash, flanked by a thick forest on one side and water on the other. The area became crowded with horsemen as the rest of the king's knights tried to get into the fray.

Natalia brought her horse to a halt. Before them, the duke's actions held the enemy horsemen at bay. "This won't work," she called out. "That stream is too close to our own horsemen."

Athgar looked over at the Orcs, uncomfortably riding double with the help of the general's men.

"There," said Natalia, pointing. "Will that do?"

He followed her gaze to where a mass of enemy knights clustered around the pond's easternmost point, Dagmar's standard amongst them.

"Perfect," he called back. "We just have to get to it. How close do you need to be?"

"Within range of a bow," she replied.

"Therengian, or those smaller ones they use in these parts?"

She laughed. "Therengian, of course."

He turned to the general's man, pointing. "You see that area over there? That's where we need to be."

The man swallowed hard. "It'll be difficult, but I'll get you there." He raised his sword on high and swept it down. Moments later, the general's horsemen surged forward, splashing into the edge of the pond.

They paralleled the shoreline, staying in the shallower sections whenever possible, but even so, they lost three riders, unhorsed as the water grew too deep or the bottom too uneven. They soon turned inland, coming out of the water and forcing the enemy back. It was a shallow and precarious foothold, for the enemy quickly recovered, reinforcements rushing forward to make up their losses.

Athgar dismounted, moving to the pond's edge and gazing off towards the enemy horsemen clustered in the distance.

"I'll hold them off as long as I can," said the captain, "but it won't be long before their numbers overwhelm us."

Natalia stepped back as a horse ran past, then moved to stand beside Athgar. Enemy knights packed the area she'd chosen: the perfect target had they been in the water. Rather than doubt him, she began her spell, concentrating on the destination.

She closed her eyes, visualizing the water turning. At first, waves appeared, and then a small whirlpool, its edges moving ever faster. As the power surged through her, she began the incantation to make the whirlpool spin more, a thin mist forming on its surface even as the water rose. She heard Athgar talking to the Orcs but ignored it. Faster and faster, the water spun, the sides of the vortex growing until a spiral of water reached into the sky, whipping around like a tail.

Those around her looked on with interest, but there was little danger to those ashore. The Orcs started chanting, and she risked a glance Athgar's way. The Ashwalkers were tossing a small ball of flame back and forth, its centre glowing brighter and brighter with each passing. They finally threw it to Athgar, and he held it a moment, suspended in the air above his hands. He turned to Natalia, nodding, and she poured every ounce of energy she could muster into the vortex.

The waterspout thickened as it sucked so much liquid from the pond that it temporarily lowered the water level. Athgar threw the ball of fire, using his magic to guide it. He knew it wasn't the most accurate of spells, but it didn't need to be. It struck the edge of the vortex and exploded, sending super-heated steam flying in all directions.

The effect was immediate and terrifying as the cloud expanded, scalding everything it touched. At first, little could be seen of the carnage, for a fine mist covered the area, but as it blew south, it revealed utter devastation. Dozens of knights were down, the steam penetrating visors and any other exposed area. Many staggered around in a blind panic, clutching at their helmets, screaming in pain.

Having ended her spell, Natalia turned her attention to the enemy horsemen pressing in on their position. She thrust out her hands, sending ice flying towards them. This new onslaught, piled on top of the sudden explosion of steam, was too much to bear. Some gave up where they were, dropping their weapons and raising their hands in surrender, while others made a mad dash for the safety of their own lines, far to the south.

"There," shouted Athgar. "It's Dagmar!" The king's standard had fallen and now lay discarded, even as a trio of knights tried to lift their injured king.

Natalia saw their chance and moved to the water's edge, touching the surface and calling on her magic once more. The water, now returned to its original level, suddenly stilled, then began freezing, the ice thickening quickly.

"Take the horsemen," she called out. "Go, now!"

Athgar ran across the surface, his feet occasionally slipping on the ice. An enemy knight, seeing his approach, turned to intercept him, but a blast of fire from Marag took the rider in the chest, pushing him from the saddle.

Athgar was soon across the water and back on land, running past the dead and wounded. Ahead of him, the three knights struggled to put their king onto a horse.

Athgar shot a bolt of fire over them, spooking the mount. The creature ran off, leaving the three knights to turn and face him, their king discarded in their need to protect themselves.

In his haste to get to Dagmar, Athgar had rushed ahead but now found himself outnumbered. He backed up, readying his axe, when a dozen horsemen, Reinwickers all, charged past him, taking their fury to the enemy. He looked over his shoulder and spotted Natalia crossing the icy pond.

"I thought I'd come and join you," she said. "I hope you don't mind?"

"Mind? Not at all. I welcome your company."

She halted by his side. "That was some trick. Whatever made you think of it?"

"I'm not sure. I remembered you using your Water Magic to stop me from immolating back in Ord-Kurgad, and it made me think."

"About what?"

"About what can happen when we combine our magic."

"But we are two different schools of magic. We can't combine the effects —it goes against all the rules of magic!"

"Then perhaps it's time we changed the rules?"

She was about to argue the point but then thought better of it. "I must apologize. My training at the Volstrum runs deep, and I sometimes forget there are other approaches to spellcasting. The combination of our magic worked well here. I look forward to exploring more such possibilities in the future."

He noted the horsemen's return, the King of Andover amongst them. "It appears Dagmar is now a prisoner. It will be interesting to see what the duke does with him."

"He must be lenient, if there is to be a lasting peace," said Natalia.

"Something tells me the duke is not a forgiving man."

"Then it will be our job to convince him. Now come. We should seek His Grace before he lets his emotions get the better of him."

They picked their way north, soon coming across a knot of warriors gathered in a circle, the object of their interest hidden from view.

"What's this, now?" called out Athgar.

The group parted, revealing the duke lying on the blood-soaked ground, his loyal retainers standing around him with tears in their eyes. Lord Fernando knelt beside his father, looking up as Athgar and Natalia pushed their way through the crowd.

"My father is dead," he said. "He gave his life to buy us time."

"We captured Dagmar," said Natalia. "Victory is yours, Lord."

"It is a shallow victory indeed when one must lose their father." He paused a moment to compose himself before letting his gaze wander over those gathered. "We won a tremendous victory this day, but the war is far from over. We must march home and wrest control of our realm back from the men of Abelard."

"What of Dagmar?" asked one of his knights.

"We shall take him with us."

"And his army?"

"Those who haven't fled will be disarmed and sent on their way. I doubt they'll put up much resistance with their king in irons."

The men went about their business, collecting the wounded and seeing to the prisoners. Lord Fernando finally stood, releasing his father's hand. "Athgar, a word, if I may?"

"Most certainly, Your Grace."

"Please, we both know we are equals. Call me Fernando."

"I shall be pleased to do so," he replied. "What is it you'd like to speak of?"

"I saw you burning on the battlefield."

Natalia wore a look of shock. "What?"

Athgar grinned. "I learned much from the Ashwalkers, including how to resist fire."

"Remarkable," said Fernando. "Does that mean you are now impervious to flame?"

"Hardly. The spell has a reasonably short duration, no more than the count of ten."

"Yet you were afire for easily twice that."

"I was, thanks to the Ashwalkers. Once I exhausted my energy, they used their own magic to keep the flames at bay. You might say it was a group effort."

"Incredible. I would never have thought such a thing possible. We shall talk more of the Orcs, that I promise you, but now we must hasten back to Korvoran and discover what damage has been wrought in our absence."

In the north, a calm descended off the shore of Reinwick, broken only by one man's voice.

"I demand to see your superior!" raged the admiral. He stood near the *Ardent's* bow, two Temple Knights watching him.

Farther down the deck, a tall knight removed her helmet, revealing short, blonde hair. She took one look at the admiral, then walked up to him, her bloodied weapon still clutched firmly in her hand.

"What do we have here?" she asked.

"How dare you interfere with my fleet," he ranted. "Such action is unconscionable and against the Church's principles."

She remained calm. "Are you an expert on such things?"

"I know the Church is sworn to abstain from becoming involved in local matters! Who do you think you are, breaking the Church's rules? Your head will roll for this!"

"My name is Grazynia, Temple Captain Grazynia, to be precise, and I have the honour to be the acting admiral of this fleet."

"I demand you release me at once. You had no right attacking our ships. The Church is sworn to neutrality."

"You appear to be under the illusion that this is a Church Fleet. Let me assure you it is not. We operate under the exclusive command of the Temple Knights of Saint Agnes. As such, we are not bound by orders relating to the Holy Fleet."

"This is outrageous. You can't just attack my fleet and get away with it."

Grazynia looked aft and watched as her knights hauled down the flag of Abelard.

"Well?" he demanded. "What have you got to say for yourself?"

She returned her gaze to the admiral. "You are under arrest on the charge of piracy."

"Piracy? Don't be absurd. We are the Kingdom of Abelard's flagship, and—"

She raised her finger, cutting him off. "I shall give you a choice, Admiral. You can, if you like, admit your king sanctioned this illegal attack, in which case I'll confiscate all of your ships in the name of the order, or..." She let her words trail off.

"Or what?"

"I'll hang you all for piracy and take them anyway." She took a moment to peruse the rest of her fleet in amongst the invasion force. "Actually, it looks like most of the work is already done."

"You wouldn't dare!"

She moved to tower over him. It had been a tough fight, and the sweat rolled off her face, dripping onto the front of his jacket. "I'm sure I don't need to remind you, but I'll do it anyway. Temple Knights don't lie."

The admiral paled even more. "W-w-why?" he stammered. "Why in the name of the Saints would you interfere in something that is none of your business?"

"None of our business? Keeping the Petty Kingdoms safe is one of our most sacred vows."

"But your order is dedicated to protecting women?"

"And did you suppose your warriors would simply leave our charges unharmed when they stormed the capital? No, Admiral. We did what we should have done decades ago—prevented strife within the Petty Kingdoms."

"And what is to happen to me?"

"Once we have your confession, you are free to go."

"Just like that, I am to be released?"

"Naturally. We have no desire to take your men into custody or have a place to hold them. Don't worry. We'll arrange to drop them off on the coast of Abelard, but as to these ships..." She took another look at the mass of vessels behind them. "Well, we'll take some of them into service, but we'll sell the bulk of these merchant ships off."

"But they belong to the king!"

"Not anymore they don't. I might also remind you that your release depends on your admitting the wrongful acts of your king, so I doubt he'll welcome you back to court anytime soon."

A Temple Knight rushed up to them. "Small boat approaching, Captain."

"Bring it alongside, and I'll be along shortly. Now, Admiral, do you agree to my terms?"

"Have I any real choice?"

She smiled. "I knew you'd see it my way." She turned to his guards. "Take him to his quarters and have him write out his confession. I'll look at it later."

"You promised to release me."

"And I will, once I've seen that you've carried out your part of the bargain. Oh, and one more thing, Admiral. Don't take this personally; we're only maintaining the balance of power."

"How can I not take it personally? It's my ship you took by force!"

She looked at her fellow knights and winked. "There, you see. He sees reason after all."

The boat pulled alongside, and Grazynia looked down to see a young woman staring up at her. "Captain Grazynia, I presume?"

"And you are?"

"Galina. Captain Leona sent me."

"Then welcome aboard." Grazynia waited while they helped the new arrival onto the deck. "I assume you're responsible for that skirmish ashore?"

"I helped direct it, but a local organized it, a Therengian by the name of Herulf."

"I wasn't aware descendants of the Old Kingdom were allowed to bear arms in Reinwick?"

Galina brandished a scroll. "Ordinarily, they aren't, but I have a letter from the duke authorizing just such a thing."

"And there were enough of them to repel an invasion?"

"No, not in the least, but they used their bows to keep the first wave from organizing. Had your ships not arrived, they would have overrun us."

"And had this Herulf of yours not organized a defence, the enemy would have run rampant. It appears we are in each other's debt. I appreciate the assistance, but I wonder why you chose to row out here to the *Ardent*."

"We have taken prisoners, quite a few, if I'm being honest. The problem is we have no place to put them."

"Then I shall begin preparations to take them into custody. I'll send my knights ashore, and they can march them down to Korvoran."

"And the fleet?"

"We'll join you in the capital. There are a few repairs to make before we return to Temple Bay."

"Is that your secret base?"

Grazynia smiled. "It is, but if you tell anyone else I told you, I'll deny it."

EPILOGUE

AUTUMN 1108 SR

Athgar made his way through the crowd, cups in hand. He finally halted in front of Natalia, who was busy watching something off to her left.

"Anything of interest?" he asked.

She turned, a smile breaking out. "Lots," she replied, taking the offered drink. "Thank you." She took a sip. "Captain Marwen has made Galina an offer."

"Meaning?"

"They are to be wed."

"I didn't know they knew each other that well."

"I've yet to tell you all about our adventures in Zienholtz," she replied. "Let's just say they spent a lot of time in each other's company."

"I suppose that means she won't be returning with us to Runewald."

"No, but now we have a way of keeping in touch."

"We do?"

"Yes. The same spell the family uses to keep track of its more powerful disciples."

Athgar chuckled. "You make them sound like a religion."

"If you think about it, they are. They're a group of individuals gathered together to bring about their own vision of the Continent. Yes, we call them a family, but only a few are blood relatives."

"If you look at it that way, it makes perfect sense. You could even say they have their own zealots. That enemy Fire Mage was certainly one."

"Was it a woman?"

"It was. Why? Did you know her?"

"If it's the person I'm thinking of, then yes. Her name was Ria Sartellian, and she was the family's representative in Dagmar's court."

"Really?" said Athgar. "I find it strange to think she would actively take part in the battle. I would've thought she'd be more active in an advisory capacity."

"She had a lot riding on this campaign, both for the family's sake and for her own advancement."

"I'm afraid you'll need to explain that one to me. I understand the family wanted back into Reinwick, but what did she stand to gain on a personal level?"

"Power," replied Natalia. "The family thrives on it."

Somebody rapped a staff on the ground, and the room fell quiet. Athgar and Natalia moved closer to get a better view.

Lord Fernando, now the Duke of Reinwick, stood at the top of the stairs, commanding everyone's attention.

"We have suffered much these past few weeks," he began, his voice strong and clear, "but ultimately, we triumphed over our enemies."

A rousing round of applause greeted his remarks. He waited for it to subside before resuming. "There are many to thank when it comes to this campaign, from the lowest foot soldier to the bravest of knights, but I must point out that the efforts of our allies brought us to victory. To that end, I would like to thank Lord Athgar, High Thane of Therengia, and Lady Natalia Stormwind, his warmaster, without whom we would never have captured King Dagmar."

The audience gasped as the two made their way forward.

"Be it henceforth known there will be everlasting friendship between the realms of Reinwick and Therengia for the part they played in this war."

Polite applause greeted his proclamation this time, but with much less enthusiasm.

"I would also like to thank Rugal, Chieftain of the Ashwalkers, whose timely arrival on the field of Ebenhof turned the tide of the battle. Be it known that henceforth they shall be given the Thornwood to call their own."

This resulted in many discussions, so much so that the master herald had to rap his staff once more to quiet the room.

"I must also thank the Temple Knights of Saint Agnes for their efforts in defeating the menace from the sea. In recognition of this, I bequeath them a yearly stipend to help defray the cost of maintaining their fleet."

Temple Captain Leona bowed as the applause grew.

"Lastly, but by no means least, I must thank those descendants of the Old Kingdom who rose to the challenge and fought for the security of our realm. In recognition of their efforts, they shall henceforth be granted every right and privilege afforded to the rest of my subjects."

Athgar, hearing the tepid response, scowled, an action noted by Natalia. "Don't worry," she whispered. "It takes time to make actual change. This is but the first step."

He was about to say more, but the door opened, and a squad of knights entered. In amongst them was Dagmar in chains, looking dishevelled and filthy.

They marched the King of Andover into the centre of the room, facing the duke, then forced him to his knees. Lord Fernando descended the steps, then came to a halt before his prisoner. He looked down at the pitiful creature before him.

"I have a mind to see you beheaded," said the duke, "but that, I fear, will only lead to more war." He scanned the crowd, his gaze coming to rest on Athgar. "Lord Athgar, I would have your thoughts on the matter."

"Executing him will, as you say, only lead to more war. I suggest, instead, you resist the urge to punish Andover. The time is coming when the Empire of Halvaria will finally sweep into our lands. To withstand such an invasion, the Petty Kingdoms must come together, not fight amongst themselves."

"Well put, my friend, but is that all you would say?"

"We travelled here to Reinwick to break the hold the Stormwinds and Sartellians have over the courts of the Continent. I would ask that Dagmar take an oath to never again accept the presence of that family into his court nor take up arms against the gentle folk of Reinwick. In addition, he must rescind the death sentence that plagues the descendants of the Old Kingdom."

"I freely admit I was led astray," said Dagmar. "If Your Grace would permit, I would gladly take such an oath."

Fernando stared down at the man. "Release his shackles," he commanded, then waited as a guard came forward with a key and removed the chains. The duke extended his hand, helping Dagmar to his feet.

"Let us put this animosity behind us," said Fernando. "Stand with me as a brother, and we shall begin a new age of co-operation and friendship, free from outside influences."

They shook hands enthusiastically before turning to those gathered, holding their hands in the air as a show of solidarity.

"Will it last, do you think?" asked Athgar.

"It's a start," replied Natalia. "Only time will reveal if it's enough to end the Volstrum's tyranny."

"Or Korascajan. Don't forget them."

"I could hardly do that." She took a sip of her wine. "What shall we do now? Continue our quest to destroy the family's influence or return home?"

He grinned. "Can't we do both?"

<<<<>>>>

PLEASE REVIEW VORTEX TODAY

ONTO TORRENT, BOOK SEVEN

If you liked *Vortex* then *Temple Knight,* the first book in the *Power Ascending* series awaits.

START TEMPLE KNIGHT

A FEW WORDS FROM PAUL

Vortex ends with a dramatic change in the politics of the Petty Kingdoms, which wouldn't have been possible had it not been for the actions of another individual who is only briefly mentioned in this tale—Charlaine deShandria. Her story beings in Tempered Steel, but the events of Temple Captain are what set up the situation in Reinwick. I should also point out that Andover's humiliation at the hands of the Duke of Erlingen's army was revealed in Warrior Knight.

The astute reader may also pick up on several hints concerning other things occurring in the Petty Kingdoms, especially when dealing with the Temple Knights of Saint Agnes. More details will be forthcoming in future books, but for now, you'll just have to be patient.

Athgar and Natalia's story is far from over and continues in Torrent, book seven in The Frozen Flame series.

This tale wouldn't have been possible were it not for the love and support of Carol Bennett, my wife, editor, and best friend. I should also like to thank Amanda Bennett, Christie Bennett, and Stephanie Sandrock for their encouragement and support.

My BETA team has also been instrumental in fine-tuning this story, so a big shout-out goes to: Rachel Deibler, Michael Rhew, Phyllis Simpson, Don Hinckley, Charles Mohapel, Lisa Hanika, Debra Reeves, Mitchell Schneid-kraut, Susan Young, Joanna Smith, James McGinnis, Keven Hutchinson, and Anna Ostberg.

You, my readers, also need to be thanked for your interest in my books spurs me on to tell more tales. Reviews are the lifeblood of an Indie author such as myself, so please feel free to leave a comment or review on your favourite retailer.

CAST OF CHARACTERS

VORTEX CAST OF CHARACTERS

REINWICK

Aleksy - Lay brother of Saint Mathew

Athgar - Fire Mage, Thane of Runewald, son of Rothgar, bondmate to Natalia Stormwind

Ava - Temple Knight of Saint Agnes

Barbek Stoutarm - Dwarf smith

Belgast Ridgehand - Dwarf Entrepreneur, friend of Natalia and Athgar

Berengar Koch - General, army of Reinwick

Brandis - Servant, Duke of Reinwick's estate

Egon Ahlers - Baron of Herenstadt

Enid - Servant, Duke of Reinwick

Felicity - Temple Knight of Saint Agnes

Fernando Brondecker - Son of the Duke of Reinwick

Galina Stormwind - Water Mage, graduate of the Volstrum

Grazynia - Temple Captain of Saint Agnes, Admiral of the Temple Fleet

Handley - Proprietor of the Lydia

Herulf - Therengian, Korvoran

Katrin Stormwind - Water Mage, former student of the Volstrum

Kurlan Stratmeyer - Baron of Blunden

Larissa Stormwind - Water Mage, formerly at Court of Reinwick

Leona - Temple Captain Temple Knight of Saint Agnes, Korvoran commandery

Lofwine - Therengian, Korvoran

Natalia Stormwind - Water Mage, bondmate to Athgar, Runewald

Osbert - Therengian, Korvoran

Stanislav Voronsky - Former Mage hunter, friend of Natalia

Wilfhelm Brondecker - Duke of Reinwick

Yelena Dreyer - Wealthy shipping merchant

ANDOVER

Dagmar - King of Andover

Deveral - Head servant, assigned to Natalia

Greta - Messenger assigned to Natalia

Viktoria - Sister of King Dagmar

Volkard (Deceased) - Previous King of Andover

ORCS
Agar - Youngling, son of Shaluhk and Kargen, Red Hand Tribe
Artoch (deceased) - Master of Fire, Athgar's mentor, Red Hand Tribe
Gharog - Shaman in training, Ashwalkers
Grazuhk - Chieftain, Cloud Hunters
Grundak - Hunter, Red Hand Tribe
Kargen - Chieftain, bondmate to Shaluhk, Red Hand Tribe
Kragor - Hunter, Red Hand Tribe
Laghul - Shaman, Black Axe Tribe
Laruhk - Hunter, Red Hand, brother of Shaluhk
Marag - Master of Flame, Ashwalkers
Rotuk - Master of Air, Cloud Hunters
Rugal - Chieftain, Ashwalkers
Rugg - Master of Earth, Stone Crushers
Shaluhk - Shaman, bondmate to Kargen, Red Hand Tribe
Snaga - Master of Flame, Ashwalkers
Tonfer Garul - Scholar, Ebenstadt
Vagrath - Shaman, Ashwalkers
Zahruhl - Chieftain, Stone Crushers
Zhogral - Hunter, Ashwalkers

THERENGIANS AND ALLIES
Byrnwold the Brave - Former king of Therengia
Dunstan - Bard, Runewald villager
Harwath - Therengian guard, younger brother of Raleth
Hilwyth - Thane Guard, wife of Raleth
Maurice - Temple Knight, Saint Mathew
Oswyn - Daughter of Athgar and Natalia, Runewald
Raleth - Commander Thane Guard, older brother of Harwath
Rothgar (Deceased) - Father of Athgar
Weyland - Warrior of Runewald
Wynfrith - Thane of Bradon
Yaromir - Temple Captain, Saint Mathew

NOVARSK
Oleg Kolkov - Son of Lord Pavel
Pavel Kolkov - Baron of Nayalov
Rada - Daughter of King Vastavanitch of Novarsk
Sir Yarren of Larodka - Knight in service to Valentyn Sayenko

Taras Kirilov - Baron of Yusenka
Valentyn Sayenko - Baron of Krasnov

THE FAMILY

Ethwyn Sartellian - Therengian, Fire Mage, Athgar's sister
Graxion Stormwind - Former court mage, Zowenbruch
Gregori Stormwind - Former instructor at the Volstrum, Andover
Illiana Stormwind (Deceased) - Former Grand Mistress, Natalia's grandmother
Marakhova Stormwind - Water Mage, Grand Mistress of Stormwind Family
Nina Stormwind - Water Mage, Mistress of the Volstrum
Oksana Stormwind - Water Mage, former classmate of Natalia
Ria Sartellian - Fire Mage, Andover
Svetlana Stormwind - Water Mage, former classmate of Natalia

OTHERS:

Aeldred (Deceased) - First king of the Old Kingdom of Therengia
Charlaine deShandria - Former Temple Captain of Saint Agnes, Korvoran
Cordelia - Temple Knight of Saint Agnes, Caerhaven
Edna - Server at the Drake
Freidrich Hartman - Duke of Krieghoff
Graziano - Admiral, Abelard fleet
Gundar - God of the earth, creator of the Dwarves
Haglarith(Deceased) - Dwarf, King of Kragen-Tor
Nikolai (Deceased) - Former associate of Stanislav

PLACES:

THERENGIA

Athelwald (Destroyed) - Therengian village near Ord-Kurgad, birthplace of Athgar
Bradon - Village
Ebenstadt - City, formerly known as Dunmere
Old Kingdom - Another name for Therengia
Ord-Kurgad (Destroyed) - Former Orc Village, Red Hand Tribe
Runewald - Village, home to Athgar, Natalia, and Red Hand Tribe

PETTY KINGDOMS

Abelard - Kingdom, east of Reinwick
Andover - Kingdom, south of Reinwick and its traditional enemy

Burgemont - Kingdom, west of Andover
Corassus - City Stat, southern coast
Eidolon - Kingdom, northern coast
Erlingen - Duchy, southern border of Andover
Hadenfeld - Kingdom, middle of the Continent
Holstead - Duchy
Ilea - Kingdom, southern coast
Krieghoff - Duchy, eastern border
Langwal - Kingdom, northwest of Andover
Novarsk - Kingdom, west of Ebenstadt, occupied by the army of
Therengia
Ostrova - Kingdom, north of Novarsk
Reinwick - Duchy, northern coast
Ruzhina - Kingdom, Home of Karslev and the Volstrum
Zalista - Kingdom, west of Novarsk

CITIES & TOWNS

Blackwing - Village, Andover
Caerhaven - Capital city, Krieghoff
Draybourne - City, Holstead
Finburg - City, Norvarsk
Halmund - Capital of Novarsk, west of Ebenstadt
Herenstadt - Barony, Reinwick
Karslev - City, Ruzhina
Korvoran - Port city, Reinwick
Krasnov - Barony, Novarsk, Lord Valentyn
Ostermund - Town, Krieghoff
Porovka - Coastal city, Ruzhina
Torburg - City, Erlingen
Zienholtz - Capital, Andover

OTHER PLACES

Anchor - Tavern in Korvoran
Antonine - Headquarters of the Church of the Saints
Drake - Tavern, Andover
Great Northern Sea - North of the Petty Kingdoms
Korascajan – Family's Fire Mage Academy
Lydia - Tavern in Korvoran
Redrock River - River, Novarsk
Stormwind Manor - Large manor that houses the head of the
Stormwind family

Successor States - Precursor to Petty Kingdoms
Temple Bay - Rumoured secret base of the Holy Fleet
The Five Sisters - Islands, Great Northern Sea
Thornwood - Forest, Reinwick
Volstrum - Family's Water Mages academy, Karslev
Watering Hole - Tavern, Andover
Yusenka - City, Novarsk

OTHER INFORMATION:

BATTLES

Battle of Heronwood (1108 SR) - Therengia defeated the army of Novarsk

Battle of Ord-Kurgad (1104 SR) - Orcs of the Red Hand defeat an attempted siege

Battle of the Standing Stones (1104 SR) - Therengian/Orc army defeats Holy Army invasion

Battle of the Wilderness (1104 SR) - Human name for the Battle of the Standing Stones

ORC TRIBES

Ashwalkers - Masters of Flame, Reinwick/Andover
Black Axe Tribe - Masters of Flame, Therengia
Cloud Hunters - Masters of Air, Therengia
Red Hand Tribe - Masters of Flame, Therengia
Stone Crushers - Masters of Earth, Therengia

MISCELLANEOUS

Ardent - Flag ship, Abelard
Golarus - Therengian Place of learning
Golden Chalice - Small merchant ship, Porovka
High Thane - Ruler of Therengia
Master of Air - Orc term for Air Mage
Master of Earth - Orc term for Earth Mage
Master of Flame - Orc term for Fire Mage
Old Kingdom - Original Kingdom of Therengia by the Petty Kingdoms
Order of the Mailed Fist - Novarsk order of chivalry
Seaflower - Herb, induces sleep
Skrolling - Therengian term for a non-Therengian Human
Thane - Elected ruler of a Therengian Village
Thane Guard - Elite Therengian warriors
Thanes Council - Ruling council of Therengia

The Disgraced - Failed Volstrum Students
Tusker - Huge animal similar to a prehistoric entelodont
Valiant (formerly *Lydia*) - Flagship, Temple Fleet
Vigilant (formerly *Sea Wolf*) - War ship belonging to the Temple Knights of Saint Agnes

Printed in Great Britain
by Amazon

27839070R00175